GILDOR

THE FORBIDDEN LAND

GILDOR

The Forbidden Land

Arthur Woodring

BOOK 1

A Novel

Gildor: The Forbidden Land
Copyright © 2020 by ARTHUR WOODRING

Library of Congress Control Number: 2020903518
ISBN-13:   Paperback: 978-1-64749-066-9
              ePub   978-1-64749-070-6

Fantasy/Adventure

All rights reserved. No part of this publication may be reproduced, distributed, or transmitted in any form or by any means, including photocopying, recording, or other electronic or mechanical methods, without the prior written permission of the publisher or author, except in the case of brief quotations embodied in critical reviews and certain other noncommercial uses permitted by copyright law.

Although every precaution has been taken to verify the accuracy of the information contained herein, the author and publisher assume no responsibility for any errors or omissions. No liability is assumed for damages that may result from the use of information contained within.

Printed in the United States of America

GoToPublish LLC
1-888-337-1724
www.gotopublish.com
info@gotopublish.com

Contents

Chapter 1 1
Chapter 2 11
Chapter 3 19
Chapter 4 26
Chapter 5 37
Chapter 6 43
Chapter 7 55
Chapter 8 63
Chapter 9 72
Chapter 10 84
Chapter 11 90
Chapter 12 98
Chapter 13 109
Chapter 14 115
Chapter 15 121
Chapter 16 127
Chapter 17 131
Chapter 18 140
Chapter 19 152
Chapter 20 158
Chapter 21 167
Chapter 22 171
Chapter 23 179
Chapter 24 185
Chapter 25 194
Chapter 26 203
Chapter 27 215
Chapter 28 223
Chapter 29 236
Chapter 30 244
Chapter 31 250
Chapter 32 257
ABOUT THE AUTHOR 261

Chapter 1

Professor Stevens's eyes clouded over with weariness as he sat laboring over the complex schematic spread out on the workbench of his basement laboratory. The old man had started the tedious task of trying to create some sort of order out of the multicolored stack of papers several hours earlier. His frustration building to a head, he ran his hands through his thinning gray hair and mumbled to himself, "I know there's a way to complete this circuit, but where can I divert the power from and still retain enough to allow the rest of the equipment to continue operating without losing any of its integrity?"

Benjamin Thomas sat on a stool at the opposite side of the workbench. Although he didn't understand the complex equipment his grandfather was designing, he knew the old man was in a hurry to finish it. Glancing at the clock on the wall behind him, he spoke while fighting off a yawn at the same time, "It's almost 5:00 a.m., Grandpa. Don't you think you should call it quits and get some shut-eye? I won't be able to enjoy my party tomorrow if I'm too tired. Jack and Glenna will be here in about five hours to help me get things ready."

The professor looked across the workbench and shook his head, his disheveled hair flying about like thin blades of grass in a windstorm. "I can't stop just yet, Benjamin. I'll have these circuits figured out in another hour or so, and I don't want to stop now when I'm so close to finishing them."

"But, Grandpa—"

The old man held his hand up. "If I stop now, it'll take half the day Monday for me just to figure out where I left off. I can take these schematics to the lab later this morning if I finish within the next couple hours. I'll be back to help you celebrate your birthday by early afternoon if I can get things set up in time. My assistants will be able to start working on the equipment without me if the schematics are complete. There shouldn't be anything to keep me from coming home after they get started."

Realizing how demanding his grandfather's work must be, and that he was probably trying his best to find a way for them to spend at least part of his birthday together, Ben leaned back and nodded. "Okay, Grandpa, you win. I'll stay here with you until you're done."

"Thank you, my boy. But that won't be necessary. I can manage without you. Why don't you go upstairs and get some sleep? You'll need all the rest you can get if you really want to enjoy yourself."

Ben fought back another yawn and headed for the door. "All right, I can take a hint. I know when I'm not needed. I wouldn't be much help anyway because I have no idea what it is you're working on, and since you won't tell me, I guess I never will."

Professor Stevens took his eyes away from the schematics for a moment and looked at his grandson. "I wouldn't say you weren't any help, Ben. You helped me stay awake during the night. I appreciate your willingness to keep me company when I have long hours to put in."

Ben hunched his shoulders. "Yeah, that's me, somebody to keep you company. I can't help you if I don't know what it is you're working on."

"Trust me, son. You don't want to know. But I can tell you this: the government is willing to pay Foster Research Unlimited big bucks for what I'm working on. There could be a substantial bonus for me if everything works out. Possibly a big enough bonus that I might be able to retire early. You and I will have much more time to spend together before you leave for college this fall if that should happen."

Ben swung around and looked at the old man before starting up the steps to the main floor of the house. "I hope you're right about that, Grandpa. I guess I'll wait until I get to college before I start worrying about physics. I'll have plenty of time to study after I get there. I'll continue to work on my football skills with Jack until then, since that's how I earned my scholarship in the first place."

The professor nodded. "Now that's the right idea, Benjamin. Take a little time to enjoy life before you put your nose to the grindstone the way I did. Maybe you'll make fewer mistakes that way. Lord knows I made enough for both of us lately."

Ben wasn't sure what his grandfather meant by that last statement, and he was too tired to ask. "I'm going to bed. Try not to stay down here too much longer. Okay, Grandpa?"

"Oh, Ben," the professor called out behind him.

"Yes, Grandpa." Ben looked back over his shoulder and saw the professor rubbing his chin as if in deep thought.

"Maybe you should sleep on the sofa in the living room," the professor said thoughtfully. "That way, you'll hear Jack when he arrives. You know, just in case you sleep a little too long. I probably won't be here to let him in. I don't want you to miss him when he gets here. You can't have a party if your friends leave, thinking you're not at home."

Ben nodded. "That's a good idea. I don't know if I really want to climb both sets of stairs to my room right now anyway."

A few minutes later, Ben was sitting on the sofa in the living room of his grandfather's large house. After kicking off his shoes, he reached up to turn off the floor lamp standing behind the sofa and lay down. Sleep overcame him almost as soon as his head hit the pillow.

Ben didn't sleep well. He tossed and turned the whole time. The expectation of the party he and his friends planned kept him from sleeping. That, and the fact that the sofa was too short for him to comfortably stretch out his full six-foot frame on didn't help matters any.

He was still rolling and tossing when he felt a huge pair of hands take a firm grip on his shoulders and start to shake him. Still half asleep, he blinked his eyes open, reached up to push his thick brown locks away from his face, and found himself staring into two steel-blue eyes. "Jack! What are you doing here?"

"Sorry, buddy." The well-muscled young man chuckled, standing over him. "I thought you were going to fall off the sofa the way you were kicking around there."

Ben got up on one elbow and rubbed the sleep from his eyes. "Thanks for waking me. Grandpa and I put in a late night, and I didn't get to sleep until after five. Speaking of Grandpa, where is he? Did he let you in?"

Jack shook his head. "Nope. I found a note on the door, telling me that I should let myself in and wake you up. It said you were asleep on the sofa in the living room, so I used the key you gave me, and here I am." He shook his head again, slower this time. "My old man must really be puttin' the heat on for that government contract if he even has Professor Stevens working all night." By the way," he added as an afterthought, "the professor also wrote that he would be working later than usual today and that he would probably miss your party." He stopped to scratch the back of his head as he thought the matter over. "I sure wish I knew what it is that they're working on. Every time I ask Dad about it, he just tells me that it's classified."

"Yeah it must be," Ben replied. "Grandpa won't tell me anything about it either." Taking a quick look around the room, he noticed Jack was alone. "Where's Glenna? Didn't she come with you?"

"She's outside on the patio, starting to set things up for the party," Jack replied. "I told her we'd be out in a few minutes. Will ya hurry up? I've got a little surprise I need to tell you about."

Ben sat straight up. "Surprise? What kinda surprise?"

Jack seemed hesitant. "Well, I ran into Megan at the mall yesterday, so I invited her to the party. I hope ya don't mind. I told her that Glenna and I were planning to celebrate our graduation with you and some of our other friends. She said she'd be happy to come and that she'd be here sometime around noon."

"You mean she's actually coming here to the house?"

Jack's eyebrows raised a little. "Yeah. She seemed pretty excited about it too. Why?"

Ben hunched his broad shoulders before stretching out his strapping arms and yawning. He tried his best to act nonchalant as he answered, "Ah... no particular reason. I was just wondering." He didn't want to let on just how hard his heart was pumping at the moment. He only met Megan a couple of months earlier when she moved to Franklin with her stepfather, but he managed to become fairly good friends with her during that short time. Their brief relationship started to grow stronger when they discovered they had both lost loved ones at an early age.

Jack slapped Ben on the shoulder. "Come on, man! If we're not ready when the others get here, the party's liable to be over before it even gets started. Get movin'!"

Ben jumped to his feet and started running for the stairs, but his powerful legs were cramped from being bunched up from sleeping on the short sofa. "Give me a few minutes," he said, slowing to rub the back of his thighs. "I'll be with you as soon as I get a shower and put my swimming trunks on—and get rid of these blasted cramps."

Jack left out an amused chuckle. "Get goin'! Glena and I will be waitin' for ya outside."

Surrounded by hills covered with a thick evergreen forest, a narrow dirt road served as the only access to the Stevens' estate. The combination of the steep hillsides and the rocky shoreline surrounding his lakefront property assured Professor Stevens of almost complete solitude. All but the two- hundred-foot span of level beach behind the house was unsuitable for swimming or for boat docks. However, the good professor did allow the locals access to his dock for boating and fishing purposes. The forested hills contained an abundance of game, so certain friends were also allowed limited access for hunting. Ben and his grandfather often took advantage of the natural resources surrounding their secluded home too.

An hour and a half after he woke up, Ben was out on the beach with Jack, Glenna, and the rest of his friends as the party was just getting into full swing. It was a warm, dry summer day, and the sun was doing its best to keep it that way. It was almost noon, and the temperature was into the low nineties. Even the deep blue waters of Lake Franklin were not immune to the relentless onslaught of the solar furnace. The water temperature had risen to almost eighty degrees along the level sandy beach behind the house.

Ben sat on the beach listening to Jack and Glenna talking to each other but paid little attention to their conversation. He kept his eyes glued to the expanse of beach leading up to the house with guarded anticipation.

"Do you think Megan will show up soon?" Jack asked.

"I doubt it," Glenna replied.

"Yeah, well, what do you know anyway?" Jack retorted.

"Enough to know that she wouldn't be interested in a bonehead like you, Jack Foster," Glenna retorted. "She probably won't stay long even if she does come. It's almost twelve now, and she said she'd be here in time for lunch."

Jack gave Ben a gentle poke in the ribs before standing up and brushing the sand off the seat of his swimming trunks and the back of his heavily muscled legs. "Don't worry, Ben. She'll be here soon. She probably just got held up in some traffic in town or something, that's all."

Ben hunched his shoulders as he stood up beside Jack. "Glenna has a point," he said. "Maybe it wasn't a good idea to invite Megan. Her dad's a busy man. Maybe she stayed home to be with him. It's too late to worry about that now. Let's go for a short swim before we start serving lunch."

"Sorry, Ben. I have to learn to control my mouth better." Glenna had walked up beside him and put her hand on his arm. She was petite and had to squint into the sun when she looked up at him. She was pretty, with large green eyes that didn't miss much of what went on around her. Her short brown hair was curled under at the ends, giving her an enchanting elfin appearance.

Ben couldn't help but smile at her. "Don't worry about it. I'm sure she has a good reason for not coming. Maybe she'll show up later." He acted nonchalant, but he sure didn't feel that way; his guts felt like they were tearing themselves apart. When he felt an elbow poke lightly into his ribs, he suddenly shifted his attention back to Jack.

Jack nodded toward the house. "I think our swim will have to wait, my man. Look there! The girl of your dreams just showed up."

Ben left out a soft whistle when he saw the familiar figure coming toward them. "She sure has, hasn't she?"

"Glenna and I will leave you two alone for a while," Jack said. "We're goin' up to the patio and start serving the hamburgers and hot dogs. Come join us when you're ready."

Ben never took his eyes off Megan. "Yeah... I'll join you in a couple of minutes."

Megan's raven hair literally shone in the sunlight. That, and the bright-green blouse and trim cutoffs she wore made her an easy target to spot, along with a stunning suntan. She had only walked a few yards out onto the warm sand before suddenly stopping to look around as if confused.

Ben started waving his hands in the air to get her attention. *I wonder what's wrong,* he thought. Then he heard the wild whistling and hooting coming from some of the guys on the patio. It didn't take long for him to react when he realized what was going on. He ran to meet Megan, and she flashed a welcome smile when he finally stopped beside her. "Sorry about all that, Meg. You'd think those guys never saw a pretty girl before."

"I guess I should consider it a compliment then," she said, beaming another heartwarming smile.

"Come on," Ben said, motioning for her to follow him toward the patio. "Pay no attention to them, and they'll stop."

Megan fell in step beside him. "I'm sorry I'm late," she said. "I was trying to call Daddy on my way up here to let him know where I would be, but he didn't answer his phone. He must not be in his office right now."

"I hope everything's all right," Ben replied.

Megan nodded. "I'm sure it is. With him being a reporter for *The Fact Finder* magazine and all… I guess I worry too much. I just wish he would quit *The Fact Finder* sometimes because I get so tired of moving all the time. I guess that's the way it is when you're the daughter of one of the top-ranked investigative reporters in the country. I'm just afraid he'll get himself into a mess he won't be able to get himself out of one of these days. Sometimes I think he takes too many chances just trying to get a hot story." She paused before changing the subject. "I'm not late for lunch, am I?"

Ben shook his head. "Actually, you got here just in time. Jack and Glenna are only now starting to serve the food on the patio, and the water's just the right temperature if you'd like to go swimming later on."

Megan looked out over the lake. "I'd really like that. I haven't been swimming in open water like this since I was a little girl back in Guam where I grew up."

Ben stopped and gawked at her. "Guam? That explains it."

"Explains what?" Megan asked, seeming a bit apprehensive.

"Your looks," Ben replied.

Megan reached up and touched the side of her tanned face absentmindedly. "What's the matter with the way I look?"

Ben left out a nervous chuckle. "Sorry, I didn't mean to be rude. I just meant that you look… you know, different. I couldn't put my finger on it before, but something about you always seemed to keep me wondering. Maybe it's the shape of your eyes that kept me so confused, but at least now I know why. Your mom was from Guam, wasn't she? I know your dad sure isn't from there."

Megan slowly nodded. "Yes, Momma was half-Malay and half-Japanese. Is something wrong with that?"

"Not at all," Ben replied with a broad smile. "I was just thinking that your mom and dad made a pretty good combo because they sure have a good- looking daughter." He saw Megan blush out of the corner of his eye and pretended not to notice. He changed the subject. "Our menu is rather limited.

I hope you like hot dogs and hamburgers. You'll have to fill up on pretzels and potato chips otherwise."

"Hamburgers and hot dogs sound just fine to me," Megan replied, giggling.

Half an hour later, Ben and Megan were walking back to the beach with Jack and Glenna when they heard some of the other kids calling out to them from the water's edge. Two of their buddies were standing by the volleyball net that they and their girlfriends had erected earlier and were yelling for them to come and join them.

"That sounds like a pretty good invitation to me," Glenna said. "Come on, guys, let's play." She didn't waste any time in slipping out of the blouse and shorts she had been wearing over a provocative red one-piece swimming suit.

"I'm with you," Megan replied, stripping down to the glossy gold bikini she wore under her own clothes. She called out over her shoulder as she ran toward the net with Glenna. "Come on, Ben! Maybe we can be on the same team together."

Ben was dumbfounded as he stood watching the two girls run down the beach. Jack brought him back to his senses with a solid slap on the back.

"We better go join in the fun, old buddy, before those guys start hitting on those bodacious babes of ours."

Ben blinked and cleared his throat. "Yeah. I think you're right. Let's go!"

※

The rest of the day raced by, and the party was over before they knew it. Megan stayed to help Ben, Jack, and Glenna clean up afterward, and it was past six before they had finished. Jack made the suggestion that they all drive into Franklin for some pizza.

Beginning to feel the effects from lack of sleep the night before, Ben balked at the idea. "No can do, good buddy. Ya know I'm operating on about five hours' shut-eye. I am totally wasted."

A phone started ringing somewhere, and they turned to see where the sound was coming from.

"Oh, that's probably Daddy." Megan rushed to her purse to answer her cell phone while the others carried on their conversation.

Jack shook his head. "What a bummer. I sure was lookin' forward to haven' some pizza."

"Don't let me stop you," Ben replied. "The rest of you can go. I'm goin' to bed though."

"I'm afraid I won't be able to join you either," Megan said. She looked worried as she stuffed her phone back into her purse. "That was Daddy. He wants me to pick him up right away."

"Is something wrong?" Ben asked.

"No... no!" Megan stammered. "No! Nothing's wrong. We just had a bad connection, that's all. I could barely hear him."

Jack put his arm around Glenna's trim waist and drew her close. "Well, love, I guess it's just you and me. Do you feel like haven' some pizza with me?"

Glenna shook her head in disgust. "Honestly, Jack Foster, I don't know where you put it all. You musta ate at least four or five hamburgers and Lord knows how many hot dogs, and you're still hungry. But if you're buying, I'll go with you. Lord knows, you might founder yourself, and I'll have to drive you home."

An amused smirk crossed Jack's face as he looked back at Ben and cocked his head to one side. "That's my girl," he said, taking Glenna by the hand and starting around the corner of the house. "We'll see you two later."

"I'll see you tomorrow," Ben replied. He turned to look at Megan as soon as Jack and Glenna were out of sight. "Are you sure everything's okay with your dad? You look worried."

Megan glanced in the direction Jack and Glenna had gone before suddenly bursting into tears. "I need your help, Ben. Daddy's in some kind of trouble, and I don't have anyone else I can turn to."

Ben's heart leaped in his chest. "What kinda trouble is he in?" he asked, moving closer to Megan. "What do you want me to do?"

"He's had an accident, and he wants me to pick him up on the access road behind FRU's lab. I wanted to call the police, but he told me not to. He said he wants to report what he discovered directly to *The Fact Finder*'s main office because he's not sure he can trust anyone else, not even the local police."

"Where's their main office?" Ben asked. "Is it around here? Why didn't he call there for help?"

Megan shook her head. "It's the mountains. Daddy can't get through to them on his cell, and he said he's hurt too badly to get to a pay phone by himself. That's why I have to go get him. He sounded terrible on the phone just now. He didn't sound like himself at all."

"Can't we call the main office from here?" Ben asked. He started to go into the house, but Megan grabbed his arm to stop him. She had an urgent look on her face when he turned to look at her.

"No!" Megan wailed. "When I told Daddy where I am, he told me not to use your phone. He's afraid it might be bugged."

"But that's ridiculous," Ben replied. "Who'd bug Grandpa's phone?"

"Your grandfather works for FRU, doesn't he?" Megan asked.

Ben gave a thoughtful nod. "I get your drift. Let's get going then! It sounds like there's no time to waste. We'll have to take your car. Grandpa took his to the lab this morning, and my pickup broke down two days ago."

They ran around to the front of the house where Megan had her sleek yellow sports car parked in the driveway. She pushed the black button on the door handle twice to unlock the doors, and there was a quiet hiss before the doors began to drift slowly upward. Ben stopped her when she started to slip in behind the steering wheel.

"Better let me drive," he said. "I know these mountain roads better than you do, so I can drive on them faster."

Megan didn't argue. She handed Ben the key fob and ran around to the passenger side to get in. It only took a few seconds for them to settle in before Ben backed the sleek Yellow Jacket out of the driveway and headed down the road with the peddle to the metal and the engine winding at full speed.

They reached Foster Research Unlimited in about twenty minutes. Ben hit the brakes about two hundred feet from the gate and pulled over onto the berm of the access road without stopping. He continued to drive slowly around to the back of the building while he and Megan scanned both sides of the road looking for any sign of Mr. Dills. They didn't see any movement until after they passed by the rear gate.

Megan was the first to spot the hand waving above the high grass growing outside the fence that surrounded the lab. "That's got to be Daddy," she cried, pushing the door open and jumping out before Ben could bring the car to a complete stop.

Ben slammed on the breaks and stopped the car. By the time he managed to get out, Megan had already run to her father's side and found herself to be in serious trouble. Ben heard her scream and looked up to see her struggling with two uniformed guards.

Chapter 2

Ben ran around the car and came to a dead stop as soon as he realized what was happening. A third man stepped between him and the two restraining Megan. The third man trained a gun on Ben while the other two fought to keep the struggling girl's arms pinned behind her back. When the man with the gun turned to see how his companions were faring with Megan, Ben launched his attack. Forgetting his own safety, he ran forward and smashed his balled fist into the chin of the gun-wielding assailant and sent him to the ground in a heap. Ben turned to take on the others but stopped before he could unleash more of his burning fury when a familiar voice called out to him.

"Ben Thomas, stop!"

Ben turned in the direction of the gate and found himself staring into the face of one of his grandfather's assistants. "Ted Stoner? What's this all about, Ted?" Ben asked, fighting back his anger and allowing himself to relax.

Ted stepped forward and opened his mouth as if about to say something, but he suddenly stopped and waved his hands. "No, don't..."

Ben heard Megan scream, but before he could figure out why, a stunning blow on the back of his head sent him reeling to the ground in an explosion of blackness and stars.

"Take it easy, Ben," somebody whispered.

He could feel hands running through his hair as he opened his eyes to see to whom they belonged, but the swirling stars were slow in leaving. The back of his head felt as if it was about to split open and dump its entire contents out on the floor. He knew he was lying on his back; the voice he heard came from above him. He tried blinking rapidly to force his eyes to focus. At first, he could only see a shining blur, but then he caught the glimpse of dark hair hanging in front of his face. A beautiful face began to form as his vision cleared. *I know that face, those almond-shaped eyes. Tears? Why is she crying?* Reality suddenly hit, and he raised his head from Megan's lap and left out a low involuntary moan when a sharp pain suddenly shot through his skull.

"Oh, thank God," Megan sobbed. "I thought that ape might have killed you."

He reached back and felt a lump the size of a golf ball on the back of his head. "I'm not so sure he didn't." He glanced around at their surroundings and sat up straighter. They were in a small empty room with poor lighting. "Where are we?" he asked, trying to stand and losing his balance.

Megan reached out to steady him and helped him sit back down. "We're at FRU's laboratory. Remember?"

Ben shook his head. "I don't remember a thing after I saw Ted. How did we get in here?" He started to stand again, and Megan helped him to his feet.

"You were knocked out before they brought us here," Megan said. "You've been out for at least an hour."

Ben took a quick look around the room again. There was only one door, which he discovered was locked when he walked over and tried the knob. "What is this place?"

"We're locked in a closet," Megan replied. "There's a laboratory in the next room with strange-looking machines and other stuff in it like I've never seen before."

Ben started pounding on the door with both fists. "Maybe it's the lab Grandpa works in," he cried. "Grandpa! Hello, Grandpa! Are you there? It's me, Ben. Let us out of here if you can hear me!" He stopped pounding when Megan rushed forward and took him by the arm.

"It's no use, Ben," she cried. "I've already tried that. Either they can't hear us, or nobody's out there. Or they can hear us and just won't let us out. Either way, we're not going anywhere until they open the door for us. I looked at it when they were putting us in here. It's gotta be at least three inches thick, so you're not going to break it down."

Ben gave the door a kick and took a step backward. "They can't keep us in here forever. I'm sure Grandpa will have something to say when he hears about this. Why'd they bring us here anyway?"

Megan lowered her head. "I think it might have something to do with Daddy." She sighed.

"What do you mean?"

"He's an investigative reporter for *The Fact Finder*, remember? He called and asked me to come here and pick him up, so you drove us here in my car."

Ben rubbed the back of his head as he tried to remember. "Yeah, it's comin' back to me now. Why'd he need our help in the first place?"

Megan shook her head. "I guess he was investigating FRU for some reason that he didn't get a chance to, or didn't want to, tell me about."

Ben snapped his fingers. "Yeah! He told you he had an accident and needed your help. Those guards caught us before we could find him. Is he here too?"

Megan shook her head again. "I didn't see him anywhere. I don't know where he might be."

"So why'd they come after us then if your dad's the one they want?" Ben asked, still rubbing his aching head.

Megan threw her arms out at her sides. "I don't know. Maybe they think we know something."

"That's exactly right, Ms. Dills."

They both turned toward the door when they heard the voice. Ted Stoner had managed to enter the room without them noticing while they were talking. The three security guards who were with him earlier stood outside the open door with their guns aimed at the two teens.

Megan took a step toward him, and Ted put up his hand to stop her. "Stop where you are, Ms. Dills. My associates may get nervous if you get too close."

"Where's Grandpa?" Ben asked. "Does he know we're here?"

Ted smiled and shook his head. "Right now, Professor Stevens is hard at work at the other end of the building. He has no idea you're here, and he never will."

"We'll see about that," Ben said, putting his open hand in the middle of Ted's chest and pushing him out of his way.

Ted grabbed Ben by the arm when he tried to move around him to get to the door. "Please don't try anything foolish, Ben, or my friends here will have to stop you. I assure you they won't be as gentle with you as they were last time."

Ben backed away when he realized Ted meant what he said. "Why are you holding us here, Ted? We haven't done anything wrong."

"Sorry, but we can't afford to take any chances," Ted replied. He pointed to Megan. "We only wanted the girl there. Unfortunately, you got in the way, so we had to bring you along with her."

Megan moved closer to Ben. "Why do you want me?"

"Perhaps I should answer that, my dear," a voice said from the next room. Ben recognized Ned Foster's voice without having to see him. He knew Ned Foster very well because he was his best friend, Jack's, father. "Mr. Foster?"

A tall, heavyset man wearing wire-rimmed glasses stepped into the doorway. "Yes, Ben, it's me."

Ben took Megan by the arm and drew her close. "We'll be all right now.

This is Jack's dad. He's FRU's CEO."

Foster lowered his head and looked over the rims of his glasses at the teenagers. "I'm so sorry the two of you got involved in this. I had no other choice but to have my men lure you here when we discovered Mr. Dills lying out by the gate this morning. I wish things could have been different."

"What do you mean you found him lying out by the gate?" Megan asked. Ben felt her shudder beside him.

"Where's my daddy?" Megan cried. "What did you do to him?" She turned and rested her head against Ben's chest with her face close to his.

Ben slipped his arm around Megan and held her tight. His stomach was doing flip-flops while he waited to hear Foster's answer to Megan's question, although he already thought he knew what it was going to be.

Foster reached out to gently stroke Megan's silky black hair, but Ben pulled her away. "I'm sorry, my dear child, but I'm afraid your father is dead."

"Dead!" Megan screamed. "How?" she sobbed.

Ned Foster shook his head slowly. "It was an unfortunate accident," he began. "Somehow he found a way past our security system and broke into the lab early this morning. He managed to pilfer some classified information from our computers and download it onto his phone before one of the security guards must have happened by and startled him. Evidently, Mr. Dills stumbled and fell off the fire escape in his haste to escape, or he might have made a clean getaway. One of the other guards found his blood trail during a routine patrol around the building and followed it to the gate, where he discovered your father this morning. He was still alive when the guard found him, so we brought him back here to the lab for questioning. He was delirious and kept mumbling something about us needing to call you to come and get him. But he died shortly afterward without divulging any pertinent information. We found his cell phone was still on him when we searched his body. When we discovered the information from our computer on his phone, we had no idea what he might have told you, or anyone else, about what we are doing here."

Megan forced herself to stop sobbing and raised her head to look at Foster. "You're lying. My daddy didn't die this morning. I just talked to him before we came here."

"No one here killed your father," Foster replied. "We aren't murderers. He was already dying before we brought him back inside the lab. I'm afraid that was me, pretending to be your father that you talked to on the phone earlier. I had to find a way to lure you here before you had a chance to talk to anybody. We checked your father's phone and discovered that he had sent you a text message about the same time he would have been in the lab. The message contained top secret information about our research here."

Ben's anger kindled. "Why didn't you try to get help for Mr. Dills then, if you're not murderers? Why do your men carry guns if you don't intend to kill anybody? And why are you holding us prisoner here?"

"Because I had to find out what Mr. Dills might have told his daughter," Foster replied. "I don't know how much she knows about her father's investigation. I can't afford to let anyone find out about the research we're involved in, and I'll do whatever I must to prevent that from happening. Even if it means keeping you here at gunpoint. My company could be ruined if the general public ever found out about some of the research that has been conducted here in the past."

"So that's why you killed Daddy," Megan sobbed. "He was investigating the research you've been doing, and you killed him to keep him from reporting on your illegal activities."

Ted Stoner stepped close to Foster. "Careful, sir! Don't tell them any more than they already know."

Foster shook his head. "It doesn't matter, Ted. They aren't going anywhere."

"But we can't keep them here forever," Ted replied.

Foster held up his hand. "We won't have to. We'll send them to Gildor. They won't be coming back from there to tell anyone about our activities. They'll simply become a couple of additions to the old research facility."

"What's Gilnor?" Ben asked.

"None of your business," Stoner snapped.

"It's all right, Ted," Foster broke in. "We can tell them about Gildor. After all, it will be their new home soon. Now go prepare the equipment while I explain a few things."

Ted snorted indignantly, then turned and left the room.

Ben waited for Ted to get out of hearing range before saying anything. "Look, Mr. Foster, Megan and I promise not to tell anybody about what's going on here. We don't know anything anyway. Please let us go. You know me. I'll keep my word. What good's it going to do if you send us to this Gilnor place?"

Foster forced a crooked smile. "It's pronounced *Gildor*. Let me explain what Gildor is," he added, motioning toward the door.

Ben continued to hold Megan close as he guided her out the door. They only took a few steps into the laboratory before the two security guards grabbed them from behind. Megan screamed and started to thrash around in the first man's iron grip while the second held his arm tightly around Ben's neck and put a gun to the side of his head. While they were being held, Stoner walked up to them and gave them each a shot in the side of the neck with a hypodermic gun he had been hiding in the pocket of his smock. When the treachery was done, the guards loosened their grips and guided Ben and Megan to a couple of nearby gurneys and didn't back away until after the teens were laid comfortably in place.

It only took seconds for whatever was in the hypodermic to start taking affect. Ben's vision started to blur as soon as he was released. He tried to reach out to the guard as he backed away, but he could hardly move his arms. They felt like they were incased in cement. Paralysis rushed through his body, and he discovered that he was unable to even move his head. He managed to move his eyes in Megan's direction and saw that her situation was no better than his. She wasn't able to move either as she lay on the gurney beside his.

"Excellent," Foster said. He moved to stand between the immobilized teens and snapped his fingers in front of their faces. "Now I will tell you about Gildor while we wait for the drug to take its full effect." He waved his arms to encompass the fantastic equipment within the laboratory. "This laboratory contains such highly sophisticated equipment that most research scientists would die to get their hands on it. But this is only a drop in the bucket compared to what we Fosters have managed to accomplish over the past hundred years or so.

"You see, it all started quite by accident. My great-grandfather founded this company about twenty years before World War I started. He actually started out in the shipping business with nothing but a single freighter. Well, to make a long story short, his ship ran aground one evening on a sandbar in the South Pacific. It turned out that the sandbar was part of a little island— just a little out-of-the-way place, only a couple of hundred acres of land, far out of any of the main shipping lanes. Great-grandfather was so taken with it that he decided to claim it for his own. Being independently wealthy, he decided that the little isle would make a perfect spot to build a small farm and increase his fortune. He started out raising a few head of beef cattle and trying to improve their breed, but he didn't limit his research to just cattle. He was able to fund his own research and began experimenting with exotic floral life with the profits he gained from his shipping business.

"After he died, his son took over the business and expanded the company's research to cover thousands of varieties of flora and over two thousand forms of fauna as well. He had this strange idea that he could improve human life by conducting genetic research on animals. But people began to frown upon his work, so he was forced to stop his research for a while. Then he remembered his father's little island. The island became the main base for all his genetic research after that. No one, except those directly involved, will ever know how many people have been helped by the experiments FRU has secretly conducted since then.

"Sure, we had to do things on the sly because people didn't agree with our methods, but FRU is fifty years ahead of anyone else involved in genetic research, and we have managed to make great strides in gene-splicing as well. Scientists announced that they finally managed to break the human genetic code and map its DNA in the early twenty-first century, but FRU actually managed to do so much more decades earlier. However, we chose to keep our findings to ourselves and secretly use the knowledge we gained for the betterment of mankind. Seventy-five years ago, my grandfather and father discovered that the island was actually the cap of a long-extinct volcano that formed a mammoth cavern with only one tiny entrance to gain access to it. They moved our facility there underground and used solar energy to supply it with power. Father named the little island hideaway Gildor, short for 'Genetic Isolated Laboratory for the Development of Organic Research.' The residents there don't even realize that there's another whole world outside that vast cavern. As far as they know, the people living down there think Gildor is the whole world. It even has a man-made sun and moon to keep it warm and lighted. The place even has its own climate because of the self-sustained biosphere and ecosystem contained within it." Foster smiled deviously before continuing, "So you see, kids, no one will know where you'll be, not even Ben's grandfather."

Apparently finished with his narrative, Foster turned and nodded to Ted Stoner. "You know what to do from here on, Ted. I'll see you in my office when you're finished. I have to go and make sure our friends at the police department have successfully made Dills's death look like an automobile accident."

Ben fought to maintain consciousness until Foster left the room. Although he could barely hold his eyes open, his concern for Megan's safety helped keep him awake. He forced his tired eyes to stay open long enough to see a blurred vision of Stoner wheeling Megan's gurney toward one of the strange-looking machines. He watched helplessly as one of the guards helped Stoner lift the girl's motionless body off the gurney and lay her on a slab under the machine, but he couldn't hold his eyes open long enough to see what happened after that. A strange and distant humming reached his ears just before his eyes started to drift shut.

Chapter 3

Ben's head was spinning. He tried to lift his hands to rub the blurriness from his eyes, but his left hand was trapped behind his body. He discovered he was strapped into place on some sort of bench when he tried to lean forward. He was finally able to move sideways far enough, after a considerable strain, to free his hand and use both fists in an effort to rub the haziness from his eyes. The first thing he saw after his vision cleared was a small square of light not more than two feet in front of his face. The window was only about a foot long by six inches high, and he couldn't see anything through it but a vast whiteness. He turned his head to look for something familiar. *Where am I?* he thought. *I'm inside some sort of dark padded room. The back and front are definitely padded. I can feel the padding with my hands.* The only light inside the little room came in through the window. He thought he saw movement beside him when he looked to his left. He had to squint to get his eyes focused well enough to catch the hint of a face bordered by waves of raven hair. "Megan, are you all right?" His throat was dry, and he almost choked when he spoke.

Megan jumped, turned to face him with eyes wide as saucers, and whispered, "Don't make any noise. They might hear us."

"Who might hear us?"

She pointed a shaking finger at the window. "Giants," she whispered. "Can't you hear them?"

There was a low rumbling outside the room, but Ben didn't pay much attention to it. "Aw, that's just thunder. There must be a storm brewing outside. I'll find out where we are when I get us outta here."

Megan reached out and grabbed his arm when he started to move. "You can't open the door from the inside. I already checked. There's no handle."

Ben pulled his arm free and leaned forward, straining against the straps holding him in place, and began pounding on the door as hard as he could. The door didn't budge.

"You should listen to your girlfriend, Ben," a voice thundered from somewhere above them. "The container you're in is locked and won't open until we open it from the outside."

Ben's eyes went wide. "Who are you, and where are we?"

A huge green eye suddenly filled the window in front of them. "Why, it's me, Ned Foster. You're inside a transport box."

The teens were forced to hold their hands over their ears when Foster spoke. It was a gesture that he probably didn't see but must have guessed had taken place.

"I'm sorry about the noise," he whispered. "I suppose my normal voice is too loud for your little ears.

"What do you mean?" Ben asked.

There was a throaty chuckle, and the box began to shake violently. "Oh, I must learn to control myself, or I might accidentally hurt you. I simply meant that my voice must hurt your ears when I talk in a normal tone. People your size can't stand the volume of a normal-sized person's voice at close range. I wouldn't be able to hear you at all if I didn't have an earphone plugged into the transport box to amplify your voices.

"People our size? What are you talking about?" Ben asked.

"I think your little girlfriend had the right idea," Foster replied. "She called us giants, did she not?"

Ben left out a nervous chuckle. "You're kidding, right?"

Ned Foster chuckled again. "No, son, I'm not kidding. Right now you're only about one centimeter tall. Ms. Dills is slightly shorter. Don't worry about it, though, because that's just the right height for living in Gildor. Keeping things small is how we managed to keep the place a secret all these years.?"

"You mean you shrunk everybody on the island?" Megan asked.

Ben was happy she was finally thinking about something besides her father's untimely demise. It meant she was getting over the shock. He hoped so anyway.

"Not quite, my dear," Foster said. "It would be more accurate to say that we shrunk *every living thing* on the island that lives in that cavern I told you about earlier. Outside on the island of Gildor itself is where our genetic research lab exists. The folks who work for me there keep the facility running as well as maintaining the power plant and solar cells that supply the island's power. As far as those people working there for FRU, they know the rest of the place is just a thriving, tree-covered island jutting out of the ocean. They do their jobs and take six months a year off while another unsuspecting crew moves in to replace them for the other half of the year."

Foster fell silent for a moment. "Well, I guess I should tell you a little more about the part of Gildor you'll be living on, or maybe I should say, living in. The trees there will seem enormous to you, but in actuality, they're only scrub about two to three feet high, nothing but pesky bushes to normal- sized humans. The cattle my great-grandfather once raised there are gone now. They became part of the research facility and were mixed in with the rest of FRU's genetic and cloning experiments. I haven't visited the island myself in over thirty years, but the people I have make occasional deliveries there for me say there are hundreds of thousands of humanoids living there now. You won't have to worry about overcrowding though. The cavern under Gildor is over two and a half miles long and almost two miles wide. Considering the height you are now, that would be about the same size as an entire continent. I don't want to see either of you hurt, so I decided to deliver you there myself. This will be my last look at the island for quite a while. As of today, Gildor will no longer exist in any of FRU's computer records."

"And you're just going to leave us there with… with who knows what?" Megan yelled.

Ben caught the anger in her voice. *Atta girl, Megan. Don't let him think he's doing us a favor by stranding us on some isolated island.*

There was a short silence before Foster spoke again. The box moved suddenly when he held it out at arm's length so his huge face filled the entire window. "Considering the alternatives, I think you ought to be very happy just to be alive, Ms. Dills. You will have the remainder of your life to thank your father for this. If he would have kept his nose out of FRU's business, you wouldn't be in the predicament you're in right now."

Ben heard a quiet sob beside him and struck back with an angry reply of his own. "Somebody will stop you someday, Mr. Foster. You'll be sorry if Grandpa ever finds out what you've done. And I don't think Jack would ever let you get away with it either if he knew what you were doing."

"Leave my son out of this!" Foster's voice was loud enough to force his prisoners to cover their ears again. "Jack knows nothing of this, and he never will. All he knows is that FRU is trying to get a government contract to assist the Defense Department in prepping future special operations personnel and pilots for defense purposes. He doesn't know anything about Gildor or its inhabitants, and he never will, when it's his turn to take over the company. Our research there is finished, and all records of Gildor's existence will be destroyed by then. All Gildor will be is a lost memory when Jack takes over the company. I'm through talking now. We're almost to the island, and we will be landing soon. I'll have my people take you to the cavern and set you free once you're safely inside. There are some supplies under the floor. Remove them and take them with you when you leave the transport box. Do you understand?"

"You can't do this to us, Foster," Ben yelled while pounding on the window with both fists.

Foster gave the box a stern shake, causing Ben's and Megan's heads and arms to flop around like those of rag dolls. "Do you understand what I just told you?" Foster repeated.

Ben lowered his fists. "Yeah, we understand," he replied. "Good. Now goodbye."

"Wait! Mr. Foster, wait!" Ben's words went unheard. Silence was the only response he received. The transport box shook and rolled for a few seconds and then became still.

"It's no use," Megan said. "He's unplugged the earphone and set us down."

Ben whistled through his teeth, trying to regain his composure. "Foster said we were almost to the island. I wonder how long we were asleep."

"I'd guess at least a day anyway. There's really no way of knowing," Megan replied.

An uneasy calm fell over them after Foster set their prison down and left them alone. Ben tried counting the seconds out loud in an effort to keep track of the time that passed before they landed, but he kept losing count. Megan hadn't spoken a word for quite some time, and it was driving him crazy wondering what was going through her head. He was about to start pounding on the door in frustration when the sound of Megan's voice forced him to draw his wits about him.

"What do you think it will be like in that cavern?"

Ben turned and gave her a questioning glance. "What?" "Gildor, I mean," Megan said.

Ben cocked his head to one side and spoke through the side of his mouth. "I can't really say. Mr. Foster said there are people there, but he didn't say if they were friendly or not."

Megan's voice was quivering when she spoke again. "I hope they are." She paused a moment before going on. "I hope you don't mind me saying this, Ben, but I'm glad you're here with me."

"Yeah, so much for all those dates I was hoping to ask you out on," Ben replied. "It looks like we'll be spending a lot of time together from now on, huh?"

"I'm sorry I got you wrapped up in this, Ben," Megan said, bowing her head. "You wouldn't be in this mess if I wouldn't have asked for your help."

Ben reached out to caress the side of her face and lifted her head. "It's all right, Meg. We'll be okay. I promise I'll do whatever I have to do to keep you safe. Trust me and don't blame yourself for my being here. I would have insisted on coming with you anyway, even if I had another choice."

Megan took Ben's hand in both of hers when the transport box suddenly started to move again. Their safety harnesses were the only things that kept them from being hurled against the sides of their tiny prison. The violent shuffling lasted about a minute before things slowed down again and a white cloth fell over the window, blocking their limited view of the outside world.

"They must've put us in some sort of bag," Ben said, arching his neck trying to get a glimpse of what was happening. "They must be getting ready to take us to the cavern now."

They both screamed when a sudden sensation of flying overtook them. Ben felt as if he was going to fly up and hit headlong into the ceiling. The sensation only lasted a few minutes before they felt the box come to rest again. The inside of their little prison was soon flooded with sunlight when the cloth covering it was removed and the window was exposed to the sun. There was a sudden jerk, and they could feel themselves moving forward at a rapid rate.

Megan was the first to calm down enough to speak. "They must have put us in some kind of vehicle," she puffed.

Ben grabbed the straps of his safety harness so tight that his knuckles turned white. "Whoopee! Man, what a rush." He could feel the transport box bouncing back and forth as the vehicle ran quickly along a rough road. "I guess it won't be too long before we get a look at our new home. Right now I don't care what it looks like. I just want out of this stinking box." He guessed about fifteen minutes had passed before they felt the vehicle come to a stop. Only his harness kept him from collapsing to the floor in a heap at the sudden jerk. As soon as they came to a complete standstill, Ben turned his attention back to his companion. "You all right, Meg?"

Megan had a firm grip on her restraining straps and was holding herself in an upright position. "I'm okay," she blurted.

Once again they felt the sensation of flying as their prison was lifted out of the vehicle and carried for a short distance before being set down again. They sat motionless for a few minutes while they listened to voices rumbling outside the box. Then they heard a rattling sound for a moment before everything suddenly went silent.

"When are they going to open this thing up and let us out?" Megan screamed in frustration.

As if in answer to her question, a quiet hiss came from the ceiling of the box. "Are you two all right in there?" a low voice asked.

"Yeah... yeah, we're okay," Ben stammered.

"Good," the voice replied. "I'm going to open the door and let you out of there in a few seconds. After I release your restraining straps, open the trap door on the floor of the transport and remove the bag of supplies you'll find there. Then get out of the box ASAP. Understand?"

"We understand," Ben replied.

A moment later, he and Megan felt their restraining straps begin to loosen, and they quickly slipped out of them and stood up. Ben quickly knelt down on the floor and lifted the ring of the trapdoor on the floor of the transport box. A quick glance inside the cubbyhole revealed a large brown bag, and he grabbed it and took it out of its resting place before replacing the door. A moment later, the door to their prison popped open and fell flat on the ground in front of them, letting fresh, warm air rush into the cramped compartment.

"That's more like it," Megan said.

Ben took Megan's right hand in his empty left one and hefted the supply bag over his shoulder with his right. "Come on! Let's get outta here before they pull this thing outta this hole we're in! Run," he yelled, pulling Megan outside behind him. He spotted some rocks about fifty yards away and dragged the panting girl toward them.

After they were safely behind the rocks, Ben threw the bag of supplies down and pulled Megan close to him as they peered back in the direction of their former prison. They hunkered down and watched as the door to the box slowly lifted back up into place. A few seconds later, they saw the box slowly withdraw from its resting place, leaving a large hole leading to the outside world. Then they heard a loud rumble tear through the inside of the cavern, followed by a violent shaking of the earth when a large, heavy door filled the gap where the hole once was. The sudden shock caused a great cloud of dust to shoot high into the air. When things grew quiet, the two newcomers to Gildor sat up and looked at each other.

"Are you all right?" Ben asked, helping Megan to her feet. Megan nodded. "Yeah, I think so."

Ben took a quick look around. "W... welcome to Gildor," he stammered, reaching out to brush the dust from Megan's black locks.

Chapter 4

"Woo! Am I glad we weren't still in there," Ben said.

"Me too," Megan replied, still shaking dirt from her hair. "Mr. Foster certainly made sure he covered his tracks. Nobody will ever know we're here unless someone saw them put us in here."

Megan's inadvertent comment struck home, and Ben began scanning their surroundings for anyone who might have seen them coming out of the transport box. He didn't want to alarm Megan needlessly, but he had a feeling that Ned Foster probably wasn't worried about hiding his tracks all that well. He had taken the time to warn them beforehand that Gildor was populated with humanoids. Reality suddenly hit him. *Was that a hint that they might not be completely human?* he thought. *And if they aren't, are they dangerous?*

Megan noticed him glancing about. "What's wrong? Did you hear something?"

Ben shook his head. "I was just looking at our surroundings. They sure are beautiful."

Both of them were held spellbound by the stunning landscape. The false sunlight was at its zenith, so they could see everything in the clearing they were standing in. Directly in front of them, fifty yards beyond where they had exited the transport box, was a tropical forest of majestic trees with leaves shining light blue green in the brilliant light. Ben judged the gigantic plants to be over three hundred feet high with trunks that appeared to be at least twenty feet in diameter. He wasn't sure how tall the big trees really were, though, after considering his previous height of six feet now only equaled about a centimeter. Some quick figuring in his head proved one foot to now equal somewhere around one hundred eighty feet. It was so dark under the thick canopy of the forest that it was impossible to see more than a few yards beyond the edge of the forest.

He thought he saw the blurred movements of birds flying about in the underbrush, but there wasn't enough light to tell what they looked like or of what species they might be. The light beamed down on a small stream to their left, giving its slow, smooth surface a silver glow as the current carried it along its leisurely journey into the forest. Beyond the far bank of the stream lay a peaceful pond, the surface of which was broken only by an occasional fish or some other form of aquatic life that rose to catch low-flying insects. The forest began again on the far side of the pond and continued on behind the protective rocks where Ben and Megan stood.

They both gasped in amazement as they slowly turned to follow the contour of the forest. There, not more than thirty yards from where they were, stood an enormous woolly creature that looked to be a cross between an elephant and a water buffalo. A full twelve feet high at the shoulders and at least fifteen feet long, it stood nibbling at the leaves on the lower branches of a tree. Its body was shaped like that of an elephant. Its short, whip-like tail swished back and forth at pesky insects while the giant animal ate. Its legs were thick and long and ended with huge round feet, each one having only a single clawed toe at the front. The neck of the strange beast was short and bull-like, topped with a head the size of a refrigerator. Two long tusks grew out of its lower jaw and curled up and back toward the top of its gigantic head. The nose was broad and flat, like that of a water buffalo, only it had four distinct nostrils instead of two. In general, it wasn't hard to identify as a species that had no natural genealogy.

"Looks like we just discovered one of Foster Research Unlimited's genetic experiments," Ben whispered. Tearing his attention from the creature, he turned to his right. A low flat tract of land lay there covered with long flowing grass the same blue-green hue as the leaves of the forest. The expanse of the flat land stretched for about half a mile before ending at the foot of a row of high cliffs. The steep walls rose high enough, perhaps seven hundred feet above the grassland, to keep whatever lay beyond them a mystery.

Ben moved to sit atop the rocks that he and Megan had hidden behind earlier and wiped sweat from his brow. *Seven hundred feet*, he thought. *How many inches is that? If I weren't so doggone small, I could probably step right over them. It's hard to tell what this place might be hiding.*

Megan moved to sit beside him and pointed at the behemoth chomping on the leaves. "Do you think that thing will try to eat us?" she asked, sounding genuinely concerned.

Ben chuckled softly. "I don't think so. It seems to be herbivorous. See how it only eats the leaves off that tree. I don't think it'll cause us any trouble if we don't bother it. It must not scare easily because it didn't run away when that big door slammed shut a while ago. It had to be standing there when all that noise was being made. We surely would have heard it approaching otherwise because it's too big to walk up on us without making some kinda noise."

Megan's posture eased a little. "Well, if you say it's harmless…"

Ben shook his head and held his hands up in front of him. "I didn't say that. I said I didn't think it will cause us any trouble."

"Do you think there's anything else around here that we should worry about?" Megan asked.

"I haven't the foggiest," Ben replied. "I suppose we'll find out before too long though."

Megan continued to watch the creature and whispered, "Mr. Foster has really gone and done it, hasn't he?"

"What do you mean?" Ben asked.

Megan had a perplexed expression on her face when she turned to face him. "He's stranded us on some godforsaken island, inside some underground cave that no one but a few people even know about. How are we going to survive here?"

Ben opened his arms and turned from side to side. "We may be in the middle of who knows where, but I wouldn't say this place is godforsaken. How can you call something so beautiful god-forsaken?"

Megan suddenly popped a smile. "Ben, you certainly have a way of making things seem brighter than they really are. I hope that's a knack you never lose."

Ben stood up and offered Megan his hand. "Come on! Let's go look this place over. We need to find, or build, some sort of shelter before nightfall, or should I say, before the lights go out. I don't know exactly what they have up there lighting this place, but it sure is bright."

Megan nodded in agreement. "Yeah, and it's hot too."

Ben looked up into the bright light. "I wonder if they heat this place with that light too. Or is it because this island is tropical that it's just naturally warm underground? I guess we may never know the answer to that question." He jerked his head in the direction of the pond they had seen earlier and said, "Come on. Let's see what other mysteries this place may hold."

They explored the clearing and were amazed at the abundance of unrecognizable plant life that they found growing in such a small area. There were hundreds of varieties of flowers that neither of them had ever seen before. It was the home to thousands of insects as well, some of which had nasty bites, as Ben discovered when one of them left a good-sized welt on his hand when he accidentally aggravated it.

Ben hadn't noticed the tiny bug until he felt it crawling on the back of his right arm. Thinking nothing of it, he tried to brush the pesky thing off and received a painful bite for his effort. After letting out a surprised yelp, he pulled his left hand away and looked at it. A little red fly was still attached to where it had sunk its fangs into his palm. He carefully scraped the dead insect off with his right thumbnail so it wouldn't inject any more poison into his hand and began to examine it. It wasn't more than an eighth of an inch long. Its six multifaceted eyes took up the whole front of its head. Unlike most insects, this one had ten legs instead of six, and it had a single heavy wing on its back that appeared suited more for gliding than actual flight. Ben was beginning to suspect that a flying spider, rather than a fly, had bitten him as he had first thought. Evidently, it had to climb to a high perch and wait for an accommodating breeze to come along to carry it aloft. Whatever its means of transportation, it must have been very successful in its endeavors because its plump, little body was full of blood, and Ben was sure that it wasn't all his.

Megan walked up to Ben when she heard him yelp. "Are you okay?" she asked.

Ben brushed the spider off his hand and let it drop to the ground. "Yeah, it was just a spider."

"Just a spider," Megan replied sarcastically. "It must have had a powerful bite to make you yell like that."

"Too powerful," Ben replied, glancing up at the false sun. "It's getting hotter. If we start sweating, we might draw more of those little beasts. It's going to be hard enough getting used to this place without those things chewing on us."

Megan looked alarmed. "What about germs? What if that spider was a carrier of some sort of disease?"

Ben had already considered that. "We'll have to pray our immune systems are able to fight off infections the same as back home. There's no telling what we might run into here. Let's hope the germs are similar to those we're used to."

"Suppose they aren't?" Megan asked.

Ben threw his hands out to his sides. "There's not much we can do about it. We don't have any way of knowing what might be in the air here, or which of these plants might be poisonous and which ones aren't. We have to take some chances if we're going to live here."

Megan nodded. "You're right. I'm just frightened because this place is so creepy."

Ben held up the bag of supplies he had salvaged from the transport box. "Well, I guess I'm not so confident myself. Right now, I think we better check out this bag and see if there's anything in it that I can put on my hand. That spider's venom is beginning to burn."

"Oh my god, I hope it's not deadly!" Megan threw her hand over her mouth when she realized what she had said. "I mean… I hope you're okay. You are, aren't you?"

Ben held his hand up. "I'm okay. It feels a little bit like a beesting. See for yourself, it's not swelling or anything. It's just red and itchy around the bite. So I guess the poison isn't spreading. Even if it is, it doesn't seem to be bothering me. I'd still feel better if I had something to put on it though."

Megan took the bag from him and opened it. She rummaged through it for a few seconds before pulling out a small first aid kit. Then she took him by the hand and led him to the side of the stream where she had him sit down in the shade of some trees. "Now let's have a look at that hand," she said, popping the first aid kit open.

After Ben's hand had been treated, they stayed in the shade of the trees to inspect the remaining contents of the bag. Ned Foster didn't put any more than they needed in it for them to survive. Besides the first aid kit, the bag contained nothing more than a ten-foot length of rope, two sharp hunting knives in leather sheaths, a spool of fishing line, a package of hooks, a box of heavy sewing needles, a small magnifying glass, two pairs of thin khaki coveralls, and a typewritten letter, which Ben opened and began to read aloud.

June 4, 2020
Ben and Megan,

If you learn to use these things wisely, you will survive a long time on Gildor. The knives will come in most handy when you discover just how hostile your new surroundings can be. The fishing line and hooks will most likely supply you with your first real meal, so don't lose them. As for the needles, you will need them once you have learned to hunt. You will soon find out that the meager clothing you have on won't last forever, and there probably aren't any stores in Gildor to buy more, so you will have to supply your own. Protect the magnifying glass with your lives, for it will supply you with a means of building life-protecting fires.

You may hate me for leaving you in Gildor, but I'm sure once you get used to the place, you will agree that it was better than the only other option I had to assure your silence.

Ben, you can be thankful that your grandfather works for me. In a way, he is responsible for your being alive; it was he who perfected the technology my father developed fifty years ago that allowed me to let you live. David actually worked on the equipment that enabled me to reduce the two of you in size so that you could be transplanted in Gildor. He's been working on a way to reverse the process for the past fifteen years, and I think he is getting very close to that breakthrough. Thanks to him, we will be able to shrink future astronauts and launch them into space in vehicles much smaller than those currently in use today. And once they reach their destination, they can be returned to their normal size. Just think of the benefits the space program would gain from such technology. We would be able to completely break down anything's molecular structure and put it back together again hundreds of times, even thousands of times, smaller than it was and then break it down again and put it back together at its original size.

You will never get to see the final result of your grandfather's work, but at least this way, you and Megan will both be able to live long enough to start families of your own someday. Who knows, maybe the two of you will get together and start a family. You two make a good-looking couple, you know. I'm so sorry things turned out the way they did, but I do hope you get to enjoy a long and prosperous life together.

Sincerely,
Ned Foster

After he finished reading the letter, Ben balled it up and threw it on the ground. "He sure gets under my skin. He couldn't resist telling us that Grandpa worked on the equipment he used to shrink us so he could strand us here. Talk about rubbing your nose in it. What's he trying to prove anyway? How stupid does he think Grandpa is?" He turned to see what Megan was doing when she didn't reply.

Megan was sitting beside him staring straight ahead with her knees drawn up under her chin and her arms wrapped tightly around her legs.

"Are you all right?" he asked.

She nodded. "I don't think Mr. Foster was trying to prove how stupid your grandfather is at all. If you think about it, he said a lot of things with very few words. He told us, in a roundabout way, that your grandfather saved our lives, but he'll never know it. You can be proud of what your grandfather has accomplished, Ben. I wish I could be as proud of Daddy's." She lowered her head and let her forehead rest on her knees.

Ben put his hand on her shoulder. "You can be proud of your dad, Meg. He died trying to protect others from the likes of Ned Foster. We may be stranded here because of the investigation he was conducting into FRU's rather questionable genetic research, but at least he managed to get it stopped. Foster as much as admitted that himself. Who knows how many people your dad may have saved because of the sacrifice your dad made?"

Megan raised her head and looked at him through tear-filled eyes. "Maybe he did. But why do we have to pay the price?"

Ben thought for a moment before giving her his honest answer. "Sometimes that's the way God plans things, Meg. We may not understand why things have turned out the way they have right now, but we will in time."

Megan tilted her head to one side. "Do you really think so?"

Ben stood up and reached down to take her by the hand. "Trust me. We'll get the answers to all our questions someday."

Megan stood up and brushed the dust and grass off the seat of her shorts. "What do we do now?"

Ben looked toward the creek and pointed to a spot farther downstream. "There might only be a few hours of daylight left. I think we could both use a good bath before it gets dark. Come on, let's get the sweat and dirt washed off us before we start attracting unwanted attention from any more biting insects."

While they walked through the knee-high grass toward the stream, Megan drew Ben's attention to some strange-colored birds running in front of them. They were similar in size and shape to roadrunners. Bright-orange feathers covered their whole bodies except for their tiny skulls, which were covered with dull green flesh. They ran along in front of the two humans, gobbling up the insects that scurried out of their path. When they tried to get closer to one of them, it took off, fluttering its four wings wildly and squealing like a scared rabbit.

Ben led Megan to a spot along the stream where the grass only grew ankle high. After making sure there were no dangerous animals in the vicinity, he motioned for her to sit down on a boulder before turning to survey a section of the creek.

The water was clear and flowed over a clean gravel bed. As far as he could tell, there were no aquatic life forms in the water that might pose a serious threat to them. To make certain of that, he picked up a small stone and threw it into the slow-moving current. When he didn't see anything swimming away from, or toward, the spot where the stone had hit, he was convinced it was safe to enter the water. "We can bathe here," he said, slipping his T-shirt off over his head and stripping the rest of the way to his swimming trunks.

Megan wasted no time in stripping to her bikini and throwing her blouse and cutoffs down beside Ben's clothes. She glanced at them before turning toward the water. "We should wash our clothes after we've finished bathing. We really don't know how long we've been wearing them. Mr. Foster never told us how long we were asleep after they shrunk us."

"We can do that later," Ben replied. "Let's concentrate on getting ourselves clean first." He took Megan by the hand and led her into the cool flow of waist-deep water. He splashed a handful of water into his face and leaned forward to let the slow current flow over his overheated head and shoulders. The cool water was invigorating. He stayed under a few seconds and surfaced to find Megan standing beside him with a perturbed look on her face. "Something wrong?"

"We can't stay in this water too long, Ben," she said. "We really need to build some sort of shelter for the night. And we still need to wash our clothes."

"You're right," Ben replied. "Why don't we split the duties? As soon as we're done bathing, I'll start building a lean-to while you wash our clothes. We'll get things done faster that way."

Megan hunched her shoulders. "Okay! I'm sorry, I didn't mean to complain. I guess I have a case of the jitters. I just don't want to spend the night out in the open in this creepy place, that's all."

※

Ben had the lean-to half-finished an hour later and was busy cutting leafy limbs from a tree for the roof when he suddenly heard Megan yelling for him to hurry back to the creek. When he reached the bank, he found her standing on a huge stone in the middle of the creek, pointing downstream and literally screaming at the top of her voice. "Look, something big is coming up the creek!"

Ben didn't know what the thing was, and he wasn't going to wait around to find out. He plunged into the water and swam to the stone Megan was standing on. "Come on," he yelled, extending his hand up toward the frightened girl.

"Our clothes," Megan said, bending down to pick them up off the surface of the stone where she had laid them out to dry.

Ben yelled even louder. "Leave them! We gotta get outta here." He grabbed Megan by the arm and pulled her into the water screaming. Holding her arm tight in one hand, he kicked his powerful legs toward the bank and started swimming as fast as he could. Fear, combined with Megan's screaming, only served to make him swim faster. The time it took them to reach shore would have been good enough to set a new world record if anyone had been there to time them.

Before Ben could get to his feet, Megan was already pulling him out of the water. Something bumped his left ankle just before he stepped out onto the bank, but he didn't pay much attention to it. They stumbled and fell beside each other, puffing for air as soon as their feet hit dry ground. Glancing back at the stream a moment later, they saw the surface of the water boiling with activity where they had just been seconds earlier. It turned out that the big thing they had seen swimming upstream was many smaller things instead.

"It's a school of fish," Ben exclaimed. "There must be thousands of 'em." He started to crawl closer to the water to get a better look at the swarming mass when he heard Megan cry out behind him.

"My god, Ben, your ankle!"

Ben looked back and saw a small silver body attached to his left ankle and immediately sat up and tried to pull it off. He was surprised to feel how hard the fish's body was when he grabbed it. It was like a rock. He could feel its jaws beginning to tighten, so he turned to Megan after several failed attempts to dislodge it. "Quick, go get my knife outta the lean-to!"

Megan disappeared a few seconds and returned with both knives and the first aid kit. She gave one of the knives to Ben and kept the other one with the first aid kit.

Ben wedged the knife's sharp six-inch blade between the fish's lips and his ankle and began to twist the handle until he forced the little beast's mouth open. The little monster's jaws snapped shut with a loud crack the instant he pulled it off his angle. Blood shot from the lacerations in his ankle as soon as the fish left go. Not willing to take a chance of letting the little monster get another bite on him, he quickly drove the blade of his knife through its hard body and pinned it to the ground.

While the fish finished its death throes on the ground beside Ben, Megan turned her attention to his bleeding ankle. She wrapped both her hands around it to staunch the bleeding before taking his hands in hers and placing them just above the wound. "Keep a tight grip right here while I clean and bandage your ankle," she said, pulling a roll of gauze from the first aid kit.

After Megan finished cleaning and bandaging his ankle, Ben picked up the dead fish to examine it. It was only about seven inches long, but it appeared deadly. Its whole body was covered with thick silver scales that shone like steel. Three long fins grew along the entire length of the top and both sides of its slightly tapered body, giving it a similar appearance to that of the nock and fletching on the back end of an arrow. Its teeth were unlike anything he had ever seen in a fish before. There were no separate or jagged teeth; instead, it had two horseshoe-shaped ridges of razor-sharp bone in the top and bottom of its open maw. The mouth was massive, almost too large for the small body it accommodated. However, the strangest thing about it wasn't its mouth or the size and shape of its body; it was its eyes, or rather, the lack of eyes. The little monster was completely blind. There were two sets of nostrils located above its huge mouth, which Ben was sure more than made up for the absence of eyes.

No doubt, Ben thought, *this little fella could detect the smell of a potential meal for thousands of feet. It's a perfect representation of an eating machine. It and its little buddies could put a school of piranhas to shame.*

Megan stood beside Ben watching him study the fish. "How does your ankle feel?"

"It'll be okay." He flipped the fish's limp body into the water beside him, and the surface began to boil as soon as the bloody offering hit the surface. Then he pointed to the rock where their clothes had been. "Things could have been a lot worse if you wouldn't have called me when you did. Looks like we won't have to worry about washing our clothes anymore."

The fish must have been able to smell their clothes even though they were lying on the rock and not in the water. The little devils had leaped up onto the rock and dragged them into the stream. Half a minute later, there was nothing left but a few strands of green material from Megan's blouse and shorts, and there were no evident remains of Ben's brown T-shirt or his blue jeans.

Megan put her hands on her hips and sighed. "Could we please get out of here, Ben? I've had just about all I can stand of this place for one day."

Ben stood up and slipped his hunting knife into its leather sheath before tucking it into the waistband of his swimming trunks. "Well, we still have those coveralls Mr. Foster gave us and our sneakers," he said, stomping his feet in the grass. We'll have to hang them inside the lean-to overnight to dry. He nodded toward the unfinished lean-to. "Let's go. If I hurry, I can still finish the lean-to before dark."

"I'm hungry," Megan said.

"Me too, but we'll have to wait until morning before we can go hunting for food. It's just not worth risking our necks in the dark to satisfy our hunger. We're not in danger of starving yet." He took a step and almost lost his balance.

"Let me help you," Megan said, taking his right arm and putting it around the back of her neck to help support his weight. She helped him make his way back to the lean-to, where they set to work finishing the small shelter together. An hour later, they were nestled comfortably inside their dry shelter while a cool shower fell in the darkness outside.

Chapter 5

Ben's ankle was slightly swollen in the morning, so Megan insisted that he stay off it for a while. She checked the wound thoroughly and, after she was satisfied it was not infected, rewrapped it with a clean bandage. Unable to walk any distance, Ben was forced to stay inside the lean-to out of the hot sun while Megan went looking for breakfast. He didn't like the idea of her going alone, but there was no way he could accompany her.

They had to have weapons, so Ben kept himself busy by making a bow from a sapling he had cut while working on the lean-to the previous day. He was just finishing the primitive weapon a few hours later when Megan strolled back into camp. He had cut a length of the rope and unwound a portion of it to use as a bowstring. He was just tying the ends of the string into the notches on either end of the limber sapling when Megan approached him. "How did the hunting go?" he asked, lying the bow aside and looking up at Megan.

Megan sat down beside him and put the huge folded leaf she was carrying on the ground between them. "I found these on some bushes a few hundred yards from here." She unfolded the leaf and opened it up to reveal hundreds of plump blueberries inside. "They taste just like the blueberries back home, so I assume they're safe to eat."

Ben licked his lips as he picked up a few of the berries and popped them into his mouth. He closed his eyes and left the sweet juice of the berries flow slowly over his tongue. "Oh yeah." He sighed. "Now that's what I call good eatin'."

"I take it you like them then." Megan giggled.

"Remind me to let you go hunting for breakfast more often," Ben said, gathering up a huge handful and starting to munch on them.

After they finished their meal, Megan reached out and picked up the bow Ben had been working on. "I see you've been busy while I was out gathering food. Will this thing work?"

Ben nodded and picked up the crude quiver he made from some dry grass he wove together to hold the arrows. "It will if I can get the arrows to fly straight. I didn't have time to look for anything to use for arrowheads or fletching yet, so I'll have to get mighty close to kill anything with them if I try to shooting them as they are."

Megan pulled her legs up in front of her and lowered her chin to the top of her knees before turning to look at Ben. "Who taught you how to make a bow and arrows like that?"

Ben hunched his shoulders. "My dad taught me how to make them when I was a little boy." The mention of his father suddenly brought old memories of both his parents flooding back to him. "I wish Mom and Dad were here right now."

"Do you miss them much?" Megan asked.

Ben nodded. "Yeah, I do. I can still remember all the camping trips Mom and Dad took me on. We spent a lot of time in the woods together and had a lot of fun in those days. Dad taught me how to hunt and fish. He even taught me how to track wild game and make my own weapons, like this bow. Mom was always telling me to be patient. She always said that I had a quick trigger and that it would get me into trouble one day. We sure had fun together whenever they could get away from their business for a while. I was only twelve when their plane crashed."

"What happened?" Megan asked. "I mean… were they going someplace special when their plane crashed? Why weren't you with them?"

"They were on their second honeymoon," Ben replied. "They owned a small freight business. When one of their customers needed some cargo delivered to the West Coast one day, Dad asked Mom to go with him. He had to stay in California for a few days, so he decided to take Mom along and treat the trip like a second honeymoon. Their plane went down in the Rockies on their way home. I was staying at a friend's house while they were away. I can still remember when they told me about the accident." He shuddered involuntarily as the memory came rushing back to him. "All they wanted to do was spend a little time alone together. Now they're spending eternity together. That was almost six years ago."

Megan reached out and touched his hand. "I'm sorry if I made you talk about unpleasant memories."

"It's all right," Ben said. "I can't mourn them forever." He gave her an inquisitive glance. "You never told me much about your parents. Why not?"

Megan sat staring at her hands for a moment before answering, "I'm afraid there isn't much of a story to tell," she said without looking up. "Are you sure you want to hear about them?"

"Only if you want to tell me about them," Ben said apprehensively. "You don't have to if you don't want to."

Megan raised her eyes to meet his. "I promise, I'll tell you about my parents someday. I hope you'll forgive me, but I really don't feel like talking about them right now."

Ben nodded his head. "I understand. I think I know how you feel, just losing your dad and all."

Megan kept quiet for a moment as if trying to gather her thoughts and then shrugged. "Thanks. I will tell you about them one day. Right now just isn't the right time. I just can't help feeling ashamed when I think that we're stranded here because of Daddy," she added, lowering her eyes to stare at the ground.

Ben shook his head. "It's not your dad's fault, Meg. He was just trying to do his job. Blame Ned Foster if you have to blame somebody for our being here. He didn't have to strand us here. He could have been honest with the government people and told them about how his grandfather and father hid their illegal research. I don't think they would have held him responsible for their actions. But he didn't, and he sent us here instead to hide his own shame."

Megan raised her head and sniffed. "I don't really mean to blame Daddy. I just get so frustrated when I think that we can't do anything about the situation we're in. Thanks for not blaming him."

Ben stood up to test his ankle and quickly readjusted his weight when a sharp pain suddenly shot up his leg. "Megan, I hope you know you don't have to hide anything from me. Thanks for sharing your thoughts with me though. I'm glad that you trust me enough to do that."

Megan stood up and stared into Ben's gray eyes as if trying to read his mind. She must have noticed him shifting his weight. "Yeah, I know. You don't have to hide anything from me either. Like, for instance, that pain you have in your ankle right now." She took him by the arm and helped him sit back down. "Stay off that ankle and let me handle things around here for a while!"

Ben yawned. "I guess I could use a few more hours sleep." He rolled back into the lean-to and closed his eyes, only to sit up and reopen them a minute later when he heard Megan moving about outside. She was kneeling a few feet in front of the lean-to with her back toward him, apparently digging a hole. "What are you doing now?" he asked.

Megan held up the magnifying glass from the supply bag without looking back. "Digging a fire pit for later. We'll need a fire if we ever manage to find something other than berries to eat. Besides, a fire will help keep wild animals away." She stopped digging and turned to look at Ben. "Won't it?"

Ben wanted to laugh but had second thoughts about it. "Yeah, it will. I'll go hunting later if the swelling in my ankle goes down."

"You mean *we'll* go hunting," Megan interjected.

Ben lay back with his hands behind his head. "That's what I meant to say.

We'll go hunting later."

Apparently satisfied with Ben's reply, Megan went right back to digging for a few seconds before turning around again. "Do you think we'll find people like ourselves on this island? I mean, the animals we've seen so far seem so different from those we're used to. How different do you think the people will be?"

Ben had intended to go to sleep, but Megan's question intrigued him so much that he forgot about being tired. "I've been giving that some thought," he said. "It's a well-known fact that different environments affect the way people evolve. For instance, people have different-colored skin depending on what part of the world they're from, and the color and shape of their eyes can vary too."

"That's a fact I'm only too aware of," Megan quipped. "I'm a good example of two different races mixing things up."

Ben chuckled. *I wish she would tell me more about herself.* "Yeah, and a darned pretty one at that," he replied, giving her an emphatic nod. "Now, as I was saying, if Gildor turns out to be what it appears to be so far, my guess is there are people like us living here." He fought back a yawn while he gave the subject more thought. "We'll find out sooner or later. Perhaps as early as tomorrow when we go hunting. That is, if my ankle is healed enough for me to walk on it by then."

Megan hunched her shoulders and turned to resume her digging. "I hope they're like us," she said.

Ben watched her dig for a few minutes until his eyelids grew too heavy for him to hold open anymore and left them drift shut. Megan's back was the last thing he remembered seeing before falling fast asleep.

The sun was high in the sky when Ben awoke. He judged the time to be well past noon when he crawled out of the lean-to. He stood up beside the small fire burning in the firepit and then stretched out his arms. While twisting to and fro to loosen the stiff muscles in his back and shoulders, he looked around for Megan and spied her kneeling by the creek.

She was kneeling over with her right arm moving back and forth between her knees as she cut at something on the ground with her knife.

"Hey there," Ben shouted.

Megan looked up and waved. "Well, good afternoon, sleepyhead. I hope you slept well."

Ben stretched again before hobbling gingerly toward her. "What are you doing there?"

Megan held up a large fish that she had just finished cleaning. "I've been fishing while you were sleeping. There's more than those flesh-eating fish in this stream. I was walking by the stream hunting for bird feathers that you could use for your arrows when I spotted this big whopper swimming near the bank. I tried catching him with my hands with no success. Then I remembered the fishing line and hooks in the supply bag. I tied a short piece of the line to a hook and tied the other end to a stick and used a small bug for bait. The rest is history." She held up the fish again. "Here's dinner."

Ben shook his head. "You're a handy girl to have around, Meg. I hope I'm as lucky tomorrow when we go hunting. I hate to think that I can't help provide food. You've been doing all the work so far. First you tend my wounds, and now you supply our meals while all I've managed to do is build a lousy lean-to and let a crummy fish try to bite my foot off."

Megan washed the blood off her hands in the creek and stood up with her catch. She gave Ben a stern look and nodded toward the lean-to. "The lean-to isn't lousy," she said. "It kept us warm and dry during the rain last night, and it protected us from the hot sun today, didn't it?"

Ben glanced over his shoulder at the meager shelter and grimaced. "Yeah, but it's not the same as being able to provide a hot meal when we need one."

"Maybe not, but I didn't know how to make a lean-to, and you did. Having a good shelter is just as important as eating. We can't survive without anything to eat or without a good, sturdy shelter, can we?"

Ben shook his head. "Guess not."

Megan pointed at his ankle. "You saved my life yesterday when you pulled me off that rock and got me out of the stream. I might not be here right now if you wouldn't have risked your life to save mine. I think you've done a lot since we've been here, Ben. Besides, you'll get plenty of chances to supply food for us after your ankle heals."

"Yeah, I guess I have managed to accomplish a few things," he replied, smiling sheepishly.

Megan walked past him and slapped the fish into his midsection with a wet smack. "Don't let your deeds of gallantry go to your head, hero. I built the fire and caught the fish. Now you can cook it." She stopped and glanced back over her shoulder. "Oh, by the way, I found an old bird's nest full of big feathers out in the clearing earlier. I put the feathers inside the lean-to so you would find them when you woke up. I guess you were too sleepy to notice them."

Ben looked down at the fish in his hands and started to laugh as he turned to follow her. "Well, I'll say this about you: you sure know how to deflate a guy's ego in a hurry. I'll get back to work on the arrows right after we eat."

Chapter 6

The following morning arrived with the unusual songs of the strange birds that lived in the clearing. Ben and Megan rose early and ate a pitiful breakfast of leftover fish from the night before. Afterward, the meager meal left them almost as hungry as they were before they had eaten.

The pain in Ben's ankle had subsided enough to allow him to walk on it without causing any real discomfort, so he decided he could go hunting. "Maybe we'll find a deer or something if we follow the game trail I found down by the creek the day before yesterday," he said.

Megan's left eye closed as she screwed her face in a disgusting manner. "Can't we kill something else besides a deer? You know, like a fish or something? I mean, deer are so pretty. It would be a shame to kill one just to eat it."

Ben couldn't believe what he was hearing. "You obviously aren't hungry enough yet, or you wouldn't be talking that way. But yeah, you can try to catch some more fish if you want. I'm warning you, though, it won't be easy. Fish can't supply us with hides for clothing. I don't plan on killing a deer just for fun, you know." He shut up after that because he knew Megan would change her mind about the deer when she realized real hunger and the need for clothing.

Megan lowered her head and began wringing her hands together. "Sorry, I just don't know if I could bear to eat something as beautiful as a deer."

"It's okay," Ben replied, gathering his bow and arrows from the floor of the lean-to. "Let's go see what we can find. We may not have to kill anything. We might find some fruits or vegetables growing out there somewhere."

They were careful to keep a sharp eye out for danger as they followed the game trail into the forest. They stopped every so often to survey their surroundings until they came to a fork in the trail. The trail on the left followed the stream closely, but the underbrush growing on either side of it was so thick and thorny that they decided to take the wider, more open trail on the right. The right trail also continued to parallel the stream, but from a greater distance, so the teens were still able to follow the stream and avoid most of the thorns at the same time. The sharp thorns had started to take a heavy toll on their thin coveralls; both their coveralls had several holes torn in them already. Taking extra care not to get scratched or let their clothing be torn anymore than possible, they pushed on at a painstakingly slow pace as they pushed on deeper into the shadows of the great trees. To make sure they didn't wander too far from the stream, they stopped every few minutes to listen for the sound of running water, but it was getting almost impossible to hear anything over the constant chatter of birds and insects.

After stopping so many times, Megan tapped Ben on the shoulder. "It sounds like we're getting close to the creek again," she said, wiping sweat from her brow. "I sure could use a cool drink. Do you think the water is still okay to drink? It might be full of dirt and leaves under these trees."

Ben listened to the inviting sound of the running water and nodded. "I don't think the water will be foul. As long as it's running, it ought to stay fairly clean. This trail should lead us back to the creek soon. There's plenty of cover for whatever made it to be able to drink without being seen. If the animals on this island think like those back home, they ought to have a side trail leading back to the water somewhere."

They followed the trail until it broke into a clearing about forty yards long by thirty yards wide, with the stream flowing through it. The water ran in clear ripples over the rocky bottom and showed no signs of grayness or scum on the surface. Small clumps of blue-green algae grew along the banks and on the larger stones on the bottom: good signs the stream wasn't polluted.

Ben knelt down on one knee, scooped a handful of the lucent liquid into his cupped hands, and raised it to his nose. When he didn't smell any strange odors, he took a cautious sip. A moment passed, and then he grabbed his throat and gasped for breath. He choked a few seconds and threw his hands into the air before falling over backward to the ground.

"Very funny, Ben," Megan said, easing the toe of her sneaker into his ribs. She stood with her hands on her hips, watching him for a moment before jamming her toe into his ribs a little harder. "Okay, you can stop pretending now. You're not fooling me." When Ben failed to move, she became concerned and knelt down beside him and put her ear to his chest. When he remained motionless, she raised his arm and dropped it to the ground. "Ben, I can see you're breathing, so stop pretending." She slapped his face, but not hard enough to really hurt. "Okay, I'll just leave you here alone. I'm going hunting." She stood up and walked off into the forest, where she hid behind a tree to watch how he would react.

Ben still didn't move. The steady rise and fall of his chest was the only movement she saw for almost a minute. She decided he wasn't faking after that and came charging back. She almost fell on top of his inert form when she knelt down beside him. "Oh my god, Ben! Ple-please don't die." She tried slapping his face again. This time, she hit him hard enough to make it hurt. When that failed to revive him, she tried shaking him back to life; and when she noticed he had stopped breathing, she glanced around looking for help. "Ben, you can't die," she screamed. Desperate, she pulled her raven tresses back from her face and tried to administer CPR.

As soon as their lips touched, Ben's chest began to heave irregularly, and a low gurgling sound arose from deep within his throat before Megan could even blow the first breath of air into his lungs. Then he started laughing aloud, and his hands shot up on either side of Megan's face to hold her lips firmly against his.

As soon as Megan became aware of the cruel joke that had been played on her, she jerked away so violently that she fell back on her buttocks. "Ben Thomas, you... you pig," she stammered. "Don't you ever do that again!"

Ben sat up, still laughing. "Oh, come on, Meg! I was only kidding. I didn't mean any harm."

Megan stood up and turned her back toward him, folding her arms tightly in front of her. "That's not funny," she sobbed, glancing over her shoulder at him. "What if something really did happen to you? What would happen to me? I don't know anything about surviving in the wilderness."

Ben scrambled to his feet and turned her around to face him. "I'm sorry, Meg." He looked directly into her dark watery eyes. "I wasn't thinking. I won't do anything like that again. Will you forgive me?"

Megan looked up at him. Her eyes moved rapidly back and forth studying his face, as if trying to decide whether he was telling the truth or not. Ben thought his heart was going to give out. He hadn't realized how badly he frightened her. Then he relaxed when she moved closer and leaned her head against his chest.

"I couldn't stay mad at you even if I wanted to," she said. "Promise me you won't pull any more stunts like that again!"

He cupped her face in his hands and kissed her on the forehead. "I promise I won't pull any more bad jokes. The water's okay. You can get a drink if you still want to."

They stayed in that spot long enough to get a drink and rest a few minutes before reentering the forest at the far end of the clearing. After following the creek about thirty yards farther downstream, they were flabbergasted when they broke into a second smaller clearing.

The clearing was about twenty feet wide and ended at a sheer cliff a few yards from where they came out of the forest. The rushing water splashed lightly around the base of a huge boulder before cascading over the precipice in a misty waterfall that ended far below. Several large fruit-bearing trees grew on either side of the boulder. They stood atop the cascade like rigid guards watching over their majestic stone monarch. Some of the fruit from the trees was scattered about in the lush blue-green grass that covered the clearing.

Ben led Megan under the fruit trees and bent down to pick up a piece of the ripe fruit. It was bright pink, shaped like a kidney bean, and about the same size as his open palm.

"I don't suppose that thing is good to eat," Megan quipped.

Ben turned the strange fruit over in his hands and gave it a close inspection. "I'm not sure. There's only one way to find out."

"Just our luck." Megan scoffed, crossing her arms. "Here we are, standing in the middle of this Garden of Eden, and we can't eat the fruit because we don't know if it'll kill us or not."

Ben glanced at her and chuckled. He was relieved to see that she still had her sense of humor after being so upset with him earlier. "We'll know in a little while," he said. "We'll just take some of it back to camp with us and feed it to some of the small animals roaming around there. If they eat it and it doesn't make them sick or anything, then we'll know it's safe to eat. Okay?"

Megan considered his suggestion and smiled. "Okay. But what are we going to eat now? I'm tired and hungry."

Ben looked around the clearing and pointed toward the top of the boulder standing at the head of the waterfall. "We can rest up there if you're tired. In the meantime, I can pick some of the berries off those bushes growing on the face of the cliff beside it. They're the same as the ones you found growing in the field back at camp, so we know they're safe to eat."

Megan threw her hands out at her sides. "Sounds good to me."

Ben wrapped several pieces of the strange fruit in a large leaf similar to the one Megan had put the berries in the day before. After tying the ends of the leaf together, he took Megan by the hand and led her to the top of the boulder, where they stood watching the water flow endlessly over the high precipice for several minutes. There was a vast plain far below them, but they weren't sure how far down it actually lay because they couldn't see the bottom of the cliff from their vantage point. It was impossible to distinguish any details other than the dark-green grass that grew on the uniform flatland.

"This looks like a good place to rest before we return to camp," Ben said. "You go ahead and rest while I pick some berries! We can both take a break afterward."

"Good idea," Megan replied, yawning. "I can't think of a more beautiful place to take a nap. The shadow of the cliff will keep us cool while we rest." She gazed out at the panoramic view of the distant plains as she sat down on top of the boulder and raised her arms up over her head. Lacing her fingers together, she stretched wearily and twisted to and fro at the waist.

Time passed quickly while they sat eating the berries in the shade and enjoying the view. Megan grew weary after she finished eating and soon gave up trying to maintain a coherent conversation. She stretched out on the warm surface of the boulder and closed her eyes while they were talking and soon fell asleep. There were still several hours of daylight left, and there wasn't any hurry to return to camp, so Ben left her sleep while he stood watch. He would awaken her a few hours before nightfall, if she didn't wake up on her own by then. Although they hadn't run into any dangerous animals, Ben still didn't want to be caught out in the forest after dark. *Why take chances as long as we only have one weapon to defend ourselves with?* he thought. *I've got to make another bow for Megan and teach her how to use it.*

It was almost dusk when Megan finally awoke. Puzzled, she sat up and looked around until she was wide awake. She relaxed when she saw Ben sitting a short distance away watching her. "I must have fallen asleep," she moaned.

Ben snickered. "Yes, I guess you did. For at least a few hours."

Megan leaned back and squinted at the false sun. It had moved completely across the sky and was already beginning to dip below the horizon. "God! I didn't realize I was so tired." She got up and walked over to Ben and knelt in front of him. "What have you been up to while I was sleeping?" she asked.

Ben held the sapling up in his hand. It was almost an exact replica of his bow, only a little thinner and unfinished. "I've been doing a little whittling. This will be yours when I'm finished with it. Never know when we might need a second bow. I would have finished the darned thing, but I fell asleep for a while myself. We better get outta here before it gets much later."

Megan glanced around nervously. "I hope I never have to use that bow."

Ben smiled and hunched his shoulders. "I hope not too. I did make it just in case you ever have to protect yourself though."

"Oh." She sighed. "I thought for a minute there that you might have seen something while I was sleeping."

"No," Ben replied. "I was just passing the time creatively, that's all. And I fell asleep too." He stood up and offered her his hand. "We'd better head back to camp before it gets too dark to see where we're going."

As he led Megan toward the forest, he started to get an uneasy feeling. Things didn't seem quite right, but he couldn't put his finger on what was wrong. It wasn't until after they reached the edge of the darkening wood that he realized what was bothering him. The insects had stopped their interminable chatter. *Something big must be close by for them to shut up so fast. But what can it be?* He kept his thoughts to himself and tightened his grip on Megan's hand as he picked up the pace.

"You're hurting my hand, Ben," Megan complained, beginning to resist being dragged along the dark game trail. "Our clothes will be cut to pieces by this brush if we continue at this pace in the dark. Slow down, will ya? I can barely see where we're going."

Ben kept quiet and stopped to let his eyes adjust to the poor light. It was then that he realized they were on a different trail than the one they had followed to the waterfall. To make sure of that, he bent down to examine the path and discovered there was no sign of their passing that way earlier. He stood up and gave Megan an alarmed look. "We have to backtrack. I must have missed our trail in the dark. I don't remember it being this narrow before."

"I didn't think we were going in the right direction," Megan replied. "What's the big hurry anyway?"

Ben decided it was best to let her know why he was worried. "I don't like what I'm hearing," he said. "The insects have stopped making noise."

Megan gave him a dumbfounded look. "Yeah. So?" "So it means that something big is in the woods." Megan rolled her eyes. "Yeah, we are."

"No, there's something else here besides us. The insects shut up before we even entered the woods."

Megan's hand quivered inside Ben's as she took a fleeting look around. "What do you suppose it is?" she asked.

"Ah, probably nothin'," Ben replied, trying to reassure himself. "It's probably just a rabbit or somethin'. I just panicked for a second. Let's turn around and head back. The other trail can't be too far."

Since the trail was so narrow, Megan had to take the lead because Ben couldn't squeeze around her. They hadn't walked twenty yards before a huge white shape swung down out of the trees from above and landed with a heavy thud in front of Megan. Megan threw up her arms and screamed before turning to run. In her panic, she ran headlong into Ben and managed to push around him, but not without shoving him into the thorny underbrush on the side of the trail.

Although Ben had reacted quickly, he didn't react fast enough. He heard the thing coming through the trees long before he saw it and nocked an arrow on his bowstring. He had just started to raise the weapon before Megan suddenly turned and knocked him into the underbrush as she fled from the lumbering giant coming toward them. The creature reached out and struck Ben a tremendous blow across the left shoulder when he tried to regain his feet. The force of the blow threw him ten feet into the thick brush, and his coveralls became the merciless recipient of the spiny branches. The thin material literally tore away from his arms, legs, and chest in shreds. He was half naked by the time he stopped tumbling. He managed to scramble up onto his hands and knees as soon as he stopped rolling and crawled back to the trail in time to see the grunting, rumbling monstrosity follow the terrified girl around a bend in the trail. Then

Megan's screaming suddenly stopped. Realizing he had to hurry, Ben reached down to push himself upright when his hand bumped something on the ground beside him. Looking down to see what it was, he discovered his bow lying in the middle of the trail and hurriedly picked it up. *No time to waste,* he thought. He forced his bruised and bleeding body into an upright position and moved as fast as he could to follow Megan and her gruesome pursuer down the trail.

He only managed to cover about forty yards in the next two or three minutes because he had to stop periodically to listen, even to the faintest sounds. There was urgency for speed, but he also had to be careful. He couldn't help Megan if he ran headlong into the beast off guard. Moving slowly forward, he heard low grunting noises coming from somewhere nearby. The noises seemed to be coming from somewhere off to his left. He thought his heart was going to pound right out of his chest when he turned to investigate.

He covered the next few feet walking carefully heel-to-toe, moving through the underbrush as quietly as he could. When it sounded like he was within a few feet of the noises, he stopped to part the bushes and peered into a small moonlit clearing. The sight that met his probing eyes filled him with dread.

Not twenty feet from where Ben stood were two large, humanoid creatures. The larger of the two paced back and forth on all fours with a heavy club in its right hand while the smaller one sat hunched over beneath a tree examining some unseen object in its hands. Both were simian in appearance and sported long gray manes on their heads that resembled fright wigs more than hair. They were larger and much fiercer-looking than any gorillas Ben had ever seen in zoos. That was a fact he became aware of when the larger one stood up to its full seven feet, enabling the startled teen to get a good look at its horrifying visage. The shock caused Ben's breath to freeze in his throat. The ugly giant turned its massive sloping head toward the awestruck teen and hefted the club it held over its right shoulder and stuffed it into a crude scabbard tied on its back. In doing so, its thick mane parted for a moment. Those eyes were hard and calculating, with slit pupils like those of a cat. The mouth was wide and thick-lipped and held partly open, exposing the jagged teeth within. The nose was wide and flat with four nostrils that spread halfway across the devilish face it centered.

After his initial shock, Ben turned his attention to the second creature. Even in the dim light, he could tell that it was a female. She was built exactly like her mate, except for the two large breasts that hung from her massive chest. She was smaller than her counterpart, but she was still a giant compared to human standards. There was little doubt that she could be just as threatening. Ben watched her playing with whatever she had in her hands, turning it over and over again, but he couldn't tell what it was. It wasn't until the ape woman held the plaything up in front of her face that Ben was finally able to get a good look at it. His heart leaped into his throat when he recognized the bit of khaki material as part of Megan's coveralls.

He scanned the rest of the clearing in hopes of locating the girl. Pulling an arrow from the quiver on his back, he started to nock it on his bowstring and discovered it was broken. Apparently, it had snapped when he was pushed into the underbrush earlier. Cursing under his breath, he reached for another arrow. Then keeping a tight grip on his bow and a close eye on the two anthropoids, he proceeded to moved even closer. After skulking within ten feet of the unsuspecting creatures, he finally located the object of his search.

It was the big male that revealed where the girl was. The ape man ambled around the tree that the female was sitting under and stooped to look at something hidden between two huge exposed roots. Reaching down into the hollow between the roots, he took hold of the object of his fascination and held it up for a closer look.

Ben cringed when he saw the hulking creature lift Megan into the air by the shoulder of her coveralls with one hand while he used the other to spin her around in a circle. He heard the sound of ripping cloth just before he saw Megan tumble helplessly to the ground when the material finally gave away. When the inert girl failed to move, the ape man lost interest and turned his attention to the little gold thing still dandling in his fingers. He stood there regarding the colorful bit of material for a moment before starting to amble away. He only took a few steps and then stopped, holding the bra up to his wide nose to sniff it before throwing it to the ground with a repulsive snort.

A moment later, the female dropped the khaki material she had been holding and got up to retrieve the gold thing she had seen her mate throw down on the ground. When the huge male saw her moving toward the discarded bra, he wheeled around and beat on the ground with both fists and grunted at her in something that sounded like primitive language. The reverberations caused by the huge ape man pummeling the earth made the leaves of the nearby trees rustle in protest. His mate must have realized he meant business because she backed away, shaking her head. She seemed to answer his bellowed comment in her own softer tone before turning and walking off through the trees on all fours. Left standing in the clearing alone, the male began spinning around and sniffing the air as if he had caught a strange scent. He spun in a full circle and continued sniffing for several seconds before he was completely satisfied that there was nothing odd about the odors he detected.

Ben wiped sweat from his brow, glad he was downwind of the simian. He hoped the creature would follow his mate away and thought he was just about to get his wish a moment later, but his hopes were suddenly dashed when the girl on the ground left out a low moan and moved her arm slightly.

The ape man quickly moved to the prostrate girl's side and bent down to take a closer look. He rolled her over on her back with one hand and moved his face even closer to hers. Lifting her arms, he left them drop to the ground again, as if trying to determine whether she was alive or dead. Still not satisfied, he tilted his head to one side and began rubbing the back of his gigantic hand along the curves of her torso. When she responded to his touch by moving her head and moaning again, he realized she was alive. That must have triggered some primitive instinct within him because he quickly backed away and reached for his club. He stood there staring at the tiny unmoving figure for a moment as if unsure of what to do next.

What passed through the ape man's primitive mind during those few seconds was a mystery to Ben, but he decided it was time to act. He didn't know what the anthropoid was going to do next, and he wasn't willing to wait to find out, not with Megan's life hanging in the balance. The anthropoid was too busy concentrating on the girl to notice Ben sneaking out of the brush.

By the time the anthropoid realized Ben was standing behind him, the point of a well-aimed arrow had penetrated deep into his slow brain from just below the base of his thick skull.

The female must have remained nearby because she called out to her mate seconds after he roared out in agony. Ben barely managed to duck behind the bole of the tree Megan was lying beside a moment before the ape woman reappeared. The female anthropoid discovered her mate rolling on the ground, trying to dislodge the arrow from the back of his skull, and realized he was in trouble, but she seemed to have no idea what to do to help him. Confused, she stood by and watched her great companion roll and toss until he ceased to move. Soon after that, one anthropoid lay dead on the ground while the other stood by in what looked to be total shock.

Ben remained hidden and watched every move the ape woman made, hoping she would turn and run when she realized that her companion was dead, but she lowered her head and looked into his lifeless eyes instead. After a few seconds, she turned her face up toward the dimly lit sky and left out a long forlorn howl that sent chills up Ben's spine. Then she laid her head on the male's wide chest and started to cry, almost like a human woman mourning the death of her husband.

Ben watched the peculiar behavior for a moment before he decided to try to get to Megan. The ape woman's back was toward him, so he took a cautious step from behind the tree and almost fell when his feet became entangled in something on the ground. He glanced down and quickly kicked the tangled remains of Megan's bikini top away from his ankles before starting to sneak toward the inert girl again. Taking one last look in the grieving anthropoid's direction, he carefully lifted the unconscious girl to his shoulder and silently backed away through the trees. He could still hear the ape woman wailing for several minutes until the buzz of insects finally drowned the lurid noise out completely.

He carried Megan for what seemed an eternity before he finally laid her down on the ground with her head on his lap. He felt her wrist and left his breath quickly slip between his tightly pursed lips when he felt a strong, even pulse. A closer inspection revealed that, aside from a few minor scratches and bruises, she had no major injuries. *Thank God she's all right*, he thought. He tied the torn shoulders of Megan's coveralls back in place as best he could before he sat back to rest. After he caught his breath again, he picked her up and peered down into her beautiful face for a moment. *What would I have done if you'd been killed?* he wondered. *This is no time to waste on idle thought.* Then he turned to resume the trek back to camp with Megan cradled safely in his arms.

He had to make several stops along the way to rest and get his bearings. He wanted to make sure he didn't make another wrong turn after all the twisting and turning he did in the darkness, especially if the female ape came looking for them. It wasn't until he stopped for what must have been at least the twelfth time that he spied their previous tracks exposed by a dim patch of light on the soft soil. A wry smile touched his lips when he realized he was finally headed in the right direction. After resting a few more minutes, he forced himself to push on again.

The light had completely disappeared by the time Ben stumbled into camp with Megan in his arms. He didn't rest again until after he had laid the inert girl on the ground next to the glowing embers of the campfire and checked her carefully for any injuries he may have missed in the dark forest. When he was sure she was okay, at least as far as he could tell, he carried her into the lean-to and laid her down before allowing himself to rest for a few minutes. Then he cleaned her cuts and bruises with fresh water from the stream. When he finished tending to Megan's wounds, he cleaned his own battered body before finally giving into exhaustion and falling into a fitful slumber.

Chapter 7

Ben was awakened by hunger pangs. The rumbling of his stomach had grown so loud that he glanced over at Megan to see if the noise was disturbing her sleep. She was lying on her side with her back to him, but he could tell by the sound of her regular breathing that she was still sound asleep. He had awakened twice during the night and checked on her, only to find that she hadn't regained consciousness yet, and he wondered if he should try to wake her. He was worried that she might have suffered some sort of head injury from the rough handling the anthropoids had given her the previous night. He finally decided to let her sleep a while longer and took the fishing pole and headed for the creek.

An hour later, he was sitting in front of the lean-to cooking two large fish over an open fire. The smell of the cooking fish must have aroused Megan. Ben heard her stirring behind him. By the time he turned around, she was already sitting bolt upright. However, Megan was apparently unaware of her surroundings because she immediately began to cry out.

"N-no! G-go away!" she cried before covering her face with both hands and starting to weep uncontrollably.

Ben rushed to the delirious girl's side and took her in his arms. "It's all right, Megan," he whispered. "They're gone. They can't hurt you anymore. You're safe with me back at our camp." He took his left arm from around her for a second and waved his hand in front of her eyes. "See, we're safe. There aren't any apes here."

Megan quieted down to a subdued sobbing and raised her head to look around. The familiar setting of the lean-to and Ben's reassuring arms around her helped her regain control of her emotions. When she realized there was no danger, she hugged herself and started rubbing her hands over her arms as if trying to get warm.

"Are you cold?" Ben asked, holding her tighter.

Megan gave him a perplexed glance. "No, n-not physically anyway. I just had a sudden chill, that's all. What happened to them? How did we get back here?"

Ben lowered his head. "I had to kill one of them." He wasn't proud of the fact that he had to kill one of the first intelligent creatures they had encountered on the island.

Megan looked into his eyes. "You killed one of them?"

Ben nodded and diverted his eyes from hers. "I didn't have any other choice. I thought he was going to kill you. I had to kill him to protect you."

"How?" Megan asked. "They were both so huge."

"With my bow," Ben replied. "I didn't want to kill him, you understand, but I had to, or he might have killed both of us."

Megan tilted her head until her eyes met Ben's again. "Thank you for saving me, Ben. I don't know how you managed it, but I'm thankful that you did."

Thinking Megan must be as hungry as he was, Ben pointed to the fish cooking over the fire. "Are you ready for breakfast?" he asked, changing the subject. "This time, I caught the fish and cooked them too."

Megan held her hand over her eyes like a visor to shield them from the bright light outside as she crawled out of the lean-to. Although she still wasn't quite at full strength yet, she was able to move about without any noticeable problems. Ben figured if she could move about that easily, she, more than likely, had not suffered any serious physical injuries.

Megan sniffed at the cooking fish and licked her lips. "Emm, they smell good," she said, moving closer to inhale the delicious aroma.

Ben followed her out of the lean-to and walked over to the fire to check the fish. "They will be done soon, and then we can eat." He turned to look at Megan when he heard her suddenly squeal behind him. "What's the matter, Meg?"

Her eyes were wide, and her face was almost crimson as she stood staring at him while she struggled to hold the top half of her coveralls in place with both hands. Apparently, the knots he tied in the shoulders of the suit the night before had come undone. "My god! What happened to my clothes? An… and where's the top of my bikini?"

Feeling a little flustered himself, Ben scratched the back of his head as he answered. "One of those apes ripped it off last night when he tore the shoulders out of your coveralls. I saw him playing with it after he found it stuck in his fingers. I found it lying on the ground later, but I'm afraid there wasn't enough of it left worth salvaging. It was shredded pretty badly by then."

Megan seemed to relax after Ben finished explaining what had happened. "Oh, so that's what happened." She winced at the pain that shot through her stiff arms when she tried to retie the coveralls in place again.

Ben gave her a perturbed look. "Just what did you think happened to your clothes?" The more he thought about what she might be accusing him of, the angrier he became. "I wouldn't do anything to hurt you, Megan."

"I... I wasn't sure," she stammered. "I'm so sorry, Ben. I'm just confused. I know you wouldn't try anything. Please don't be mad. I just don't remember much about what happened last night." She bit her lip as she stood looking at him. "I remember running into the chest of one of those big ugly things while I was being chased by the other one. The last thing I recall is seeing both their hideous faces looming over me before I fainted. Everything's a blank after that. The next thing I knew, I was sitting up in your arms here in the lean-to. Maybe you can tell me what happened while we're eating?" She turned then and looked back over her shoulder at him. "Would you mind trying to tie the ends of this material over my shoulders for me? I can't hold the coveralls up and tie them in place at the same time. They're not nearly long enough for me to tie them by myself."

Relieved that Megan still trusted him, Ben nodded and started to jury-rig her torn coveralls. "I'll let you alone later so you can take these off and sew them yourself. Right now they should stay in place long enough for you to eat breakfast."

"Will you tell me about what happened last night?" Megan asked. "I want to know how you managed to get me away from those apes."

"I'll tell ya about last night, but I don't think you're gonna wanna hear it."

They were both famished enough that breakfast didn't last long at all. They had wolfed down the fish and were leaning back licking their fingers while Ben finished his account of the previous night's rescue. Megan asked a surprising question afterward.

"When are you going to teach me how to shoot my bow?"

Ben sat up and rubbed his greasy hands on the grimy legs of his coveralls. "I'll have to make you a new one first. I lost the one I was making for you in the woods last night."

Megan shot him a cynical smile. "Why can't you teach me how to shoot yours? Are you afraid I'll break it?"

Ben laughed and shook his head. "No, I don't think you'll be able to pull it back. It's all I can do to bend it."

Megan tilted her head to one side. "How strong do I have to be to shoot a bow that can kill an animal as big as a deer?"

Ben gave the natter some quiet thought for a moment. *At last, she's finally beginning to realize that she might have to kill animals to survive in this place.* "If you can pull thirty pounds back, you ought to be able to kill just about anything you hit with it. That is, if you learn to shoot straight. I thought you didn't want to kill animals?"

Megan stood up and brushed the dust off her coveralls. "I don't. But after that walk we took in the woods yesterday, I can see we'll need sturdier clothing than what we've got now. Unless you can think of something better to make them out of, animal skins seem the best bet to me."

Ben got up and pulled his knife from its sheath. "I'll go cut a sapling so we can start making your bow now."

"Not so fast," Megan replied. She put her hands on her hips. "I want to take a bath first. I smell like those ape things we ran into last night. Oh, and you need a bath too. You don't smell much better. I think we better bathe in the pond this time. Those meat-eating fish might pick up our scent again if we try to bathe in the main stream."

Ben shook his head. "Women," he grumbled. "Give 'em an inch, and they'll take a mile." He had to admit though; her thinking was still pretty sharp considering everything she had been through the previous evening.

A few minutes later, Ben was sitting under a tree by the pond, keeping a sharp lookout while Megan bathed. The shade of the tree offered little relief from the sweltering heat. While he was wiping sweat from his brow, he happened to look in the direction of the forest and noticed a quick movement in the underbrush behind him. He quickly reached for his bow and nocked an arrow on the string, thinking the female anthropoid might have found them. Then he scrambled up on one knee and aimed in the direction of the movement a split-second before two strange-looking animals wandered out of the forest and started to graze on the high grass about sixty yards away.

The two beasts munched on the grass, paying little attention to the human kneeling under the tree in the distance. It was clear that they saw him but weren't alarmed by his presence. They continued to move around the pond, grazing on the sweet grass as they went, until they had moved well out of bow range on the opposite shore.

Ben studied their features closely. They were obviously a buck and a doe of (what he could only think of as) a variety of exotic deer because he had no idea what else they could be. The buck had antlers while his female counterpart sported nothing more than a huge set of ears on her beautiful head. The buck's antlers were unlike any Ben had ever seen before. The bony outcrops didn't grow from the top of his head. Instead, they grew from behind his jaws and slanted slightly outward for a couple inches before shooting up into a curling arch over the top of his skull. The unusual set of antlers gave the strange deer an appearance of wearing an ornate crown.

Ben took note of two deer's other strange features as well. They both had long serpentine bodies that tapered to short blunt tails, and their smooth hides had a greenish hue, the doe's having more of a blue-green tint. Their sleek coats were well-suited for the tropical forest, the colors of which almost perfectly matched the grass and foliage of their forest home.

Ben marveled at the way they grazed. They didn't bend their long necks once to reach the tender grass. Both their heads remained in the upright position so they could keep a cautious lookout with their sharp eyes while they used their huge front feet, which resembled human hands rather than the split hooves of normal deer, to pull the long blades and lift them to their mouths. When they moved from one spot to another, they simply curled their fingers under and walked on their hard, bony knuckles.

When Megan finally noticed the shy animals, she ran out of the water yelling at Ben, covering her breasts with her left arm and pointing toward the deer with her right. The ruckus she raised caused the buck to snort a warning to his mate seconds before they both bolted back into the safety of the forest.

Ben watched the frightened deer disappear into the underbrush before turning to glare at the agitated girl. His eyes narrowed in anger when he stood to greet her, but when he saw the eagerness in her eyes and that heartwarming smile, he forced himself to cool down. *She has no idea what she's done.* "You shouldn't have yelled like that, Meg. I might have been able to get a shot at one of those deer if you hadn't moved and started making all that noise."

Ignoring Ben's chastising, Megan walked up and knelt down in the grass beside him before pulling her dripping raven tresses back with her free hand and allowing the false sunlight to shine full on her face. Then she turned and looked up at him. "Why do you want to kill a deer right now?"

He stopped ogling her and left his face take on a more somber countenance before throwing his bow down and walking off toward the pond. "I don't understand you," he yelled, flinging his arms around aimlessly. "First, you want me to teach you how to shoot a bow so you can kill a deer, and then you go and ask me a stupid question like that. What are you thinking about anyway? We could have used one of those deer pelts to make clothes. God only knows when I'll get another chance like that!" When he was through venting his anger, he took off his coveralls and marched off toward the pond without looking back. His head ached from the heat, and he just wanted to cool off. It was several minutes later before he finally looked back in Megan's direction.

She was just sitting there, unmoving, with her arms pulled tight around her drawn-up legs and staring toward the forest where the deer had disappeared. Ben never took his eyes off her as he stepped out of the pond and retrieved his coveralls. The water must have done its job because he felt much better as he walked back toward her. Biting the side of his lip, he stood behind Megan for a moment, wondering how to apologize for his sudden outburst. It turned out he didn't have to say anything because she turned and looked up at him with tear-filled eyes just as he was about to speak.

"I'm sorry I scared the deer away," she said. "When I saw you aim your bow at them, I knew you were going to try to kill one of them. I don't want to see anything die just yet, Ben. It reminds me of my parents when things die."

Ben's heart melted right then and there, and he sat down beside her and took her in his arms. "It's okay, Meg. I never thought about that. Please forgive me for this quick trigger of mine. Sometimes I say things without thinking. Honestly, I wouldn't say anything to hurt you on purpose. I don't want to hurt you in any way."

Megan sniffed and pushed slowly out of his embrace. "I'm okay," she said, brushing her tears away. "I've got to remember that we're not back home anymore, and that Gildor is a wild place that we have to learn to survive in."

Ben looked at the ground and folded his hands in his lap. "Would you like to tell me about your parents now? You don't have to if you don't want to. I just thought it might make you feel better. I can't help feeling like you're keeping something from me. You know, you don't have to hide anything from me."

Megan gave him a quick glance and nodded. "There really isn't much to tell. I didn't tell you that Mommy and Daddy were never married. Daddy met her when he was on assignment in Guam twelve years ago."

Ben held his hand up to stop her for a moment. "Now wait a minute. If your mom and dad only met twelve years ago, that would make you about five years old. That means Philip Dills wasn't your real father."

Megan lowered her head. "That's right, Mommy and Daddy weren't even lovers. As I said before, Daddy came to Guam on assignment for the newspaper he worked for in those days. He lived there for almost two years. He met Mommy in the market one day and found out that she needed a job, so he hired her as his housekeeper. She worked for him for almost a year and a half before she was killed in a traffic accident. I had no other relatives besides Mommy, so Philip Dills adopted me. He was the only father I ever knew. All I know about my biological father is that he was an American serviceman who refused to marry my mother before he left Guam. Mommy never told me anything more about him. She even refused to tell Daddy anything about him. Now you know everything there is to know about my past. So what do you think of me now, now that you know I'm no more than someone's unwanted illegitimate brat?"

Ben looked her straight in the eyes and shook his head. "Is that why you didn't want to tell me about your parents? Did you really think I would think less of you because your mother wasn't married to your father? That's not your fault, Megan. You can't help what some dumb guy did eighteen years ago. It's a shame he didn't marry your mom because he would have found out that he has one fantastic daughter if he had. And as far as your being unwanted goes, Mr. Dills must have wanted you. He wouldn't have adopted you and loved you as if you were his own daughter otherwise. If you still want to know what I think… well, I think I'm pretty darned lucky to know a girl like you. So what do you think of that?"

"Thanks," Megan said, smiling at him in a way he had never seen her smile before.

A funny feeling suddenly arose in Ben's chest, like his heart was flying aimlessly around inside. "You're welcome. I want you to know I meant everything I just said. I like being with you, Meg. I'm glad you're here with me."

Megan slowly rubbed her hands together in front of her and glanced downstream to where the creek disappeared into the forest. "Well then, I guess I'd better learn to defend myself in case there are any more of those apes around. Do you think there are more of them about? If so, do you think they'll come after us?"

Ben patted her arm. "Not as long as we stay close together. They'll probably leave us alone as long as we keep our bows handy. I don't think the female realized I killed her mate last night, but I don't think it would have taken her long to figure out what happened if she found my arrow sticking out of the back of his head. They both seemed reasonably intelligent. Now that they know we can kill them, they'll probably be a little less willing to attack us a second time. There's no telling when we might have to defend ourselves again though. The sooner you have a bow of your own, the safer you'll be." He patted her softly on her bare back. "Right now would be a good time for you to go sew your coveralls while I hunt for a sapling to make your bow out of."

"Good point," Megan replied, starting to get to her feet. She stood up and pointed to a sapling standing on the far side of the creek. "Would that little tree make a good bow for me?" she asked.

Ben turned and studied the sapling a moment before smiling and giving her a hard clap on the shoulder as if she was one of his gridiron teammates. "Good eye," he exclaimed. "Go on now and let me get to work!"

"Thanks, I think," Megan replied, rubbing her shoulder and grimacing as she started to walk away.

Chapter 8

Weeks passed while Ben and Megan learned more about their new home. During that time, they discovered that their camp was located in the southern end of a crater about four miles long and two miles wide. That was after Ben took their present size into consideration. In reality, the crater was only about 115 feet long by 60 or so feet wide, before converting the distance into miles, after taking into account that he and Megan were little more than a centimeter tall.

The only exit they found out of the crater was down the side of the cliff where the creek ended in the tumbling waterfall they discovered their third day in the land of Gildor. The sides of the crater consisted of sheer walls of rock and loose dirt that threatened to collapse into landslides every time they tried to scale them.

Ben guessed there was a higher expanse of land surrounding them, but he thought it would be safer if they restricted their exploration to inside the crater for the time being. He thought the safest thing they could do, when they decided to leave, was to descend to the lower plains via the crack in the face of the cliff where the waterfall broke through. However, they were still making new discoveries right where they were with every passing day, so they decided to stay inside the creator for a while longer.

The duo managed to make many more discoveries as their explorations took them farther from their camp. They discovered that the head of the creek flowing through the crater got its start at the base of a sheer wall eight hundred feet high. Bubbling up from between two outcrops of stone, the headwater of the little rill was nothing more than a small puddle. Along its course to the crack in the crater wall, the stream expanded until it grew to be over twenty-five feet wide before it plunged over the precipice into the mysterious land below.

With the stream to provide them with an abundant supply of fresh water, Ben and Megan were in no hurry to leave the crater as long as they could find food. They only ate the variety of fruits and vegetables that they saw animals eating. However, Ben continued to remain cautious. He was only too aware that the strange animals indigenous to the island might be able to digest certain things that might be deadly poison to him and Megan. It turned out that they only found a few types of fruits and vegetables to be dangerous, one of which was a certain type of tuber, which Ben discovered quite by accident, that contained a high level of poison. The plant that grew from it had distinctive, blue leaves shaped like a human hand. Ben had just dug up a few of the roots and piled them behind him when some birds landed and started pecking at them. One minute the birds were pecking happily away, and the next they were lying dead on the ground beside the toxic pile. His most dangerous discovery, however, was the small red berries he found growing on a bush a short distance from the camp. They were not only poisonous; they were even dangerous to touch, as he found out when he picked one of them with his bare hand. As soon as the juice from the berry ran out over his fingertips, it burned his flesh as if he had grabbed the lit end of a match. He was able to rub most of the poison off on the damp grass before any permanent damage was done, but he was left with very sensitive fingertips for the next few days.

One day, Ben decided to test the acidic juice of the red berries on a swarm of stinging ants and found it to be extremely deadly indeed. He smashed some of the berries with the end of a stick and poked the dripping end into the insects' nest. The ants that came in direct contact with the end of the stick died almost instantly, and the others that managed to avoid the red death on the stick died as soon as they came in contact with their contaminated fellows. It was then that he got the idea of dipping two of his arrowheads into the poison.

Ben had been teaching Megan to shoot a bow for the past few weeks. She caught on fast after he taught her how to handle the weapon properly. No matter how good either of them ever got with their primitive weapons though, they knew that they would never have the killing power of a high-powered rifle. And since they had no rifles, poison arrows would give them the advantage they needed if they ever got into a life-threatening situation. As an extra precaution, Ben filled a small hollowed-out log with the deadly berries so they would have a ready supply in case they ever needed them.

Besides fruits and vegetables, they found the animal life within the crater to be an excellent source of nourishment. Ben finally managed to kill one of the strange deer with his bow. After butchering the animal, he saved its hide and started curing it so they could make clothes and moccasins to replace their rapidly deteriorating coveralls and sneakers when they finally wore out. Megan still had a problem with killing any of the beautiful animals, so she made Ben promise not to kill any more of them. He reluctantly agreed to her demands, although he was sure she would change her mind when the need for food and clothing grew even greater.

They continued to keep a sharp lookout for more of the giant apes, but they never saw any more of the repulsive creatures roaming within the crater. It was a complete mystery to them as to how the anthropoids and other animals ever got into the crater in the first place. The elephantine creature they saw their first day on the island would never have been able to scale the sheer walls of the crater, but it too had managed to disappear along with the anthropoids somehow. They never saw hide nor hair of it again. Ben was sure there had to be an opening in the walls somewhere, but no matter how long or how hard he searched, he never found one.

A couple more weeks passed before Ben grew tired of exploring the crater and wanted to move on. It was early one afternoon when he suggested to Megan that they try to descend to the lower grasslands. They had just finished eating a lunch of fresh fruit and dried fish when he brought the subject up to her for discussion.

"What do you think about us trying to go down to the lower plains?" he asked as he sat sharpening his hunting knife on a stone lying on the ground beside him.

Megan looked across the campfire at him and shrugged. "I guess we might as well go down there. We've explored just about every inch of this hole in the ground for the past two months and found no real good reason to stay here."

Ben had to agree with that. "Well then, when do you want to leave?"

"How about tomorrow morning?" Megan replied. "It's too late to leave now. It'll be dark before we reach the bottom if we leave now, and we won't be able to see what we're doing. It's much too dangerous to climb down that cliff in the dark."

Ben rubbed his chin and nodded. "I was kinda hoping you'd say that. It'll probably take us most of the day to reach the bottom."

"We can start gathering the supplies we'll need now," Megan said. "There's no reason to put that off until morning. We probably won't be able to take much with us. We'll have our hands full just climbing down."

Ben got up and went inside the lean-to and returned a few seconds later with a long, thick rope in his hands. "I made this from some vines I found growing in the forest. It's strong enough to hold our weight and just about anything else we might want to take with us. This stuff's pretty tough. It was tough enough to dull my knife blade while I was cutting it."

Megan shot him a wry smile. "That's good. We can wrap our things in the other half of that deer hide you saved to make a skirt for me out of. I can carry it like a knapsack after I tie the ends shut."

He glanced at the vest Megan was wearing and smiled. It took a few weeks to cure the deer hide properly, but when it was finally ready, he gave it to Megan, and she started to work making the new vest.

Megan had removed the tattered top half of her coveralls and replaced it with the vest as soon as she finished sewing it together. Then she cut the legs off the coveralls and took the seams in on the remainder of the garment to make a trim pair of shorts. She also managed to salvage enough of the discarded material from the legs of the coveralls to make a bra that replaced the bikini top that was lost the night Ben rescued her from the apes.

Ben gave Megan's new attire an appreciative nod. "It's a good thing you didn't have time to make that skirt yet, or we would have to leave a lot of things behind," he said. "Let's get started gathering the things we'll need together so we can get an early start in the morning."

They spent the next hour sorting through their meager belongings and carefully packing them for their descent of the cliff the next morning.

Ben wanted to make sure that he and Megan ate a large breakfast before heading for the waterfall, so he got up before dawn and went fishing. An hour before sunrise, he was cooking a large fish that he caught in the stream along with a couple of the strange four-winged birds that he had shot with his bow the night before. He wasn't sure if they would get a chance to stop and eat later on but he prepared enough food to last them the whole day anyway. After they finished eating their breakfast, they packed the extra food. Then they prepared to leave camp for what they hoped was the last time.

They stopped on their way to the forest to bid the little pond a final farewell before leaving. The pond had been a lifesaver during their stay in the crater. It hadn't only been a constant supply of freshwater but a good place to take a cool bath for fast relief from the continuous heat during the day. They lost count of how many fish they had taken from its cool waters. There was no doubt they would miss the little pond and the comforts it provided, but they were confident they were doing the right thing in leaving. After all, they didn't want to spend the rest of their lives alone on the island. They were growing weary of living alone, and it was time to go find out if there were any more people like themselves living in Gildor.

Ben noticed Megan was acting rather strange after they abandoned their old home of almost two and a half months. She walked beside him with her head down and hadn't spoken since they left the clearing. "Something bothering you, Meg?"

Megan never looked up, and Ben could barely hear her when she answered, "Do you think we can find a place to climb down safely?" she asked. "It looked to be an awfully long way to the bottom of that cliff as I recall."

Ben put his hand on her shoulder and turned her to face him. "I know it's scary, Meg, but we've gotta do this. We can't stay on this mountain forever. Sooner or later, more of those apes might come along, and who knows what they might do if they find us. This crater is only so big, and it won't take them long to find us if they ever decided to come looking. We've been pretty lucky so far, and I don't want to take any more chances."

"I know," Megan replied. "I really don't want to stay up here any longer either, but I've never climbed a mountain before. Aren't you afraid of falling?"

Ben pulled her into his arms and held her tight for a moment. "We'll be all right. Just stick with me and do what I tell you to, and everything will be fine. I'll use the rope to help lower you down in short intervals if it gets too rough for you to descend by yourself." He held her out at arm's length and looked into her eyes. "Do you trust me?"

Megan took a deep breath and nodded. "Yes, with my life," she replied.

"That's my girl," he said, slipping his arm around her waist before starting for the waterfall again.

They started their descent of the cliff half an hour later. It was less steep on the right side of the waterfall, so Ben chose to descend from there. The whole side of the cliff was covered with thick vines and creepers, which made the first four hundred feet of their descent easy. However, it became considerably harder below that level. The face of the cliff suddenly became devoid of any plant life and took on a whole new aspect. Rocky outcrops with sheer drops of over sixty feet between them took the place of the lush green vines and creepers that grew higher up the face.

Without the vines to hold on to, Megan suddenly became frightened, and Ben had to use the rope to lower her to the next rocky shelf. It was still over nine hundred feet to the bottom, and from that point on, the descent became considerably tougher for both of them. Although they were both exhausted by the time they reached the bottom, they managed to do so without any serious incidents. The closest either of them came to falling was when Megan's left foot slipped over the edge of a rocky shelf, but thanks to the safety rope Ben had tied around her waist, she was able to regain her balance without falling over the edge. She did lose one of her sneakers in the process, however.

They both shook from fatigue as they sat on the stony ground watching the waterfall a short distance from where they finished their descent. The base of the falls was hidden in a dense white mist that rose two hundred feet into the air. The creek flowed from beneath the mist and continued on a winding course around the base of the cliff and out of sight.

"That sight makes the climb down here all worthwhile, doesn't it?" Ben gasped.

Megan remained silent, captivated by the beauty of the falls. She turned to look at Ben after a few seconds and asked, "Do you think there's a pond hidden under that mist?"

Ben slipped the deer-hide bundle with their belongings in it off his back and stood up to get a better look. "I can't tell from here. If I had to guess, I would say there is, but we won't know for sure unless we go find out? Shall we go investigate?"

Megan spent little time in scrambling to her feet. She flinched when her bare foot pressed down on a sharp stone. "Let's look for my shoe on the way. I think it fell over there somewhere near the base of the falls."

Ben removed their bows and quivers of arrows from the bundle before replacing it on his back. "I hope we won't need these down here, but we better keep them handy just in case," he said, handing Megan her bow.

Megan took her bow from him and automatically nocked an arrow on the string. The primitive weapons had become a part of their everyday life since their run-in with the apes weeks earlier. They never left the safety of the camp without them.

The oncoming darkness prevented them from seeing any great distance, but they could still see most of the natural beauty within the immediate vicinity. Not wanting to waste what was left of the rapidly diminishing daylight, they fell silent and hurried to discover what lay hidden beneath the veil of mist. Their eyes gradually grew accustomed to the darkness as they walked toward the waterfall, and they were soon able to see a great distance in the glowing moonlight. It wasn't until they were close enough to feel the cool dampness of the falls that they happened to notice the animal life on the plain to their left.

Standing a short distance away was a small herd of the strange deer like the ones living in the crater. The animals grazed on the long grass of the plain, hardly taking notice of the humans invading their feeding grounds. Ben saw a couple of the dominant bucks glance up at them as they passed by, but they resumed their nonchalant eating, almost as if they were used to the presence of humans. He continued to lead Megan toward the falls, never giving the matter much thought.

The panorama behind the herd of deer was breathtaking. The vast plain spread on for miles. Only low rolling hills lay between them and the high mountain range, barely visible on the distant horizon. The dim false moon was beginning to rise from behind the lofty peaks, giving them the appearance of magnificent spires from some ancient city of the Middle East.

Ben and Megan were so busy taking in their exquisite surroundings that they both neglected to keep an eye out for danger as they walked toward the base of the waterfall. By the time they reached the base of the falls, the fine mist which rose above the pond they discovered there had soaked through their clothing. Ignoring the dampness, they walked on around the pond and stepped into the mouth of a cave they found in the base of the cliff behind the falls.

"It's wonderful down here," Megan squealed with delight. Her voice was barely audible above the sound of the pounding water.

Ben looked around and studied their surroundings closely. "It sure is. It's too bad Foster's men didn't release us down here in the first place. We might not have bumped into those apes if they had, and we could have used this cave for shelter."

Megan shuddered at the mention of the apes. "Do you think some of those apes might be down here, Ben?"

Ben shook his head. "I doubt it. If they're like most apes, they'll prefer the forests on the mountain to these flat grasslands." He paused a moment in deep thought before adding, "However, they are more developed than normal apes, but I can only guess how much more."

"I, for one, don't intend to find out how smart they are," Megan replied. "As far as I'm concerned, I hope I never see any more of them ever again."

"That makes two of us," Ben replied.

They remained in the mouth of the cave for a few minutes and discussed its options for shelter for the night, completely ignoring any threat of danger that might be lurking in the advancing darkness.

"You know, we could stay in this cave for the night," Ben suggested. "It beats staying outside in the open."

Megan turned to look into the dark interior of the cave and shook her head. "I don't think that's a good idea. We don't know what might be lurking around back there. Since it's too dark to use the magnifying glass to build a fire, I think I'd rather take my chances outside where we can see better, if you don't mind."

Ben hunched his shoulders. "Suit yourself. If that's what you want, then that's what we'll do. Come on then! We'd better go find a place to sleep for the night."

Megan started to follow him out of the cave and stopped to look at the pond. "Do you think we could go for a swim in that pond in the morning?" she asked. "This appears to be the first really deep water we've come across since we came to Gildor. The pond up on the mountain wasn't really deep enough to dive in, but this one looks as if it might be."

Ben stared at the pond's shimmering surface. "It looks okay. I'll have to check it out closer in the morning. We don't want to run into any more meat- eating fish like the ones that tried to take us apart our first day here."

Megan started to tremble and rubbed her hands over her arms. "I'm freezing in this cold dampness," she said. "Let's get outta here and find a warm place to camp for the night before we both catch cold. Oh, and we still haven't found my shoe yet."

Ben double-checked the arrow on his bowstring before stepping from behind the tumbling water. Then he waved for Megan to follow him back the way they came. "Come on, let's try to find your sneaker and get outta here!"

When Ben was clear of the falls, he stopped on a flat rock and turned to offer Megan a hand up onto its slippery surface. As soon as she hopped up beside him, Ben noticed the terrified expression on the girl's face and spun around to look behind him.

At least ten fierce-looking apes had surrounded the pond. The anthropoid closest to them stood only a few yards from the surprised humans and was holding a heavy cudgel high over his sloped head, ready to strike a killing blow the moment either one of them moved within his reach.

Chapter 9

Megan pulled Ben to one side and caused them both to lose their balance and fall. Although he had been taken by surprise, Ben instinctively rolled over onto his back and stood up in the waist deep water to face the ape again. The water was cold, and the soaked pack on his back felt as if it weighed a ton, but the adrenaline charging through his system allowed him to pull the pack off his back, grab another arrow from his quiver to replace the one he lost after falling into the water, nock it on his bowstring, and aim the weapon at the oncoming ape with lightning speed.

When the ape saw his intended prey fall off the slippery stones, he rushed forward, ready to bludgeon him to death. However, the slow-witted creature didn't count on Ben's quick reactions. Before the ape could take more than a couple of steps, Ben had released his arrow, which hit the surprised creature in the right shoulder, causing him to lose his grip on his cudgel. The stunned beast man stopped his charge long enough to jerk the arrow from his shoulder and bellow in agony. Then he threw the bloody shaft to the ground and charged again with open hands thrust forward.

That brief pause was long enough to allow Ben to nock another arrow on his bowstring and take a truer aim at the ape's massive chest. The second arrow buried itself deep into the anthropoid's chest and forced him to take a step backward. His whole body shuddered spasmodically before he fell over and lay still while his life force quickly drained away. A second ape suddenly came running out of the shadows toward Ben, and the young man quickly raised his reloaded weapon and, in one fluid motion, released the arrow. The bowstring twanged, and the deadly missile was launched, striking the ape squarely between its wide-set eyes and killing it instantly.

With a brief break in the action, Ben turned to find out what had happened to Megan. He spun around just in time to see the girl take careful aim with her own bow and shoot at an ape standing at the far side of the pond. Considering that she was standing waist-deep in cold water, her shot was a good one: the arrow struck the ape square in the chest.

The stunned ape grabbed at the shaft and tried to pull it out with a feeble attempt, but the arrow's tip was embedded deep within his primitive heart. His life ended before he could dislodge the arrow, and he toppled facedown into the dark water a split second later.

The attack suddenly ended when the rest of the anthropoids realized the deadly effect the humans' weapons were having on their ranks. They had stopped their attack after Megan killed the third member of their party and fell back before turning to run away when it became apparent that their crude weapons were no match for those of the humans.

While the rest of the anthropoids turned to run, one stayed behind to face the humans alone. He stood on the far side of the pond, pointing an accusing finger at them, and grunted in some sort of guttural language before turning to lumber off after his comrades.

Ben turned to help Megan out of the pond while maintaining a watchful eye on the retreating apes as he did so. As soon as Megan was out of the water, they both turned and ran toward the flat plain. Neither of them spoke until after they ran for well over sixty yards. They didn't waste time in idle chatter because they were both too busy looking behind them to assure themselves that the apes weren't following.

Ben was the first to speak after they stopped running. "That was a good shot you made back there." He puffed.

Megan was panting so hard she had to bend over while looking back toward the waterfall with wide dark eyes. After she caught her breath, she turned to look up at Ben. When he noticed the look on her face, he reached down to place a hand on her shoulder. "Are you okay?" he asked. "You're not hurt, are you?"

"No, I'm just scared to death." She panted.

"We're safe now," Ben said, trying to reassure her. "Those things are more afraid of us than we are of them now."

Megan straightened, still regarding him with wide eyes, and shuddered violently. "They're afraid of us now, but what about later? They're smart, Ben. Did you see how that big one pointed at us while he was yelling? He knew exactly what he was doing."

Ben stepped back and glanced toward the waterfall. "We'll get out of here in the morning, just as soon as it's light enough to see. We should be safe enough for now. I don't think they'll follow us out onto the plains."

Megan moved close and leaned into his arms. Resting her head against his chest, she slipped her arms around his waist and drew even closer. "I hope you're right. I don't want to be caught by those things again."

Ben raised his hand to run his fingers through Megan's silky hair and stroked the back of her neck. "You're freezing," he said, hugging her tightly. "We should get these wet clothes off and lay them out to dry. We can cut some of this long grass and dry ourselves off with it. Then we can pile some of it around us to help keep us warm while we're waiting for our clothes to dry."

Half an hour later, they were sitting together in the tallgrass stripped to their swimwear with a large pile of grass stacked around them to keep them warm. Ben was studying the distant mountain peaks across the plains while Megan sat beside him staring back at the waterfall.

Megan moved farther under the grass and lay down with her head resting on Ben's lap. "Are you still planning to go back there in the morning?" she asked.

Ben nodded as he leaned forward to push grass away from the girl's face. "I think it would be safer if we headed for those mountains. But I have to return to the pond and retrieve our things before we leave. And to fill this," he added, holding up the makeshift water bottle he made from a small hollow log and sloshing its contents. "We drank most of our water when we were climbing down the cliff today. We'll set out for those mountains as soon as I get back." He pointed his thumb over his shoulder at the lofty peaks looming in the distance.

The mountains were deep purple against the darkening sky. He wasn't sure, but he thought he saw shadows of valleys in the highlands earlier when they were descending the face of the cliff. "That looks to be as good a place as any to start exploring. If those dark lines I saw are valleys, they just might have streams or rivers running through them. I don't think we'll have a hard time finding water once we get there. Where there's water, there's game. I'm hoping we find plenty of both there."

Megan smiled and stretched her arms up over her head. Yawning, she rolled over on her side and closed her eyes. "I want to be fresh if we're going to leave first thing in the morning. We'll have a long trek ahead of us when we set out for those mountains. I hope you're right about the game. We need some leather to make some new shoes too. I don't have any shoes at all now. I lost my other one when I fell into that pond." She no sooner finished that statement than the world around them suddenly started to shake violently. Her eyes flew wide, and she sat bolt upright. "What's happening?" She gasped.

Fighting to maintain his balance, Ben pushed himself up onto his hands and knees. "I don't know, maybe an earthquake," he yelled above the rumbling. "Almost sounds like a stampede." Bewildered, he popped his head above the tallgrass and looked around. A series of loud bellows came from the direction of the waterfall, and he pivoted in that direction. His jaw dropped in disbelief at what he saw. He quickly recovered his wits and grabbed Megan by the shoulders and yelled again. "Run!"

When Megan saw the look on Ben's face, she got up on her knees and turned to see what had caused him to become so alarmed. She screamed and started thrashing her hands and feet to rid herself of the grass piled around her as soon as she realized what was happening.

A little more than a hundred yards away and approaching fast was a herd of the strange elephantine creatures like the one they had seen their first day in Gildor. The creatures themselves weren't as frightening as what they carried on their backs. Every one of the behemoths had an ape on its back driving his mount straight toward the two humans.

Megan finally managed to kick her way out of the pile of grass and stood up. As soon as she gained her footing, Ben shoved her bow and quiver into her hands and took her by the wrist before starting to tow her toward the mountains as fast as they both could run.

The bellowing of the great beasts behind them seemed to be getting closer. Ben chanced a glance back over his shoulder and saw that the charging herd was gaining fast. Realizing the huge animals in the angry ape's herd would overtake them in seconds if he didn't do something fast, he let go of Megan's wrist and stopped running. When Megan stopped to look back, he slapped her on the backside and yelled, "Keep going! I'll catch up."

Confused, Megan glanced toward their pursuers and then shot Ben a questioning look, as if to ask what he intended to do.

Ben pushed her ahead of him and yelled again, "I said keep going!" He watched her for a moment to make sure she kept running while he nocked an arrow on his bowstring. Then turning around, he took careful aim at the lead animal and quickly left the poison-tipped missile fly before spinning on his heels and taking off again. He had no way of knowing how long it would take the poison to kill something as large as the behemoth or if he even managed to hit it. He had no other choice but to turn and run before he found out if his aim was true or not. By the time he caught up with Megan, the noise of the thundering herd had lessened, but he didn't want to risk stopping to look back, so he kept running. He continued to run until Megan became so exhausted that she had to stop to catch her breath and fell to her knees, panting in front of him. He stopped beside her and loaded another arrow before spinning around to shoot again. There was no need for the second arrow, however, because their pursuers had stopped seventy-five yards behind them.

It became obvious right away that Ben's arrow had veered off course. The behemoth he had aimed at was still standing, but its rider was slumped across its back with an arrow protruding from his left shoulder as he desperately fought to maintain control of the great beast. The ape's mount was agitated and reared up on its hind legs as it tried to turn and run in the opposite direction, but its rider struggled to prevent it from doing so. Then they both suddenly became very still, and there was no movement from either one of them for a few seconds before the anthropoid fell to the ground beneath his great mount. The confused animal stood over his fallen rider for a moment, looking down at the ground, before its knees suddenly buckled, and it collapsed on top of the dead ape.

Ben realized what must have happened while he watched the scene unfold. His arrow had struck the mount in the head first and ricocheted off its thick skull before traveling on and embedding itself into the rider's shoulder. Amazing as it seemed, he had killed both the rider and his mount with one arrow.

When the army of apes saw their leader and his powerful mount die from the wounds they had received from the horrible weapon, they panicked and turned their mounts back toward the cliffs, howling in terror.

Megan stood up and looked at Ben. "What happened?"

Ben took her hand in his and started at a brisk pace toward the mountains again. "We got lucky," he said.

Megan glanced over her shoulder and shook her head. "We aren't that lucky," she replied. "We just lost our clothes along with the rest of our supplies. The deer hide is still back there in the pond, and you never did get a chance to fill the water bottle."

Ben patted the water bottle secured to a piece of rope tied around his waist. "We still have a little water. Hopefully, it'll be enough to get us to the mountains."

They continued their trek in the moonlight for almost another hour before stopping to bed down in the high grass. They were too exhausted to care about the lost deer hide or the other supplies by then. The ground was cool, so they covered themselves with a thick layer of the long grass to help them stay warm and to help keep the biting insects off them. They fell asleep huddled close together a few minutes later.

A beam of bright light shot through a hole in the grass Megan had covered herself with and hit her full in the face. As the light grew brighter, it also grew hotter and awakened her. She sat up and threw her arm over her eyes to shield them from the blinding rays and turned her face away from the uncomfortable heat. When she opened her eyes again, she discovered Ben was already up.

Ben had awakened earlier and slipped from under the grass blanket to check their surroundings. He had seen Megan get up a moment later and walked over to sit down beside her. "It's an awful long way to those mountains. It didn't look half that far in the moonlight last night."

Megan turned to look at the remote mountain range. "How far do you think it is?"

Ben squinted as he tried to determine the distance. "Maybe seventy-five or a hundred miles. It will probably take five or six days to get there if we push it. It all depends on how far and how fast we'll be able to travel in this heat."

Megan tugged at her deerskin bra. It was beginning to grow hotter fast, and her meager clothing wasn't much help in protecting her from Gildor's manufactured sun. "Do we have to move on now, Ben? I don't know how much more of this heat I can take. It's beginning to get really hot already. At least we could take cover in the shade of the trees or in the lean-to when it got this hot back at the crater. Can't we wait here under the cover of the grass until it cools off later, or do you think those ape things are still following us?"

Ben fingered the frayed hems of the legs of his swimming trunks as he stared back in the direction of their old home. He hadn't noticed before because the heavy mist from the falls had kept it hidden from him, but the crater they had been living in was positioned on top of a broad, flat plateau. "Well, I'll be," he said. "No wonder we couldn't find another way out of that crater except down the face of the cliffs. We were stranded on a plateau the whole time."

Megan stood up and stared in disbelief. "Do you think those apes live up there? Maybe that's why we never saw any more of them in the crater because they actually live on top of the plateau."

"That could be. Or maybe they live somewhere inside the plateau. I don't think they'll come looking for us though. They probably prefer to stay in the safety of their own homes as far away from danger as possible. That would explain why we never saw any more of them in the crater after I killed one of them. They probably came after us last night because they thought we were going to invade their home."

Megan tilted her head to one side. "Do you think it's safe to rest here for a while?"

Ben nodded and looked up into the brightly lit sky. "We'll stay here until nightfall and head for the mountains just before dark. It might be more dangerous traveling at night, but it beats being slowly roasted to death by whatever it is up there that they call a sun."

They cut more of the long tough grass to cover themselves with while they waited for the sun to go down. Before they tucked themselves in, they went looking for something to eat. Luckily, Ben found a bush with a few edible berries on it that the birds hadn't eaten, so they were able to eat a paltry meal before going back to sleep. Unfortunately, the only freshwater they had was what was left in their water bottle, so they had to ration what little remained. It promised to be a long hot wait until nightfall.

They waited until an hour before sundown before scrambling from beneath the grass. Before setting out for the mountains, they each took one swig from the water bottle, but it wasn't nearly enough to quench their thirst. However, it was enough to sustain them for a while at least. They could only hope to find a stream somewhere along the way where they could replenish their water supply later.

After they had walked a while, Megan touched Ben's arm, and he turned to see what she wanted.

"What are we going to do when we get to the mountains?" she asked.

"Find a new home, I hope," Ben replied. "Maybe we'll find people there.

It's pretty evident there aren't any back where we came from."

"Do you think we could build a real house?" Megan asked hesitantly.

Ben shrugged. "Don't know. Maybe someday. It won't be too soon though. We'll have to make tools first. We don't have anything to work with but our hunting knives. Maybe we can find a cave to live in until we can build a house."

Megan forced a wry smile. "So we'll be forced to live like Neanderthals as well as having to dress like them."

Ben shook his head and chuckled. "Not exactly. We'll be living more like the American Indians of the Old West. I can cure animal hides to make new outfits with. You've already proven that you can sew a deer hide into better clothing than any Neanderthal ever could. And I can make leather for moccasins."

His statement made Megan glance down at her bare feet. "I'll make our clothes if you make the moccasins. Please make the moccasins first though."

Ben had to smile at that remark. "Good idea. I'll make you a pair with straps that you can tie around your calves so they won't come off so easily next time."

Megan giggled as she stepped around him and started walking faster. "You'll have to find some animals willing to give up their hides first."

Ben threw his hands out at his sides and hunched his shoulders. "So I will, so I will." He knew it would take several days for them to reach the foothills of the mountains, and he realized that they had to find food soon after they got there. It was even more important for them to find a good water supply. The water they had left would have to be used sparingly. He was almost sure there would be an abundant supply of both once they reached the mountains. *There has to be streams flowing through those mountains somewhere. The only problem will be finding them after we get there. In the meantime, I hope I can squeeze enough moisture out of the plant life growing on the plains to keep us alive until we reach them.*

The mountains appeared to be no closer than they were when they first set out for them three days earlier. The terrain had changed. The grass on the plains dwindled in height until it grew only a few inches high on the hard, rocky ground. Without the long grass to cover them during the day, they were forced to sleep out in the open and cover themselves with dry dirt and as much of the short grass as they could pick. The insufficient cover didn't protect them very well from the relentless heat of the sun, and they both soon started to suffer from severe sunburn. Ben's deep-tanned upper body had turned crimson, and his skin started to peel and itch as it dried out. Although he was itchy and sore, his companion suffered far worse than he did.

Megan's suntan had turned from an unblemished brown to cherry red. Not only was her skin beginning to dry and peel, she had a far worse problem: blisters had started to form where sun poisoning was beginning to set in.

Ben's compassion for the poor girl grew even more when he accidentally bumped into her arm while walking beside her. Even though it was the slightest of touches, Megan screamed out in agony and fell to the ground crying. Ben decided that they should rest in that spot for the rest of the night and remain there all of the next night as well. He tried to keep Megan's skin moist by applying as much dew-moistened grass to it as possible during the night and early-morning hours. It took several hours to cool her down after he started applying the damp grass, but she finally managed to fall into a fitful sleep. While Megan slept, Ben gathered as much of the sparse long grass as he could find and wove it into a small blanket. After he finished weaving the makeshift cover, he spread it over Megan before lying down beside her and falling asleep himself.

The following day brought more heat with it, so they remained where they were until sundown. Ben didn't like the idea of forcing Megan to go on so soon, but they simply couldn't afford to stay on the open plain any longer than they had to; their need for water was just too great. That night, they set out for the mountains again. Megan had become so weak that Ben had to help support her by holding her arm around the back of his neck while they pressed on through the cool night air.

Over half the evening still remained when he could no longer support Megan's dead weight. He found a large depression in the ground and laid her down on the short soft grass growing on its bottom and then sat down beside her. When he noticed how the poor girl was shivering, he covered her feet and legs with the grass blanket and lay next to her. Then he gently started to rub her sunburned arms and shoulders in an effort to keep her warm. "I'm so sorry I ever got you into this mess, Meg," he whispered. "I swear I'll get you to those mountains, even if it means I have to carry you the rest of the way." Then he moved even closer and looked up into the star-filled sky as he wrapped his arms around her. "God help us," he pleaded before closing his eyes and falling asleep.

There were purple clouds in the sky when Ben awoke a few hours later. The sun was hidden behind them and prevented most of its heat from beaming down on him and the girl. The air had a slight chill to it, so he sat up and reached for the blanket to pull it up over Megan's shoulders, but he was astonished to discover it was missing. He thought his eyes were playing tricks on him, so he shook his head to clear his vision and looked again. The blanket just wasn't there. Thinking he must have misplaced it, he got up on his hands and knees and spun around in a full circle looking for it. When his quick search of the depression proved unproductive, he popped his head above the edge of the hollow and slowly turned in every direction, searching for a clue as to how the precious possession had disappeared. He continued his slow rotation until his eyes came to rest on a lone figure standing about thirty feet to his right.

Ben was totally astonished at the sight that met his eyes. For the first time since arriving in Gildor, he was looking at what appeared to be one of the humanoids Ned Foster had told him and Megan about.

She was the most exquisite creature Ben had ever seen. Although her back was turned toward him, her scanty attire did little to hide her femininity as she held the woven square of grass up in her hands to examine it. When she accidentally dropped the blanket on the ground, the beautiful creature turned to the right as she bent down to pick it up and exposed her profile. The unexpected action allowed Ben to get a better look at the stunning creature. The longer he studied her, the more he thought she seemed to be equine in appearance, but he still wasn't quite sure. Her face remained hidden from him while she stood up straight again to examine the crude blanket. She twisted the slack material in every direction while thoroughly testing its strength and weight with her small hands. Ben got a quick look at the side of her bare midriff when she held the blanket up in front of her face to sniff at it. He also managed to catch a glimpse of a small tight-fitting vest that barely covered the upper half of her torso as she raised the blanket even higher.

Her hair was a peculiar shade of dark red. It wasn't auburn or a typical carrot color but, rather, the color of a ripe apple. The remarkable tresses grew short on either side of her head and high and long over the top before dropping down the back of her neck between her shoulder blades, sort of like the mane of a horse. Her ears were long and pointed, standing straight up from the sides of her head and ending an inch above the highest point of her thick mane. She wore a dark-green G-string that was fashioned in such a way to allow her flowing red tail to hang freely behind her.

Ben knelt silently watching the strange female for several seconds, hoping she would lower the blanket so he could get a better look at her face. He remained there, unmoving, until Megan suddenly appeared beside him. Before he could warn her to be quiet, she spoke out loud enough for the equine girl to hear her.

"What's going on?"

Ben turned toward her and put his finger to his lips. She didn't realize her folly until he pointed toward the strange girl standing out in the grass. By the time they shifted their gaze toward her, the equine girl had lowered the blanket and was staring directly at them. They realized she had spotted them by the terrified look on her face.

"Ben, she... she's human," Megan stammered.

Ben whistled in disbelief when his eyes met those of the strange girl.

The equine's gaze locked on Ben for only a split second, but that short time was long enough for his quick eyes to take her completely in. He took note that her eyes were large, almost too large for the exquisite face they were situated in. The pupils were dark liquid pools in the center of a splash of watery blue irises. Her bangs grew to a point between thin eyebrows, making her face appear almost heart-shaped. That face was uncommonly gorgeous: with high cheekbones, a delicately rounded chin, and a small slightly upturned nose. Unlike those of the anthropoids, Ben was glad to see that her delicate nose had only two nostrils instead of four.

The two humans had only seconds to make all these observations because the equine beauty dropped the blanket as soon as she became aware she had been seen. In a flash, she ran off across the rolling plain at a speed neither of them could hope to match in their weakened conditions.

Ben hopped out of the depression and went to pick up the blanket. He turned to watch the fleeing girl until she vanished over a distant knoll before returning to the depression where Megan waited for him.

"I'm so sorry, Ben. I didn't mean to scare her off." Her eyes suddenly went wide as she became more excited. "My god, was that a tail I saw? I thought she was human when I first saw her."

Ben turned to look at Megan and smiled. "She wasn't quite human, but she wasn't far from it either. I haven't seen anything so beautiful in my life. Except for you, that is," he added as an afterthought.

Megan smiled weakly. "Thanks for the compliment."

Ben winked at her and said, "You know, if there's one of her kind around here, there just might be others. Surely a young girl like that wouldn't be running around out here all alone. Maybe we'll find out where she came from tonight when we move on."

Folding the grass blanket over his arm, Ben took one last look in the direction the equine girl had disappeared before he jumped back into the depression beside Megan. He took her gently by the arm and said, "Come on. You'd better lie back down and cover up. You certainly don't need any more exposure to this sun."

Chapter 10

Ben and Megan slept the day away and awakened that night with the dampness of a light rain soaking through the grass blanket spread over them. The depression they were lying in was beginning to collect water, so they climbed out and found some higher ground to lie on. With nowhere else to go, they stayed under the inadequate protection of the saturated blanket while they waited for the drizzle to stop. However, the light drizzle suddenly turned into a heavy downpour that lasted almost two hours and drenched them both. One good thing happened during the cold driving rain though. Ben had set the water bottle out during the hardest part of the deluge and managed to catch almost half a bottle of freshwater.

As soon as the rain stopped, they went to the place where they last saw the equine girl that morning, only to discover that they couldn't find her trail in the darkness. They talked it over and decided to wait until morning before trying to track her for fear of losing any chance of discovering her whereabouts altogether. Although it meant adding another delay in reaching the mountains and taking a chance of dying of thirst or starvation, they figured it would be worth the risk if they found a village of friendly equine people. Ben hoped they would be friendly, but if it turned out they weren't, he and Megan at least had enough water to continue their trek for another couple of days if necessary.

They were devastated when they returned to the sight the next morning. The deluge of the previous day had washed the equine girl's trail completely away. Not willing to risk any further delays, they continued their trek in the daylight. They slowly pressed on with a dreadful sadness in their hearts, not knowing if they could even reach the mountains. That was why they had put so much hope in finding an equine village in the first place, even though they didn't know if one existed. Their last hope had been dashed when they realized how alone they really were.

The sun flooded the vast grasslands with welcome warmth. It wasn't quite as hot as it had been on the previous days because the rain had been followed by cooler air flowing throughout the great Gildorian cavern. They were able to travel in relative comfort by keeping their blanket draped over their heads and shoulders as they walked. The rain had helped soften their dry skin and relieve the intolerable discomfort they had been experiencing from their sunburn. No matter how much physical relief they experienced, nothing could take away the dreaded loneliness they felt off their minds. The sighting of the equine girl had perked their spirits, but their short-lived enthusiasm disappeared right along with her. Ben continued to keep a constant vigilance for the strange girl, hoping to catch some sign of her, as they trudged relentlessly onward.

Two more days passed before they could actually tell they were drawing closer to the mountains. There was very little to be happy about, though. They hadn't eaten for almost three days, and as far as Ben could tell, they had at least two more days of walking ahead of them. They were already weak from hunger, and it would be a long, hard trek if they didn't find something to eat soon.

The water ran out the following day. The severity of Megan's sunburn and her weakened condition forced her to drink more than anticipated to keep from dehydrating. Ben had cut his own ration of water in half in hopes of saving enough for them to finish their trek, but the water ran out anyway. It was then that he realized his plan to squeeze moisture from the plant life was a folly. The only plant life that grew on this part of the plain was the dark-blue-green grass, and it was almost dry. In spite of its rich color, the grass didn't hold enough moisture to waste energy on. However, they did cut some of it and roll it up to chew on whenever their mouths dried out. What little moisture they managed to get from the grass was by no means enough to sustain them for the remainder of the trek to the mountains.

They switched back to traveling at night a few days after the water ran out so that they wouldn't sweat so profusely. Even so, it only took a few hours of walking before they began to suffer from thirst again. They literally had to force themselves onward each night until the sun rose above the horizon the next morning in order to survive.

They looked up at the looming mountains one morning before covering up with their crude blanket and going to sleep. The mountains were very close now. Ben wondered if they would be able to reach them by the following morning. *If we can only manage to walk that much farther*, he thought. He and Megan were so exhausted that they were barely able to stand, let alone walk for any great distance.

They stopped several times the following night to allow Megan to rest. Each time they stopped, Megan required more time to recover before being able to move on. Ben practically had to carry her the last mile before they finally stopped for the day, at least one more night's travel from the foothills.

A light rain started to fall during the day, and Ben woke Megan when he felt the droplets hitting his face. They both slipped from beneath their blanket and tried to catch some of the rain on their parched tongues. They barely managed to get their tongues wet before the rain stopped and the sun came out again with all its burning fury. Ben managed to wring some water out of the damp grass before it dried out again, but it wasn't nearly enough to satisfy their dreadful thirst.

He kept his eyes fixed on the outline of the nearest mountain that night as he and Megan trudged slowly toward it. About two hours into their trek, Megan had fallen to the ground, exhausted, after which Ben took the blanket and empty water bottle off his left shoulder and replaced them with Megan's bow and quiver. Then after tying the water bottle around his waist, he wrapped the tattered remains of the blanket around the exhausted girl and lifted her up into his arms before pushing on while keeping eyes intensely fastened on the mountain.

It took a Herculean effort, but Ben managed to carry the unconscious girl all the way to the foothills before collapsing, parched and completely worn out. He forced his overtaxed body to its knees one more time, just long enough to pull Megan under the cover of a bush that grew near the base of a large boulder. After pulling her into the protective cover beside him, he lay back and fell into a deep sleep with the notion that he might never awaken.

It was late afternoon when Ben was suddenly awakened by the sound of thunder. Reverberations of the oncoming storm rang throughout the mountains like cannon fire. The thunderclaps were strong enough to cause the very ground beneath him to shake with every peal of the mighty thunderheads. He scrambled from beneath the boulder, untied the water bottle from around his waist, and wedged it between two heavy stones with the open mouth facing upward toward the darkening sky, hoping to catch some of the welcome offering. Then he returned to the protection of the boulder and waited for the deluge to start. A few minutes later, the torrential rain fell so fast that the leaves of the sheltering bush hung heavy with cold water in a matter of seconds. The weight of the rain soon bent the bush's fragile limbs and left some of the cold water drip onto Megan's face and waking her from her unchecked sleep.

Alarmed, Megan sat up and turned to look at Ben. "What's happening?"

The straining bush suddenly gave way to the increasing weight and snapped in half, dumping water over both of them before Ben could answer. Megan left out a squeal as the cold water poured over her head and left her gasping as the sudden chill took her breath away.

Ben moved as fast as his exhausted body would allow. He slid through the mud to huddle next to the drenched and shivering girl and put his arm around her shoulders. Moving his mouth close to her ear, he spoke in a loud voice. "Huddle close to me, Meg. Our combined body heat will help keep us warm until this storm passes."

They sat under the boulder through the remainder of the storm with the broken half of the bush propped up in front of them in an effort to keep the rain from blowing in on them. They cupped their hands to catch some of the cool water and drank ravenously while they waited for the storm to take its destructive force to some other part of the underground world.

Tiny rills still flowed down out of the foothills hours after the storm had passed. It would take days for the sun to dry up the mud and water the tempest left behind.

Ben and Megan welcomed the warmth of the glaring sun for the first time in days. They threw the remains of the ruined bush on the ground and climbed out from under the boulder to let the sun warm their chilled bodies.

Ben led his companion to where he left the water bottle standing between the rocks, and they were both elated to find it filled to the brim with freshwater. They drank half the contents of the bottle before forcing themselves to put it down. The cool liquid gave them new vitality. However, Ben knew that drinking too much of it at once could be harmful, so he took the bottle and set it aside before they were tempted to empty it completely.

They found another boulder to take shelter under while they waited for the temperature to rise. Although the water had given her new vitality, Megan was still very weak. Ben knew she wouldn't be able to go on without something to eat. He felt the pangs of his own hunger as he watched Megan's reclining figure under the boulder.

"Megan, stay here while I go search for food!" He realized the girl was sound asleep when she failed to reply. He could see the steady rise and fall of her chest as she lay in the shade of the boulder. Thinking she would feel safer with her weapon within reach if she awoke while he was gone, he placed her bow and quiver on the ground beside her before leaving. Then he gathered his own weapons and headed up the hillside in search of food.

It was dark when Megan awoke. The day had dwindled away, and the air was cool with a slight breeze. The breeze carried a delicious aroma on it, and she licked her lips as she sat up and looked around with a baffled expression on her beautiful countenance. It didn't take her long to zero in on the pile of fresh fruit lying nearby in the moonlight. She started to crawl out of the protective cover of the boulder and shivered when the cool air began to waft around her half-naked body.

"That bikini can't be very warm," Ben said. "This might help keep you warm. I made it while you were sleeping," he added, offering her the bundle he held in his hands.

Megan peered at him through the darkness before she slipped the rest of the way from under the boulder. "Thanks," she said, smiling as she reached out to take the new grass blanket from him. It was slightly larger than the original but just as sturdy. "I'm sure it'll help. I hope you made one for yourself too. I don't want you freezing during the night. It looks like you're going to be doing most of the hunting for a while until I regain my strength."

Ben nodded. "No problem. I managed to patch the old one up and enlarge it with some new grass. That one I just gave you is for draping over your shoulders during the day. You don't have to worry about the hunting either. After all you've been through the past few days, you could use a good rest. I'll hunt if you're willing to stay here and watch the camp.

You'll be warmer and gain your strength back sooner if you stay out of the damp forest for a while."

Megan sat down and sniffed at a piece of the softball-sized fruit stacked in the pile beside her. "These sure smell good. What are they?"

Ben shrugged. "Don't really know. I saw an animal that looked kinda like a big mouse with long ears eating them, so I figured they were safe enough for us to try. Hope you don't mind me bringing the fruit back instead of the animal. I didn't think you would want to eat anything that cute. Especially since we would have to eat it raw."

Megan wrinkled her nose and shook her head, sending her hair flying about her face in a swirl of dingy dark waves. "I don't care what it looked like. One can't afford to be very picky when you're starving. But you're right. I probably wouldn't be able to eat it raw. Not yet anyway."

Ben held his empty hands out at his sides. "We don't have the magnifying glass anymore to start a fire with. I can't build a fire with wet wood without it. I could try striking my knife off a rock to make sparks and get a fire going that way, but there isn't enough dry tinder lying around to even try that. I sure hope I can find some flint somewhere. It would be a lot easier getting a fire started if we had some."

Megan picked up a piece of the fruit and turned it over in her hands. "Maybe we can find a way to build a fire tomorrow. Right now, we need to concentrate on gaining our strength back." She patted the ground and motioned for Ben to sit down beside her. Then she took a large bite out of the fruit and looked at him. "Whatever this is, it's pretty tasty," she said, wiping juice from her lips with the back of her hand. "Tastes a little like grapes. Lord knows I love grapes."

Ben figured she must have been telling the truth because she ate her fair share without a single complaint.

Chapter 11

The two explorers were climbing farther up the mountain several days later. It was the middle of the afternoon, and the temperature was so hot that they chose a slow, gradual ascent rather than a more direct steeper path to wind their way up through the foothills. The ascent was much easier when they stuck to the natural valleys that cut through the mountains, so they only climbed steep areas when they couldn't find any other way to avoid them.

Ben wanted to find a permanent home in a valley with a stream flowing through it. A stream would be a constant supply of freshwater, as well as a drawing force for game. That way, they could hunt in either the foothills or the higher mountain range without having to roam far from home. All they had to do was follow the stream. It would be advantageous if they could find a cave or some other form of natural shelter, especially if it was in the lower elevations where they could live in the comfort of the warmer foothills and still be able to hunt in the cooler mountains without straying too far from their home.

Ben hadn't seen any extremely large animals since they parted company with the anthropoids. He knew from experience that larger game animals liked to live in the mountains around his grandfather's estate. He hoped the wild game of Gildor had a similar preference.

They traveled a long way during the day, and it was getting late. The temperature would drop rapidly after the sun went down. They would be left out in the cold without any protection from the elements if they didn't find some sort of shelter soon. It had rained almost every day since they reached the mountains, and there wasn't any dry wood to build a fire with, even if they had the means to start one. A heavy rain fell during the day, and it thoroughly soaked any wood lying on the ground, so they had no other choice but to continue their search for shelter or take their chances in the cold open air.

They were about to give up for the day when Megan slipped on some loose stones and grabbed Ben's arm to maintain her balance. When Ben looked down to see what she had slipped on, he instantly recognized something that made his heart jump. He picked up two dark palm-sized stones and tested their weight in his hands. Unsheathing his hunting knife, he struck one of the stones with the dull side of the blade and whooped with joy when a shower of sparks flew into the air.

"Yes," he cried, hoisting the stones in his hands. "Good work, Meg."

"Well, thank you," Megan replied, giggling. "I wish I knew what I did to make you so happy though."

Ben held the stones out for her to look at. "These stones you just slipped on are flint. I can start a fire with them now, if we can just find enough dry tinder to get one going."

"What are we waiting for?" Megan cried. "Let's get looking!"

They searched the area for bushes and trees that had dead branches hanging on them and, fifteen minutes later, had managed to gather a sizable pile of dry touchwood to start a fire with. However, they still needed larger logs to feed the fire after they got one going.

"What about that high grass over there?" Megan asked, pointing to a tuft of brown grass protruding from between two large stones. "Do you think that is dry enough to burn?"

Ben nodded. "Yeah. It will burn, all right, but it will burn too fast to make a good warm fire that will last. We need logs for that, but I don't know if we'll be able to find any dry enough to burn."

"So what do we do?" Megan asked.

Ben turned his eyes skyward and noted the position of the sun. "We still have a couple hours of daylight left. The temperature will drop fast after the sun goes down. Without warm clothing, we'll have to huddle together to stay warm by the small fire I do manage to build with what little dry wood we've got. I'm afraid it won't last more than an hour or so. We might be in for a long, cold night if we don't find shelter soon. It wouldn't take much of a fire to keep us warm if we could find shelter, but we might still have to huddle together to stay warm if it burns out. Or we could turn around and go back down to the foothills. It'll be warmer down there than it is up here. We can come back here tomorrow if you want."

"I don't much care for that idea," Megan replied, plopping down on a nearby stone and looking up at Ben. "I don't care if we have to huddle to stay warm. We've been huddling together ever since we were brought to this stupid place. What difference does another night make? Why are you so worried about it anyway? It took us all day to get this far, and I don't feel like going back now. I really don't want to walk all the way back down through that valley again just to turn around and walk back up here in the morning. And besides that, I'm tired," she added indignantly as she crossed her arms in front of her.

Ben hated it when she pouted like that. It made him feel as if he had done something wrong when all he was really trying to do was the right thing for both of them. *I care*, he thought. *If you only knew how much I care. If you only knew how hard it is for me not to take advantage of our situation sometimes.* He shook his head. "Well then, if you really don't want to go back, I suggest you get up and help me find shelter." He offered her his hand, which she reluctantly took, and he pulled her to her feet.

They started their search along the base of the valley's sloping walls. After half an hour of fruitless searching, they climbed farther up the mountainside, where they discovered a small canyon. Ben hoped they would find a cave or recess in the rocky walls there large enough to offer them a temporary shelter for the night.

The sun was almost to the horizon line, and they were about to give up the search when Megan spotted a large catlike creature skulking along near the bottom of the rocky escarpment of the canyon wall. She called Ben's attention to the animal as soon as she saw it. The big cat ambled on into a thicket and disappeared without even seeing them.

Ben motioned for Megan to stand still and turned to whisper into her ear. "There might be a cave behind that brush. Stay here while I check it out!"

"Be careful," Megan said, sounding truly worried. "That thing looked to be as big as a lion."

Ben winked at her before sneaking off toward the thicket. After he reached the bushes, he proceeded with extreme caution as he tried to see what lay behind them.

The mouth of a cave was hidden behind the thick growth. The opening was almost three feet wide and over five feet high. A well-worn path through the middle of the thicket served as the sole access route in and out of the hidden den, assuring the huge cat of its privacy, as well as protection from unwanted visitors.

Ben started to lean forward to get a better look, and his heart nearly burst from his chest when something touched his shoulder. He spun around on his heels with his fist ready to deliver a vicious blow until he recognized Megan standing behind him. "Meg!" His voice was a harsh whisper. "What are you doing here? I told you to stay where you were."

The girl ignored his scolding. "Don't go in there, Ben. That lion will tear you apart."

He slapped his hand over her mouth and led her several yards from the cave's entrance. Fighting down his anger, he spoke in a softer tone, "I don't intend to go in there. I intend to make that cat come out to us."

Megan shook her head in disbelief. "And just how do you plan on doing that?"

Ben turned his quiver upside down and dumped out a piece of the flint they had found earlier. "With this," he whispered. "I'm going to try and set fire to the damp brush in front of the cave and smoke him out. Then I'll shoot him when he comes out. He might try to come back here later otherwise. We don't want that now, do we?"

Megan slipped her bow off her shoulder and started to nock a poison-tipped arrow on the string. "I'll help," she said.

Ben started to protest but thought better of it. The memory of how she shot the anthropoid through the heart at the waterfall still lingered fresh in his mind. She learned how to handle a bow rather well for someone who had never shot one before being stranded in Gildor.

"Okay," he said. He pointed at a boulder about fifteen yards away. It was on the far side of the cave's mouth and looked to be as safe a place as any for her to stand if the big cat came charging from the cave. "Stand on that boulder over there and be prepared to shoot in a hurry if you have to!"

While Megan was getting into place, Ben piled the dry grass they found earlier under the brush in front of the cave and prepared to light it. After checking to see if Megan was in position, he held the flint close to the grass and struck it with the blade of his knife. A shower of sparks fell into the grass, but nothing happened. He struck the flint again and again until the sparks found a patch of grass dry enough that it started to smolder. Bending down on hands and knees, he blew on the smoldering embers until the grass burst into flame. Then he pushed the ball of flame farther into the brush with a stick before standing up and turning to wave at Megan. Then he stood back and waited for the brush to catch fire.

Megan acknowledged Ben's wave and took another arrow from her quiver and laid it on the boulder beside her. She knelt down on one knee and silently held her weapon at the ready.

Ben nocked an arrow on his own bowstring and prepared to draw it back as soon as he saw any movement in the mouth of the cave. He held his breath while he watched the brush slowly start to burn. A pillar of thick smoke wafted into the air as the flames began to spread through the brush aided by a light breeze. The breeze soon changed direction and started blowing toward the mouth of the cave and forced the smoke inside.

It must not have taken long for the lion's den to fill with smoke because it only took a few minutes before Ben could hear angry growls coming from the cornered animal inside. He signaled for Megan to get ready when he heard the padded footfalls of the fear-crazed beast running back and forth inside the cave. "Get ready, Meg. Here he comes," he yelled, pulling his bowstring back and aiming toward the mouth of the cave.

The burning brush suddenly flew into pieces when the panicked animal charged from the den. Ben dropped his bow and covered his face and eyes with his hands to protect them from the shower of hot sparks and burning debris that flew into the air around him. A split second later, he heard a scream and hurriedly brushed the glowing embers away. He turned just in time to see the big cat charging directly at Megan.

Megan still remained at the ready, however. As soon as she saw the crazed beast break from the cave and charge at her, she quickly let her arrow fly. The poison-tipped projectile flew straight and true, hitting the lion squarely between the top of his shoulders and just behind the base of his massive neck, continuing downward and severing his spine.

When Ben finally managed to completely clear the embers from his face, he saw the mortally wounded feline lying on the ground a few feet from the boulder Megan had been kneeling on. The big cat wasn't moving, and Megan was standing over it, ready to shoot again if she had to.

After retrieving his bow, Ben nocked the arrow back on the string before rushing forward and slowly circling the prone animal with his weapon at full draw. A few tense seconds passed before he bent over the body of the motionless cat and moved the tip of his arrow close to one of its glazed eyes. He didn't lower his weapon until he was sure the lion was dead. "Woo, that was close." He sighed. He knelt down beside the beast and gave it a pat on the side of the head. "You can put your bow down now, Meg. He's dead."

Megan relaxed and knelt down beside Ben to stroke the lion's massive head with shaking fingers. She turned slowly to look at Ben. "I thought it was going to kill you when it broke through the brush the way it did. It turned toward me when I screamed." She looked away and turned her attention back to the dead cat. "I've never seen anything like this before."

"Neither have I," Ben replied. He moved his hand along the lion's lean body, stroking its beautiful coat. Its hair felt like fine thread as it passed between his fingers.

The big cat resembled an African lion more than anything, but there were several differences. The fur was light red, with two four-inch-wide yellow stripes running horizontally along either side of its serpentine body's entire length. Its eyes were light blue with slit pupils like those of a regular feline. When Ben pried the sagging mouth open with the blade of his knife, he left out a soft whistle when he saw what lay hidden within. The gaping maw was full of teeth over an inch long and ran in double rows along both its upper and lower jaws. It resembled a shark's mouth more than that of a lion. As he left his gaze drift, Ben gasped in awe when his eyes came to rest on the lion's feet. All four were at least ten inches long and six inches wide with five toes on each front foot. The three middle digits of the front feet extended three inches beyond the two on either side of them, giving the strange members the appearance of huge grasping hands with two opposing thumbs. Ben pushed on one of the cat's feet, and a set of two-inch claws automatically extended from the end of its toes. The strange beast must have grasped its prey with its front feet while ripping it apart with its sharklike teeth and hind claws. Considering its environment, the big cat seemed much better equipped than an African lion would have been. Although its head was about the same size and shape as that of an African lion, its body was much different. The Gildorian lion's body was thin and serpentine and almost eight feet in length, not including its four-foot-long tail. Although it was longer than an African lion, it wasn't nearly as heavily built.

"So many strange animals, and now this lion," Megan breathed. "None of them look like the ones we're familiar with, and yet they seem very much alike in some ways. What other surprises do you think FRU might have come up with?"

Ben shook his head. "Hard to tell. Gildor is probably full of FRU's genetic experiments. Who knows how many kinds of animals, insects, and plants they've messed around with? God only knows how they might have evolved after having all those years to develop." He stood up still staring at the lion. "If the rest of the animals are as highly evolved as the ones we've seen so far, what're the people going to be like?"

Megan shrugged and stood up. "If they're anything like that pony girl we saw, I'd guess this is a very primeval place. I was planning to major in history when I got to college, but I'll probably be writing the history in this place."

"Come on." Ben laughed. "Let's check out our new home. We better make sure this big fella lived alone."

The mouth of the cave was only a few feet from the right wall, so the entire inside was hidden in darkness except for the small area in front of the opening. Ben made a crude torch with a stick and some dry grass and lit it so they could see inside. They cautiously stepped inside to have a look around after they cleared the burned brush away from the entrance and were happy to find that the lion had been the sole occupant. They were astounded by the size of the grotto they found themselves standing in. It was roughly thirty feet long and fourteen feet wide with a domed ceiling resting twenty feet above a spacious uneven floor. A rock ledge, which could easily be reached by climbing a set of natural stone steps along the left wall, rose almost to the ceiling. The former resident had used the ledge to store his kills until he was ready to finish eating them. The remains of a deer were still hanging over the edge of the uppermost point, and there were piles of bones scattered on the floor below, serving as testimony of the meals that had been eaten there. All in all, the young couple thought the cave would make them a perfect home. Although it smelled of smoke and the lion's excrement, they both realized that the odors would dissipate in time after it was cleaned out.

Megan set to work cleaning the inside of the cave while Ben went looking for kindling to build a fire. Darkness had fully set in before he returned with the kindling and piled it inside the entrance. After he managed to build a small fire, he went back outside to gather some larger pieces of wood and returned a few minutes later with a bundle of damp logs. He stacked the logs neatly beside the fire in hopes that they would dry enough to be burned later.

After stacking the wood, Ben began working on a crude door to cover the entrance of the cave with. He cut some saplings that he found growing in the canyon while Megan cut vines to bind them with. It only took them a short time to tie the saplings together after that and secure them over the entrance. Ben made sure he left a small opening near the top of the entrance to allow the smoke from the fire to escape. When the door was finally in place, they sat down by the fire and waited for sleep to overtake them. Both of them fell sound asleep within minutes after the cave was filled with comfortable warmth.

Chapter 12

Ben removed the carcass of the deer from the ledge the next morning and took it out into the forest to bury so wild animals wouldn't be drawn to the cave by the smell of carrion. He also buried the body of the lion, but not before removing its pelt, which he thought would make a warm blanket after it was properly cured.

After burying the lion's carcass, Ben set out in search of food and was happy to find several kinds of fruit-bearing trees growing on the hillside above the cave. He also discovered a large herd of deer living in the lower valley. He and Megan had no real concern for water either because a stream of cool, clean water ran down the mountainside no more than seventy yards from the cave.

They both rejoiced at the abundance around them after Ben returned to "the lair" (the name Megan gave their new home) with an armload of fresh fruit and the water bottle full of sparkling water. They actually started to feel safe again because they didn't have to worry about how long it would be between meals anymore.

Several weeks passed since they moved into the lair, and Megan did her best to make it as livable as possible. She made a broom out of dried grass tied to a stick and swept the inside of the cave every day for almost a week. It was an impossible task to remove all the dirt the cave had collected over the eons, but her patience paid off, and she managed to rid it of almost all the loose dirt and dust. Ben had killed a piglike creature while hunting in one of the upper valleys one day and was about to throw its useless hide away when Megan stopped him and made him cut a portion of it off before letting him dispose of the rest. Consequently, the frugal young woman was able to make a bristle brush, which she was able to use to scrub the blood off the ledge where the lion had stored its victims. It took hours, but with a lot of hard work and elbow grease, she almost managed to make it sparkle.

While Megan kept herself busy preparing the lair for human habitation, Ben busied himself making furniture. With nothing more than a stone ax and his hunting knife, he managed to build a small table and two benches out of logs. Two small log beds stood at the rear of the grotto and were covered with thick grass mats and blankets made of animal hides. Ben's was covered with the lion's pelt while Megan's had two soft deer hides she had sewn together thrown over it.

A large clay jar filled with water stood near the entrance of the lair. Megan made the jar, along with several smaller ones, out of clay she found near the bank of the stream. Ben fired them for her in an oven he built out of stones. It took a few tries, but he finally managed to keep the jars from cracking when he fired them. Only four of them were left undamaged by the time he figured out how to control the fire properly.

Ben added one more touch he thought was absolutely necessary if they were going to continue to have a fire inside the cave. He dug a hole through the left wall above the ledge where the rocky shelf ended four feet below the ceiling. The hole would serve as a chimney to rid the lair of smoke.

As the lion had done previously, they used the ledge to store the meat of the game they killed. The smoke from the fire would rise to the ceiling and slowly swirl over and around the meat stored on the ledge before continuing on its course out through the hole in the wall. This also helped to dry and preserve the meat so it wouldn't spoil quickly. The wood smoke even helped improve the meat's flavor as well.

Smoking meat, tanning leather, and curing hides were only a few of the skills Ben's parents had begun to teach him while he was still a little boy. He had gone on many camping trips with his mother and father before the tragic accident that claimed both their lives. It was during those trips that his father taught him the skills of survival, including the skill of making log furniture. He carefully followed his father's instructions when he built the rough furnishings and smoked the meat. If it hadn't been for his father's tutoring, he and Megan might very well have perished after being left to fend for themselves in Gildor.

Not to be overlooked were the lessons his mother had taught him as well. She constantly warned him about his hot temper and how it could get him into trouble. She taught him to read and write and even how to sew. Sewing was a skill he never really took interest in, but his mother insisted that he learn how just the same. She taught him how to sew leather because that was how she made her living. She made leather goods and sold them through the family freight and wholesale business. The skills he learned from his mother were quite evident every time he and Megan slipped their moccasins on in the mornings.

As a whole, the lair turned out to be a comfortable home for them. Most of their needs seemed to be met in the little valley. Food and water were in abundance, as well as peace and quiet. They had just about everything they needed, except the one thing they both missed the most: *friends*. They had each other to talk to and keep each other company, but they still missed the companionship of other people. Even if the life-forms they discovered might only be partly human, they just longed for their friendship.

Ben was aroused one morning from a deep sleep by the loud rumbling of his own stomach. His hunger was more demanding than usual, and he wanted to eat as soon as his feet touched the dirt floor. He would normally have gone outside to fetch a fresh supply of water first, but this morning was different. He wanted to eat before starting his daily chores.

He quickly slipped his moccasins on and climbed to the top of the ledge, where he hacked a generous portion of meat off the shank of a deer he had killed a week earlier. Lifting the meat to his nose, he sniffed it to make sure it wasn't spoiled before taking a nibble.

"Hey, bring some of that down for me too!" Megan must have awakened about the same time he did. She was sitting up on the edge of her bed, watching him.

Ben figured she watched him climb to the top of the ledge while she stayed under her blanket. Flashing her a wry smile, he called down from his lofty perch. "So you waited for me to climb up here to get breakfast so you wouldn't have to get out from under your nice, warm blankets. Is that it? Now you've got the guts to ask me to bring your breakfast down to you."

"Why not?" Megan retorted. "You would have done the same thing to me if the situation was reversed."

Ben chuckled as he hacked off another generous portion of meat. "I suppose you're right. Only, I would have asked you to cook it for me too. In this case, I'll volunteer."

"I'll fetch some wood for the fire," Megan said, slipping her feet into her moccasins and wrapping the long straps up around her calves before tying then in place.

A short while later, after Megan had fed the fire and the venison had been impaled on the spit over it, the young couple munched on some fruit while they watched the meat cook. Ben started to tell Megan about his plans for the day while they waited. "Our supply of meat is dwindling fast. I thought we might try one of the lower valleys instead of hunting in the canyon today. I don't know if there's a wet season here inside this cavern or not. During the five months we've been here, it hasn't rained very often, but when it has, it's been mostly in downpours. If the seasons are going to change, they might do so soon, and then the weather could get really bad. I don't want to kill too many of the deer in this valley because we may need them later. We may not be able to roam very far from the lair if the weather gets too rough, and I'd like to leave the herd here undisturbed for as long as possible."

Megan handed him his portion of venison on a wooden plate. "Do you really need me to go with you?" she asked. "Neither of us has ventured very far without the other going along. I'm not sure that I like staying here alone, but I don't want to go with you either. I have some sewing I'd like to finish if you don't mind."

Ben considered what Megan was suggesting for a moment. *We really could use some warmer clothing. Our clothes are shot, and we haven't replaced them yet.* "Well, we haven't seen anything dangerous in the canyon since you killed that cave lion over a month ago. And we really haven't seen what I would consider any dangerous animals on our hunting trips lately. I'm sure you can handle anything that might come up while I'm gone. You proved that already. What are you gonna sew anyway?"

"It's a surprise," Megan replied. "I'll show you when you get back."

Ben nodded and let the subject drop. *If she wants to surprise me, then I'll let her,* he thought. He went about his daily chores without asking any more questions, and after he was finished, he prepared to set out for the lower valley. He stacked some greenwood a safe distance from the cave before leaving and told Megan to light it if any trouble arose while he was gone. He promised to return as fast as possible if he spotted the dark smoke of the signal fire.

Ben entered the mouth of the lower valley an hour later. The only animal life he had seen during his short trek through the foothills was a few small mammals and an occasional bird or two. Pushing on through the valley, he became alarmed when he happened to come across a set of tracks. It was the spoor of a giant elephantine creature like those the anthropoids rode when they chased him and Megan from the plateau. The tracks were fresh; the behemoth had passed that way within the last hour or so. He still wasn't sure if the creatures were dangerous or not, but he was certain that he and Megan would be in danger if any anthropoids were roaming about. During the time they lived on the plateau, they had seen but one of the huge animals and two apes. Although the apes they ran into later used a herd of the beasts to chase them from the base of the plateau, the beast they encountered by itself appeared to be fairly docile. Nevertheless, he decided that caution was always the best policy concerning things he was unsure of. He was about to turn and head in a different direction when he noticed a second spoor beside that of the giant quadruped.

These footprints were almost the size and shape of a human woman's. They were only about two-thirds the size of his own and seemed to have been made by naked feet, but he was puzzled by the strange impressions left at the front of each print. They looked almost as if whoever or whatever made them wore some sort of hard coverings over the front halves of their feet. The creature that made the tracks was bipedal; only a left and right foot had made the strange impressions, and its stride was equal to that of a woman or a half- grown boy.

Ben found himself wondering what kind of people would wear footwear that covered only the front half of their feet. His curiosity aroused, he decided to follow the strange tracks. He only followed them about a hundred yards before a second set of tracks joined those of the creature he was already tracking. The second spoor was identical to the first, except that they were slightly longer and deeper than the first. Judging by their depth, he guessed the first creature to weigh about 95 to 105 pounds, and the second to be somewhere around 120 to 130. They weren't huge animals by any means, but Ben still followed the trail with caution.

After following the tracks another five hundred feet, Ben finally came across the elephantine creature browsing leisurely under some high trees. He was convinced that the beast was alone after giving the area a careful scan. It was evidently wild and not one of those belonging to the apes, so he was extracareful not to disturb it as he passed. The trail of the creatures he was looking for led off in a different direction.

It was midday when Ben sat down under a small fruit tree to eat his lunch. He had barely taken the first bite when he heard a noise off in the distance. As far as he could tell, it sounded like a roar. It came from the forested hills to his right, the same direction the tracks he followed were leading. A second roar erupted from the forest a few seconds later and was immediately followed by a woman's scream.

Ben's heart jumped into his throat as he quickly snatched up his bow and started running toward the commotion as fast as he could. He ran through the trees until he came to the crest of a hill where he stopped to scan the other side. His heart almost stopped when his eyes took in the extraordinary scene below.

The roar had come from a cave lion much larger than the one Megan had killed. That lion must have weighed over four hundred pounds, but this one looked to weigh well over six hundred, and it was circling two of the most beautiful creatures Ben had ever seen.

Two equine women were caught in an ever-tightening circle that the big serpentine cat was walking around them. One woman was on the ground, apparently unconscious, or dead, while the other stood over her fallen comrade, trying to hold the lion at bay with a long stick. Every time the lion attempted to close in, the equine woman prodded the infuriated beast with her stick. Ben realized that she wouldn't be able to hold the ravenous beast off much longer, especially if it ever figured out that she could do very little physical damage to him with the flimsy weapon.

It only took a second for Ben to react. He drew back his bow and took careful aim, then left the arrow fly as soon as he was sure of his target. Almost faster than the human eye could follow, the arrow flew straight to its intended target. Its poison tip drove deep into the lion's side.

The big cat roared in agony and jumped high into the air, twisting and turning. Landing flat on its back, it continued to kick frantically in a futile attempt to regain its feet, but the poison on the arrowhead took its deadly toll in a matter of seconds. As suddenly as the lion reacted to the shock of the arrow hitting him, he stopped moving and fell into an endless sleep.

The equine woman stood in open-mouthed silence as she watched the wounded cat kick its life away in front of her. She seemed bewildered by the beast's sudden demise. However, her fear of the lion soon passed and was replaced by yet another.

Ben saw the look of terror that crossed the beautiful creature's face when he started down the hillside toward her. At first, he thought she was afraid the lion might get up and attack again, so he paid little attention. She remained frozen, watching him draw nearer. Then Ben soon realized that the fear in her huge liquid eyes was directed at him and not the lion. He didn't want to panic her by moving any closer, so he slowed his pace and turned toward the lion's body. After cautiously approaching the carcass, he bent down beside it, pretending to ignore the equine woman completely. When he chanced to glance in her direction a moment later, she was kneeling beside her fallen comrade, examining the back of the prone woman's right leg.

The prone girl had regained consciousness and tried to sit up, but her companion's firm hand on her shoulder held her down until she could finish examining the injured limb. When the wounded girl propped herself up on her elbows, Ben finally got a good look at her face. She was younger than the other woman, but no less beautiful. Her hair was the same apple red as the girl he and Megan had seen out on the plains a couple months earlier, and he wondered if it might be the same girl. When he saw her torn and bleeding right thigh, Ben could control his impatience no longer. He left his bow lying on the ground beside the dead lion and started walking slowly toward the two women.

When they noticed him approaching, the two equine's faces were immediately masked with fear. The uninjured woman hurriedly tried to help her companion to her feet, but the girl screamed out in agony and fell back to the ground, grabbing at her wounded thigh. Realizing her companion couldn't move, the older woman stood up and pointed her crude weapon at Ben in a threatening manner.

Ben stopped and smiled while holding his arms out at his sides. He didn't know if they could understand English, so he spoke softly as he pressed forward, hoping the soft tone of his voice would help reassure them. "I mean you no harm. I only want to help. I'm a friend."

The equine held her ground and continued to wield the stick with a determined look on her face. She shifted her weight from one foot to the other and crouched as if getting ready to thrust the end of the stick into Ben's chest, but she wavered when he continued to move forward with his empty hands extended outward. Ben wasn't sure what was about to happen next, but he did know that the wounded girl's leg needed immediate attention. He pressed slowly onward until the jagged end of the stick touched the front of his bare chest. Then he stopped to stare into the wide green eyes of the cowering woman. *What's she going to do now?* he wondered, getting his first close look at her.

Her hairstyle was the same as her friend's: bangs to her eyebrows, a high carrot-colored mane that swept up over the top of her head and down between her shoulder blades, with shorter hair growing on either side. She had the same heart-shaped face, only with more mature features. She looked to be in her mid- to late thirties. Like her younger companion's clothing, her apparel consisted of a dark-green G-string and tight-fitting vest made of what appeared to be soft tree bark or some other plant material.

Ben remained perfectly still, letting the equine have time to make up her mind about what to do. She finally stood up straight and tilted her lovely head to one side, giving him a perplexed look. As if on cue, the girl on the ground moaned in pain, and her comrade threw her weapon down and knelt beside her. She glanced up at Ben a moment later with pleading eyes. It was then that he realized he had won her confidence.

He knelt down beside the wounded girl and quickly surveyed her damaged leg. Three ragged gashes ran across the back of her right thigh about ten inches above the knee. The lion had evidently been chasing her and tried to grab her leg with its front feet but had only managed to rake her leg with the claws of its three longest front toes. Ben whistled when he realized how close the big cat had come to hamstringing the girl and causing her to permanently loose the use of the leg. He shook his head. *Why that lion didn't kill her is a mystery to me. Perhaps the intervention of her friend kept him from killing her. Maybe they'll be able to tell me what took place here someday.*

He sat down and placed the girl's wounded leg across his lap and washed the claw marks out with clean water from his water bottle.

After carefully inspecting the ragged wounds, he wrapped them with a makeshift bandage made from the buckskin bag that he had carried his lunch in. Although the wounds were deep, they wouldn't cause any disabling injury, but there would definitely be scars after they healed.

After he had finished wrapping the girl's leg, Ben sat back and looked at his handiwork. He happened to glance at the feet of the two women while he sat there and realized they were the ones who made the tracks he had been following earlier. Their feet were bare and shaped similar to those of humans, except they didn't end with five toes. They were graced with a single toe ending in a thick, hard hoof instead. *How strange, and yet how beautiful these two are*, he thought. When he realized they were watching him, he shook himself out of his daydream.

The younger equine was lying on her side with her head in her companion's lap. When Ben's eyes locked on hers, the girl tried to force a smile through her mask of fear and pain, and he could not help admiring her courageous effort to put forth a false front of well-being.

It was almost evening when Ben and the equine women finally broke over the crest of the hill below the entrance of the little canyon.

It had taken several hours to make the return trip, and Ben knew Megan would be worried. As a rule, he would have been back long before nightfall, but his progress was hindered by the need to travel slowly in order to prevent the wounded girl's leg from bleeding. He had no idea how much blood she may have lost, and he didn't want to risk her losing any more. The litter she was on bounced more than he liked as he pulled it along behind him. The older equine tried to help him, but she was unable to support the weight of the other end of the litter for very long before she became exhausted and had to put it down again. It was evident that neither of the equines had eaten a hardy meal in quite some time. The paleness of their faces and the rumbling he heard coming from their bellies convinced him of that. He ended up giving his bow to the older woman to carry while he took on the chore of getting the wounded girl to the canyon by himself.

Megan must have spotted them as soon as they topped the hill because she came running almost as soon as they stepped into view. There was a look of concern on her face as she ran toward them with her bow in her hand. She didn't slow down until she had covered over half the distance between them. She soon realized Ben wasn't in any danger when the equine woman strolled up beside him without threatening him with the bow she was carrying.

Ben noticed a sudden swish of the equine's tail when she saw Megan approaching. She balked and dropped the bow so she could hold her own crude weapon up as protection. Ben stopped pulling the litter and left one handle rest on his hip while he reached out to slowly push the alarmed equine's spear down with his free hand. "Friend," he said, smiling and pointing at Megan. The frightened equine turned to look at him and tilted her head to one side. Ben took his hand off her spear and tapped himself on the chest. "Friend," he repeated. Then he pointed to Megan and repeated the word again.

The equine slowly lowered her stick and looked at Megan, who had stopped a short distance away when she saw the fear in the horsewoman's eyes. "Free... freend," she said hesitantly.

"Yes, that's right," Ben replied, still smiling.

"Is there anything I can do?" Megan asked, beginning to draw slowly nearer.

Ben nodded. "You can try giving our friend here a nice smile. She could use a little encouragement right now."

"*Right*," Megan replied. She turned to face the startled woman and flashed her one of her friendliest smiles. When the beautiful creature smiled back, Megan left out a sigh and stepped around her to get a better look at the girl on the litter Ben was pulling. "Well, now I know why you're so late. Just where did you find these two?"

Ben started to drag the litter toward the cave again. "It's a long story. I'll tell you about it later. Right now, we have to get this girl to the lair. Her leg was clawed by a lion."

Megan bent down to pick up the other end of the litter and was surprised to discover that she had help.

The equine woman had taken a position on the far side of the litter and grabbed the other handle. She looked at Megan and nodded. "Freend," she said.

Megan nodded. "That's right. You're learning fast." The equine smiled again. "Laaarrnning fats," she said.

"Close enough." Megan giggled as she and the equine both fell in step behind Ben while he led the way up the hill with the litter.

That evening they had a meal of boiled vegetables and roasted venison. Ben and Megan had helpings of both meat and vegetables, but the equines ate large helpings of mostly vegetables, hardly touching the meat.

After they all had finished eating, Megan checked the wounded girl's leg again. While she was changing the dressing, Megan spoke to the girl in a mild tone. The sound of her voice seemed to soothe the girl's nerves and help her relax.

The older equine insisted on helping Ben gather firewood and fetch drinking water from the creek. He tried to get the persistent woman to stay in the lair, but she insisted on helping him. He figured there was no use arguing with her because she couldn't understand a word he said anyway.

Before turning in for the evening, Megan took one of the doeskins off her bed and laid it on the floor beside the fire for the two women to use. It wasn't long after Ben secured the door over the entrance of the cave that the two equines, with their bellies now full, fell sound asleep.

Before turning in themselves, the young couple discussed trying to teach their newfound friends English.

"Perhaps it would be better if we tried to learn their language instead," Megan said. "It won't do us any good if we never learn their language and it turns out that English isn't spoken anywhere in Gildor."

Ben thought the suggestion over and nodded. "You're right. I think it would be best if we started first thing in the morning. The sooner we learn to communicate with them, the better off we'll be."

They retired to their own beds after their short discussion and turned in for the night. The next day promised to be an eventful one because they were sure they had a lot to learn from their new friends. They certainly realized that they had much to teach the equines as well.

Chapter 13

Ben marveled at the equines' ability to comprehend and retain almost everything he and Megan had taught them during the month they had been living with them. They managed to learn enough broken English to make themselves understood whenever they chose to use the strange language. However, the fillies (as the two humans began to refer to them) were excellent teachers as well. The two humans discovered this when they learned the solitary language of Gildor in a relatively short time. It was no easy chore for the fillies to learn the English language, though, because they weren't used to using contractions. Their own Gildorian dialect was a simple language devoid of any such shortcuts, but it was easy for the two humans to make them up as they learned to speak it. Sometimes the fillies had trouble understanding them when they inadvertently made contractions out of certain word combinations. Nevertheless, they soon grew used to their new friends' inappropriate use of their language and were able to understand almost everything they said.

It wasn't until after Ben and Megan started to learn the Gildorian language that they learned who and what the fillies really were. The elder of the two was named Mota, and the younger was her daughter, Tala. They were members of the race of equine people called Pack, and they told their new human friends that the land within the cavern, oddly enough, was called Gildor. The fillies also told them that the Packs were the slaves of the race of pure humans who ruled all of Gildor.

Ben was surprised to learn that pure humans actually existed in the forbidden land. When Ned Foster described the place, he made it sound like there were no pure humans living there. When Ben asked Mota to tell him more about the humans, she refused. She claimed that she was afraid if he and Megan learned too much about the humans, they might become as evil as they were. She did, however, consent to tell him the legend of how the Pack race had come to exist.

The Packs were a special people bred and raised by the humans for use as beasts of burden. According to Gildorian legend, the Great Creators found a way to combine the traits of humans with those of certain types of beasts, producing more intelligent races of slaves that were easier to train than dumb animals. The Great Creators' evil experiments turned out to be very successful. Their creations, the Pack being one of them, were doomed to living their entire lives as slaves. After all, what else could those produced by mixing the bloodline of a mere, dumb animal with that of the superior human ever be, but slaves to the pure-blood descendants of those who created them?

Mota told Ben about more experiments the Great Creators had tried that failed miserably. She went on to explain the origin of the race of beast people, or the Bondo, as she called them.

The Bondos didn't respond well to the training or harsh discipline of their human masters. One day, the humans lost control of them, and they revolted. Many of the Bondos managed to escape before the humans could smash their revolt. A few of them were never captured, but those who were unfortunate enough to be caught were destroyed. As far as Mota knew, the remaining Bondos still lived in the wilds of Gildor. Humans only hunted them for sport because they had no other use for them.

Ben finally understood why the apes had chased him and Megan from the plateau after hearing Mota's story. He shuddered to think about what might have happened to Megan in the hands of the two Bondos he had rescued her from months earlier. He was thankful that he was fortunate enough to have rescued her before any harm came to her. Still, he couldn't help pitying the poor beasts, and he wondered if they would have reacted the same way if they had known that he and Megan meant them no harm. He figured he would never know the answer to that question.

Early one morning, while Ben was filling the water jars at the stream, Tala unexpectedly appeared beside him. It wasn't a total surprise to him, however, because he was quite used to the equine girl's presence by now. He didn't mind her following him around because he didn't realize at the time just how infatuated with him she was.

While Ben filled the jars with water, he asked Tala how she and her mother came to be in the foothills the day he rescued them from the lion. He thought if he could get the girl talking that she might divulge more information about the pure humans of Gildor. Without her mother around to stop her, Tala let the information slip out freely. Talking as best she could in broken English, she started telling Ben about the fateful day she and her mother were taken out to work in the fields on their master's plantation.

There were several other Packs in the work party that day, including Tala's father, Tolan. Their overseer was a mean and burly man named Dang, who was well-noted for his ill treatment of the Packs and for taking his pleasure with their women whenever he pleased.

On that particular day, while the packs were allowed to stop working long enough to drink their daily allotment of water, Dang ordered Mota to fetch him a drink from the water cask. Mota obediently did as she was ordered. When she took the water to Dang, the brute grabbed her and tried to draw her to him. She struggled free and tried to run away, only to be caught from behind by Dang's huge outstretched hand. He had taken hold of her tail and pulled the screaming filly back to him. Once he had her in his grasp again, he threw her viciously to the ground and dropped down on top of her. While he was busy trying to wrest Mota's meager clothing off her, Dang failed to notice the hulking figure running toward them. Before he could carry out the despicable act he had in mind, he was lifted off Mota by the gigantic figure that had rushed to her aid.

Tolan, Mota's mate, lifted Dang up by the throat until his feet dangled inches from the ground. Although Dang was a powerful man, Tolan was much larger and considerably more powerful. The overseer dangled in the giant Pack's hands with horror-filled eyes as he tried to call out to the other plantation guards for help. But try as he might, he couldn't made a sound. His bull neck snapped in Tolan's grip as easily as a dry twig under the hooves of a heavy ox. He was already dead on the ground by the time the other four guards ever realized anything was wrong.

The two guards who arrived on the scene first tried to force Tolan to his knees on the ground at spearpoint, but before they could get him under control, Tolan turned on them, shoving their spears aside and then smashing his balled fist into one man's face before kicking the other in the stomach.

When the other two guards finally reached the scene and tried to help their fallen comrades, they discovered that several more Packs had already intervened. While the guards were busy struggling with the enraged Packs, the rest of the work party made good their escape into the wilderness.

Not waiting to see the outcome of the fight, Mota quickly grabbed Tala's hand and dragged her along as she ran for the safety of the forest. They never knew what happened to Tolan.

The two equine women wandered through the mountains for weeks before they finally descended into the plains. It was there that Tala came across Ben and Megan sleeping under the blanket one morning while she was searching for water. She told Ben that she thought he and Megan might be humans searching for her and her mother at first but dismissed that idea when she saw their ragged condition. Their strange blanket of grass intrigued her so much that she could not resist taking it. She thought that if she could show it to Mota, she might be able to make clothing out of it for them to wear before they returned to the cold mountains. However, when she stopped for a moment to look at the blanket, she realized that Ben and Megan had discovered her. Fearing that they might try and capture her, she dropped the blanket and ran back to where her mother was sleeping in the grass several hundred feet away.

Oh, how things might have been different if we had only known, Ben thought when he realized just how close they had been to the fillies when he and Megan were too weak to follow Tala's trail.

Tala continued, stating that her mother decided to return to the mountains that night because she was afraid the humans might try to capture them. So it was with great caution that they took a different path back to the mountains instead of the one they had followed when they descended into the grasslands. They were able to find an ample supply of food and water when they returned to the mountains, so Mota decided they would remain there for a while. They roamed up into the higher valleys where they rested for several days, but they were forced to return to the foothills when they were unable to find an adequate shelter to spend the cold nights in.

Suffering from spending too many nights out in the cold mountain air, they decided to try to kill a wild animal and use its hide to make warmer clothing. The vests and G-strings they wore were only intended to help maintain their modesty, not for warmth and comfort. Their master never gave them warm clothing. As far as he was concerned, they would never need more than the sparse garments they were supplied with when they had his warm barn to sleep in at night.

Tala stopped talking long enough to run her hands over the pair of soft doeskin shorts she was wearing. The shorts were a gift from Megan. Megan originally made two outfits, one for her and one for Ben; but when she saw the petty garments the fillies wore, she decided to give the shorts and matching vests to the Packs instead. The outfit Megan had made for herself was an almost-perfect fit for Tala, but she had to alter the one she originally made for Ben before giving it to Mota. Although Mota was slightly larger than Megan, she was nowhere near Ben's size. Megan had to add one very important detail to both outfits before giving them to the fillies though. She had to cut holes in the back of the shorts for the fillies to put their tails through before they could wear them.

Ben's mind wandered while he watched Tala admiring her new clothes. They must have seemed like a grand treasure to her. Although Mota's outfit was meant as a surprise for him, he thought it looked much better on her beautifully sculpted figure than it ever would have on his. He was drawn back to reality when Tala continued telling the rest of her story.

The fillies were following a herd of aboks (or Gildorian deer) the day they accidentally roamed into the hunting territory of a cave lion (or mithor, as the huge serpentine cats were called). They immediately set off in pursuit of an abok when they flushed it from its bed. They had followed the frightened animal only a short distance before they heard the mithor roar behind them. Becoming instantly aware that they weren't the only ones following the abok's trail, the equines took off running. The mithor must have thought the two women would be much easier pray to catch than the fleeing abok because he turned and began to chase them as soon as he saw them.

Acting hastily, Tala threw her crude spear at the charging beast, only to see the poorly thrown weapon go wide of its mark and fall harmlessly to the ground. She turned to run again just as the mithor sprang at her, and the big cat managed to rake her thigh with his claws before she could get out of the way. She fell to the ground screaming and thinking she had only seconds to live. She closed her eyes and waited for the killing blow, which never came. Mota had arrived and fended the mithor off with her spear before it could finish her daughter.

※

Tala slowly shook her head as she finished the story. "That when you save us, Ben. Tala not member more." She looked at him with her big blue eyes and exposed her excellent white teeth with a bright smile. "You save Tala from mithor. Now Tala belong you."

Ben's eyes shot wide, and he waved both hands in front of him. "Whoa there, girl! I don't want any slaves. You're a free woman as far as I'm concerned."

Tala lowered her eyes and shook her head before replying in a small voice, "Tala not want be slave. Want be mate."

Ben shook his head more vigorously than before. "You… you don't want to be my mate. You… you only think you do. You will find a man of your own kind one day and fall in love. Just wait and see."

The filly's eyes were brimming with tears when she looked up again. "All Packs slaves," she sobbed. "Only way Tala can have Pack mate is go back master's plantation. Be whipped if return to master now. Not want whipped." She stopped speaking for a moment and rubbed the small brand on her upper left thigh.

Mota also bore the same mark on her left leg. She had informed Ben earlier that it was the sign of their master's plantation. All Packs were branded when they became old enough to work in the fields or after they were sold at the auction, depending on whether their original master intended to retain possession of them or not.

Tala looked up at the morning sky. "It is no good!" she exclaimed in Gildorian. "I will never have a mate if you do not want me, Ben. And I will never return to Plantation Quander to be a slave," she added, jumping to her feet and running back toward the lair.

Ben called out after her, but she never slowed her pace and soon disappeared over the top of the rise between him and the cave. He quickly gathered up the water jars and put them into the pannier before lifting the heavy burden to his shoulders and rushing off after the disappointed girl.

Chapter 14

Tala was still in her mother's arms by the time Ben returned to the lair. Megan was standing beside them, stroking the weeping girl's mane with a gentle hand. Mota saw Ben first and whispered something into her daughter's ear. Then the young filly backed away from her mother and glanced up at Ben through tear-filled eyes before shaking her head and running off into the forest, leaving her Mota and Megan to face him alone.

Ben could still hear Tala crying as she ran off. Having no idea what else to do, he carried his burden to the cave and set it down inside the entrance. When he stepped back outside, he found Megan and Mota waiting for him with what he thought looked like annoyed expressions on their faces. *Well, you've gone and done it this time, Ben,* he thought. *Might as well face the music.* He walked up to the equine woman and threw his arms out in a helpless gesture. "I'm sorry, Mota. I'm afraid I've hurt Tala's feelings."

Mota turned and looked in the direction Tala had run before speaking in an even, controlled tone. "It is not your fault. She thinks she has fallen in love with you. I think she is infatuated with you because you saved our lives. That, and the fact you are one of only a few humans who never treated her like a worthless slave has confused her. She is coming of age, and her interest in men is peaking." Mota's eyes brimmed with tears, but she managed to continue in a controlled tone. "Tala thought she would never meet another man since we escaped from the plantation, where the only ones she ever knew lived. She was beginning to think that she might have to spend the rest of her life without a mate until she met you. Now she thinks you may be the only man she will ever meet who will be kind to her. Do not worry about her, Ben. She is very young and has a long life ahead of her. I am sure that the opportunity for her to meet the right young man will come someday. She must learn to be patient." The filly spun on her heels and looked back over her shoulder before trotting off into the forest after her daughter. "I have to go find her now and try to make her understand that you already have a mate."

Ben stood and watched Mota run into the trees with his mouth hanging open. It took a few seconds for him to find his voice again. "I don't get it," he said, turning to Megan. "I didn't say anything to make Tala think I was in love with her. And where did Mota get the idea that I already have a mate? Surely she doesn't think that you and I—" He stopped short when he noticed the look on Megan's face. Her perturbed look had softened, and she was definitely blushing.

"You didn't try to make me fall in love with you either, but I have," she said, turning her eyes toward the ground.

Ben thought his chest was about to explode as he stood looking at his beautiful companion. "Megan, are you trying to tell me that Mota got the idea that you and I are mates from you?"

Megan nodded and started to wring her hands in front of her without looking up. "I told Mota and Tala that I thought of you as my husband. I'm sorry if that bothers you. I'll tell them the truth when they come back."

"What truth is that?" Ben asked, trying not to sound like a total idiot. He wanted to take her in his arms and kiss her just then, but he fought off the temptation with super effort. He caught the hint of tears in her eyes when she glanced up at him for a second before biting her lower lip and turning away again.

"That… that we are just good friends an-and not lovers at all," she stammered.

Ben couldn't take it anymore. His heart was breaking as he watched Megan struggle with her emotions. He reached out to caress her face and turned it up so that she was looking directly into his eyes when he spoke. "You are my best friend, Meg. But you mean so much more than that to me. You see, I'm in love with you too. If you only knew how many times I wanted to tell you that. But I was afraid of scaring you off."

Megan's brow wrinkled as she stood with her face still resting in Ben's hands. "Scare me off?"

Ben nodded. "Yeah, scare you off. Shoot! We're only eighteen years old, Meg. I've wanted to take you in my arms and kiss you a good many times, but I was always afraid I'd lose control of my emotions. Good Lord, I'm so afraid of hurting you that I have to force myself to keep my distance sometimes. My parents and my grandparents raised me to respect women, not to take advantage of them when they're stuck in a crazy situation like the one we were forced into." He pulled his hands away from her face and shook his head as he turned to sit down on a nearby stump. "I have a lot to learn about love yet. And the worst thing is, we can't have a proper marriage ceremony because the inhabitants of this Godforsaken hole in the ground don't even know about God. For cryin' out loud, they think the FRU scientists who created them were gods."

Megan walked over and dropped to her knees on the ground in front him. "Is that what you think, Ben? That I fell in love with you just because I was stuck in Gildor with you? Well, I want you to know one thing right now. I started falling in love with you long before we ever came to Gildor. You are the first boy I ever met whom I could feel comfortable around. Unlike most of the others that I dated, you were very easy to get to know. And you were one of the very few that didn't try to get me out of my clothes on the first date." She suddenly fell silent, and her face lit up as she cocked her head to one side and shot him a confused look. "Why... why, Ben Thomas, did... did you just ask me to marry you a moment ago?" she stammered.

Ben's mouth suddenly jerked to one side, and he raised an eyebrow. "Yeah, I guess I did. It may have sounded silly, but I really meant what I said. Will ya marry me if we ever find someone to perform the ceremony for us when the time comes?"

Megan got up and flew into his lap so fast that she almost knocked him off the stump he was sitting on. She threw her arms around his neck before he knew what was happening and pressed her moist lips to his. They remained in that position for quite a while before Megan gently pushed away and sat up straight with her arms still wrapped around Ben's neck. "You said you have a lot to learn about love. Well, you're learning fast, Ben. You know more than you're giving yourself credit for. We both know that there's no one here to perform a Christian marriage ceremony from what Mota and Tala have told us about Gildor, but what's to stop us from performing one of our own? Mota and Tala can be our witnesses. It will do them good to learn about the God we believe in. It certainly won't hurt them to learn about him."

Ben cupped her face in his hands and kissed her again. "I really do love you, Megan," he whispered. "When do you want to get married?"

She stood up giggling. "How about this afternoon?"

Ben forced himself to swallow the dry lump in his throat. "This afternoon? But… but I… I thought that we would wait until we were a little older at least. You know, maybe a year or so anyway."

A dejected look crossed Megan's face. "Do you really want to wait that long?" she asked, staring down at her feet. "It's not like we have to wait until we finish college or anything." She held her arms out and turned from side to side. "It looks like this place is going to be our home for a long time. I have learned to accept that fact. Why can't you?"

Ben thought about what Megan was saying and found himself agreeing with her. "I was just thinkin' about how young we are, Meg. Are you sure you want to get married now? We still might get out of this place someday. And then you might find someone else you'd prefer more than me."

Megan shook her head. "That's not going to happen, Ben. It could take years for someone to find us. We're only a centimeter tall, remember? Who's going to find us anyway? Mr. Foster already told us that he was through using Gildor as a research facility. I doubt that anyone he may send here from now on will ever be leaving again. The one thing I am sure of is, I love you, and I want to share the rest of my life with you. Who knows how long that will be in this primitive land? I just want us to spend as much of that time together as we possibly can, that's all."

Ben got up and took her in his arms again. She felt so warm and inviting when she leaned against him. "Okay," he said. "You're right. I want to spend as much time as I can with you too. We'll get married this afternoon, if that's what you really want."

Megan looked up at him and smiled. "I have some important business to take care of first," she said.

Ben nodded again. "Me too. We're almost out of fresh meat, so I need to go hunting while we're waiting for Mota and Tala to get back. Maybe while we're taking care of those necessities, it'll give us some time to think and get our heads straight."

Megan nodded back at him. "I have some sewing I need to finish while you're gone. I'm making a new outfit for you out of the pelt of a buck you killed. Then you can replace those old worn buckskin shorts you're wearing. It should be ready by the time you get back. I'm planning to replace my own outfit with a nice, soft doeskin dress I've been working on, but it isn't quite finished yet either."

Ben looked at her worn shorts and vest and nodded. "You stay here and finish your dress. I'll send Mota and Tala back to stay with you if I run across them while I'm hunting. I really don't like the idea of leaving you here all alone."

Megan smiled and shook her head. "Go ahead, darling. I'll be fine. I'm sure the girls will be back soon enough."

"Okay, but I won't be gone very long," Ben replied before turning to leave. He heard Megan call out after him as he made his way to the cave to get his bow.

"Take your time, I'll be all right."

Ben was gone the better part of the day before he finally managed to get close enough to a fat, little buck to shoot with his bow. He started a hasty retreat back to the lair after field-dressing the animal, keeping a watchful eye out for the two fillies along the way. His vigilance didn't pay off, however. The Packs were nowhere to be found, and he was beginning to get worried.

Megan was sitting outside adding the finishing touches to her dress when Ben returned. She looked up when he stopped beside her on his way into the cave. "I see you had another successful hunt," she said, glancing at the deer draped over his shoulders.

"Not all that successful," Ben replied. "I didn't see the fillies anywhere.

I'm worried that something might have happened to them."

Megan smiled and jerked her head toward the cave entrance. "Not to worry, love. The girls returned shortly after you left. They're inside preparing dinner now."

Ben readjusted his burden and left out a deep sigh. "Thank God. I'd feel terrible if anything would'a happened to either one of 'em."

When he took his fresh kill in to hang it on the ledge and skin it, he discovered Mota and Tala gleefully stirring a pot of boiling vegetables. Tala's mood had improved dramatically since he last saw her. In fact, she seemed downright jovial, smiling the whole time she worked beside her mother. Ben took the hide outside after he finished skinning the abok and whispered to Megan, "I wonder what Mota said to Tala that's made her so happy all of a sudden?"

Megan shrugged. "I don't know. Maybe she's so happy because I told her that you and I are going to get married before dinner. You can bet I'll find out for sure sooner or later."

Ben noticed Megan was fondling her new dress like it was an exclusive designer original. "Is that your wedding dress?" he asked, raising his eyebrows.

Megan quickly finished folding the garment and laid it on her lap. "Yes. And you can't see me in it until the wedding ceremony." She got up and stepped inside the cave for a moment before returning with another bundle in her hands. "Here, take these and go get a bath in the creek! I refuse to marry a man who smells like an old dead abok."

"Okay, I can take a hint," Ben replied. He took the outfit from her and turned to leave. "I'll go take a bath just as soon as I finish stretching this new hide out on the curing rack. I should be back in half an hour."

Megan called out to him as he walked away. "You better make that an hour. It's going to take me a while to get ready. The girls and I will be waiting for you up on the hillside where you proposed to me this morning."

"I'll see you there," he yelled, spinning around and waving. He shook his head as he spun back toward the curing rack. *Oh God, am I doing the right thing?* he thought. Then he smiled when a small voice seemed to answer, *If you believe in me and trust me, then know that you're love for Megan is a good thing.* His nerves suddenly settled, and he looked up at the clear sky where he could barely distinguish the dome of the great Gildorian cavern above. "Thank you, Lord," he breathed freely.

Chapter 15

After Ben finished bathing and putting his new clothes on, he still wasn't sure if he had been gone an hour yet, so he forced himself to wait an extra few minutes, just to make sure he wasn't rushing things. He set out at the slowest pace his excited mind would allow him to go when he finally started back to the lair. *Can't appear to be too eager, or Megan will try to wrap me around her little finger in no time,* he thought. *I'll be scrubbing floors and washing dishes for the rest of my life if I let that happen.* Then he laughed at his simpleminded jape and quickly picked up the pace.

Only Mota and Tala were standing there when Ben reached the stump on the hillside. Confused, he started looking about for Megan. *Surely I didn't get here before her. She'll never let me forget it if I did*, he thought. He turned and noticed the amused looks on the fillies' faces and made an ill attempt to clear his throat. "Uh… hum… where's Megan? She didn't change her mind, did she?" he finally asked.

Tala broke out laughing and pointed behind him. "Megan did not change her mind. She is hiding from you over there."

Ben spun around to see Megan step from behind a tree, and his mouth suddenly went dry. It was as if he was seeing her for the very first time all over again. He remembered that day well.

It was the latter half of the school year when he first saw the new girl. She was hard to miss, wearing that short blue dress that flattered a showcase figure and showed off just enough of those fabulous legs to catch the attention of most of the school's male population. Her shoulder-length jet-black hair, combined with those unique dark almond-shaped eyes certainly didn't make her hard to look at either. Oh, and that smile… she had a smile that melted his heart every time he saw it, especially after he got to know her and how cordial she was. She wasn't just your everyday looker either. She actually turned out to be a very nice, intelligent girl. She was definitely a girl he was eager to get to know better.

❧❧

I didn't think it was possible, but she's more beautiful now than she was then, Ben thought. The greenish doeskin dress wasn't any shorter than the blue dress he first saw her in, but it seemed to hug the contours of her lovely figure much better. Her raven locks had grown during their stay in Gildor, tumbling down over her shoulders almost to the middle of her back in billowing waves. She reminded him of a beautiful wood sprite as she approached, flashing him that enchanting smile of hers. She had changed during their time in Gildor, both physically and mentally. She grew to be tougher than he ever thought she would, but her sweet personality never changed. That's why he loved her so.

"How do you like my new dress?" Megan asked, spinning around for Ben to get a better look at it.

Ben cleared his throat. "You're beautiful in doeskin, Meg," he replied.

She bent at the waist and curtsied. "Thanks for the compliment, kind sir. Do I look good enough to marry?"

He gave her an enthusiastic nod and felt the corners of his mouth twitch when he smiled. "You bet."

Megan's smile disappeared as she grew serious and moved closer to look directly up into Ben's cool gray eyes, as if searching for something there. "Are you sure, Ben? Be-because I don't want you to do something you'll regret later if you're not."

Ben took her hands in his and gave them a gentle squeeze. "I'm sure. I've never been so sure of anything in my life. I love you, Meg."

Megan turned her eyes toward the ground. "I was worried that you might have changed your mind after you had time to think about it. I want you to be sure of your true feelings for me. That's why I told you to take your time getting ready."

Ben wanted to take her in his arms and hug her, but he had something more important to do first. He gently pushed her chin up until she was facing him again. "Megan Dills, before these witnesses," he said, nodding in the direction the fillies were standing, "and before the eyes of Almighty God, I take you to be my wife if you will have me. I vow to love you from this day forward until the end of my days. Do you accept this pledge of my love, Megan?"

Megan sniffed and slipped her hand out of his for a second to brush away a tear. Then she looked up at him and smiled. "Ben Thomas, before these witnesses and before the eyes of Almighty God, I do accept your pledge and vow to be your faithful wife from this day forward until the end of my days."

A hand suddenly slipped between them before the young couple could embrace to seal their simple marriage vows with a kiss. They both turned to discover the fillies had moved into position beside them.

"There is something Tala and I must do before the end of your ceremony," Mota said. She held up a slender white tree root that she had dug up earlier and gave one end to her daughter to hold while she held the other. Together, they wrapped the tender root around the wrists of the newlyweds and stepped back. "May your love grow as great and strong as the tree from which this root came," she said. After that, she turned and led Tala toward the lair, leaving Ben and Megan behind to finish the ceremony by themselves.

After a long kiss, the young couple stood staring into each other's eyes for a moment before Ben slipped his arm around Megan's waist and turned to lead her down the hill behind the fillies. "Come with me, Mrs. Thomas! Our wedding feast waits."

Megan put her hand over Ben's arm and looked up as she walked beside him. "Mrs. Thomas. I like the sound of that," she said.

Ben glanced at her and smiled. "Me too, love. Me too." He slowed the pace a little and suddenly became somber. "You know, our life here won't be all fun and games, Meg. Just because we're married now doesn't mean we aren't going to suffer some bad times."

"Yes, I'm aware of that," Megan replied. "I know there's a lot to learn, even though I never got to experience a true family life myself. We would both be too young to get married if we were still back home, but things are different here. When a man and a woman spend as much time alone together as we have, it almost always leads to something else eventually. It did with us, and I didn't want to risk anything further happening between us unless we were properly married."

Ben nodded thoughtfully. "I agree with everything you just said, Meg. I just didn't want you fantasizing that the rest of our lives will be lived happily ever after like some fairy tale." He fell silent for a moment before continuing, "Do you think God really recognizes us as husband and wife now? I mean... well, we did have to conduct the ceremony ourselves. And it was kinda short."

Megan stopped and looked into his eyes again. "It probably wouldn't be considered a proper ceremony back home, but it's the closest thing we'll ever get to have as far as a Christian ceremony here. Or would you rather wait and marry me in some pagan ritual the Gildorians could perform for us?"

Ben suddenly felt more at ease and smiled. "You're right. I don't think God minds a short ceremony. I think that he's probably pretty happy that we took the time to do things the way we did." He pulled Megan into his arms and kissed her tenderly. "Come on," he said, taking her by the hand. "Let's catch up with Mota and Tala."

They both started to laugh and ran down the hillside hand in hand.

Ben stepped outside and sat on the boulder beside the entrance of the lair after he finished eating his dinner. While he sat there staring up at the stars, his thoughts were of his grandfather and what he might be doing at that moment. As usual, his eyes started to mist, like they always did, whenever he thought of the old man. He wondered how his grandfather reacted when he heard of his and Megan's sudden disappearance. *I hope you don't think we ran off together, Grandpa,* he thought. *You know me better than that. God, please let him find us.*

His private thoughts were suddenly interrupted when he heard someone approaching. He turned to see Megan step out of the cave smiling, and he quickly blinked away his tears before standing to greet her. "You sure look pleased with yourself. Mind telling me what made you so happy? It wouldn't be because you just got married today, would it?"

Megan hunched her shoulders and took Ben by the arm. She motioned for him to sit back down before sitting down beside him. "I'm very happy to be married to the most wonderful man in the world right now, but that isn't the only thing making me smile."

Ben cocked his head to one side and raised an eyebrow. "Oh? And just what have you been up to then? You look as if you just won the lottery or somethin'."

"Maybe I did in a way," Megan quipped. "Remember earlier this afternoon, when I told you that I would find out what Mota said to Tala to make her so happy all of a sudden."

Ben shook his head in disbelief. "I don't believe it. You just came right out and asked her, didn't ya?"

Megan started to giggle. "Yes, I did," she replied, slapping her hand over her mouth to stifle her sniggering.

Ben started to get slightly irritated. "Well, what's so funny?"

Megan stopped giggling and took her hand away from her mouth. "Mota told me that she had talked to Tala about finding a mate. She told Tala that it would be extremely hard to find one out here in the wilds and that she should bide her time, and you might be able to find her one. She even went so far as to suggest that if you weren't able to find Tala a mate, you might be willing to take her as a second wife because it isn't unheard of for some Gildorian men to take two wives."

"What?" Ben's face flushed as comprehension sank in. "Do you mean to tell me that Tala still thinks that I might marry her someday?"

Megan was unable to control herself any longer and burst into such a fit of hysterical laughter that she had to bend over when her ribs started to ache.

"What's so funny?" Ben asked, staring at her in total disbelief.

Megan forced herself to stop laughing long enough to point a shaking finger at him. "You… you should have seen your face just now. You looked just the way I thought you would when I told you what I found out." She tittered before falling into another sequence of uncontrollable laughter. Then Ben began to laugh along with her, not knowing exactly why but enjoying the contagious joy.

The young couple stayed outside and talked a while longer before going back into the lair. Mota and Tala were already asleep nearby fire, so Ben stayed up front to secure the door over the entrance while Megan walked to the back of the lair alone. After he finished securing the door, he turned and walked to the back of the cave, where he sat on the edge of his bed and started to undress.

"I finished my outfit today while you were gone," Megan whispered.

Ben nodded. "Yeah, you've been wearing it ever since we got married. I told you already that it looks great on you."

There was a moment of silence before Megan spoke again. "Not that one, silly. I'm talking about the one I'm wearing now."

Ben had taken his vest off and was in the middle of slipping out of his breeches when he turned to look in Megan's direction. "There couldn't have been enough of that doeskin left to do anything with. I can't imagine what—" He stopped dead when his eyes finally focused on her in the dim firelight.

"I didn't need doeskin to make this," Megan said, holding her arms up over her head and turning around to show off the extremely brief light-green nightie she was wearing. "Do you like it?"

Ben kicked his legs out of his buckskin pants and rolled over on the bed. It wasn't until then that he noticed their beds had been pushed together. Apparently, the fillies had been at work while she and Megan were outside. "Ye... yeah, I sure do," he stammered, lying back on the bed and ogling her. "I... I like it a lot. What's it made outa?" The nightie wasn't only short; it was transparent as well. He could plainly see the outline of Megan's figure beneath it, even in the dim light at the back of the cave.

Megan giggled as she lay down beside him. "Mota and Tala showed me how to make the material out of the bark of a tree we found up on the mountain a few days ago. The material feels like light cotton, but it's much stronger. I had to pound the bark with a stone to soften it, but I must have pounded it too much. I had originally used the material to make a new dress, but most of the color had faded out of it before I could finish it. I decided to throw the dress away since it was impractical to use as a dress anymore, being so transparent and all... but then I got another idea after you proposed to me today. Since the material is so easy to work with, I decided to shorten the dress and make a baby doll out of it while you were getting your bath. You don't think it's too revealing, do you?"

Ben gave his head a quick shake as he reached out to touch the hem of the translucent garment. It may have felt like cotton, but it sure didn't look like it. "Not as long as you promise not to go parading around in public with it on."

"You don't have to worry about that. I made it just for you," Megan whispered, slipping into his arms. "Besides, there's a fat chance of anyone other than you ever seeing me in it out in this wilderness," she added before flashing him a sly wink and snuggling closer.

Chapter 16

The night passed quickly. Neither Ben nor Megan heard the fillies moving about the next morning. The newlyweds were still fast asleep in each other's arms when Mota and Tala opened the door and flooded the front of the lair with sunlight.

The fire had been attended to, and breakfast was already cooking before Ben finally awoke. He gently slipped out of his new wife's embrace and sat up on the edge of the bed. After putting his breeches on, he sneaked a peek in the fillies' direction to see if they were watching him while he bent down to slip his moccasins on.

Tala sat eying him with a wry smile while she tended the fire, and her mother added fresh vegetables to the pot. When she saw him look in her direction, she turned and whispered into her mother's ear. Then both women fixed their gaze on Ben and started giggling before continuing on with the business at hand.

Ben stood up and glanced over his shoulder to see if Megan was still asleep. A sheepish grin touched his lips when he turned his eyes back toward the fillies. *I wonder if they were really asleep when we went to bed last night*, he thought.

"Good morning. I trust that you slept well?"

Ben turned back to look at Tala again. "Why, yes, I did. I slept very well, as a matter of fact." *Oh, why did I say that?* He could feel his face turning color.

Mota flashed Ben an all-knowing smile as she carried a full plate to the table and motioned for him to sit down. "Your breakfast is ready. There is more in the pot if you are still hungry when this is gone. We will have another plate ready for Megan when she wakes up."

Ben tried not to look at Tala as he made his way around the table. "Thank you, Mota," he said before sitting down. "It smells wonderful."

Mota leaned close to Ben after he sat down and whispered into his ear. "Please forgive my daughter for asking such an inappropriate question. She is very young and has not learned that such things are none of her business. I am sorry if she has caused you any embarrassment."

Ben shook his head and winked at the filly. "No harm done. There is no need to apologize. People are always kidding newlyweds about their honeymoons where I come from."

Mota straightened up and shot him a bewildered look. "I must remind you to tell me more about that place someday," she said before returning to join Tala at the fireside.

Ben and the two fillies were sitting at the table talking half an hour later when they heard a quiet rustling in the rear of the cave. They turned to see Megan sitting up on the bed with her doeskin blanket wrapped firmly around her while she searched for something under the rest of the furs with an uneasy look on her face. She continued her diligent search for several seconds before finally looking up and flashing the others a shy smile when she noticed they were watching her. Her hair was a mass of black curls twisted about her face and shoulders, and she reached up to brush a stray strand of the dark fluff away from her eyes before she locked the dark slanted orbs on Ben.

He marveled at her delicate beauty while she sat there holding her blanket up in front of her. He couldn't help laughing when he saw her lean slowly over the edge of the bed to look down at the floor. Finally, he got up to help her locate what she was looking for after she diligently started rummaging through the blankets again. It didn't take him very long to find the object of her search because he already knew what and where it was. Still laughing, he walked straight to his side of the bed and reached under the roll of furs that served as his pillow and pulled out her new doeskin dress. "Is this what you are looking for?" he asked, holding the neatly folded dress up in front of her.

Megan shot him a surprised look as she pushed another strand of unruly curls from her eyes. "Thanks. I don't suppose you know how it got under there, do you?" she asked.

Ben pointed to himself and opened his eyes wide. "I haven't the foggiest," he answered, turning around and walking away snickering. "Oh, by the way, your breakfast is on the table," he said, glancing over his shoulder. "I'll be outside with Mota and Tala if you need me."

Mota and Tala followed Ben out of the cave when he walked past them. While they waited for Megan to dress and eat breakfast, they decided to walk up the hillside and pick some fresh fruit for their lunch later. Tala spent as much time close to Ben as she could and spoke to him only when he spoke to her. Even then, she would only say a few words. It was apparent that the filly still thought she was in love with him. Not wanting to cause her any more anguish than he already had, Ben didn't try to avoid her.

Although he loved Megan with all his heart, the beautiful filly did stir strange feelings within him. He cocked his head to one side as he thought about what Mota had told Megan the previous da: "It is not unheard of for a man of Gildor to take two wives." He shook his head a moment later. *No! What are you thinking?* He went back to picking fruit, but his mind continued to dwell on the Pack girl beside him.

They were headed back to the lair after they filled their baskets with fresh fruit and were almost halfway down the hillside when they heard Megan cry out from inside the lair.

"Help, Ben!"

Ben dropped his basket and ran for the cave as fast as a hungry fox chasing a rabbit. His heart pounded like a jackhammer as he raced down the hillside. When he was about thirty feet from the entrance of the lair, he heard Megan cry out again. This time, it was a warning.

"Look out, Ben! It's a trap!"

He instinctively reached for his bow and then realized he'd left the weapon in the lair. It was the first time he had ever forgotten to take it with him since they left the plateau. Cursing his stupidity, he reached for his hunting knife and crouched into a fighting stance before moving cautiously onward toward the cave. He heard a muffled scream behind him just before he reached the entrance and wheeled around on his heels. Mota and Tala were both on the ground, fighting frantically to break free of a heavy net that had been thrown over them. Two men with metal-tipped spears were standing on either side of them, holding the ends of the net in place.

Someone yelled, "Halt, thief!" Ben turned to look up and saw a man standing on the hillside above the entrance of the lair. All he could see was an outline because the man was standing in a direct line with the sun. He stood there holding a spear with its butt resting on the ground and its metal point gleaming in the bright sunlight beside his head.

"What do you want?" Ben asked.

"I want you, Pack thief," the man replied gruffly. "And the slaves you stole."

Ben put his hand up to shield his eyes so he could get a better look at the stranger. "Who are you calling a thief?"

His accuser pointed a finger at him. "You are a Pack thief, and I am arresting you and your accomplice in the name of Lord Quander, master of Plantation Quander. It is his Packs you stole." He bent down and yelled into the mouth of the lair. "Din, bring the girl out!"

There was a moment of confusion while Ben watched a scrawny young man pull Megan from the cave kicking and screaming. Ben didn't know whether to rush to Megan's aid or play it safe and stand fast. In the end, he made no decision at all because during his brief uncertainty, a hidden assailant had skulked up behind him and hit him a glancing blow on the back of his head with something heavy. The jarring impact sent Ben to his knees with the world spinning around him. He reached behind his head with his right hand and saw blood on his fingertips when he pulled it away. Then a second blow suddenly sent him reeling facedown on the ground. While he lay there, he heard the stranger order his men to get the prisoners ready to move out. He heard Megan call out to him again an instant later, and then everything went suddenly black when consciousness abandoned him.

Chapter 17

Ben's head felt as if someone had hit him with a sledgehammer. When he fully regained consciousness, he realized he was lying on his back and that he was moving. His body bounced around heavily as the litter he was stretched out on was dragged over the hard rocky ground. He remained still and kept his eyes tightly closed, although he had regained consciousness a few minutes earlier. After the grogginess finally passed, he tried to open his eyes slowly. He only managed to raise his eyelids a tiny crack before blazing sunlight flooded into his them and sent a new wave of pain shooting through his head, forcing him to squeeze them shut again. He shook his head and tried to open his eyes a second time and was successful in doing so. The throbbing in his head started to subside a little, so he decided to rub the back of his neck to help relieve the pain, but his hand didn't move when he tried to raise it. In fact, he couldn't move either of his hands. He blinked, trying to clear his blurred vision, and turned his head to one side.

Booted feet walked beside the litter. Shifting his gaze upward, he discovered they belonged to a handsome young man about six feet tall with a muscular build. He had dark-brown hair and a thick neatly trimmed mustache. When the stranger finally looked down, his green eyes showed no animosity in them toward the captive.

The young plantation guard called to one of his companions when he noticed Ben had regained consciousness. "Yo, Calor, your prisoner is awake."

Ben raised his head to look down the length of his body to see what kept his arms pinned at his sides. A heavy, wide iron band was fastened around his waist with manacles attached to either side of it, and his wrists were clasped in the manacles to prevent him from moving his hands more than a few inches. *No wonder I can't move my hands*, he thought. His memory suddenly came charging back to him, and he began to worry about the women. He arched his back so he could look up over his head, and his eyes came to rest on Mota and Tala. They were pulling his litter.

The fillies stopped when they were suddenly ordered to halt by one of their captors. Turning in unison, they peered back at Ben with tired and drawn faces.

The man who ordered the fillies to stop walked back to the side of the litter and knelt down beside Ben. His face had sharp angular features with close-set eyes and a hawk nose. His black eyes took in the supine prisoner with a single glance. When the homely fellow leaned closer, Ben could see that he hadn't shaved in a while; sparse black whiskers covered the lower half of his ugly face. He threw his head back to clear the long black dreadlocks away from his face and leaned even closer. His unpleasant odor drifted into Ben's nostrils and made him nauseous.

"You are a thief," the ugly specimen of manhood grumbled. The disgusting smell of his breath was even worse than his body odor.

"I don't know what you're talking about," Ben said, shaking his head. He rolled over on his side and tried to sit up, but the ugly brute grabbed him by the arm and pulled him to his feet before he could gain his balance. The world started spinning as the pain in Ben's head suddenly came rushing back with a vengeance. The only thing that kept him from falling over backward was the grip his captor had on his arm. The angry plantation guard was about to deliver a vicious blow to the side of his head when someone spoke up.

"Take it easy, Calor! You do not want to kill him. Lord Quander will want to question this one himself." The speaker's voice was deep and clear and yet not too harsh.

Calor gave Ben a quick glance and grunted as he lowered his fist. "You are right. I will not beat the truth out of him just yet. From now on, he walks with the rest of the prisoners. These lazy Packs are in no condition to haul his backside any farther." With a final nod, he walked up beside Mota and Tala and ordered them to drop the litter.

After Ben's head had cleared enough for him to move without falling over, he turned to see who had prevented Calor from beating him.

The handsome young fellow whom he had first seen when he opened his eyes was standing beside him. He took Ben's arm and held him steady until he was able to walk without swaying. The young guard remained close by until he was sure the prisoner could continue on without his help.

Then he spoke to Ben in a low whisper, "It would be wise on your part if you do not try to anger that one," he said, nodding in Calor's direction. "Calor would just as soon run you through with his spear as look at you."

Ben nodded. "Thank you for the advice. I will try to stay clear of him from now on." He cut his eyes away from the young guard and looked for Megan in the column of captives in front of him. *Where is she?* The fear in his heart subsided when he spotted her familiar raven tresses farther up the line. He wanted to move up beside her, but his restraints prevented him from doing so.

Altogether, there were seven captives in the column, including Ben. They all had their hands secured in manacles attached to iron bands that were clasped around their waists. Short lengths of heavy chain linked the manacles to either side of the iron rings and allowed the prisoners very little hand movement. Their captors didn't have to worry about any of them trying to escape by running off in different directions either. All the prisoners had a third loop attached to the right side of his or her waistband with a long chain strung through it that kept them all bound together. Both ends of the chain had huge padlocks through the loop on the waistbands of the first and last prisoner in the line. Their captors seemed to have thought of everything to keep them from trying to escape.

Megan walked with downcast eyes while one of the guards stayed in step beside her with his eyes fastened on her the whole time. The little man would reach over occasionally and take Megan's chin in his hand and force her to look at him. Then he would say something to her, and she would jerk her head away and look at the ground again to avoid looking into his wicked little eyes. Whenever the girl reacted to his advances in a negative manner, the little rat would laugh shrilly and smack her across the back with a slender stick he held in his hand.

Ben could see welts on the upper half of Megan's back where her dress didn't cover. Anger began to well up in him while he watched the scene unfolding before him, and he strained to free himself until his wrists started to bleed from the chafing manacles. All he could think of was getting his hands on the little beast tormenting Megan.

"Take it easy in those manacles, friend!"

The young guard walking beside Ben noticed him straining against his bonds. In his anger, Ben had forgotten all about him. Without thinking about the harsh punishment his brash remark might bring, he let the guard know just what he was thinking. "I'll kill that little rat up there if he touches my wife again," he said venomously.

The guard turned his eyes in the direction of the abusive little man. "The beautiful one with the dark hair is your woman?" he asked in a soft tone.

"Yes," Ben replied, still straining at his manacles and gritting his teeth at the sharp pain that shot through his arms. The manacles were rough around the edges and started to peel the skin off his wrists. He could feel the warm blood running down over his hands. "If that punk touches Megan again, I swear I'll kill him."

The guard put his hand on Ben's arm to stop him from struggling. "Keep your voice low, friend! I will see what I can do to stop Din from bothering your wife any further. We will be stopping to make camp soon. When we do, I will bring her to you. I will make sure she walks with you tomorrow."

Before Ben could thank him, the young guard marched up the column toward Din and grabbed him by the shoulder just as he was about to bother the girl again. The muscles in the young guard's arm flexed with power when he squeezed the imp's shoulder and spun him around to face him. It was clear that he said something threatening by the fear that registered on Din's face. When the bigger man finally released him, Din hurriedly moved off toward the front of the column.

The guard was smiling when he returned and fell in step beside Ben again. "Din will not bother your woman anymore today," he said.

"Thank you, friend," Ben said breathing easier. "Do you mind me asking what your name is?"

The guard looked at him and smiled; his even white teeth seemed to shine in the brilliant light. "My name is Bander."

Ben introduced himself, forcing a nervous smile as he did so. "My name is Benjamin Thomas, but you can just call me Ben. I am glad to meet you, Bander. I wish I knew why my friends and I are being treated like criminals."

"Because in the eyes of my people, you are criminals," Bander replied.

The two young men walked along beside each other and talked for over an hour. Ben had just finished explaining to Bander that his speech sounded odd because he was not from Gildor moments before their conversation was interrupted. Calor ordered the column to halt so they could set up camp for the evening. Bander seemed to be shocked when

Ben told him that he was not from Gildor. By his expression, Ben guessed that Bander thought he was either lying or crazy. However, the young guard never said a word after Calor gave the order to halt. Instead, he gave Ben a puzzled look and glanced back over his shoulder more than once while he walked away to help the others set up camp.

The seven captives were ushered to one side of the campsite where two trees grew several yards apart. They were then lined up between the trees while the ends of the chain holding them together were fastened around their thick trunks. The prisoners' wrists were released from the manacles as soon as they had been tethered between the two forest giants.

While Ben sat waiting for Bander to come and move Megan next to him, he took the time to check out the rest of the captives. In front of Mota and Tala were two other Pack women, both appearing to be about Mota's age, although neither of them was quite as beautiful as the filly. Mota was in front of Ben and next to last in the line. The second prisoner in the line was a young Pack who appeared to be in his early teens or even younger. Megan was situated at the front of the line. She and Ben were the only pure-blood humans in the group.

About an hour later, Bander and another guard carried baskets full of food over to the line of prisoners. Bander set his basket on the ground and motioned for his companion to do the same. Then he knelt close to Ben and whispered, "I will have Bodon move your woman behind you in the line now."

Ben looked at the guard standing behind Bander. He was a short powerfully built man with a balding head. Although he looked fierce at first glance, his gleaming blue eyes betrayed the kindness in his heart. His wide mouth formed a smile that exposed the empty spaces on either side of his two front teeth. *He might be friendly, but he must be able to defend himself,* Ben thought, nodding toward the guard. "Thank you, Bodon."

Bodon raised his right hand with the fingers spread wide apart and the palm forward. He silently nodded his balding pate before turning to move to the end of the chain where Megan knelt beside the tree.

Ben guessed the quick hand signal was the Gildorian sign for okay. "I want to thank you for making my wife's life a little more bearable today," he said, turning back to Bander again.

Bander never replied verbally. Instead, he reached out and took Ben's forearms in his strong hands and shot him a quick smile before bending down to pick up the basket of food he had set on the ground earlier. He had a bewildered look on his face when he stood up to leave. "I was thinking about something you said earlier. About your not being from Gildor, I mean. I do not understand how that can be. But when I see the extraordinary beauty of your wife, I am inclined to believe you. I have never seen a Gildorian woman with such strangely shaped eyes before. Most Gildorians would think she was a crossbreed with some animal, like the Pack and Bondo, but I do not believe this to be so. She seems to be too human to be a half-breed. I do not recognize any animal traits in her."

Ben sighed deeply. "I was afraid you didn't believe me, Bander. I'm glad you do because everything I told you is true. Megan looks the way she does because she is part Malaysian and Japanese. That's the name for two of the races of humans her mother was from. Her father was Caucasian, or a white man, like you and me."

Bander shook his head. "That is very strange. In all the known lands of Gildor, there are only white and black people, as far as I know. If there are any of these people you call 'Malaysian' or 'Japanese' living here, I have never seen or heard of them."

"Perhaps there are other races of humans here that you don't know about yet," Ben replied. "Maybe in some far-off land you haven't discovered yet."

"Maybe so," Bander said. "Perhaps we will talk more about that later." He didn't bother asking any more questions. He just stood up and walked down the line, handing the food in the baskets out to the captives.

While Bander was busy handing out the food, Ben turned and watched Bodon prepare to move Megan next to him in the line. The kindhearted guard gently loosened the end of the chain, unwound it from around the bole of the tree, and then slowly pulled the free end through the loop on the side of Megan's waistband. He was so careful in trying not to make Megan move unnecessarily that Ben began to worry about the severity of the wounds on her back.

Megan remained quiet while she knelt on the ground, waiting for Bodon to lock the end of the chain back around the tree again. After the powerful little man finished securing the chain, he moved to stand beside Megan and helped her to her feet. There was a look of intense pain on Megan's tearstained face as she got up and straightened very slowly.

Ben's heart ached to see her in such a condition. And then hot anger welled up within him. *If I ever get my hands on Din, I'll kill him for sure,* he thought.

Bodon led Megan down the line and gently helped her kneel beside Ben before tethering her at the end of the chain.

Megan never spoke while she was being tethered. She just knelt there silently with her head hung low until Bodon walked away. It wasn't until Bander brought them their ration of raw vegetables and water that the stricken girl finally raised her head. "Thank you," she said in a barely audible voice.

Bander glanced at the beautiful young woman and nodded. He turned to Ben, who was busy examining Megan's wounds. "I have to make a poultice for the young Pack's leg. He fell and cut his leg open two days ago when he tried to escape from Calor. Now the wound is beginning to make his leg stiff and sore, so I must put a poultice on it to keep it from becoming infected. Does your wife require one also?"

Ben tore his attention away from Megan's back and looked at the young guard. "Din managed to do a nasty job on her back before you stopped him," he replied, fighting hard to control his anger. "There are at least six welts on her mid and lower back. Two of them have broken open and are bleeding. Yes, I'd say she could use a poultice," Ben snarled. When he remembered who he was talking to, he suddenly felt sorry for answering the way he did. *After all, Bander is the one who stopped Din from beating Megan.* He shook his head and lowered his voice. "I'm sorry, Bander. I didn't mean to talk to you that way. It's a terrible thing to have to watch someone you love take a beating and not be able to do anything about it."

Bander turned and stared down the line of prisoners as if in deep thought. When he finally spoke again, he had a far-off look in his eyes. "I know how you feel, Ben Thomas. There is someone I love for whom I can never reveal my true feelings. Until a few months ago, I used to see her every day, and yet I dared not talk to her for any length of time, lest she receive a beating." He lowered his head and sighed deeply. "I wish I had your courage, my friend."

Ben slipped his arm around Megan and kissed her on the cheek. "You can really hurt someone you love by staying silent, Bander. You should speak up if you love this girl as much as you say."

Bander turned back toward Ben and nodded. "Perhaps you are right. But there are also times when you must remain silent to protect the one you love," he added. Standing up, he quietly moved on down the line to help Bodon serve the water to the rest of the prisoners.

Ben turned his attention back to Megan. "Are you all right, darling?" His words were a soft whisper in her ear.

There were tears running down Megan's tanned cheeks when she turned to look at him. "I'm tired, stiff, and sore," she moaned. "Besides that, my back feels as if it's on fire." She tilted her head to one side and tried to smile as she reached up to touch the side of Ben's face with her fingertips. "How does your poor head feel now?"

Ben shook his head. "To tell the truth, I forgot my pain when I saw the way Din was treating you. I guess somewhere along the way, it was replaced with my concern for your safety."

Megan forced a weak smile. "I guess love has a way of doing strange things like that."

Bander returned with the poultices for Megan and the injured Pack boy about twenty minutes later. He stopped in front of Ben and knelt down. "Do you want to apply this poultice to your wife's wounds, or do you prefer that I do it?" Although Bander asked the question in all seriousness, Ben couldn't help snickering when he saw the look on Megan's face. Her mortification was quite evident when she heard Bander offer to apply the poultice to her back.

"I'll do it," Ben replied, still snickering. "Just tell me what to do."

Bander handed him the poultice on a slab of thin bark. "Place the side with the medicine on it over her wounds. Use this to hold it in place by wrapping it around her chest and tying it," he added, handing Ben a long, thin vine he had cut for just that purpose. After finishing the set of brief instructions, Bander moved on to tend to the youth's injured leg.

Ben held the hot poultice out in front of him at arm's length and grinned sheepishly at Megan. "I'm sorry for laughing, Meg. Please turn your back toward me, and I'll tie this in place for you, okay?"

Megan rolled her eyes and turned painfully around until her back was toward Ben. "Please hurry," she hissed, clenching her teeth. "The pain caused by even my slightest movement is almost unbearable. I hope this thing works. It just has to, if I'm going to get any rest tonight."

Ben was awakened by the sound of a rough voice the following morning. He opened his eyes to see Din moving along the line of captives and kicking each one lightly in the ribs to stir them into wakefulness.

He hesitated when he came to Ben and noticed the baleful look in the prisoner's eyes. Moving back a couple of steps, Din nodded at Megan, who was still asleep with her head resting in Ben's lap. "You better wake your woman," he hissed callously. "You only have a short time before we march again." He started to walk away and stopped to look back over his shoulder. "We will reach Lord Quander's plantation in two more days. After that, you will both be found guilty of Pack theft and will be sold as slaves for your crime. Who knows, maybe I will buy your woman at the auction myself? She will be mine to do with as I please then."

Ben's revulsion for Din welled up in him, and he swore under his breath that if the little rat ever touched Megan again, he would surely kill him one day.

Chapter 18

The next two days passed slowly while the six guards led their prisoners through the high mountain passes toward Lord Quander's plantation. Ben talked with Bander whenever a chance presented itself while they marched. He hoped his new friend would give him a clue as to what might lie in store for him and Megan. The remark Din had made to Ben about him and Megan being sold as slaves bothered him, so he made it a point to talk to Bander about the subject whenever he got the chance. He always made sure they were out of earshot of Megan before bringing the subject up though; he didn't want her getting any more frightened than she already was.

Bander told Ben that it would not be easy for him to convince Lord Quander that he and Megan were not Pack thieves, but the friendly guard promised to speak in their behalf at their hearing.

Ben realized that there was nothing he could do himself to help his and Megan's plight, so he decided to trust Bander and hope that he could convince Lord Quander that they were not Pack thieves. He considered Bander's friendship an asset that might help him and Megan eventually regain their freedom.

It was early afternoon on the fifth day of their march when the band of plantation guards led their prisoners to the top of a hill overlooking Plantation Quander. Bander told Ben that all the land that they could see around them, from the top of the hill they stood on, belonged to Lord Quander.

Ben was awestruck by the immensity of the mysterious lord's holdings. To his right lay a ridge of high hills that seemed to extend on forever. Bander informed him that Lord Quander's holdings extended at least two days' march beyond those hills. To their left were hundreds of acres of neatly plowed fields that ended at the edge of a forest of gigantic trees. Ben could see at least fifty Packs working in the fields under the watchful supervision of plantation guards. Directly in front of him, near the base of the hillside, stood the main buildings of the plantation, including Lord Quander's house. There were five buildings in all: Lord Quander's huge stone house stood at the base of the hill; an enormous barn stood about sixty yards to the right of the main house; and two smaller outbuildings, which he guessed were the bunkhouses for the plantation guards, stood on either side of the barn. One outbuilding was situated halfway between the barn and the main house while the other stood directly across from and facing the front of the barn. The fifth structure had a low roof and was smaller than the others. It stood out in the open sunlight and apart from the main house and the rest of the buildings. *Perhaps that is where they house their prisoners*, Ben thought. All the buildings were still too far away for him to tell what kind of shape they were in, but he had a fairly good idea of how much work it took to keep them properly maintained. After the guards led them down the hill, the Packs were promptly led away and tethered to a wooden post at the far end of the barnyard while Ben and Megan were led before a crude wooden throne on the veranda in front of the main house.

The entire house was built with heavy granite blocks. Its large windows were adorned with wide yellow shutters made of wood. White curtains were hung on the inside of every window. The floor of the veranda was made of flat fieldstone that had been painted yellow to match the wood trim on the exterior of the house. The roofs of the veranda and house were both covered with dark slate shingles. The roof of the veranda rested at least ten feet above the fieldstone floor and stood over a huge oaken door with black iron hardware and appeared to be the only access to the house from the veranda. Ben could not help but marvel at the intricacy of the workmanship that had been put into the building. The house and most of the barnyard were located in the ever-looming shadow of the hill behind them so the immediate area stayed relatively cool in the midday heat. Ben understood why Lord Quander had built his home there the moment he and Megan stepped into the cool shadow of the hill and out of the burning heat of the Gildorian sun.

The young couple was forced to stand in front of the empty throne for almost half an hour before Lord Quander finally stepped out of the house onto the veranda. Megan gasped, and Ben could only stare as they watched the hulking figure draw nearer. Lord Quander was well over six feet tall; the top of his head was only about three feet lower than the rafters of the veranda. His huge form was a mass of flabby, loose flesh that rolled like water in a balloon under his thin clothing when he moved.

The giant shot a quick glance at the two prisoners when he walked over to his throne and sat down. The wooden seat made loud cracking noises, straining under Quander's enormous weight, as he settled into a comfortable position. After he made himself comfortable, he motioned for Calor to step forward and spoke to the plantation guard in a low tone.

Calor turned around a moment later and pointed a finger at the young couple kneeling on the ground. Quander sat quietly regarding the two while Calor introduced them as the thieves who stole his packs. After telling Quander how he and his men had discovered the Pack women living with Ben and Megan, Calor finished his story by informing him how the two humans had been hiding out in a secluded cave in the mountains. The ugly guard glanced at the prisoners and smiled wickedly. "The way these two were hiding out in that cave should be more than enough proof to make you believe that they are the ones who murdered your brother and stole your Packs."

After allowing Calor to finish his interpretation of the tale, Quander leaned forward in his throne. The crude wooden structure strained under his immense weight again as he pointed at Ben. "Tell me how only the two of you managed to kill my guards and make off with my Packs," he demanded. His flaccid jowls quivered as he spoke.

Ben thought for sure he could convince the plantation master that he and Megan weren't thieves now. It sounded as if he really didn't believe Calor's story. Ben began by gesturing back and forth between Megan and himself with his hands. "How could my wife, who is not even half my size, and I kill your guards and steal your Packs? We cannot answer your question, Lord Quander, because we did neither." He turned toward the plantation guards. "We could not even manage to put up much of a fight against these men before they captured us and brought us here to your plantation."

"He lies, my lord," someone shouted from behind Ben. Calor was red-faced as he stepped forward again. "He lies, Lord Quander. He and his woman had to kill your brother and the other guards. They must have had help. Why else would they have had the two Packs living with them if they did not steal them?"

Ben angrily challenged Calor's accusations. "If we had help, why didn't you find the rest of the thieves, and where are the rest of the Packs we stole?"

Calor glared at Ben without speaking. He stood fast and clenched his fists as if getting ready to take a swing at him if he dared speak out again. Then he turned back in Quander's direction. "They probably split up, and the others took the rest of the packs with them," he said.

"Enough," Quander bellowed, his voice reverberating through the barnyard. "Bander, take these prisoners to the slave quarters! Calor, bring Mota and Tala to me. Now! I wish to hear their part of this story."

Ben opened his mouth to protest, but Bander stepped in close beside him. "Careful, my friend, now is not the time," he whispered.

Ben heeded the warning and remained silent.

Bander ushered the young couple across the barnyard to the long brown low-roofed building that stood by itself. It looked to be nothing more than a shed with only a single door and two barred windows in its front. Bander guided them up a set of rickety steps, which creaked noisily under their feet, to the door. After quickly ushering them inside, he closed the door behind him. "I am not sure what Quander believes yet, my friends," he said. "Perhaps he will make his decision concerning the two of you after he hears what Mota and Tala have to say. I will let you know when I bring you your dinner later." Without saying another word, he held his hand up with the palm forward and the fingers spread wide before leaving the building.

After she heard Bander lock the door and walk away, Megan took Ben by the arm and leaned close to him. She had a worried look in her eyes as she stood gazing up at him. "Do you think Mota will be able to convince Lord Quander that we didn't have anything to do with his brother's death or his missing Packs?"

"I don't know," Ben replied, kissing her lightly on the cheek. "I sure hope so." He walked over to the window on the right side of the door and leaned on the sill before glancing back at her. "We must keep in mind that if Mota tells the truth, she could be condemning her own mate to death. The only thing I can think that might have happened is that Tolan and the other Packs killed the guards and escaped. If Mota thinks that is what happened too, she may not be able to tell the truth, even if it means you and I have to suffer for it."

"Who's Tolan?" Megan asked.

Ben looked at her sheepishly and gritted his teeth. "Oh yeah! I guess I forgot to tell you about him. He's Mota's mate. Tala told me about him the other day when she got so upset with me. She told me that her father killed one of Lord Quander's men when he tried to rape Mota. Tala and Mota managed to escape with some of the other Packs working in the fields that day during the ruckus that followed."

Megan tilted her head to one side as she stood looking at Ben. "Why do I have this funny feeling that there's more to this story than you're telling me?" she asked.

Ben hunched his shoulders and held his hands out at his sides. "Okay. I asked Tala about the full-blooded humans who lived in Gildor while we were alone at the creek that day. She obliged by telling me about them. She divulged a little more information than I expected to hear. You already know the rest of the story." He turned and looked out the window without saying another word.

Megan silently nodded and walked over to the window and stood beside Ben. When he turned to look at her, she glanced up at him and smiled. She slipped her hand into his before they both turned to watch the proceedings on the veranda through the window.

They saw Calor drag Mota before Quander's throne and force her to her knees. When Lord Quander spoke to her, Mota shook her head so violently that her carrot-colored mane flew about her face as if it had been whipped by a wild prairie wind. She spoke with her face turned toward the ground.

Although Ben and Megan couldn't hear any of the conversation that took place between Mota and her master, they could tell that the hulking thug terrified the equine woman. Ever since they had been captured, neither Mota nor Tala had spoken to anyone unless they were ordered to. They both exhibited tremendous fear of the guards, and they appeared utterly terrified of Lord Quander himself.

"Poor Mota," Megan whispered. "She looks so afraid."

Ben put his arm around his wife's waist and drew her close to him. "I hope she isn't so afraid of him that he thinks she might be lying," he said under his breath.

Mota continued to talk for a while until Quander suddenly silenced her by delivering a brutal kick to her shoulder with his booted right foot. The unexpected kick sent the poor filly flying backward to land flat on her back in the dust at Bander's feet.

Bander bent down and helped the shaken filly to her feet and then took her by the arm and walked her to the barn, where the rest of the Pack herd was housed.

At a signal from Quander, Calor led Tala before his throne and forced her to her knees with her eyes turned toward the ground. When the frightened filly refused to look up at Quander, Calor took hold of her flowing red mane and jerked her head back until her eyes were focused on the fat nobleman. The frightened filly only spoke after Lord Quander ordered her to.

Quander listened to Tala for even less time than he listened to Mota. After he had heard enough, he suddenly pushed his flabby bulk up out of his throne and reached out with a meaty hand to grab a handful of Tala's apple-red hair and, in one fluid motion, pulled the screaming girl to her feet with a quick jerk.

Tala's terrified screams were so loud that Ben and Megan could hear them from their remote prison. The two onlookers watched in stunned silence while the horrible scene unfolded on the veranda.

Quander held Tala at arm's length as he vented his anger in her face. Then with all his brute strength, the hulking mountain of flesh hauled her off the ground and lifted her over his head before flinging her body ten feet through the air, to land on the ground at the feet of the guards who stood watching the proceedings. Considering the hearing ended, the plantation master waved his hand and ordered Calor to return Tala to the barn with the rest of the Packs. Considering the hearing over, he turned around and walked into the house and slammed the door behind him.

Ben and Megan remained glued to the window and watched Calor step forward, grab a handful of Tala's long mane, and start dragging the stunned filly toward the barn. Before Calor could drag the poor girl five feet, he was knocked face-first to the ground by a vicious blow from behind. Spitting dust, he sprang to his feet and wheeled to face his assailant with his spear raised and ready to fight. Before he realized what was happening, the stunned guard found himself on the ground again when his assailant planted a hard open hand in the middle of his chest. His spear was jarred from his hand and went bouncing harmlessly across the ground, out of his reach. Shaking oily dreadlocks out of his eyes, the ugly guard looked up into Bander's angry face.

Even without being able to hear Bander's words, Ben and Megan knew that whatever he said to Calor was definitely a threat to his future health and well-being. The newlyweds watched in surprised silence as Calor scrambled to his feet, bent down to pick up his spear, and hurriedly shuffle off toward the bunkhouse to join his comrades.

After he made sure Calor wasn't coming back, Bander knelt down beside Tala and stroked the pony girl's hair with a gentle hand. Tala tried to stand, but dizziness had overtaken her, and she stumbled into Bander's embrace. The young guard dropped his heavy spear and scooped the swooning filly up in his strong arms before carrying her off toward the barn.

Several minutes passed before Bander reappeared from the barn. After retrieving his spear, he glanced in the direction of the building where Ben and Megan stood watching before he turned to walk off toward the other bunkhouse.

Ben and Megan remained at the window until they saw Bander disappear into the bunkhouse. With the activity in the barnyard over, they turned and walked toward the middle of the room where they finally took the time to survey their surroundings.

The inside of their quarters consisted of a single small room about ten feet long and twelve feet wide. The furniture consisted of two beds standing near the back wall and a little round table with four chairs placed in the middle of the floor. Evidently, the building hadn't been used for quite some time: the beds were unkempt and filthy, and the table and chairs were covered with a thick mantle of dust.

After finishing his brief examination of their meager accommodations, Ben ventured over to one of the beds, pulled off the dusty blankets, and shook them vigorously, raising a cloud of dust that nearly choked both of them. When the dust settled, he sat down on the edge of the bed and leaned back with his head resting against the wall.

Megan took one final look around the room and shook her head. "What do you suppose they used this building for?" she asked before sitting down on the bed beside Ben.

Ben sat upright and put his arm around her shoulders. "I don't know for sure, but judging by the bars on the windows, I'd say they used it for a jail. All I know is, I don't have a very good feeling about any of this. The ceiling is low, and the building is standing out in the sun, so I'm guessing it gets pretty hot in here during the day. We'd better prepare ourselves for the worst. It's pretty late now, so I don't think Lord Quander will have another hearing until tomorrow. We'd better be prepared for anything the next time he talks to us. He just might try to sweat a confession out of us."

Megan leaned her head on Ben's shoulder. "I'm really scared, Ben." He hugged her and kissed her on the forehead. "Me too, love. Me too."

Megan looked up into his eyes and shook her head. "We only got to spend one night together after we were married. Do you think we will ever get to spend any more nights like that together again?"

Ben hunched his shoulders. He didn't have an answer for her, but he knew what she was thinking. He drew her closer to him and leaned back on the bed with her wrapped tightly in his arms. "I don't know how many nights we'll have together after tonight, love. Maybe we should make the best of what time we have right now."

The newlyweds were suddenly awakened when they heard a key rattling in the lock of the door. There was an anxious moment while they sat up on the bed, waiting for the door to open. Ben put a protective arm around Megan when it started to swing slowly inward. They both held their breath while they waited for their unexpected visitor to enter and were greatly relieved when they saw Bander sneak into the room.

Bander quickly shut the door behind him and, with a quick touch of his finger to his lips, warned Ben to remain silent when he turned to see that the prisoner was about to speak to him. The young guard moved silently to the middle of the room and laid a sack on the table before glancing back at the closed door. Then he turned to the young couple sitting on the edge of the bed. "I am sorry for bringing your dinner so late, my friends," he whispered. "Lord Quander gave orders that you were not to be given food or drink until after he interrogates you tomorrow afternoon."

Megan got up and walked over to the table. "How did you manage to bring us this food then? Lord Quander didn't change his mind, did he?"

"No," Bander whispered. "It just so happens that the plantation cook is the wife of my friend Bodon."

"Oh yes," Megan whispered. "The stocky, little man who was so kind to me when he moved me next to Ben in the line a couple of days ago."

Bander nodded. "Yes. It was his wife, Yanal, who prepared this food for you. Even now, Bodon stands guard at your door tonight. I would not have been able to bring this food to you if it would have been otherwise. If Lord Quander ever finds out that Bodon and his wife helped me to feed you, he will have us all killed."

"We won't say anything," Ben said, breaking his silence. "Megan and I will eat quickly so you can take the sack away with you when you leave. Thank you for your kindness."

Megan sat down at the table and opened the sack. "Aren't you afraid of Lord Quander?"

"Yes," Bander replied. "I would be a fool not to fear him. However, I think he would discover that I would not die so easily if he did try to kill me," he added with a sly grin. He pointed to the sack and spoke in an urgent tone, "You must eat now before Bodon's replacement comes to relieve him."

They found Bodon's wife to be an excellent cook. She had sent them two small loaves of bread and a sizable amount of roasted venison. The meat was covered with a delicious sauce that tasted like nothing they'd ever eaten before. The kind woman was also thoughtful enough to send a goatskin full of water for them to drink.

After he had finished eating his hurried meal, Ben leaned back in his chair and rubbed his belly. "My compliments to the chef," he said.

Megan quickly swept the crumbs into the empty sack after they finished eating and handed it back to Bander. "How are Mota and Tala? We saw how roughly Quander treated them earlier."

Bander seemed thoughtful before answering, "Mota has a nasty bruise on her right shoulder where Quander kicked her. She will be fine." His tone grew very somber as he continued. "As for poor Tala, she will be fine too. She has deep bruises on her left arm and shoulder where she hit the ground after Quander so brutally threw her." His voice had become strained as his anger grew, and he punched his right fist into the palm of his left hand, sending a resounding crack throughout the room. He glanced over his shoulder at the door, as if afraid someone might have heard him. His face was red with burning fury when he turned to face them again. "The Packs may belong to Quander, but not even he should be allowed to treat them that way. I would free them all if I had my way. I wanted to run up and thrust my spear into Quander's evil heart when he abused Tala the way he did."

Megan's eyes flew wide at Bander's bold remarks. "Why, Bander, if I didn't know better, I'd say you sounded like a man in love." She shook her head and smiled deviously. "But that can't be. A handsome young man like you surely couldn't be in love with a beautiful young Pack like Tala. Right?"

Bander glanced at the door again. When he turned back to Megan, his tone was much milder. "I have always had strong feelings for Tala," he replied. "We have known each other since we were very young. My father owned the plantation next to Plantation Quander for many years. The two plantations have adjoining fields, and I would go over and talk to Quander's guards whenever they brought the Packs out to work in the field bordering ours. That is how I first met Tala. I was too young to help my father's men work in the fields, and Tala was too young to be of much help to the older Packs, so Quander's guards used to let us play together. We played together for three years before the guards finally forced Tala start working in the fields with the other Packs."

He walked over to the window and looked out to check the barnyard, making sure that Bodon's replacement wasn't coming yet. He continued his story when he was sure he had time.

"I did not see much of Tala after that, and the few times that I did, she was always working too far away for me to speak to her. I knew that I dared not keep her from her work, or she would be punished, so I tried to avoid distracting her. However, when she would happen to see me in the fields, she always had a warm smile for me. Four years passed before we had an opportunity to speak to each other again."

Bander took a seat at the table before continuing, "One day, my father sold his plantation to Lord Quander and moved to Jando Village, where he and my mother opened a store and warehouse. Because my father and Lord Quander were such good friends, Lord Quander hired me to be a guard on his plantation when my parents moved. I saw Tala again shortly after I started working for Lord Quander." He stopped talking for a moment and looked thoughtfully down at the floor before going on, "Only this time, instead of being her playmate, I... I was her taskmaster." The words seemed to stick in Bander's throat.

Ben gazed quizzically at his friend for a second before asking what was on his mind. "Did you and Tala stay friends after you became one of Lord Quander's plantation guards?"

Bander shook his head. "Not the way we were when we were children," he replied somberly. "I would speak to her whenever I could, even if it was only to ask her to fetch me a drink of water. I am afraid we have not been very close for over four years now."

There was a sudden knock at the door. It was Bodon's signal that his replacement would be coming soon.

Bander hurriedly stuffed the empty sack under his vest and started for the door. "I must be on my way before the new guard arrives." Megan suddenly ran up beside Bander and put her hand on his arm before he could open the door. "Is there something more I can do for you?" he asked.

"We want to know one thing before you go," Megan said. "What do you think will happen to Ben and me when Lord Quander calls for us tomorrow?"

Bander turned away and looked at the door as he answered, "I hoped that you would not ask me that question," he replied sorrowfully. "I heard some of the other guards talking. One of them is Lord Quander's personal bodyguard. He told the other guards that Lord Quander would probably find both of you guilty of aiding the Packs in avoiding capture, even if you did not steal them or kill his brother." He fell silent for a moment as if contemplating whether to say anything more. Then he suddenly turned to face them both. "The punishment for such an offense is enslavement for three years. First, he will sentence you, and then he will send you to Jando Village to be sold on the auction block to the highest bidders."

"Slavery!" Megan covered her mouth to muffle the sound of her voice. "He... he can't do that."

Bander lowered his head. "I'm afraid it will be worse for you than for Ben."

Ben stepped forward. "Why is that?"

"Because you are a full-blooded human, some wealthy man or woman will probably buy you to be a houseboy," Bander replied. "But Megan has a mysterious beauty about her. The people of Gildor have never before seen a human with such strangely shaped eyes and beautiful facial features like hers. She will probably be bought by one of the brothel owners and remain a slave for the rest of her life."

Megan turned and threw herself into Ben's arms. "Oh my God," she cried. "Isn't there something we can do, Bander?" Ben asked, hugging Megan protectively.

"I am afraid that I alone am willing to stand and defend you," he replied. "If I could just find Mota's mate, Tolan. Only he has the strength to defeat Lord Quander in battle. If the other Packs that escaped are still with him, Tolan just might be willing to help us. I think Tolan would be more than happy to help the people who saved his mate and daughter from the jaws of a mithor. After the hearing tomorrow, Lord Quander is going to send a search party into the mountains north of the plantation to try to recapture Tolan. That is the only place where we have not searched for him yet. I will be leading a work party into the mountains myself tomorrow. My men and I are supposed to take inventory of the stores in the supply sheds bordering the plantation there. But we intend to try and find Tolan first before Calor's search party does. If we find him, I will try to persuade him to help us. He will return here sooner or later anyway. Just as soon as he finds out that Mota and Tala have been recaptured."

Ben nodded. "Thank you, Bander. I'm glad we have you for a friend."

The young guard reached out and placed his hand on Megan's shoulder. "Have faith that I will find Tolan and bring him here to help you. Even if Lord Quander does decide to sell you as a slave, it will be a few days yet before the auction is to take place in Jando Village. I will try to find Tolan before time runs out." Giving them both a final nod, he quickly turned and left the building.

Chapter 19

It was midday before two guards came to the jail to fetch Ben and Megan and lead them before Lord Quander's throne. The two sweating prisoners were ushered to the veranda, and like the two Pack women the night before, they were shoved to their knees at the corpulent lord's feet.

The massive mound of flesh leaned forward in his throne and peered at the young couple with bloodshot eyes. It was clear that he had been drinking heavily. His labored breathing pushed the smell of sweet wine into the faces of the prisoners. His angry mood had only been worsened by a nasty hangover. He pointed a meaty finger at Ben and ordered him to stand, but not before heaving out a loud rolling burp that sent a gust of alcohol-laden breath into his face.

Ben turned his face away and shook his head to clear the fumes from his nostrils.

"Look at me when I speak to you, boy!"

Ben turned his face toward the plantation lord and held his chin high while he waited, unmoving, for the hungover giant to speak again.

Quander shook the finger he still held pointed at Ben. "The Packs Mota and Tala told me that you did not steal them. They said that you only provided them with food and shelter for several weeks. Now I want to hear your version of the story, and you better tell me the truth."

Ben looked directly into Quander's eyes and spoke in a derisive tone, "What Mota and Tala have told you is the truth, Great Quander. I saved them from a mithor one day while I was hunting, and I took them to my home after that to have Tala's wounds tended to. From that time on, my wife and I provided them with food and shelter until your men attacked us for no reason."

Quander rubbed his hand across the thick stubble on his chin and eyed the youth suspiciously. "So you admit to giving them refuge and helping them avoid capture?"

Ben shook his head. "No, sir. We only gave them food and a place to stay. They both would have perished if we had refused them that."

"Do not bother me with minor details, boy. You gave them refuge from their rightful owner. For doing so, I find you guilty of aiding escaped slaves, and I sentence you to three years in slavery. You will be taken to Jando Village and sold on the auction block. Your sentence will begin the moment you are sold, four days from tomorrow."

Having passed sentence on Ben, he waved his flabby arm as a signal for the guards to take him away. Two guards immediately stepped forward and grasped Ben firmly by both arms and started dragging him toward the post in the middle of the barnyard. He heard Quander order Megan to step forward while he was being dragged away. "Be strong, Meg!" He was trying to sound unafraid for his wife's sake because he thought he knew how terrified she might be of being sold into slavery. When they reached the post, the two guards locked Ben's wrists into manacles attached to a ring pinned to the top of it, forcing him to stand with his hands over his head.

After seeing Ben dragged away by the two guards and shackled to the post, Megan's fear of Quander must have increased dramatically. Her quiet sobbing irritated Quander, and he became even more irritable. "Control yourself, woman," he roared. "I only stayed to question you because you are so uncommonly beautiful," he said. "And I thought that you just might agree to the deal I have to offer you if I do not sell you as a slave," he added, raising his eyebrows in eager anticipation. "I have some questions I want answered, and you cannot answer them for me if you continue to cry like a lost cub."

Megan forced her gaze toward Quander's throne and pressed her lips tightly together in an effort to stifle her sobbing.

Quander motioned for her to stand up. "Come closer!" Megan stood up and took a hesitant step forward.

Quander leaned forward in his throne with his left hand on his hip and his right elbow resting on his knee. "Tell me, girl, is what your man just told me the truth?"

"Ye... yes, Lord Quander," Megan stammered.

"Then you do not have anything to add in your defense against the charges that have been brought against you?" Quander asked, trying his best to smile. Megan thought for a moment before answering in a shaky voice, "Only th-that we are not familiar with your laws here. Any laws that my husband and I may have broken, we did so out of ignorance."

Quander leaned back in his seat. "I see," he retorted. "And what do you have to say in defense against the charges of your being a crossbreed mated with a human?"

Megan's fear was quickly replaced by anger at that insinuation. The impertinent remark only served to fuel her anger the more she thought about it. "I'm not a crossbreed," she screamed abruptly. "I'm as human as you are, you... you fat ugly pig," she screamed.

Quander pushed himself up out of his seat with such force that the heavy throne toppled over backward as he rushed forward and grabbed Megan by both shoulders. His fingers tightened like a pair of vises as he lowered his hairless head to gaze closely into her wide eyes. Then he relaxed and gave her a cruel smile. "No true woman of Gildor has such features as yours. The blood of some animal must be running through your veins."

Wincing at the pain shooting through her shoulders, Megan cried, "I am not an animal! The place I came from was bad enough when people there called me a bastard."

Catching Megan's slip of the tongue, Quander pulled her close to him, and his attitude became one of a victorious warrior returning from battle. He held the squirming girl tightly against his massive chest. "There! Did you all hear that, men?" he yelled, looking up at the guards attending the hearing. "She admits to being a bastard. She said it with her own tongue. Is a bastard not one born with questionable blood lines with an unknown father? Surely then she must be the product of one of the Great Creators' experiments. A crossbreed of some wonderful animal and a human woman."

He eased one arm from around Megan's waist and took her chin in his free hand. Tilting her head until her eyes were looking directly into his, he passed sentence on her. "I find you guilty of being a crossbreed and of helping escaped packs to avoid capture. Therefore, I sentence you to the same fate as your mate. Only, your sentence is not for three years but for life. No crossbreed is allowed to mate with a full-blooded human in this kingdom." He paused, and his eyes narrowed as he regarded her candidly. "However, I did tell you earlier that I might be willing not to sell you into slavery. All you have to do is agree to be my personal slave."

Megan's eyes suddenly widened, and she shook her head so violently that she momentarily broke the grip Quander had on her chin. "I will never agree to be the slave of a beast like you."

Pure rage took over Quander's countenance, and he pushed her away from him so hard that she fell to the ground. He shook his fist at her and roared, "Then you shall live the rest of your life as a slave." When he finished sentencing Megan, he turned to go back into the house. Before he stepped through the doorway, he turned to his guards and gave one last order. "Return this woman to the jail by herself! She can spend the rest of the day alone in that hot cell while her mate stays out here shackled to that post. They are to remain separated until you leave for Jando Village in the morning!"

While he watched the guards towing Megan away, Ben heard Bander call out to Quander. "My Lord, may I speak to you about the strangers?"

Ben turned to watch the proceedings between Bander and Lord Quander. Although Bander stood slightly over six feet tall, the hulking frame of his employer, who was a full head taller, dwarfed him. However, Bander's body was a pillar of hard rippling muscle compared to Quander's mass of soft, pudgy flesh. Both men were strong, but due to his size, Quander's natural strength had to be three times that of a normal man.

Neither of them appeared to be angry with the other, but it was quite evident that they were not in agreement with each other either. Although Ben couldn't hear everything that was being said, he did manage to hear the last word of their conversation. Quander threw his heavy arms into the air and yelled, "No!" The conversation had ended as quickly as it began when Quander suddenly turned and stormed into his house, leaving Bander standing there alone on the veranda.

The small group of guards who had stayed to listen to the conversation broke up and left to go about their routine duties. However, one of them walked over to relieve the guard standing watch at the door in front of the jailhouse.

Ben clinched his fists in anger when he saw who Megan's new guard was and hissed his name through clenched teeth, "*Din.*" When he turned his attention back to Bander, he saw him stroll over to the Pack barn. After the way Quander had ended their conversation, Ben felt there was no further use in hoping Bander could help him and Megan regain their freedom. *I wish Megan and I could go back and live on the plateau again,* he thought. *Not even the threat of being captured by Bondos seems as bad as being sold as slaves.*

Bander brought Ben his dinner after sundown. He unlocked one of the manacles so he could use his free hand to feed himself. Holding the food and water in a basket, he held it in place so Ben could eat his fill. Ben stopped eating long enough to ask his friend a single question.

"Are you still going to search for Tolan tomorrow, Bander?"

A sudden look of alarm crossed Bander's face, and he immediately motioned for Ben to remain silent. After checking to make sure that no other guards were around to overhear their conversation, he whispered, "Please be careful, my friend. Other ears may hear you. No one knows that we are going to search for Tolan tomorrow. We are supposed to be taking inventory of the stores in the plantation's boarder stations so we can restock them before the rainy season begins. We are not supposed to be looking for escaped Packs." He lowered his eyes and stared at his empty hand while he opened and closed it in a nervous gesture. He looked up again a few seconds later. "Since I am to lead the group, I will pick the four men I trust the most. They will be men Tolan has learned to trust and respect over the years. Not all of us treat the Packs like animals."

Ben nodded slowly. "I think I know how you feel, Bander. I want to thank you for trying to help Megan and me. I don't understand why you chose to befriend us the way you have, but we are thankful for your friendship."

Bander grasped Ben's forearm in a gesture of friendship. "Stay strong, my friend! Pray to the Great Creators and ask them to guide us to Tolan and his followers. You see, I really have no intention of leaving you here. I am going to loosen the pin holding your chains to the top of this post while you eat. It will look like you worked it loose during the night and escaped. My men and I will meet you tomorrow morning in the mountains north of the plantation. We will find Tolan together. I plan to join forces with him so we can overthrow Lord Quander once and for all and set his Packs free. Before we can do that, though, we must help your wife. If we do not find Tolan in time to prevent Megan from being taken to Jando Village, we will have to find a way to help her there before she can be sold."

After Bander finished explaining his plan to Ben, he pulled a long metal bar from his pant leg and started prying at the pin that secured the chains to the top of the post. He left out a grunt of satisfaction a few seconds later. "There, the pin is loose," he whispered. "You should be able to pull it out with ease when the time comes for your escape. Be careful though. If you are captured trying to escape, there will be nothing further that I can do to help you."

Ben looked up and gave the chains a light tug and felt the restraining pin give a little. He smiled and gave a satisfied nod before allowing Bander to lock his wrist back into the manacle. "I'll be careful," he whispered.

"I must go deliver Megan's dinner now," Bander said, leaning closer. "I will try to inform her of our plans if I get the chance to be alone with her for a while without Calor or Din listening in on our conversation. I will see you next in the Northern Mountains, Ben," he whispered before turning to walk away. "May the Great Creators watch over you."

Ben watched him walk away and shook his head. *Bander, my friend, the first thing I'm going to teach you is that your gods are false. If you only knew that they were just men of science and not gods at all.*

Chapter 20

Ben's wrists were rubbed raw by the time it grew late enough for him to try to escape. The barnyard was black as pitch. There were rain clouds in the night sky, and the moon was hidden behind them. He took a quick look around to make sure there were no guards wandering about and, when he was satisfied that he was alone, gave his manacles a hard pull. He felt the pin in the top of the post move, but the chains still held. After taking another quick look around, he put his foot against the post and yanked even harder. This time, the pin gave, and he flew five feet backward and landed on the muddy ground with the chains jingling in his lap.

A steady drizzle had started over an hour earlier, and his hair and clothing were soaked. The drops of water that ran down over his forehead and face annoyed him while he was forced to stand with his hands over his head. He was unable to wipe the water away then but wasted no time in ridding himself of the irritating droplets after he managed to free himself. He jumped to his feet and turned to run in the direction of the jail where Megan was being held, but he remembered what Bander had told him: if he was captured trying to escape, there would be nothing anybody could do to help him. Realizing he had to trust his new friend, he gathered the chains to his manacles up in his arms and turned to run toward the Northern Mountains.

It took almost all the strength he had left to climb up the muddy slopes of the mountain. The two hours it took him to get there through the cold rain had sapped his strength, but he knew he had to find a good hiding place farther up the steep slopes until Bander and his friends could catch up with him. He literally willed his exhausted body to move the last two hundred yards up the slope, where he finally found a hollow tree to duck into out of the driving rain. As he sat there staring down the mountainside and shivering in the cold, his thoughts were of the woman he loved. *Megan, I love you, and I will do whatever it takes to rescue you from a life of slavery. That I promise you.*

Most of the day was gone, and Ben still hadn't seen any sign of Bander or his friends. He was beginning to wonder if the young plantation guard was ever going to show up. All kinds of thoughts started to enter his mind. Panic almost overtook him when the thought that he may have been tricked into abandoning Megan suddenly crossed his mind. He pushed his way out of the hollow tree and was about to start back toward the plantation when he heard voices on the mountainside below. Jumping behind the bole of the large tree, he chanced a peek down the mountainside to see who had ventured so close to his hiding place.

Two men, both appearing to be plantation guards armed with spears, were coming in his direction. They talked to each other in a normal tone, so Ben guessed they had no idea that he was in the vicinity. He started to wonder if they were even searching for him. They continued to walk toward him without concern, which made it quite evident they had no idea he was there. It took a few minutes for the guards to get close enough for Ben to hear what they were saying, but when he heard one of them mention his name, his feeling of dread increased. He was sure they had been sent by Lord Quander to hunt him down and bring him back. He was about to turn and try to sneak away when he heard one of the guards say something that caused him to change his mind.

"This Benjamin Thomas has certainly managed to find a good hiding place," said a short muscular man with a shaven head. "Bander managed to convince Calor that he escaped and has tried to return to the Southern Mountains, where they captured him and the woman, but he told us that he came this way instead. If that is true, it will not take Calor long to figure out that he has been tricked."

"You may be right about that, Nexal," the second man replied, brushing long strands of thick black hair away from his face. "Bander told me if we cannot find his friend soon, we will have to give up the search while there is still enough time left to rescue the half-blood woman from Din and his men before they deliver her to the slavers in Jando Village. It would be a shame if we lose both of them."

Ben had heard enough. He was sure now that the two guards were friends of Bander and that they were truly trying to help him. He stepped from behind the tree in plain sight of the two guards and hailed them in a low voice. "Are you two looking for me?"

The startled guards looked up the hillside at him, and broad smiles immediately shot across their faces. The shorter of the two slapped his companion on the back and started to laugh. "By all the names of the Great Creators, we have found him, Bistan," he cried.

The guard with the long black hair dropped his spear before running up the mountainside to take Ben's forearms in his hands. "Thank the Great Creators we found you," he said. "We were beginning to think that you might have gotten lost or that some wild beast may have killed you. Your trail was completely washed away by the rain last night, and we had no idea where to find you. Bander was willing to continue searching for you as long as he could, but time is running out fast."

Ben gave the man a quick lookover and nodded. The guard had already dropped his spear and wasn't carrying any other weapons, except a short hunting knife, which remained in its sheath attached to his belt. "I'm sorry I made it so hard for you to find me," Ben replied. "I had to make sure you were not Calor's men trying to find me. I cannot risk being captured again if I want to rescue my wife."

"You did a good job of hiding," Bistan replied, stepping forward to unlock Ben's manacles with a key he had pulled from the pocket of his buckskin breeches. After removing the chains, he threw them on the ground and kicked leaves over them before turning back to face Ben. "We will not be needing those anymore," Bistan added with a quick wave of his hand.

A piercing whistle suddenly sounded through the forest. Ben turned to look at the short guard standing on the slope below him. "What does he think he's doing?" he asked, glancing nervously about.

Bistan smiled and put a reassuring hand on Ben's shoulder. "Nexal is signaling Bander that we found you. He will be overjoyed to know that you are all right."

They silently watched as Nexal listened for a few seconds before lifting the wooden whistle tied around his neck and blowing it again. A few more seconds passed before an answering whistle came from somewhere far below them. Nexal turned and looked up at them. "Bander and the others will be joining us shortly," he said.

They spotted three men walking up the slope toward them a short time later. Nexal put his hand on Ben's shoulder and pointed down the slope toward the advancing party. "That would be Bander and the others," he said. "Shall we go meet them?"

With Bistan and Nexal in the lead, Ben followed them down the mountainside to meet the rest of the search party. Ten minutes later, Ben and Bander were standing face-to-face with Bander holding Ben's forearms in his hands in the traditional Gildorian greeting.

"I am happy to see that you survived the night, Ben Thomas," Bander said. "I was beginning to worry that we might have to go on to Jando Village without you."

Ben smiled and shook his head. There is nothing in the world that can prevent me from trying to rescue Megan. I would have found the way to Jando Village by myself if I had to."

Bander put his hand on Ben's shoulder and laughed. "Yes, I think you would have at that. But now there are five more of us to help you now. However, there are not enough of us to assure Megan's rescue. For that, we must find Tolan and his followers and enlist their aid because without them, our task will be almost impossible. I intend to free the rest of Lord Quander's Packs, along with Tala and Mota, after we rescue Megan."

Ben rubbed his hands together to ease the tension building up within him. "When do we get started, my friend? The sooner we get Megan back, the sooner we can free the girl you love."

Bander suddenly stood back and gave his men a worried glance. They all seemed to have the same expression of awe on their faces.

"What's the matter?" Ben asked. "Did I say something wrong?"

Bander shook his head slowly. "No. It is me who must apologize to my loyal friends. I did not tell them that I am in love with Tala. They just thought because she is the daughter of Tolan that I wanted to free her if he was willing to help us."

"So what's the big deal?" Ben asked, hunching his shoulders. "She's a woman, and you're a man. There is nothing wrong with that."

Bander nodded. "I am afraid there is, Ben. You see, it is unlawful for full-blooded humans to mate with crossbreeds. I could be enslaved for three years for such a crime."

Ben looked at the other plantation guards and shook his head. "Although we do not have crossbreeds of humans and animals where I come from, we do have many different races of humans. Those humans have all intermixed with one another. There are some people who think that is wrong, but the God I worship does not care which humans choose to love each other. He is happy as long as they worship him, and he blesses those who do."

Bistan suddenly stepped forward with his spear held up over his head in both hands as he turned to address his fellow guards. "Benjamin Thomas speaks wisely. We have known Bander for many years, and he has never let us down. He has been a good friend and companion to all of us. I, for one, plan to stand by him no matter what woman he chooses to love."

The rest of the guards looked at one another and nodded in unison. "We are with you, Bander," they cried. Then they all rushed forward to congratulate him on his courageous, although ill-advised, declaration of love for a Pack woman.

Bander turned to Ben and smiled. "Thank you for your words of wisdom, Benjamin Thomas. I think I would like to know more of this God of yours. He sounds like a much kinder and wiser God than the Great Creators."

"I'll tell you more about him anytime you want me to, Bander. But I think we better get moving if we are going to find Tolan in time to help Megan."

Bander nodded. "You are right." He turned and pointed in a northerly direction. "We go that way. We must hurry because we only have two days to find Tolan"

It took the rest of that day, but thanks to Ben's tracking skills, they managed to find the trail of the escaped packs. The trail was fresh, so they were able to follow it through most of the night by torchlight until it started to rain again. They tried to pick up where they left off at first light the next morning, but the trail had been washed out by the rain. Bander decided they should split up into two groups in hopes of finding the trail again. He, Ben, and Bistan would search the lower slopes while Nexal would lead the second group over the higher ground. Every man had a wooden whistle on a string tied around his neck. If any of them found the Packs' trail, they were to signal the others by blowing their whistles.

Several painstaking hours of searching later, Bander's group heard three whistle blasts. The shrill blasts had come from somewhere to their right and about two hundred yards higher up the mountainside.

Throwing caution aside, they started to run in the direction the sounds had come from. They found two guards waiting for them with perplexed looks on their faces when they arrived at the scene. "What did you find, Nexal?" Bander asked breathlessly.

Nexal looked at him and shrugged. "Nothing," he blurted, sounding just as much out of breath as Bander.

"Why did you blow your whistle then?"

"Neither of us blew our whistle," the second guard announced. He was a tall, thin young man with short black hair.

Bander glanced up the mountainside. "If it was not Nexal or Phlander, it must have been Strill. I wonder where he is."

The answer to Bander's question came in total silence and with the speed of a diving eagle. Before the five unsuspecting men could move, a large capture net was dropped over them from above. The weight of the net, combined with their own jerking movements, caused them to fall to the ground in a tangle of thick ropes and human limbs. They struggled to free themselves for several seconds before they managed to untangle and crawl out from under the heavy net and immediately found themselves surrounded by seven equine men armed with heavy spears as soon as they stood up.

The leader of the Packs stepped forward and looked at the captives. His broad chest and bulging muscles gave aid to a menacing appearance, and he looked like he could, and would, kill them if he wanted to. His face was adorned with a neatly trimmed beard that had a slight tint of gray in it. His thick mane was as black as a moonless night, growing high at the top of his head and flowing down the middle of his back in long waves that almost reached his tail. His overall height was greater than Bander's six feet by over eight inches, forcing the young plantation guard to look up when the giant moved closer. "So, Bander, you are the one Lord Quander sent to capture me. Now you have been captured by the one you sought to capture." His voice was soft, and he spoke with a slight lisp.

Ben knew only too well the reason for Tolan's lisp. Tala had told him earlier back at the lair that Tolan had been born almost deaf and learned to talk by reading lips and using what little hearing he had to learn his enunciation. Ben found himself admiring the Pack, even though he had never laid eyes on him before.

"You are right about one thing, Tolan," Bander replied. "I have been searching for you. But not for the reason you think. There is another reason altogether that I have been looking for you."

A thin ring of white appeared around Tolan's large liquid black eyes as they widened in surprise. "Your man here," he said, pointing over his left shoulder to where Strill stood with his hands bound behind his back and his mouth stuffed with wet grass, "has already told me the same lie. You wanted to capture me and my followers to take us back to Lord Quander's plantation. Is that not the truth?"

"No," Bander cried. "Please let me tell you the truth before you decide what my intentions really are."

Tolan crossed his arms and stood his ground while closely studying Bander's face. "Very well then. Tell me your story!" His voice still had a ring of disbelief in it.

For the next several minutes, Bander narrated the story of how Mota and Tala had escaped and ran off into the mountains. He told Tolan how Ben had saved them from the mithor and how Megan had nursed Tala's clawed leg back to health. He also informed him of how the two strangers had taken the starving fillies in, fed them, sheltered them, and supplied them with warm clothing.

Ben noticed that Tolan listened to the tale with what seemed to be great interest. It was clear that his attitude toward Bander was changing while listening to the young plantation guard's story.

Tolan suddenly became bitter when he heard how Mota and Tala had been captured along with the two humans and mistreated by Lord Quander and his men after they were brought back to the plantation. Then he shouted and raised his arms into the air and cried, "I have heard enough. Now you tell me why I should believe your story, Bander! How do I know that you are not trying to trick me into going back to Quander's plantation with you so his guards can trap me and enslave me again?"

Bander started to speak, then hesitated as he glanced around at his captors, and then at his own men.

Ben leaned forward and whispered into his ear, "You've got to tell him about your feelings for Tala, Bander. It's the only way he's going to believe you."

Tolan moved closer when he saw Ben talking to Bander. "Who is this guard? I know the others, but I have never seen this one before."

"He is the man I just told you about," Bander replied, turning and placing his hand on Ben's shoulder.

Tolan backed away from Ben and looked straight into Bander's eyes. "What did he just whisper to you? Tell me the truth, or I will rip his heart out and stuff it down your throat."

Bander suddenly drew in a deep breath and spoke loud enough for all to hear. "He told me that I should tell you that I love your daughter, Tala. And that if I can manage to free her from Quander's clutches, I intend to make her my wife. Was that loud enough for you to hear, or would you like me to repeat it for you?"

A dazed look crossed Tolan's face, and he stepped back while the other Packs mumbled excitedly among themselves. The four guards under Bander's command stared in complete amazement at their friend's incredible courage.

Tolan slowly moved forward a moment later and spoke again. The anger seemed to have drained from him, but his disbelief was still evident by the sound of his voice. "How can a human take a Pack for a wife? Such marriages are forbidden."

"I can only repeat what Benjamin Thomas told me," Bander replied. "He said the place he came from has many different races of humans and that they intermarry there. And that it is not against their laws to do so. If they can do that, then why can we not do the same here in Gildor?"

Tolan stepped back in surprise again. "Just when I start to believe you, you tell me that your new friend comes from another place. Are you crazy, Bander? Why should I believe you now?"

"Believe him, Tolan," Nexal shouted, opening his arms as if to encompass his fellow plantation guards. "We have all seen this man's wife. She is very beautiful, yet her features are very strange. I have never seen anyone with such strange features before. She does not appear to be a half-blood though."

Tolan looked at Nexal. "You have never lied to me before, Nexal." He looked at the faces of the other three guards before turning back to face Bander again. "You have never lied to me before either, my friend. Why would you do so now?"

Bander shook his head. "I am not lying to you, Tolan. May the Great Creators strike me dead if I am."

Tolan rubbed a rough hand over his left cheek while he stood in deep thought. "You take mates from different races, you say?" he asked, moving close to Ben again. "You are all full-blooded humans in this place you claim to be from?"

Ben nodded. "Yes, but not all humans there have the same color skin. Nor do we all have round eyes. My wife is of mixed blood. Her skin color is not much different than mine, but her eyes are more, shall we say, slanted than mine. She is part-Malaysian, part-Japanese, and part-American. I guess you could say she is Amerasian."

"But the Pack are not human," Tolan retorted with a grimace.

"You are half-human, Tolan," Bander's response was quick and loud. "As far as Benjamin Thomas and I are concerned, you are more human than Quander, or any of his cruel guards. We see no difference between Packs and humans," he added. "Like Megan Thomas, a physical appearance is the only difference between you and us."

"He makes sense," Nexal said. The guard seemed to be saying his thoughts aloud and not to anyone in particular. Even so, everyone in the group turned to gaze in his direction.

A sudden roar of laughter brought their attention back to Tolan. "Well then, Bander," he said, slapping the young guard on the shoulder with his huge hand, "I do believe you. Surely, you did not come all the way up here into these mountains just to tell me that you wanted to marry my daughter. Why are you really here?"

Ben spoke up before Bander could even begin to answer Tolan's question, "Because my wife and I need your help, Tolan. Lord Quander has sentenced my wife to a life of slavery for being a half-breed married to a full-blooded human. We need your help to rescue her before she's sold at the auction in Jando Village and it's too late for anyone to help her."

"And for aiding escaped packs," Bander interjected, "she and Benjamin Thomas were both sentenced to slave time for helping Mota and Tala."

"Will you help us?" Ben asked.

Tolan was dumbfounded as he stood regarding Ben for a moment. "Why did you not let this one talk earlier?" he said, turning to look back at Bander. "He speaks the language like I have never heard it spoken before. I can tell that no one else from Gildor speaks like this one, even with my poor hearing. It would have been much easier for me to believe you before if you would have let him speak for himself earlier." Turning to look at Ben again, he nodded. "Perhaps you will help us find a new country of our own after we help your woman escape from Jando Village. Someplace where no one will ever bother us and we can all live in peace and freedom."

Ben broke into a broad smile. "I will try, Tolan. But we will have to return to Quander's plantation as soon as possible after we rescue Megan because we will still have to free Tala, Mota, and the others before Lord Quander hears about what will have taken place in Jando Village by then."

"So be it," Tolan exclaimed. He pointed at Strill, still standing with his hands tied behind his back. "Free that man! He is our friend."

Chapter 21

The false sun had hidden behind the horizon long before Din and his men prepared to escort their prisoners down the trail leading into Jando Village. The trek had been hard on the two prisoners the plantation guards were leading. Both prisoners appeared to be women, and Ben Thomas's mood darkened when he saw the shape they were in as he peered over the edge of the boulder he and his friends lay on top of. While he watched the guards forcibly march the women toward the city, he wondered if Din had beaten the defenseless prisoners because they walked as if they had suffered some sort of abuse. He couldn't see their faces because they wore heavy cloaks with hoods drawn up over their heads to protect them from the rain, but they certainly didn't appear to have been taken very good care of during the three- day journey. The women moved with weak and haggard steps as they trudged along in their bonds. He was sure one of them had to be Megan, but he had no idea who the other woman might be.

Ben, Bander, and Tolan remained hidden atop the large boulder near the side of the trail while they counted the plantation guards in Din's party. Their position was about a mile outside Jando Village where they knew the plantation guards would have to pass by on their way into the city. They couldn't believe their luck as they counted the men in the approaching party. Lord Quander had only sent five men to escort the prisoners to the slave auction.

Bander put his hand on Ben's shoulder and leaned close to his ear. "The thirteen men in our party should be able to easily overpower Din's men if we take them by surprise now," he whispered.

Tolan, who had been watching Bander, read his lips as he spoke to Ben. "I agree. We should take them now before they get any closer to the village. It is too bad that the weather delayed us from catching up to them sooner. We would not have to take such a chance of being seen or heard if we could have surprised them higher up in the mountains."

Ben never turned his eyes away from the short column as it marched down the hill. He wasn't sure why, but something didn't seem quite right to him. He shifted his gaze from one prisoner to the other trying to get a look at their faces. The first in the line was Megan. He finally recognized her when he caught a flash of her face when she tilted her head back to take a deep breath. She was apparently exhausted from the long journey and was breathing heavily.

Ben forced himself to take his eyes off Megan long enough to focus on the second prisoner, and he finally caught a glimpse of her face when she drew near enough for him to get a better look at her. He immediately realized they were being baited and turned to warn Bander and Tolan of the danger. "It's a trap, Bander. We can't do anything now, or we might all be captured, or even killed."

"What do you mean?" Bander replied. "If we do not rescue your wife now, we may never be able to."

"What is wrong?" Tolan asked.

Ben turned and pointed toward the column. "Take a closer look at the other prisoner."

The plantation guard and the giant Pack both turned to look in the direction of the prisoners for a moment and whispered the same name in unison when they recognized her. "Mota!"

Tolan became so upset that he almost stood up and rushed the group of plantation guards by himself, but Bander managed to restrain him with considerable effort. "Do not do anything foolish, my friend, or you could get us all killed."

Tolan pounded the top of the boulder with his fist. "That is my mate down there," he hissed. Tolan's voice was loud enough that Bander had to put his hand over his mouth.

Ben put his hand on Tolan's shoulder. "And mine, Tolan. We can't just rush down there, or they could both be lost to us forever. We'll just have to come up with another plan to rescue them, that's all."

"I agree," Bander replied. "Lord Quander must have guessed what my plans were somehow. All we can do is watch and wait for now. I am sure if we attack, it will be exactly what they want us to do."

Tolan nodded and pulled Bander's hand away from his mouth. "How do you know this?" he asked.

Bander put his finger to his lips to signal Tolan to remain silent before mouthing his answer without saying the words aloud. "Because Lord Quander is using Mota as bait. Think about it. He is trying to draw you out so he can recapture you. You know Lord Quander as well as I do. He is a vengeful man, and he would never sell the Packs responsible for leading a successful escape from his plantation. He would rather keep you and make your lives as miserable as possible before he kills you himself."

Tolan lowered his head and nodded.

Ben, who had been watching Bander's silent explanation, turned to watch the approaching column in silent thought. *Evidently, they both know how Lord Quander thinks*. He felt a hand on his shoulder a moment later and glanced back at Bander.

"Tolan and I are going down to warn the others," Bander whispered.

"Okay," Ben replied. "I'm going to stay here and watch what happens next. I'll try to signal to the girls and let them know that we're here if I can."

Bander glanced up the hillside and nodded. "Please be careful, Benjamin Thomas. Do not let anyone see you. There might be others lurking about. It might be better if you do not let the women see you."

Ben waved and winked before turning to watch the approaching column again. It only took a few minutes for the plantation guards to usher the prisoners beneath his hiding place.

When they were directly below Ben, Din walked up beside Megan and jerked the back of her cloak. Megan spun away so fast that the heavy garment was almost pulled off her. "I told you not to touch me, you slimy little pig," she hissed.

Din laughed and tugged at the cloak again until the strings holding it around Megan's neck drew tight, and she couldn't resist being pulled toward him. When she was close enough, he slipped his arms around her waist and pulled her to him. "I may be under orders to let you alone for now, but I will be able to do whatever I please with you after I buy you at the auction." To enforce his point, he held up his moneybag and jingled its contents in her face before pushing her on down the trail backward while keeping her in front of him. "It is beginning to look like your man has abandoned you. I was almost sure he would try to rescue you somewhere along the trail, but he must be an even bigger coward than I gave him credit for."

"Ben is no coward," Megan spat, turning to avoid looking into Din's evil eyes. "He will show up sooner or later. Just you wait and see."

Megan's statement must have made the scruffy little guard nervous because he stopped to take a quick look around before following her down the hillside. He hefted his spear in his hands and continued on hesitantly, "It is a shame he did not try to rescue you because I would have enjoyed killing him."

After Din and Megan had moved on, Ben started to get up to leave, but he suddenly stopped and ducked down again when he heard a man's voice a short distance below him, coming from the trees on the opposite side of the trail.

"If you would not have managed to kill him, little brother, my men and I would have." Calor stepped out on the trail to greet Din. Then he turned and signaled for the rest of his men to come out of hiding. "You can all come out now. We are close enough to Jando Village to stop hiding."

Ben swallowed the lump in his throat as he quickly counted the men as they began to appear out of the forest. There were over twenty of them.

Calor looked around and shook his head to relieve his face of the heavy wet dreadlocks sticking to it. "Lord Quander must have underestimated the loyalty of Bander and his men. They must have really gone about their business of taking inventory of the stores in the border stations. I must remember to recommend Bander for a promotion when I get back to the plantation."

Din started to laugh again. "Careful, brother, or you may find yourself reporting to Bander one day."

Calor slapped him on the back as he fell in step beside him. "That is not very likely. I am afraid I would have to make sure that our friend Bander had a very serious accident before I could ever let that happen."

Chapter 22

Ben waited until Calor and his men were well down the hill before he climbed down from atop the boulder and made his way back to where Bander and the others were hiding. A few minutes later, he was finishing his account of what he had just seen and heard. "I knew it was a trick the moment we saw Mota was also a prisoner with Megan," Ben said, shaking his head. "Calor must have realized Bander sent him in the wrong direction looking for me sooner than we expected and returned to the plantation. Lord Quander must have sent him out to follow Din and the prisoner escort to Jando Village in hopes of catching Bander in an act of treason."

"Calor has no reason to believe that I have done anything wrong," Bander replied. "He does not even think we're in the area since we did not attack the prisoner escort."

Tolan stepped forward and spoke in a disheartened tone. "That may be true, but he still has our women," he said, shifting his eyes back and forth from Ben to Bander. "What do you suppose he plans to do with Mota? Do you think he will still have her sold at the auction since we did not try to rescue her? You said earlier that Lord Quander is a vengeful man, and he would like to punish Mota and me for escaping. Well, I cannot think of a better way to punish us than by selling my mate so that we will never see each other again."

Bander pursed his lips and nodded. "You are right, Tolan. It appears that Lord Quander planned things very well. No matter what the outcome, he knew he would manage to get back at you one way or the other. Either his men would kill or capture you, or Mota would be sold, and you would never see her again."

"Surely he hasn't won yet," Ben said. "There must be something we can do."

Bander nodded as if in deep thought. "Perhaps there is. My father owns a storehouse in Jando Village. Maybe he can come up with a plan to help. That is, if he is willing to help us."

"Will you take us to him then?" Ben asked. "All three of us stand to lose someone we love by not asking and everything to gain if he agrees to help us."

Bander stepped between Ben and Tolan and put a hand on each of their shoulders. "I will do as you ask, but I must talk to my men first. They have already put their lives on the line for us, and I cannot ask them to put themselves at any further risk."

Ben looked up at Tolan. "Maybe you should talk to your men too. They may not be willing to risk their hard-fought freedom for us either."

Both men took Ben's forearms in their hands and nodded before walking away. After watching them go, Ben looked up at the darkening sky. "God, if you're listening, I sure could use your help right now." After a moment's thought, he looked up again and added, "We all could."

Bander and Tolan had come up with a simple plan during the march to Jando Village. Every man in the group had agreed to stay and help their gallant leaders in the rescue attempt with the understanding that if they were captured, they might be condemned to a life of slavery or worse. All of them stated that they were willing to give up their lives for their leaders and that if Bander and Tolan felt that the two women they were planning to rescue were worth risking their lives for, that was a good enough reason for them to risk theirs as well. They swore to fight to the death for them because they knew that Bander and Tolan would be the first ones to give them aid if any of them ever needed help. That was a fact both Bander and Tolan had proven to be true time and again in the past.

Bander's father owned a warehouse, which was one of the buildings surrounding the square where the auction platform stood, and it was from there that the thirteen would-be rescuers planned to launch their rescue attempt. It was a well-known fact that Bander's father refused to open his storehouse on auction days. Zalon hated slavery, so he refused to be anywhere near the square while men and women were being sold. Instead, he and his wife, Xanet, would stay home in their house on the outskirts of the city.

Bander told Ben that his father was the only man he could think of who had never owned human slaves or Packs when he was a plantation lord. Zalon chose to use horses and oxen to do the heavy work on his plantation, and he paid free men to do the labor instead of owning slaves. It was true that it cost him more to operate his plantation by paying free men as his main source of labor, but Zalon's conscience was clear when he went to bed at night. However, other plantation lords in the kingdom were able to offer higher wages to his laborers for positions as plantation guards, so Zalon was forced to sell his plantation by order of the high council when production suddenly dropped off.

Tolan placed firm hands on Ben's and Bander's shoulders after darkness finally fell over the village. "We must move quickly, my friends," the big Pack whispered.

Bander glanced over his shoulder at the giant equine. "You are right. The auction is tomorrow morning, and we do not have time to waste. Tell your packs to remain silent and to give their spears to my men. We will enter the city with my men posing as plantation guards leading a group of Packs to my father's warehouse for supplies. We will enter from that street over there." he added, pointing to a narrow street at the farthest end of the city.

Confused, Tolan asked, "Why from that direction? We will have to travel halfway around the city to enter on that street."

"Because that is where my father lives. I want to warn him to stay away from the warehouse tomorrow in case he decides to open it after all. He usually keeps it closed on auction days, but he could change his mind for some unknown reason."

Tolan pondered the proposal before nodding his approval. "I understand. There is no need to put your parents in danger. My men and I will follow your lead."

He didn't see anyone roaming the streets when they entered the city, so Bander had his men return the Packs' spears to them. It only took him a few minutes to lead them to Zalon's house after he located the right street in the darkness. It was almost pitch-black outside when he finally knocked on the door. The young guard waited for a minute and was about to knock again when he noticed the dim light of an oil lamp moving around inside the house through a crack in the window shutters. The door opened a few seconds later, and a tall man about the same height as Bander stood in the doorway. Even though he was about twice Bander's age, the resemblance between the two was remarkable.

"Hello, Father," Bander said in a low tone.

The older man's eyes opened wide. "Bander... son! What are you doing here at this time of the morning? Your mother will be so pleased to see you." Zalon's eyes cut away from Bander's and took in the men standing behind him. "Son, why are all these men here? And Packs carrying spears?"

"Please, Father, may we come in?" Bander asked. "The lives of two of my friends will depend on these men tomorrow. You need not fear the Packs. I am sure you remember Tolan. He is their leader. Let us in, and I will explain everything to you."

Zalon held the door open and allowed them to enter the house, looking them all over closely as they walked past him. He took Tolan by the arm and quickly pulled him inside when the Pack was about to stop and speak to him. "Please hurry inside before someone sees you, Tolan. There are reward posters for you hanging all over Jando Village. Quander is offering a considerable sum of money for your capture."

A woman walked out of the bedroom into the kitchen after the group had assembled inside the house. "Bander," she squealed, ignoring the rest of the men in the room and running over to throw her arms around Bander. She left him go after a moment and stepped back in obvious fright. "What are these Packs doing in our house? And... and what are they doing with spears?"

Bander smiled as he led her to a chair by the kitchen table. "They are my friends, Mother. Please sit down while I explain to you and Father why we are here."

Twenty minutes had passed, and Bander was just finishing the tale of Ben and Megan and how they had helped Mota and Tala in the wilderness and were wrongly accused of Pack theft and how Lord Quander had sentenced them to slavery. He also told his parents how he helped Ben escape from the plantation and that he and Tolan were also planning to help Megan and Mota escape from the slave house too.

After patiently listening to the complete narrative, Xanet sat studying her son's face for a moment before breaking the short silence that followed. "I understand why you want to free your friends' wives, Bander, but why not just buy them their freedom instead of trying to fight your way out of the city with them?" She stood up and walked over to the fireplace at the end of the kitchen and poked the dimly lit embers of the dying fire back into life. When she turned to face her son again, her lovely face was masked with confusion while she stood waiting for him to answer.

Ben couldn't help noticing how beautiful Xanet looked standing there in front of the fireplace. She appeared to be about the same age as Mota, but no less attractive than the Pack woman. Her short brown hair was without gray, and her true age was impossible to determine, if one didn't already have a fairly good idea. She wore a sleeping shift that hung to her knees and was drawn tight about her waist with a thin belt of rawhide. The garment did little to conceal the rounded curves of the exquisite figure hidden beneath the thin material.

She stepped closer to Bander and stared at him with intelligent green eyes. "You have not answered my question, son," she said impatiently.

"How can I buy their freedom, Mother?" Bander exclaimed. "I do not even have enough money to buy one of them?"

"Why not try asking your father and me for the money?" Xanet said. "We have always had enough money to buy slaves if we desired to do so."

"But you both hate slavery," Bander replied.

"We will buy the slaves for you if you plan on setting them free afterward," Zalon said.

Bander shook his head. "I know that you both mean well, and I am happy to accept your help, but I doubt that even you have enough money to buy both of them. Megan Thomas is a beautiful young woman. She has a rare and mysterious beauty about her that is sure to bring a very high price at the auction. Few women in all of Gildor are as exceptional as she is. Her price will be triple that any of us can afford."

"Then we must do our best to try and buy her," Xanet replied. "If we cannot buy her, then you and your friends can try to free her by other means. At least try a more peaceful method first."

Bander gave her a thoughtful nod. "Very well. We will try it your way first."

Xanet's quick eyes took in her son again. This time, her face had a different expression on it when she tilted her head to one side and stared into his eyes. "There is something else you are not telling us. What are you keeping from us?"

Bander glanced back and forth between his mother and father and then finally shrugged. "I was never any good at hiding things from either of you." He fell silent for a moment, as if trying to think of what to say next, and then he spoke again in a serious tone, "Mother, Father, what do the two of you think of Packs, as far as being people, I mean? Do you think of them as men and women? Or do you think of them merely as animals intended, only useful, for servitude to humans?"

Xanet looked at Bander in surprise, and then glanced at Zalon before answering, "I think your father and I both agree on that matter, son."

"Yes, we do," Zalon broke in. "Your mother and I have thought of the Pack race as intelligent people for quite some time."

"We have felt that way most of our lives, as a matter of fact," Xanet added.

Zalon nodded in agreement. "That is why I would not use Packs to work on my plantation. Xanet and I both hate slavery of any kind, and that includes the ownership of Packs. Most full-blooded humans think of the equine people only as beasts of burden, but we prefer to think of them as men and women."

Ben thought all of his friends seemed to breathe easier after hearing Bander's parents' answer. It must have made Bander's next question much easier to ask.

"How do you feel about a full-blooded human marrying a Pack?"

"But... but the law forbids such a marriage!" Zalon's loud response was heard clearly by all within the room. He cleared his throat and spoke in a softer tone when he realized that every eye in the room was on him. "Remember, most people think of Packs as animals. Whenever most humans take Packs into their homes, it is only as master-slave relationships and no more than that."

Bander got up out of his chair so quickly that it almost fell over. "It is time that law was changed then, Father," he protested angrily.

Zalon raised his hand to calm his son. "Easy, son, I was just stating the law. I have no animosity toward Packs myself."

Bander curbed his anger after hearing Zalon's remarks and smiled at both his parents. "I told you that my friend Ben Thomas comes from a land where different races of humans live together as equals. It is a land where slavery is outlawed. Why can we not then find a land to settle ourselves where full- blooded humans and all the other races of Gildor can live together in peace and freedom?"

Xanet nodded toward Ben. "Your friend here sounds like a wise man," she said. She turned to stare at Bander and asked him again, "Now, what is it that you are keeping from us? You answered my question with another question earlier."

Bander glanced at her, and his face turned crimson. "I have fallen in love," he announced softly.

Xanet nodded in acknowledgment. "I thought so," she cried, clapping her hands. "You have the eyes of a lovestruck puppy."

Zalon stepped beside Bander and put his hand on his shoulder. "Tell us who the lucky woman is!"

Bander lightly touched his father's hand and looked up into his eyes before turning to look across the kitchen at Tolan, who was watching the conversation with great interest.

The expression on the Pack's face seemed to beam with understanding when he realized how complicated Bander's plight was. He walked briskly across the room and stood close to Zalon and Xanet. Then kicking his heels together and firmly pounding the butt of his spear on the floor, he stood at attention before the parents of his friend. "May I have permission to speak freely?" he asked; his lisp was barely noticeable as he spoke.

Zalon and Xanet stepped back and looked at the towering Pack in surprise. "What do you want to speak to us about, Tolan?" Zalon's voice had an edge to it; he didn't like having the conversation with his son interrupted.

"It concerns the woman your son is in love with, Master Zalon," Tolan replied in an even more subdued tone.

Xanet spoke first, "What about her, Tolan? Do you know who she is?" "Yes, mistress, I do," Tolan said. "The woman your son spoke of is my daughter, Tala."

The silence that followed Tolan's announcement must have become unbearable for Bander. "Does this news disappoint you?" he asked, looking intently at both his parents. His question was answered with a quick and totally unexpected reaction when Zalon and Xanet both broke into broad smiles and threw their arms around his neck and hugged him tightly. When they finally let go of Bander, they turned to Tolan and took the Pack's forearms in their hands in an unexpected gesture of friendship.

Xanet turned to speak to Bander again, "Your chosen bride must be a beautiful young woman by now, son. I still remember how pretty she was as a child. I think you have chosen well. You will be the first full-blooded human to marry a Pack girl in this new country you and your friends plan to settle."

"I am glad you approve of my choice in women," Bander said, greatly relieved. "I really do love her, Mother. But I have never had the opportunity to tell her so. We must free Megan and Mota first before I can do that. Only then can I return to Lord Quander's plantation to free Tala."

"I have an idea," Zalon exclaimed. "I think we can free your friends without using force of any kind. Quickly, everyone gather around!" He motioned for everyone to form a circle around the kitchen table so he could reveal his plan to them.

The better part of an hour passed before Zalon silently led the band of fifteen rescuers from his home through the dark empty streets toward his warehouse in the central square of the city. The warehouse was the closest place to the auction block from which they could direct their daring rescue attempt without being seen and drawing unwanted attention to themselves.

Chapter 23

Part of Zalon's plan was for Ben and Bander to check in at the local inn posing as plantation guards who came to Jando Village to buy slaves for their home plantation. They were to stay at the inn overnight and join the assembly of prospective buyers in the central square the following morning. Before sending them on their way to the inn, Zalon opened the coffers of the warehouse and gave Bander and Ben enough money to buy six common slaves, hoping that would be enough to buy both Mota and Megan.

On their way to the inn, Ben and Bander had to pass through the central square where the auction would be held. Ben put the hood of the mithor vest Zalon had given him up over his head to hide his face. His vest and leather pants were relics from Zalon's plantation-lord days. Zalon insisted that Ben had to wear the traditional uniform if he was going to pass as a plantation guard. The legs of the pants were a bit too long, but Xanet quickly rectified that problem with a needle and thread. However, the open vest fit as if it was tailored for him. Although, his legs were shorter than Zalon's, his chest was the same size, if not bigger.

As he walked through the square past the auction platform, Ben had time to study the ominous structure closely. It was nothing more than a raised wooden platform standing eight feet above the ground on four heavy pillars, the floor of which was about ten feet long by four feet wide. A single set of narrow steps led up to the heavy plank floor. A four-foot-high railing surrounded the floor of the eerie stage of bondage and had sharp six-inch spikes imbedded into the entire length of the balustrade at intervals of ten inches to deter any slaves from trying to escape by jumping over it. Ben thought it looked more like a gallows of death than a stage used for displaying slaves for sale. He shuddered involuntarily when the thought of Megan having to stand up there before a crowd of excited bidders entered his mind. Shaking his head to clear the unpleasant image away, he stepped up beside Bander. "How long will it be before the auction starts?" he asked.

"I do not know for sure," Bander replied, stopping at the foot of the steps leading up to a large three-story building. "I have only been here once before when an auction was taking place, but I did not come near the square that day. I was visiting my parents. Do not worry. I will leave instructions for the owner of the inn to awaken us in plenty of time before the auction starts." He motioned for Ben to follow him up the steps to the door and rapped on its metal kickplate with the butt of his spear. He waited a few seconds and knocked on the door again, even harder with his fist.

A moment passed before the door slowly opened to reveal a woman standing in the entrance hall. She was young, a few inches over five feet tall, and wore a brief open red vest that left the expanse of her chest between her breasts and most of her flat midriff exposed. The rest of her apparel consisted of a light-blue wraparound, which rested low on the curve of her hips and was arranged to allow a shapely left thigh uncovered. She threw her head back to rid her face of a wayward strand of long raven hair and looked at the two men at the door. Her bright-blue eyes shone like diamonds in the dim light.

Bander made a clumsy attempt to clear his throat when he realized he was staring with his mouth open. "Good… good evening, my good woman," he stuttered. "I am Bander, overseer of Plantation Zalor. My friend Benjamin and I are here to acquire slaves for our home plantation at tomorrow's auction. We would like two rooms for the night if you still have any available."

"Come in, Bander and Benjamin," the young woman said, pulling the door the rest of the way open to allow them to enter. After the two men stepped inside, the young woman closed the door and bolted it behind them before turning to look them both over approvingly as she walked by them. "I will fetch my husband for you," she said, speaking to Bander. "In the meantime, you and your friend may wait here while I go tell my husband we have more guests. I will show you to your rooms and see to any other needs you may have after you are checked in." She disappeared a moment later through a curtain hanging over the doorway leading into the adjoining room.

Ben tapped Bander on the shoulder when a disturbing thought suddenly came to his mind. "Bander, what if Calor and his men are staying in this inn? They'll see us for sure."

Bander chuckled and shook his head. "There is no need to worry about that. They could not afford to pay for so many rooms. Besides, they will have orders to guard the prisoners until they are sold. Trust me, I know how Lord Quander's mind works."

Ben breathed a little easier until another thought hit him. "What if they see us tomorrow? How are we supposed to keep them from recognizing us?"

Bander was about to answer when the curtain over the door to the next room suddenly parted, and the young woman stepped through the opening with a tall, muscular man carrying a thick book right behind her. Bander immediately stopped and turned to greet the innkeeper and his wife.

The innkeeper nodded at the two men and yawned. "Both of you sign the register and write the name of the plantation you represent beside your names. Then we will see to your needs. I wish you would have gotten here earlier." He gave his wife an angry look before turning to look at Bander again. "I have an inn full of customers to tend to in the morning, and my wife is almost useless at taking care of business properly without my help. I will get very little sleep tonight."

"I am sorry for awakening you, Porat," the girl said, sounding truly apologetic. "I did not think you would want me to register them into the inn without letting you know first."

Porat slammed his hand down on the desktop and glared at her. "That is just your problem, Tanel," he replied, anger growing in his tone with every word. "You do not seem to be able to do anything without my help. I do not know why I ever bothered saving you from the auction block in the first place."

The dejected girl looked at the two plantation guards and bit her lip. Ben thought he saw her tremble for just a second but passed it off as his imagination. *Why doesn't she just tell the old buzzard to kiss off,* he thought.

Porat stood up and closed the register. "Now, gentlemen," he said in his most cordial voice, "if you will kindly follow my wife, she will show you to your rooms." He walked over to the curtain and held it back for Tanel to lead them to the inner chambers of the inn. "Your blankets will be delivered to your rooms in a few minutes. I do hope your stay with us will be a pleasant one."

They followed Tanel to a set of stairs that led to the upper floors of the inn and proceeded to climb them to the third floor. She guided them down a candlelit hallway to a plain door with the number 315 carved into it and turned to Bander. "This is your room," she said, opening the door to let him in. "I will arrange to have one of the maids deliver your blankets to your room in a few minutes. Sleep well, sir."

Bander gave her an approving nod. "Thank you. I am sure I will find the accommodations most suitable. Would you please leave word with your husband that my friend and I would like to be awakened at dawn?"

Tanel bent down and picked up the oil lamp sitting beside the door of the room. "I will tell him," she replied before lighting the lamp with one of the burning candles used to light the hallway. Then she handed the lamp to Bander.

Bander took the lamp and nodded in Ben's direction before going into the room and closing the door. "Good night, Benjamin Thomas. I will meet you in the dining room at the crack of dawn."

"Yes, at the crack of dawn," Ben replied with a wave of his hand.

"Your room is right around the corner," Tanel said, motioning for him to follow her around a bend in the hallway. "It is room number 327."

Confused, Ben looked at all the other doors in the hallway they had turned into. "Are all of these rooms occupied?" he asked. "I thought I might get a room closer to my friend's."

Tanel shook her head. "The maids have not had time to properly clean these rooms yet since they were last rented. It has been a very busy week for my husband and me. I hope it is not too great an inconvenience."

Ben figured Tanel had already heard enough complaining from her husband for one night, so he let the subject drop. "No, I am sure this room will be fine. Thank you."

Tanel flashed him a wry smile as she lit the oil lamp sitting inside the door and handed it to him. "I will be back with your blankets in a few minutes."

He stood for a moment watching Tanel walk away and then stepped inside the room. The first thing he noticed when he closed the door was the lack of a lock. He hefted the heavy spear in his right hand as he turned to survey his accommodations. "I guess you're my only means of security for tonight," he whispered at the spear before turning to look the room over.

The room was small, only about eight feet square, with all four walls and the low ceiling painted a drab green. Completely devoid of any adornments, the room appeared to be even smaller. There was only one small window, which, he discovered, overlooked the central square when he opened the shutters to look outside. He could barely make out the auction platform when he strained his eyes to see through the darkness. Turning from the window, he walked to the bed and tested its firmness with his hand. It was nothing more than a wooden bench with a grass-filled mat thrown over it. "Hmm," he moaned. "My bed back at the lair was more comfortable than this thing will ever be."

He was about to return to the window to get a breath of fresh air when he heard a noise behind him. Wheeling around, he discovered the beautiful wife of the innkeeper standing behind him holding a bundle of blankets in her arms.

"Here are your blankets," she said. "If you need more, I will be happy to get them for you."

Ben quickly took the blankets from her and stepped back to unfold them and spread them out on the bed. "I do not think that will be necessary," he said. "These look as if they will be plenty warm. Thank you."

Tanel nodded silently while she stood watching him with an odd look on her face.

When Ben finished spreading the blankets, he sat down on the edge of the bed and looked up at her. "Is something wrong?" he asked.

After a moment's silence, Tanel suddenly knelt down on the floor in front of him and put her hands on his forearms. "You are young and strong," she said, eyeing him openly. "I was just wondering, if perhaps... perhaps you might take me with you when you leave Jando Village."

Ben was dumbfounded for a moment before he found his tongue again. "I cannot take you with me. Surely your husband would never allow that. Why would I want to take you with me anyway?"

Tanel stood up and walked over to the open door and peeked out into the hallway. "Perhaps I have a way of convincing you to take me with you," she tittered. She stepped away from the door and untied the knot in her wraparound before allowing the loose skirt to tumble to the floor around her feet. She whirled around in a tight spiral in nothing more than her red vest and a pair of blue panties before the wide-eyed dumbfounded plantation guard. After spinning around a few times, she stood directly in front of him and smiled. "I will do more than just dance for you if you will take me away with you," she said. To indicate her willingness to try and please him, she started to untie the retaining string at the bottom front of her vest, but Ben finally came back to his senses and stopped her.

"I... I stand by what I said before, Tan-Tanel," he stammered. "I will not take you with me. I know Porat may not treat you right all the time, but staying here with him will certainly be better than coming with me."

The young temptress tilted her head to one side while she retied the front of her vest. "Oh, we shall see about that when the time comes," she spat, bending down to pick up her skirt and securing it back around her hips. After she was fully clothed, she stepped out into the hallway and slammed the door behind her.

Ben remained quiet while he sat on the edge of the bed, waiting to see if Tanel was coming back. When he heard her rapid footsteps going down the hallway, the astonished youth shook his head in dismay and leaned back to lie down on the bed. "Man, that was just too close," he breathed uneasily. "Now I know how poor Joseph must have felt around Potiphar's wife."

Chapter 24

A knock on the door stirred Ben out of a fitful sleep. He sat up on the edge of the bed and pushed a thick mass of brown hair out of his face. "I've got to get a haircut," he mumbled, stretching lazily. His joints cracked softly from the tension of the previous day's exhausting march when he reached down for his breeches. He had just started putting then on when a second knock came at the door. "Yeah, yeah, I'm comin'," he yelled in English, and then sat bolt upright and stroked his chin when he remembered where he was and realized what he had done. *You fool! You'll give yourself away for sure if you don't start using your head.* He rolled his eyes and blinked away the drowsiness before getting up and walking to the door. *I hope whoever it is wasn't paying any attention to what I said, or I could be in hot soup.* He opened the door a crack and looked out into the hallway to see the stern face of Porat staring back at him.

"My wife left instructions for me to awaken you at dawn," Porat said. "Ah yes, thank you," Ben replied with a nervous smile.

The innkeeper nodded and turned to walk away. "Breakfast will be served in the dining room in half an hour," he said, not bothering to look back.

Ben closed the door and blew out a deep breath. Evidently, Porat didn't hear him yelling in the strange language. He could hear voices when he leaned back against the door for a moment to give his knees a chance to stop shaking. At first, he thought the voices were coming from the hallway, but he soon realized they were coming from outside when he noticed he had left the window open the night before. He walked briskly over to the window and peered down into the central square, which was bathed in a dim predawn light.

From his vantage point, he could see everything going on in the square below. The auction platform stood about forty yards away giving him a clear view of it from the window. The square was far from empty, as it had been the night before, when he and Bander walked through it on their way to the inn. Crowds of people were assembled in front of the village shops waiting for the proprietors to open the doors. Men, women, and children were walking and running up and down the streets as they went about their daily business. The whole scene was a mass of fluid motion with all the people scurrying about like the occupants of an anthill.

Ben had just turned his attention back to the auction platform when he heard someone speak behind him. He turned around to find that Tanel had silently entered the room.

"The auction will not begin until after the livestock and Packs have been fed and watered," she said. She held out a tray with a small bowl of broth, some bread, and a wooden spoon on it. "Take this and eat now! You will not get another chance to eat until after the auction, and that could be several hours from now."

Ben walked over to her and took the tray, thanking her for her kindness before sitting down on the edge of the bed. He started sipping bleakly at the warm broth when he chanced to look up again and noticed Tanel was still standing by the door, watching him. All the while, she kept biting her lower lip.

"I was supposed to meet my friend in the dining room for breakfast," he said. "I should be going because he will be wondering where I am."

Tanel started to twist to and fro at the waist. She stopped the pivotal movement after a few seconds and leaned back against the door with her hands braced on either side of the frame. She smiled and spoke in a hushed tone, "Do you remember what we talked about last night?"

"Oh, I have not forgotten," Ben replied flatly. "And my answer is still the same. You cannot go with me. Your place is here with your husband."

Tanel moved closer and bent down in front of him. She thrust her head forward until her face was only inches from his. She kept smiling as she reached out to touch the side of his face with her hands. Ben pulled away and slapped the tray into her outstretched palms. She shot him a mystified look and smiled again.

"I showed you why you should take me with you," she retorted. "Oh yes, I know how to make my men happy." She stood up and took a quick step backward. "Think about what I offered you last night, Benjamin Thomas, and remember what I promise you now! If you take me with you, I will be eternally grateful and promise that I will be there for you whenever you want me."

Ben got up and walked back to the window and gazed down into the square. "Go to your husband, Tanel! No wonder he got so mad at you last night. If you are always chasing after other men, I do not understand why he continues to put up with you. Maybe he should have let you be sold as a slave like those poor devils down there."

"How dare you," Tanel hissed. "You do not know anything about me, or where I came from, or the way Porat treats me. The auction will start as soon as the livestock and slaves have been fed. I hope you and your friend fail in your task to acquire slaves for your home plantation, and I hope your plantation lord decides to make you his slaves instead."

Ben never bothered to reply. He ignored her and continued to stare out the window until he heard her walk away. He didn't bother turning to see if she kept going; his main concern was what would be going on down there around the auction platform later. He stood there a few minutes longer before finally turning to pick up his spear and heading down the hallway to meet Bander in the dining room. They were to meet there and then return to the warehouse as soon as they had finished establishing their cover as plantation guards.

※

Ben watched the proceedings from Zalon's warehouse window while the auctioneer stood atop the platform in his multicolored coat accepting bids for the last ox. A large crowd had started to gather close around the base of the stage earlier when the tall, thin auctioneer slipped his colorful coat on and began to beckon the onlookers to move in closer to the platform. The skillful man had already dispensed of over thirty horses and twenty other oxen before the bidding started for the last ox. Ben noted how the auctioneer managed to keep the crowd's attention. He not only worked at getting high bids for the livestock; he also worked on getting the crowd more excited by hinting about the Packs and beauteous female slaves he would be offering for sale later. Now there was only a small herd of sheep remaining to be sold before the Packs would be brought out for sale.

From his vantage point, Ben could see the Packs being led up the street toward the platform. When the equines were about thirty yards from the base of the stage, the men guarding them ordered them to stop. The packs stood with their faces turned toward the ground while they waited for the herd of sheep to be sold. There were seven packs in the line: five men and two women. Mota was the seventh, which meant she would be the last to be sold. Evidently, the keeper of the Pack barn decided that placing her last would give the crowd time to observe her before she went up for sale. Zalon explained that the tactic was used by auctioneers to help drive up the selling price of superior slaves and livestock.

It only took about five minutes for the crafty auctioneer to sell the remaining livestock to eager bidders. After he finished selling the sheep, he clapped his hands and called out to the men guarding the Packs, motioning for them to bring them closer to the base of the platform. This done, he called out to the people in the crowd, telling them to draw nearer so they could get a better look at what he was about to offer.

"Now, my friends," the auctioneer yelled, "we will start the bidding for the packs. Everyone gather close now because we only have a handful of these fine creatures for today's auction. I do not want anyone to miss out on the bidding." He turned to the line of heavily guarded Packs who were moved behind the platform by this time and pointed to the first male in the group. "You, lad, come up here and stand in the circle beside me!"

Ben watched the young Pack climb the steps to the floor of the platform. He judged the boy to be about ten or eleven years old. The boy stepped into the circle beside the auctioneer and raised his face toward the crowd, his eyes full of fear.

The auctioneer looked out over the crowd and smiled. Ben thought the thin man's face resembled a living skull when he saw the way his teeth flashed between his thin lips.

"Now," cried the auctioneer, "you all have seen how obedient this young fellow is, so now you know that he is trainable." His comment brought a roar of laughter from the crowd. "So… who will be the first to bid on this fine young Pack?" He had to speak rapidly when the bids started to rise for the young offering. The auctioneer was truly a master of his trade because the youth had a new master within minutes.

Judging by the comments Ben heard from various members of the crowd standing near the open window of the warehouse, the boy brought a very high profit for his previous owner. The skill of the auctioneer truly had to be appreciated by those who contracted him to sell their property. Ben's heart began to pound like a drum as he stood helplessly watching the Packs being sold off one after another. Only two Packs remained standing behind the platform fifteen minutes after the bidding had started. One was a middle-aged woman with a lame left leg, and the other was a younger beautiful woman with a thick carrot-colored mane. *Mota*. Ben saw the old woman begin to slowly limp up the steps to the raised floor of the platform while Mota stood silently awaiting her turn. However, he never got to see the bidding for the old woman get underway because the sound of the warehouse door opening caused him to turn away from the window.

Bander stepped inside the warehouse and joined the others behind Ben at the window. He nodded toward Ben and asked, "Are you ready, my friend? Mota will be going up for sale in a few minutes, and we should be there before the bidding starts. The auctioneer must not think it will take long to sell her because he has ordered the slave-house guards to bring out the full- blooded male slaves already."

Ben stood up straight and adjusted his mithor-hide vest. I am as ready as I will ever be," he said.

"Good. We are ready to go then," Bander replied, turning to address the others in the room. "Wish us luck and pray that the Great Creators are willing to help us."

Xanet suddenly stepped in front of him and held up her hand. "Just a moment, Bander." She reached behind him to flip the hood of his vest up over his head. "It would not be good if one of Quander's men should happen to recognize you while you are out there bidding on Mota."

Ben immediately reached back and flipped his own hood up. "It's a good thing you reminded us about that, Xanet," he said. "Our rescue efforts will be foiled for sure if we're recognized."

Zalon held two spears out to them. "You better not forget these either. You never know when you might need them."

Everyone's attention was suddenly drawn to the window when they heard a commotion coming from that direction. They turned to see Strill feebly trying to pull Tolan away from the window.

Bander rushed to help his friend gain control of the huge Pack. He grabbed Tolan's shoulders and started to turn him around to face him and was almost knocked to the floor for his efforts, but the mighty equine caught him by the arm and stopped his fall when he saw it was his friend who held him.

"I am sorry, Bander," Tolan puffed. "I did not mean to harm you."

Bander straightened and readjusted his vest. "What made you so upset that it caused you to react that way, Tolan?"

Strill answered for Tolan. "He became furious when he saw the way the guards pushed his mate up the steps of the auction platform. I cannot blame him. They were not very kind. They hit her in the back with the butts of their spears, and she almost fell over the railing."

"If the auctioneer would not have caught her, she would have been impaled on those spikes," Tolan added, shaking free of their grip.

Bander took Tolan's forearms in his hands. "She is all right, my friend. Thank the Great Creators that nothing happened to her. Please be patient. I promise you that Ben and I will return here with her shortly."

Ben reached out and put his hand on Tolan's shoulder. "Please believe me, Tolan, when I say we will return your mate to you. Mota has become a very good friend of mine, and so has Tala. Remember, Bander and I stand to lose loved ones too if anything goes wrong, so we both know how you feel."

Tolan relaxed after he read Ben's lips. "Mota and Tala were most fortunate to have found such good friends as you and your wife, Benjamin Thomas. Thank you for offering to try to reunite us. If the two of you succeed in your mission to rescue Mota, I shall remain ever indebted to you and will do whatever I can to repay your kindness."

Zalon stepped between the three friends and motioned toward the door. "You three can continue this conversation later. Right now, Benjamin Thomas and Bander must be on their way. The bidding for Mota is about to begin."

While he followed Bander through the square toward the platform, Ben took the time to look over the short line of male slaves being marched to the foot of the steps. There were four of them. The first two were elderly and walked with slow shuffling steps. He wondered what crime the poor, feeble souls could have committed that would have condemned them to slavery. The next in line was a youth who appeared to be only about twelve or thirteen. Ben heard one of the guards saying something to the boy about not having to spend four years as a slave if his parents would only pay the taxes they owed the king. The fourth man had a long flowing mane of dark-brown hair. Like most Packs, his hair grew short on both sides of his head, high on top, and on down the middle of his back in thick rolling waves. However, he didn't have the long pointed ears or the tail of a Pack. He was definitely a crossbreed, a phenomenon that automatically earned him a life sentence of slavery. Ben learned later that the man was the illegitimate son of a plantation lord and a Pack woman, thus earning him the privilege of being sold with the full-blooded humans.

The young man's presence reminded Ben of Megan. Lord Quander had sentenced her to a life of slavery for being a crossbreed. The thought that he might never see his beautiful wife again was almost more than he could stand. He was suddenly jerked back to reality when the noise of the excited crowd drew his attention to the raised floor of the platform.

A furious bidding war had begun. It couldn't have been more than a minute since he and Bander left the storehouse. He had been so absorbed in his private thoughts that he had forgotten about the events taking place on the platform. He looked up to see Mota standing beside the auctioneer.

She stood quietly as the skillful auctioneer teased the men in the crowd into raising their bids for her. He ran the end of a wooden pointer along Mota's fine form and commented on how shapely she was for a Pack. That started another surge of impulsive bidding.

Ben's heart sank in despair as he watched his friend being treated like some kind of animal, and his mood sank even lower when he thought of Megan being treated in the same manner.

It didn't take long for the bidding to reach an extraordinary price. Bander poked Ben in the ribs with his elbow. "If this keeps up, we may not have enough money left to buy Megan. What do you want me to do?"

In his heart, Ben wanted to tell Bander to stop bidding, but he made a promise to Tolan. "Keep bidding! We both promised Tolan that we would bring Mota back for him."

Bander nodded and quickly turned to call out another bid. The bidding continued for another minute or two before they were sure of the outcome. It had taken almost half the money Zalon had given him, but Bander's final bid was higher than anyone else's. Ben heard Bander breathe out a loud sigh of relief when the auctioneer finally clapped his hands and pointed at him and yelled, "Sold to that fine young plantation guard over there for eight hundred twenty dinots."

The auctioneer escorted Mota to the steps a moment later and motioned for her to go down to where armed guards would lead her to the clerk's table near the base of the platform. She would wait there for her new master to come and claim her. Remain here," Bander whispered, glancing at Ben from under his hood. "There is no need for both of us to risk being seen by Calor and his men. I will go pay the clerk for Mota and escort her back to the warehouse. Follow along several paces behind us after we walk past you and make sure no one suspects anything."

Ben nodded and took a few steps back into the crowd while he waited for Bander to make his way to the clerk's table. He pulled his hood tighter around his face and stretched his neck to watch as his friend went to collect Mota. He felt his stomach muscles tighten for a moment when he saw Calor step forward to give the clerk some papers while Bander was paying for Mota. In turn, the papers were handed to Bander, and Ben thought he was about to lose his breakfast before he finally relaxed when the unsuspecting plantation guard turned and walked away without even looking in Bander's direction. Once the papers were transferred, Mota was escorted forward, and her new master quickly secured her wrists in manacles before starting to lead her away.

It took a few minutes for Bander and Ben to make their way back to the warehouse through the crowded square with Mota, but that time must have seemed like an eternity to those waiting inside for their arrival. When the knock at the door finally came, Xanet was quick to open it and let them in.

Tolan was the first to greet them when they stepped through the threshold. He had been standing close by the door, waiting for Bander to usher Mota inside. Upon seeing her mate, Mota broke into tears and rushed forward into his open arms.

"How can I ever repay you for returning Mota to me?" Tolan exclaimed, his voice quivering with excitement.

Bander smiled as he watched the happy couple embrace. "There is no need for that, Tolan. You are my friend, and I think one friend should be willing to help the other when he needs it."

"Nevertheless, you have our eternal gratitude," Tolan replied *before* pulling Mota close and kissing her tenderly on the lips.

After the Packs eased their embrace, Ben moved to stand beside the reunited couple and put a hand on Mota's shoulder. "Do you know where Megan is?" he asked.

Mota eased her arms from around Tolan and wiped tears from her eyes. "I saw her standing behind the platform with the other human slaves. She will be the last to be offered for sale after all the others have been sold."

Ben nodded and turned to Bander and Zalon, who were standing by the door with Xanet. "Do you still plan to try and buy Megan?" he asked.

Bander nodded. "After that, we are going to Quander's plantation to get Tala."

Mota's face suddenly contorted in fear. "But, Bander, you may be captured by Lord Quander's men. Tolan and I love our daughter more than anything in the world, but we cannot ask you to risk your life trying to free her. Tolan and I will go and try to free her by ourselves."

Bander shook his head. "No, Mota. We will go back after Tala together. You may love your daughter, but I also love her. I intend to make her my wife if she will agree to marry me."

Mota's mouth flew open in shock as she glanced back and forth from Bander's face to Tolan's.

Tolan looked down on her beautifully puzzled countenance with smiling eyes. "I have much to tell you, my love," he said.

Before Tolan could begin to tell Mota about Bander's plans for their daughter, everyone's attention was suddenly drawn to Strill when he called out from his vantage point at the window. He had been watching the activity in the square through the cracks in the shutters. "The bidding for the men has already begun."

Zalon rushed to the window and looked out into the square. "One of us should go out and pretend to bid on some of the men," he said. "Perhaps no one will get suspicious of him when he bids for Megan later. His guise as an interested buyer will already be established by the time the women come up for sale."

"Perhaps you should go," Xanet suggested. "Quander's plantation guards may not recognize you after all these years."

Bander started to protest, but Xanet raised a hand to silence him. "It only makes sense that your father should be the one to do the bidding this time, Bander," she said firmly. "Calor and the other guards have already seen you buy one of Quander's slaves. They may get suspicious and decide to investigate if you try to buy another."

Bander knew Xanet was right and reluctantly agreed to her plan. "Very well, Mother. Ben and I will accompany father to the square, but we will not bid. We will remain a safe distance away and watch the proceedings in case trouble arises."

Zalon turned to look at Ben. "Will you be able to contain yourself if the auctioneer decides to fondle your wife? If she is as beautiful as Bander says she is, the auctioneer may decide to handle her in front of the crowd to tease potential buyers into raising their bids."

Ben hesitated a second before answering, "I'm willing to do whatever is necessary to get Megan back safely," he replied.

Chapter 25

Although he had been with Bander during the bidding for Mota earlier, Ben hadn't managed to get a real good look at the auctioneer. It wasn't until he and Bander accompanied Zalon across the square to stand near the base of the platform during a period of hot bidding for a young boy that he finally got the chance to study the face of the master salesman.

As soon as the boy was sold and escorted off the stage to the clerk's table, the auctioneer motioned for a young man, who looked to be in his early twenties, to come up the steps and stand in the small red circle painted on the floor. The young man obediently did as he was ordered and took a quick sideways glance at the auctioneer, as if to ask if there was anything else he wanted him to do.

Ben looked up at the auctioneer and studied the man closely while he prepared his next offering for sale. He was an older man with a large hawk nose and jet-black hair that looked as if it had recently been dyed. When he turned to look out over the crowd, he pulled a small flask out of his back pocket and took a sip of its contents. He spent his spare time between each sale nipping at the contents of the flask, which he had periodically been drinking from since the beginning of the auction. After tucking the flask back into his pocket, he ambled to the edge of the stage and looked out over the railing to see if the clerk was finished with his business. Then he returned to the side of his next offering with a staggering gait that left no doubt to anyone watching that the contents of the flask were of an intoxicating nature.

"Just look at this one, my friends," the auctioneer yelled. "Not only is he big and strong, he is young and good-looking as well. So come on, ladies, and let me hear your bids on this one."

The young man's face flushed when a woman suddenly yelled from somewhere out in the torrent of faces. "He looks strong enough to handle any chores I have around my house and still have enough energy left to keep me happy at night."

This brought a roar of laughter from the rest of the crowd, and the auctioneer had to clap his hands again to regain their attention. "There you have it, folks. That fine lady knows a great value when she sees it. Who will be the first to bid on this strong young fellow?"

There was a constant flow of bidding for several minutes before it finally started to slow down. Ben wasn't familiar with the form of money used in Gildor, but he knew enough to realize that the bids were high.

The auctioneer used his pointer to draw the crowd's attention to the slave's various assets and drive the bids even higher. "Oh, come on, people," he bellowed as he moved the tip of the pointer to the front of the slave's chest. "Look at the expanse of that chest. Look at those muscular arms and legs. Ladies, you can only guess what pleasures may await you with this one in your possession?"

Ben shot the auctioneer an angry look and then caught himself. He wouldn't be able to help Megan if he was killed trying to choke the auctioneer to death. *God! If he treats the men this way, how will he treat the women when he starts selling them?* He became so absorbed in his thoughts that he forgot he was standing close to the platform. Reality didn't strike until he heard another volley of laughter from the crowd. Apparently, the auctioneer had made another suggestive remark while he wasn't paying attention. The only thing he was sure of was that the bidding had started anew, with considerably more vigor than before.

Ben turned and looked toward the back of the crowd trying to see who was bidding on the young man. Most of the bidders were women, although there were still a few men bidding as well. Most of the men stopped bidding when the women began driving the price higher than any of them were willing to pay for a mere working slave. The bidding slowed when the number of prospective buyers dwindled, making it easier for Ben to concentrate on those who were still making offers. The number of bidders continued to slowly drop until only three women continued to make offers.

A short, heavyset woman finally threw her arms into the air and cried out, "I cannot afford to bid any higher. One of those two ladies will have to bed that pretty boy tonight."

Another roar of laughter exploded from the crowd while a few jeered at the fat woman's remark. The auctioneer raised his hands to quiet the crowd so he could hear the offers of the two remaining bidders. "Now, now, friends, there is no need to scorn that fine woman. She has made her final offer and can simply afford no more." He pointed his finger toward the last two bidders. "Now it is up to these two fine ladies to finish the bidding. The last bid offered was one thousand dinots. Do I hear a higher bid?"

"One thousand five hundred," yelled a tall blonde woman dressed in the traditional short vest and wraparound worn by most Gildorian women. "I want him for my houseboy."

There was a short silence before the second woman stepped up to the foot of the platform and looked up at the auctioneer. "One thousand six hundred dinots," she said.

Intrigued, Ben stared at the woman. Although the tall blonde woman was beautiful, this woman was even more comely, although she appeared to be a few years older. Her attire was of similar fashion to the blonde's, except for a short robe she wore over her clothing. Her short red hair showed no sign of graying, yet Ben guessed her to be in her late thirties to early forties. He wasn't sure how he knew; perhaps it was the way she carried herself. It really didn't make much difference because she was apparently going to be the young man's new owner no matter what her age. The members of the crowd suddenly grew quiet when they heard the last bid. There were low murmurs among the throng, and Ben heard enough of the comments to know that nobody had ever paid so much for a male work slave before.

The auctioneer clapped his hands again and looked in the younger woman's direction. "Do I hear any more bids for this fine specimen of manhood?" he yelled.

The young blonde hunched her shoulders and shook her head.

"Very well then," the auctioneer exclaimed. "I declare this good woman to be this fellow's new owner."

Ben leaned close to Bander. "Who is that red-haired woman?" he whispered.

Bander nodded in the redhead's direction. "You better hope that she does not bid against my father for Megan," he said. "She is Sintha," Bander replied. "She is the owner of the biggest and most expensive bordello in the city. Few can afford to bid as high as she can. You better hope she is only looking for male slaves today, or we could be in big trouble."

Ben cringed involuntarily at Bander's answer. "Do you think she might bid on Megan?"

Bander hunched his shoulders. "We can only hope that she leaves before she sees any of the women going up for bid. If she does, it means that she is not interested in buying women today. We will know in a little while. There are only a few men left in the line."

Ben paid little attention to the rest of the proceedings on the platform from that time on. He kept a constant eye on Sintha until the last of the male slaves was sold. He breathed a sigh of relief after he saw her and her armed entourage escort her three new male prostitutes out of the square and up a side street.

Bander patted him on the shoulder. "I think you can relax now, my friend. It looks as if Sintha is done for the day."

Ben rolled his eyes and blew a strand of stray hair away from his face. *Thank God.* He jumped when a hand suddenly reached out of the crowd behind him and touched his shoulder, but relaxed when he recognized Zalon's familiar face. "Why have you come so close to Bander and me, Zalon? I thought you wanted us to stay clear of you so we wouldn't be recognized."

Zalon nodded. "That was my original intention, but I have a good reason to change my mind."

"Why is that?" Bander asked.

The older man scratched his chin in deep thought. "I want you to return to the warehouse and bring Strill and Bistan back here with you. We may need their help if the bids go too high."

Bander held out his hands. "What can they do? They have very little, if any, money to add to what you already have."

"I know," Zalon replied. "But we may need their help to rescue Megan later if someone raises the bid for her so high that I cannot afford to pay for her with the money I have on hand. We may have to take her by force, but I do not want to do that if I can avoid it. That is why your mother and I have decided, if we cannot match the entire amount someone else may be willing to pay for Megan, that I should leave them the papers to our business to cover the expense."

Ben had heard enough. "I can't ask you to do that, Zalon. After all, you hardly know me, and you don't know my wife at all. I can't ask you to give your business away to help us, even if it means losing my own life to save Megan."

Zalon shook his head and put his hand on Ben's shoulder. "No, my friend. Bander has explained to Xanet and me how you want to find and settle a new land with no slavery or bitterness toward others because they are different. That is a noble and wonderful idea. We have decided to throw our lot in with you. If we go with you, we will have no further need of the warehouse. I can think of no better sacrifice than to give it away in order to save the wife of the man with such a noble cause in mind."

Ben considered what Zalon was suggesting and asked, "How do you plan to rescue Megan?"

Zalon stepped closer to Ben and put a reassuring hand on his shoulder. "We will have to follow Megan and her new owner until they are out of sight of the crowd before we can take her from him. We will leave him all the money and the papers to the warehouse to pay for his loss. With any luck, he will be satisfied and not sound an alarm. We will restrain him long enough for us to make good our escape from the city if we have to."

Ben didn't like the plan; there were just too many things that could go wrong. *Suppose we are caught trying to rescue Megan?* he thought. *What if Megan gets hurt or killed during the rescue attempt?* No, he didn't like the plan, but he kept his thoughts to himself because he couldn't think of a better one. "How much do you think the price for Megan will be?" he asked.

Zalon thought for a moment. "At least 50 or 60 percent higher than the price she brings at auction. But I think my business will more then cover the difference."

Ben considered Zalon's plan and nodded. "How do you plan on getting out of the city without being caught?" he whispered.

Zalon pointed back toward the warehouse. "I have a stable below the warehouse. Even as we speak, Tolan and Mota are readying enough horses for our escape. After we rescue Megan, we will return there to join the rest of our band of outlaws and ride out of the city together.

Hopefully, any people remaining in the streets at that time will think we are a group of plantation guards returning to their home plantation."

Ben rubbed his chin. "It's a solid plan, and it sounds like it'll work. I guess all that remains for us to do now is to free Megan."

"It is settled then," Bander said. "I will go fetch Strill and Bistan and return here with them in a few minutes."

Before Bander could turn to leave, Zalon grabbed him by the arm and stopped him. "Do not bring them back here, son. Station yourselves near the entrances of the streets leading into the square. At least that way, one of us will be able to follow the person who buys Megan and return for the others in case we lose them in this crowd."

Bander nodded. "I understand, Father," he said before turning to hurry off toward the warehouse.

The auctioneer had already signaled for the bidding to begin on the first woman before Bander had reached the door of the warehouse. Ben and Zalon literally had to push their way to the entrance of the street where they intended to take up their position to watch the proceedings. Two women had already been sold before they saw Bander return with Strill and Bistan. Ben couldn't force himself to relax until he saw his friends take up their positions around the square. Within minutes, all five of them were stationed at strategic locations. Zalon and Ben stood together at the entrance of one street while Bander and the others covered the entrances of the three remaining streets leading into the square. Whoever bought Megan would have to leave the square by way of one of those streets after the auction because there were no other thoroughfares in or out.

After he saw everyone was in position, Ben could finally focus his attention on the base of the platform. He had taken little notice of the dark-haired woman standing in the red circle beside the auctioneer atop the platform because he was too busy stretching his neck trying to get a glimpse of Megan. When he finally managed to spy a familiar patch of wavy raven hair through the movements of the crowd, his heart jumped in his chest. It wouldn't be long now before Megan would be ushered to the raised floor and offered for sale. Forcing himself to be patient, he leaned against the wall of the building he was standing beside and turned his eyes toward the auctioneer and the young woman being offered for sale. His eyes went wide when he recognized the black-haired beauty as Tanel, the innkeeper's wife.

His initial shock soon turned to pity when he saw the tears streaming down Tanel's face while the auctioneer's hands roamed over her curvaceous form. The alcoholic contents in the flask were beginning to have an effect on the auctioneer. He had laid his pointer aside and started using his hands to show the slave's points of interest. The effects of the liquor had slurred his speech, but it certainly didn't affect his capability to drive the bids higher for his precious offerings.

Bids were being called out from every direction, most of them from men. However, there were two women bidding as well. Ben knew the women were owners of bordellos because Bander had pointed them out to him during the earlier bidding sessions for the men. He tried his best to forget the plight of Tanel and focus his mind on Megan, but he couldn't force his eyes off the poor girl on the platform no matter how hard he tried.

Tanel stood rigidly in place while the auctioneer pointed out her splendid features to the crowd with his roving hands. She was dressed in the customary garb that all the comely female slaves were required to wear by order of the Jando Village hierarchy. If Tanel had been fat or ugly, she would have been required to dress in a straight black shift, which would have been far less provocative, rather than the skimpy attire she had on.

It was clear that the flimsy top half of her attire was meant for display and not support. The tight-fitting red vest was made out of some shiny sheer material that reflected the light of the midmorning sun and did little in the way of supplying any hope of true humility for its wearer. Her shapely frame was packed so tightly into the frail garment that it looked as if the single strand of rawhide holding it shut might pop at any moment.

The bottom half of her ensemble wasn't much better, consisting of an extremely short skirt that rode low on the graceful incline of her hips and was slit halfway up the front from the hem. The slit was also adorned with wide reveres so Tanel's exquisite thighs were left exposed for the public to admire.

Ben lost track of the bidding when he became caught up in the plight of the innkeeper's young wife. Before the bewildered teen knew what was happening, the auctioneer had clapped his hands and called out, "Sold to that fine-looking man in the blue shirt."

Cutting his eyes in the direction the auctioneer was pointing, Ben saw Tanel's new master pushing his way through the crowd toward the platform. He cringed when he got a good look at the man.

Tanel's new master was fat and had bushy red hair and a stubbly silver-streaked beard. A patch covered the empty socket of his left eye. The huge greasy-looking character forced his way through the pressing throng and stopped near the base of the platform, where he quickly pulled out a large moneybag and counted out the sum of his bid. Then he placed the money in the clerk's outstretched hand. After the clerk handed him the girl's ownership papers, the one-eyed man stepped back and looked up at the frightened young woman still standing on the floor of the platform.

Tanel stood looking down at him with wide eyes as he yelled up at her in a deep, commanding voice, "Come down here, girl! You belong to me now."

Frozen with terror, Tanel locked her hands tightly around the railing at the rear of the platform. She was unable to budge when the auctioneer tried to get her to walk back to the steps.

When he saw the way his new slave was behaving, One Eye waved for the auctioneer to step aside. "Never mind," he yelled. "I will take care of her myself."

Pulling up on the waistband of his breeches, the annoyed fat man forced his huge bulk to the back of the platform and up the stairs to where the horrified girl stood at the rail. With little effort, he managed to pry the screaming girl's hands off the railing and throw her over his right shoulder like a bag of flour. Then he proceeded to pelt her backside, to the delight of the cheering crowd, with the palm of his rough hand while he carried his squirming prize down the stairs. Tanel had stopped struggling by the time they reached the bottom of the stairs; the poor, fear-stricken girl had fainted. The hulking redhead suddenly stopped and glanced in Megan's direction before spinning around to look at Calor. Pointing over his shoulder with the thumb of his free hand, he asked, "Do you intend to sell that beautiful wench next?"

"Yes, I do," Calor replied, grinning evilly. "I do so by order of Lord Quander."

"Umm, I think I will stay a bit longer and bid on that one as well then," the burly beast replied.

Ben's heart sank when he heard the unpredicted remark from the greasy blob of manhood. The evil beast stood his ground and watched with a devious grin on his face as Calor escorted Megan up the stairs.

Chapter 26

The inebriated auctioneer wasted no time in walking up to Megan and wrapping his arm around her waist after she reached the top of the stairs. He drew her to his side and kissed her lightly on the left cheek while he ushered her toward the center of the selling circle. After positioning the girl inside the circle, he leaned close and whispered something into her ear.

Ben didn't know what the auctioneer said to her, but it had a disgusting effect on Megan. The outraged young woman suddenly twisted out of the drunken man's wanton embrace and punched him in the face as hard as she could before turning to run back toward the steps and was immediately confronted by Calor. The plantation guard quickly grabbed Megan and held her there until the auctioneer could take her by the hand and forcibly drag her back to the center of the red circle, kicking and biting. The auctioneer slapped her hard across the face after he finally managed to get her back inside the circle. The blow was hard enough that it staggered the girl and made her obediently stand still. Then she remained inside the circle and stared silently down at the floor of the platform.

Ben started to move toward the platform with murder in his eyes, but he didn't take more than a solitary step before he felt the point of a spear pressed lightly against his spine.

"Do not force me to stop you, Ben Thomas," Zalon whispered. "You cannot do anything to help your wife just yet. You will certainly be captured if you reveal yourself to Calor and his men now. Stay put, or you both might end up spending the rest of your lives as slaves. No one will ever be able to help you then."

Ben wheeled around to face the elder man. "I'm sorry, Zalon. I saw red for a moment when I saw the way that guy was manhandling Megan."

Zalon lowered his spear. "I am sorry that you have to watch this, but we must have patience. Whatever happens to your wife on that stage will never be as bad as what will happen to her if our plans are foiled before we have a chance to help her."

Ben wiped beads of sweat from his forehead with the back of his hand. "Thanks for keeping me in check, Zalon."

"I will stay close by, but you must learn to control your own emotions. I cannot do that for you."

Ben nodded and turned his attention back to the platform.

Megan stood with her eyes turned toward the floor while the auctioneer stirred the excited crowd into a bidding war. The women's slave keeper had taken great care in preparing Megan for the auction. Her hair was tied back in a ponytail so that her immaculate black tresses wouldn't hide her beauty from the crowd. Even though she stood with her head lowered, her face was still visible to the crowd of hopeful bidders. Her doeskin dress had been replaced by slave's attire, which was almost an exact duplicate of Tanel's, the only difference being Megan's outfit was light blue instead of bright red, and the hems of her vest and skirt were decorated with yellow tassels.

The slave keeper had carefully chosen attire for Megan, which left much of her unblemished tanned skin exposed but still allowed her to retain some modesty. Her uncommon beauty would bring a high price as long as the crowd could get a good look at what was being offered, so she was forced to wear an outfit that would normally be worn by brothel slaves.

The auctioneer was too busy working the excited multitude into a bidding frenzy to notice that Megan was trying to hide behind him. When he finally realized what she was trying to do, he stepped back, took her delicate chin in his rough hand, and forced her to raise her face so the crowd could get a clear view of the exotic beauty.

"As you can see, ladies and gentlemen, this young woman is one of the most beautiful crossbreeds I have ever had the pleasure of selling. She is a very exotic beauty, is it not? What will you bid for this most beauteous creature? Come now, I know there is not a man or woman among you who would not like to own such a beauty as this. Give me your highest bids now!"

A flurry of new bids started, which lasted for only a few seconds before the number of hopeful buyers had dwindled to a few men and one woman.

Zalon moved close to Ben and whispered into his ear, "I fear that Bander was right. Your wife's beauty has driven her price higher than I expected. Her new master may not be satisfied with mere money and property. She will bring a higher price than I have ever heard of any slave being sold for in the city before. We will most definitely have to leave the city immediately after we free her, if we manage to do so."

Ben half-turned and looked at Zalon out of the corner of his eye. "Whatever it takes," he replied. His anger grew deeper when he turned back toward the platform and discovered that the auctioneer was now fondling Megan to the delight of the cheering crowd.

The drunken seller of slaves and livestock had moved behind the beautiful offering and started rubbing his hands over the round curves of her hips and outer thighs in a circular motion. He poked his head from behind Megan's and peered out at the crowd over her left shoulder. "Now, gentlemen, just imagine yourselves in my place right now. What is it worth to you to own a woman of this caliber?"

A rough voice called out from the base of the platform, "I bid three thousand dinots."

Ben quaked with anger when he recognized the voice as that of the same one-eyed man who had bought Tanel earlier.

"We have a bid of three thousand dinots," the auctioneer yelled. "Do I hear higher?"

The other three bidders remained quiet for a moment before a woman suddenly called out from far back in the crowd. "Three thousand one hundred dinots." It was the blonde woman who had bid on Tanel earlier.

The intoxicated auctioneer shook his head in disgust and cried out in a slurred voice. "Surely this beautiful treasure is worth more than a mere thirty- one hundred dinots. I think I will show you just what you are bidding for." He quickly moved his roving hands up over Megan's flat stomach and attempted to unfasten the front of her vest with fumbling fingers.

Megan bent over and screamed. Twisting out of his drunken grasp, she darted across the platform with the auctioneer at her heels. He caught her before she could reach the top of the steps and wrapped his long arms around her. Holding her with one arm wrapped tightly around her waist, he quickly pinned both her arms at her sides with the other and spun her back around to face the cheering throng. He continued to hold the squirming girl with his right arm while he caressed her face with his left hand. "Now, what are the bids for this scrappy young female?" He had to yell out in his loudest voice to be heard above the angry girl's protests.

"Let me go, you filthy pig," she screamed, trying desperately to kick free.

The exhilarated multitude responded with another barrage of furious bidding until the selling price for the beautiful slave was driven up to five thousand dinots.

Zalon had to physically hold Ben back twice while they were forced to watch Megan's mistreatment on the auction platform.

The wild bidding ceased as quickly as it had started. One last bid had been offered, and the crowd quieted. Ben had been unable to see or hear who had made the final bid.

The auctioneer relinquished his hold on the squirming girl and left her to drop to her knees on the floor of the platform where she remained, exhausted and gasping for breath. The auctioneer leaned out over the railing of the platform, he himself exhausted from his struggle with Megan, and weakly clapped his hands. "Sold to that very generous gentleman in the blue shirt for six thousand dinots," he gasped.

Ben quickly started moving toward the platform, but a firm hand on his shoulder jerked him to a sudden stop again. "Do not move, Ben!" Zalon's voice was low and calm. "Your wife has been bought by Smandit, the village blacksmith. His shop lies on this very street. We will wait here for the others to join us before we follow him."

Ben relaxed when he realized Zalon knew the man who had bought Megan. He figured if Smandit was a friend of Zalon's, they might not have a hard time persuading him to sell her to them once he knew what the circumstances were. He leaned back against the building, let out a deep sigh, and waited to see what the man looked like when he came forward to pay for Megan. He was totally unprepared for the shock he received when he finally saw the successful bidder moving through the crowd. It was the same hulking barbarian who had bought Tanel.

With Tanel in tow, Smandit walked up to the base of the platform and took out his moneybag once more. The smithy counted out the large sum and handed it to Calor. After obtaining the bill of sale for the precious gem, he strode over to the stairs of the platform and motioned for her to come down.

Megan slowly descended the stairs while readjusting her twisted vest with shaking fingers. She finished adjusting the flimsy garment before reaching the bottom step, but Ben thought it appeared to be much tighter than it had been before. He was beginning to fear that her protuberant breasts might burst through the thin material at any moment.

As soon as Megan stepped down on the ground, Smandit took her by the hand and started off in the direction of his shop with her and Tanel both in tow. He guided them right past Zalon and Ben. Megan had passed within three feet of Ben with her face turned downward, so she didn't even notice him. Since Ben was wearing the hood of his guard uniform over his head, he knew it would have been almost impossible for her to recognize him even if she would have looked in his direction.

Bander and Strill joined Ben and Zalon at the corner a moment later. Zalon looked around for the fifth member of their party before turning to Bander. "Where is Bistan?"

"I sent him back to the warehouse after I saw who had bought Megan," Bander replied. "When I realized it was Smandit, I thought we had better warn the others to get ready to leave the city as soon as we get back."

"Very good," Zalon replied. "I already told Ben we would probably have to leave the city as soon as we freed Megan because of the high price she brought. Now I am sure we must leave as soon as we free her because we will most certainly have to use force to take her from Smandit."

"I thought Smandit was a friend of yours by the way you talked earlier," Ben said. He was beginning to get an uneasy feeling in the pit of his stomach.

Zalon looked at him and shook his head. "Quite the contrary, Ben Thomas. Smandit has very few friends in Jando Village. He is one of the most disliked men in the city." Without saying another word, Zalon whirled around and motioned for the rest of them to follow him in the direction of Smandit's shop. The four would-be rescuers only walked about one hundred yards up the block before Zalon signaled for them to stop and pointed at a large building across the street. "That is Smandit's shop."

"We need a plan before we go in there," Bander said. "He will know something is not right if we do not have a good reason for disturbing him this late in the day."

Ben hesitated for a moment. Then he lowered the point of his spear to the surface of the cobblestone street and raised his right foot above its metal spearhead before slamming the heel of his boot down on it with all the strength he could muster, bending the point to a slight angle. "Is this a good enough reason to visit Smandit's shop," he asked, holding the damaged spear up for Zalon to see.

"Very good," Zalon said. "Remember not to act too anxious, or the smithy may realize that we are up to something. Now, let us get moving before it is too late!"

As they started across the street, Ben wondered what Zalon meant when he said, "Before it is too late." *It's only been a few minutes since Smandit bought Megan. What could happen in such a short time?*

The four plantation guards stood on the front stoop of Smandit's shop a few seconds later. A woman's scream came from inside the building just as Zalon raised his hand to knock on the door. After hearing the scream, Ben rushed forward and started pounding on the door with such force that he almost shook it off its hinges. He would have kicked it in if Bander and Zalon wouldn't have restrained him.

"Who is out there?" the voice sounded cold and harsh.

"We are guards from Plantation Zalon," Zalon answered. "We have a spear that needs mending before we leave the city for the plantation."

"Go away! Come back tomorrow, and I will repair it then," the voice replied, sounding irritated.

"We need it repaired now," Ben yelled.

"I'm too busy to repair it now," Smandit yelled. "Go away!"

Ben was about to give another angry retort when Zalon laid a hand on his shoulder and gave him a stern look.

"We are willing to pay you three times your normal fee if you will repair it now," Zalon replied calmly.

There was a brief silence before Smandit answered again, "Three times the normal fee, you say?" His tone had suddenly become more civil.

The door suddenly flew wide open, and the portal was filled with the blacksmith's immense form. "Come in, gentlemen. Welcome to my humble shop."

It didn't take them long to figure out who the author of the scream was after they entered the building. In the center of the single large room, Megan and Tanel were bound with their backs toward each other on opposite sides of one of the heavy wooden pillars that supported the weight of the building's roof. Their wrists were clamped in manacles attached to iron pegs driven into the pillar a foot above their heads. Smandit had wrapped leather straps around them from their waists to their ankles in order to hold them tight against the pillar to restrict their movements. The straps were pulled so tight that neither of them could move their legs more than a fraction of an inch.

Tanel was unconscious with her chin resting on her chest and her body hanging limp in her bonds. A brand of ownership had been seared deep into the side of her left thigh just below the hip. The vicious wound was still smoking when the four men entered the building.

Megan never tried to turn to look at the strangers; she was too busy struggling to free herself from her bonds. Ben could hear her weeping through the gag that was stuffed in her mouth.

Smandit walked over to his beautiful new possession and slapped her roughly across the face. "Be still, wench, or I will brand you now," he grumbled. He turned back to face his customers when the girl stopped squirming. "Now which one of you has the spear that needs mending?"

"I do," Ben replied, holding the heavy weapon out for Smandit to take. After he handed the weapon over to the smithy, he deliberately stepped up beside the pillar so Megan could plainly see him. He saw her eyes grow wide and gave her a quick wink while the smithy had his back turned to them while he examined the spearhead in the light of a nearby window.

Smandit was already preparing to straighten the spearhead by the time he had turned back around. He had taken it off the wooden shaft and placed it in the hot coals of his forge. As he did so, he worked the billows over the forge to make the coals burn hotter. It took hardly any time at all before the spearhead began to glow bright red from the intense heat generated within the firepit. After it became hot enough, the smithy withdrew it from the hot coals with a pair of tongs and placed it on a huge anvil and skillfully started to hammer it back into shape. He had to repeat the procedure several times before he finally managed to straighten the point to his satisfaction.

Ben's mind was racing while the blacksmith labored over the spearhead. He looked at his companions several times, hoping to catch a sign from them that they were ready to make their move. When he got tired of waiting, he walked over to Zalon and whispered to him in an annoyed tone, "Why don't we make our move now before the smithy begins to suspect us?"

Zalon shot him a quick glance and shook his head. "We will wait until he has finished repairing your spear first. We may need that weapon later."

A gruff voice suddenly spoke up behind Ben, causing him to jump unwillingly.

"Does this suit you, young man?" Smandit asked. He slapped Ben on the shoulder as he held the glowing spearhead only a foot from his face with the tongs.

Ben felt the intense heat from the hot metal splash into his face and stepped back. "Please, sir, the heat from that thing is unbearable."

Smandit quickly lowered the spearhead and turned to plunge it into a bath of water. The water hissed and bubbled as a cloud of steam rose to the ceiling. "Sorry about that, lad. I keep forgetting most people cannot stand as much heat as I can. I have grown used to it after so many years." He turned and held the spearhead up again for Ben to examine a few seconds later. "The blade is a bit dull. Would you like me to sharpen it for you?" Without waiting for a reply, he strode to the back of the shop where his grinding wheel was set up near the wall. Straddling the seat, he sat down and started honing a keen edge on the broad blade.

Ben spoke to his friends while the smithy couldn't hear him over the noise of the grinding wheel. "Do you think we should try to buy Megan from him?"

Zalon shrugged. "We can try, but I doubt that it will do much good. He paid a huge sum for her, and I doubt that I can offer him enough money to convince him to sell her. I'm afraid we will have to take her from him by force."

Bander leaned close to Ben and Zalon. "We may have to kill him in order to take Megan with us," he whispered. "The clumsy dolt has already burned a brand into the leg of that poor girl there." He nodded his head in the direction of Tanel's limp form.

Ben swung around and gazed at the unconscious girl's leg. The burn was deep. The edges of the brand were surrounded by charred flesh, destroyed by a severely overheated branding iron. Although the brand itself wasn't over half an inch high by three-quarters of an inch wide, the area of burned flesh around it was almost three times that size. It was clear that Smandit had held the hot iron in place too long, either on purpose or by mistake. It really didn't matter which was the case; the damage to Tanel's thigh was considerable.

Ben cringed when he thought of Megan going through the same torture. The thought of the blacksmith branding either of the women stirred his anger into a red rage. "If we have to kill him, let me do it," he said in a tone as cold as ice.

Zalon casually strolled over to Megan and pretended to survey her comely attributes. "I see you have bought two slaves today. I do not suppose you would like to sell this one," he asked, trying to sound apathetic.

Smandit remained silent while he tested the sharpness of the spearhead with his thumb. Then he strolled over to his workbench and started to mount it back on the wooden shaft.

Ben watched the smithy work on the spear with a puzzled expression. He wasn't sure what was wrong. He knew Smandit had to have heard Zalon's offer.

When Smandit finished mounting the spearhead, he turned toward Zalon and pointed the spear at his chest. His single eye seemed to gleam bright with recognition. "I know you. You are Zalon, owner of the warehouse in the town square. Why are you so interested in this slave? I heard that you do not care for slavery, so why should she be of any interest to you?"

Zalon smiled politely and answered in a level tone, "Because I wish to buy her from you."

Smandit shook his head. "She is not for sale. You could not offer me enough money to buy her. She is mine now, and she will always be mine. I spent most of my life's savings for these two beauties, and now that I have them, nobody is going to take them from me. Is that clear?"

The discussion was suddenly interrupted by a low moan from Tanel when she started to regain consciousness. She raised her head slowly and opened her watery blue eyes. With a mask of pain on her face, she shook her head and shuddered violently before starting to sob quietly. Her vision must have cleared for a moment because she seemed to see the strangers standing in front of her. "Please help me," she pleaded. Her voice was but a hoarse whisper.

Still holding the spear on Zalon, Smandit walked over to Tanel and looked into her glassy eyes. "Very good... she will be fine now," he said with a wicked grin. "That brand will bother her for a while, but it will heal in time. I can teach the other one how to please me while I wait for this one to heal." He nodded his head toward Megan and added, "I will brand her too later."

Ben clenched his hands into tight fists. "You will not consider selling that woman to us then?" he asked, quivering with rage.

The huge smithy swung around to look at the angry young man. "Why would three plantation guards and a warehouse owner want to buy this slave?" he asked. "I am sure the three of you could afford to buy another slave. Why do you want to buy mine?" An idea seemed to suddenly form in his dull brain. "Unless you are not plantation guards at all. Perhaps you are outlaws trying to free a friend. I think that is it."

He suddenly turned to look at the others and pointed at Bander. "Now I remember! It was you who bought the Pack woman from Lord Quander's plantation today?" He rubbed his chin thoughtfully as he slowly put the rest of the pieces of the puzzle together. "I think Lord Quander's guards would be very interested in what is taking place here."

When Smandit turned toward the door, Ben quickly stepped into his path. "You aren't going anywhere, blacksmith. You will either hand over my wife to us now, or we'll take her by force."

"Out of my way, boy," the burly blacksmith yelled, giving Ben a shove that sent him flying into the closed door of the shop. The force of the impact knocked the wind out of Ben, and he fell to the floor, gasping for breath.

Before Smandit could reach the door, Bander and Strill were upon him. With the speed and agility of a cheetah, the huge smithy swung the spear he was carrying and knocked his two assailants' spears out of their hands, forcing them back by sweeping the razor-sharp point of the weapon in a wide arch in front of them. As soon as the two guards fell back, Smandit pointed the spear at Bander's midsection and lunged at him.

Strill's quick reaction was the only thing that saved Bander's life, but it cost him his own. When he saw the smithy lunge at his friend, Strill pushed Bander out of the way. The spear caught him under the ribs of his right side and drove through his body, exiting the left side of his chest two inches below his armpit. The thrust was so powerful that the point of the spear lodged into the wall behind him and pinned the plantation guard's body to it in a standing position.

Bander fell to the floor and rolled over on his back just in time to see Smandit bend over and pick up one of the fallen spears. Before the stunned guard could get to his feet, the smithy was already lumbering toward him with the spear aimed at his heart. Bander started crawling backward in a desperate effort to avoid the deadly thrust, sure that he would soon join his friend in death. But before Smandit could carry out his deadly intentions, a heavy hunting spear flew across the room and embedded itself deep into his broad chest with such force that it drove him backward against the wall, where he slumped to the floor with his single eye staring in amazement. He opened his mouth and tried to speak, but only frothing blood came from between his parted lips. He coughed once before slumping over on the floor as the life-giving liquid drained out of him.

Ben was still on the floor gasping for breath when he finally managed to sit up. He glanced at Bander and was relieved to see his friend sitting up unharmed. When he cut his eyes to Strill's body pinned to the wall, a sudden pang of sorrow shot through him. He slowly turned and looked at Smandit's corpse lying on the floor beside him and shook his head. "That fat man had more speed than I gave him credit for." He gasped.

"Yes," Zalon replied. "Unfortunately, he took one of our friends with him to the other side before I could stop him."

Bander stood up and slowly walked over to where Strill's body hung on the wall. He slowly pulled the spear from the lifeless remains and carefully eased the body to the floor. "We had many good hunts together, old friend. I will miss you more than you ever would have believed."

Zalon moved close to his son and put a hand on his shoulder. "I know how you feel, son. The loss of a good friend is never easy to take. However, Strill knew he was giving up his own life to save yours. It should give you some comfort to know that he wanted you to go on living, even if he had to die. Now it is up to you to do something good with the life he has given you. We must concentrate on getting out of here so we can make good our escape from the city before anyone finds out what took place here."

Ben scrambled to his feet and ran to the pillar where Megan and Tanel were bound. He wasted no time in removing Megan's gag and freeing her wrists from the manacles. After he unwound the leather straps from around her, she threw her arms around his neck and started to cry freely. He held her close for a moment and then kissed her passionately. Her moist lips pressing tight against his gave him a warm feeling deep down inside. It seemed such a long time since he'd had an opportunity to really kiss her. *Now maybe we can start to live our lives together the way we planned*, he thought.

Megan was the first to speak when they finally broke their embrace. "Oh, Ben, I thought I would never see you again. I thought I was going to die after that animal bought me."

"I'm here now, Meg," Ben replied. "I'll never leave you again."

They turned their attention to the door when they heard Zalon speak up, "I know you two would like to talk, but whatever you have to say to each other will have to wait." He pointed at Tanel. "That poor girl needs our help right now."

Ben moved around the pillar and removed Tanel's bonds while Zalon held her in an upright position. The two of them slowly lowered the girl's limp form gently to the floor.

Zalon peered into her eyes and felt her forehead. "She has suffered a great shock, but she will be all right if we can get her out of here and get that wound treated right away."

Bander stood behind his father, watching him as he examined the young woman. "Are we taking her with us then?" he asked.

Zalon glanced back over his shoulder. "She will only be resold as a slave if we leave her here."

Megan spoke out in a quivering voice, "If another monster like Smandit buys her, she might be branded again. Nobody deserves that. We cannot allow that to happen to her again."

Zalon looked up at her and nodded before turning to face Bander. "It appears the young lady has decided for us."

Four plantation guards left the blacksmith's shop ten minutes later. Two of them supported a drunken comrade between them as they walked up the street joyously singing the garbled words of an old Gildorian folk song while the fourth followed close behind, towing a heavily veiled slave girl by a chain connected to a thick leather collar fastened around her neck. The motley group continued up the street leading to the town square where they entered Zalon's warehouse.

Half an hour later, the same group rode out of the city on horseback as part of a larger band of plantation guards heading back to their home plantation. One of them still appeared to be so drunk that he had to ride double with one of his friends so he wouldn't fall off the horse.

There were two women with the group. The first was a very comely woman with short brown hair and dressed in the traditional short wraparound and brief vest of a Gildorian free woman. The second was a younger woman wearing the gaudy tasseled garments of a brothel slave with her head and face carefully hidden behind a dark veil.

Chapter 27

The company of plantation guards rode on for almost three hours after leaving Jando Village until they came to a place where high forested hills bordered the road on both sides. Darkness had fallen upon them an hour earlier, so Zalon decided to call a halt to their travels for the night.

Ben and Bander reined their horses in beside Zalon's after he stopped the march. "Why are we stopping here?" Ben asked. "It will only take a few more hours to reach Quander's plantation on horseback if we keep going."

Zalon looked at the two younger men and nodded. "That may be true, but I prefer to wait here until morning so we can clearly see how heavily the plantation is guarded when we arrive. There is a good chance that Calor and his men will remain in Jando Village for the night and start back for the plantation in the morning. I thought we could spare at least a few hours rest before moving on again if they do. We will leave the road here and ride up into the hills to find a campsite for the rest of the night. That way, if Calor and his men should happen to pass this way before morning, they will not see us and warn Lord Quander that we are coming. That is not very likely though since Quander doesn't own horses. It should take Calor and the other guards at least three days to get back to the plantation on foot. We should have time to make our strike and be long gone before they return. Besides, we need to get that poor girl's leg treated before we can go much farther."

Ben saw the wisdom in Zalon's reasoning. If nothing else, he learned from experience that thinking things over was always the best approach before any serious undertaking, especially if someone else's well-being was at stake. In this case, Tala's safety and Tanel's future health would both be affected if their plan failed.

"Shall I tell the others we are turning off the road here then?" Bander asked.

Zalon gave a solemn nod. "Yes. Give the order, but be quiet. We do not want anyone who might be close by to know we are here."

A few minutes later, Zalon led the band of rogues up into the dark, forested hills to find a campsite for the evening. An hour after that, a circle of eight small tents stood in a hidden clearing on the hillside with a small campfire burning at its center.

Ben stood watching Xanet as she sat stirring the contents of a small pot resting over the fire. "How soon will the herbs be ready?" he asked, bending down to check the pot's smelly contents.

"Not for a while yet," Xanet replied. "The oil has not started to come to the surface of the water yet. It will be a few more minutes before I can prepare the poultice for Tanel's leg."

Ben straightened and returned to the tent where Megan was busy tending to the delirious young woman. He knew Xanet would bring the poultice in with her when it was ready. He just hoped that it would be soon because he was really beginning to get worried.

Earlier, during the ride from Jando Village, Tanel had awakened twice. Both times, the poor girl had cried out because of the excruciating pain in her charred thigh. It was all Bander could do to prevent her from falling off the horse when she began to squirm and wriggle, trying to break free of her invisible tormentor's embrace. When Bander finally managed to convince Tanel that she was safe and that Smandit couldn't hurt her anymore, she quieted down and dropped back into a red-hot stupor.

Ben and Megan helped Bander pitch a tent and lay the comatose girl inside it while Xanet started to prepare the poultice for her leg. After Bander left to attend a meeting that Zalon was holding with the rest of the men to discuss plans for Tala's rescue, Ben chose to stay behind and help Xanet and Megan take care of Tanel.

Half an hour later, Ben was kneeling on one side of Tanel while Megan knelt on the other as they carefully removed the plantation guard's pants and hooded vest that had served as her disguise when they left Jando Village. Zalon had cleaned the burn before he and Bander had slipped Strill's clothes on over Tanel's slave garments so they could transfer her from Smandit's shop to the storehouse without her being recognized by any of the townsfolk. Further treatment of the wound had to wait until they made good their escape from the city.

"She's as hot as a rock in a firepit," Megan exclaimed, pulling her hand away from Tanel's forehead. She had started to administer cold, wet compresses to Tanel's head and face while Ben did the same to the wicked burn on her now-infected thigh.

Ben shook his head in pity as he applied another compress to the infected area. "It's a good thing we didn't leave her back in Jando Village, or she would probably be worse off than she is now."

Megan didn't say anything for a moment and then breathed out deeply before allowing the lingering horror in the back of her mind to surface. "It could just as easily have been me," she said.

Ben glanced at her with a somber look in his eyes. "Smandit would have died a lot sooner if it would have been," he replied bitterly.

Xanet slipped quietly into the tent carrying the hot poultice of herbal oil on a thin piece of cloth and knelt down beside Ben. She glanced back and forth from him to Megan and said, "One of you will have to leave. There is not enough room in here for more than two of us to work on Tanel's leg properly. The other must stay and help me hold her down. She will experience a great deal of pain for a few seconds after I apply the poultice to the wound. She might thrash around and hurt herself if she is not restrained properly."

Megan gave Ben a meaningful glance and nodded. "I'll go. You're stronger than me, so you should be the one to stay." She patted him on the shoulder before standing up and disappearing through the tent flaps.

"Hold her arms," Xanet ordered. "I will sit on her legs and tie the poultice over the burn. Now get ready. This should only take a moment."

Ben positioned himself with his knees resting on the ground on either side of Tanel's head before leaning over to pin her elbows down with his hands. When he had a solid grip on her, he nodded toward Xanet, who had already positioned herself over Tanel's legs.

"Okay, hold on to her tightly now." With the skill of a practiced physician, Xanet applied the cloth and poultice to the seeping burn and quickly tied it in place with two strips of cloth.

Tanel remained still for several seconds before the herbal oils started to do their work. As soon as the oils seeped into the burn and on into her bloodstream, Tanel's eyes opened wide, and she screamed in agony. She began to twist and writhe violently on the floor of the tent as spasms of pain shot through her tortured leg. Ben almost lost his grip on her elbows as he fought to restrict her movements but managed to hold on when he doubled his efforts. Xanet had fallen off Tanel's flailing legs, and a loose knee caught her under the chin, but she recovered quickly and managed to seize the girl's ankles. Holding them tight in her hands, Xanet was able to climb back over Tanel's thrashing legs and restrain them again. The delirious girl continued to scream and wriggle for several more seconds before her body convulsed with one last spasm of pain and went limp under Ben and Xanet's combined weight. She started to breathe in deep rhythmic gasps. Although her eyes had opened for a brief time, she showed no sign of recognition before they slowly closed again as a calm and peaceful sleep finally overcame her.

"She will sleep now," Xanet whispered as she crawled off Tanel's legs. "You can go join Megan and the others at the meeting. I will stay here with Tanel."

Ben headed for the tent flap but suddenly stopped and wheeled around before leaving. "Will she be okay?" he asked.

Xanet shook her head. "I have no way of knowing right now. I will know better in the morning. I am only guessing, mind you, but I think she will be all right if we managed to catch the infection in time. If we did, her leg will be sore for a while, and she will find walking difficult for a few days, but it should heal quickly after that."

Ben cast a worried look at the unconscious girl. "What if we didn't catch it in time?"

"Then we will be forced to take more drastic measures to save her life," Xanet replied glumly.

"You mean you may have to amputate her leg?" Ben gasped. Xanet nodded. "If that is what it takes to keep her alive."

It will be a terrible shame to have to amputate her leg, Ben thought.

Xanet reached out and touched Ben's arm as if she knew what he was thinking. She had the hint of a smile on her face when he turned to look at her. "I do not think we will have to amputate her leg, Benjamin Thomas. The infection did not have much time to travel very far yet. Zalon did a good job of cleaning the wound before she was moved from the blacksmith's shop."

The corners of Ben's mouth twitched up in a nervous smile. "I'm glad to hear that," he replied before leaving the tent.

Zalon was waiting for him when he stepped outside. "How is the girl?" he asked.

"Xanet thinks she'll be fine," Ben replied. "She is sleeping peacefully now."

Zalon shook his head. "It is a shame that such a lovely creature had to suffer a disfigurement like that. I am not sure she will ever be able to adjust to the fact that the scar will be permanent. Perhaps we will know better tomorrow." He clapped his hand on Ben's shoulder and smiled. "Right now, we have very important business to attend to. Come with me back to the meeting and join the others around the campfire to discuss our plans to rescue Bander's intended bride!"

It took almost an hour to formulate, but the plan to rescue Tala was finally completed and agreed upon by all the men in the camp. The plan would be set into motion before first light the next morning.

After the meeting ended, the group broke up, and the men headed for their tents. Ben went to the tent he and Megan had erected for themselves earlier, only to find it empty and Megan nowhere around. Thinking she had gone to check on Tanel, he walked over to the tent where she was housed. He was surprised to discover that the only other occupant of the tent with the comatose girl was Xanet.

Xanet had apparently lain down beside her patient and fallen sound asleep. When Ben heard the regular sound of their breathing, he realized his assumption was correct. He turned around and quietly stepped out of the tent to discover Zalon waiting for him.

The older man bent down and peered into the tent. "They will probably both remain asleep until morning," he whispered.

Ben nodded. "No doubt. They both have had a full day of it and will need all the rest they can get. We'll have to come back here and get them ready to move out as soon as possible after we attack Quander's plantation tomorrow."

Zalon smiled and clapped him on the shoulder. "You are learning fast, Ben. I have seen your youthful impatience begin to grow into wisdom during the very short time I have known you. This is a good thing. Our newly formed tribe should have a very wise leader one day." Ben didn't give very much consideration to what Zalon was saying; he was too busy looking around for Megan. When Zalon noticed his odd behavior, he reached out and shook him lightly to get his attention. When Ben turned to look at him again, Zalon asked, "Is something wrong?"

"I don't see Megan anywhere about," Ben replied. "She's not in our tent. I thought she might have come to check on Tanel, but she isn't here either."

Zalon just smiled and whispered, "She is safe. She is sitting over there in the woods by herself." He pointed to a large tree near the edge of the campsite. "I have been watching her to make sure she does not stray too far from camp. Sometimes women like to be alone after they have been through a trying experience, like the one Megan went through today. However, I have found that Xanet is always ready to talk about such things after she has had a little time to herself. Take an older man's advice and let her have a few more minutes to herself before you go to her."

Ben decided to heed his new friend's recommendation not to go rushing off after Megan just yet. "Thanks for the advice. My grandpa had to give me a short talk every once in a while to remind me not to go rushing off without taking time to think things over first. I guess this is one of those times."

Zalon glanced at the tent where his wife was sleeping with her patient. "Perhaps you can answer a question for me while you are waiting."

Bewildered, Ben gave him a puzzled look. "What do you want to know?"

"Why do you think Porat sold his young wife? What could she have done that would have made him angry enough to condemn her to years of slavery?"

Ben shrugged and cleared his throat. *If Tanel wants to tell these people why she was sold as a slave, it's up to her. I won't be the one to tell them about her lasciviousness. Maybe now that she knows what kind of trouble her lust can get her into, she'll think twice before she ever sets her designs on another man. Besides, I don't really know why her husband sold her. I can only guess the real reason, although I have a good idea.* "I really don't know," he replied.

"I guess she will tell us sooner or later if she wants us to know," Zalon said. He pointed toward the giant tree near the edge of the camp again. "Go to your wife now! You will find her sitting just a little way beyond that tree."

Ben walked off into the dark forest in the direction Zalon had pointed. He stopped under the trees for a few seconds to let his eyes adjust to the darkness before he spied Megan sitting on a log beside a bubbling brook. The dim moonlight reflected off the shiny blue material of the brash slave garb she still wore. She was sitting with her eyes closed tight when he walked up and sat down beside her. She held them shut for a moment longer and then finally turned to look at him. She gave him a weary smile when her eyes came to rest on his shadowed face.

Ben was completely absorbed with taking in her beauty. Her skin seemed to glow in the dim light as he sat staring at her. She had removed the binding that held her hair in a ponytail and left it tumble down over her shoulders in dazzling smooth black waves. *I don't know what I would ever have done if anything would have happened to her.* The thought unnerved him and caused an involuntary shudder to shoot through his whole body. "I wish you wouldn't go off alone like that without telling anybody, Meg," he scolded softly.

Megan lowered her head and looked into the sparkling water of the brook. "I'm sorry, love. I was thinking of home, and I just felt like being alone for a while."

Ben leaned closer and slipped his hand up under her thick hair and gently began to massage the back of her neck. She sat still for a moment, letting the tension drain from her, and then she raised her head and turned to look at him with her left cheek resting in his open palm.

"I really miss home, but I don't miss it half as much when I'm with you." She sighed.

Ben caressed the side of her face. "Is that what you were thinking about just now?"

She nodded. "That. And something else."

"Something else?" Ben asked.

"Yes," Megan replied. "I was praying when you sat down beside me just now."

"May I ask what about?" Ben asked.

Megan nodded slowly. "I was thanking God that you came to get me so quickly after I was sold to that animal today. I don't know if I could have survived knowing that I might never see you or feel your touch again, especially now that I might be…"

"Now that you might be what?" Ben asked, giving her a puzzled look.

Megan shook her head and frowned. "Never mind," she said hesitantly. "It isn't that important."

Ben kept his hand on her cool cheek and continued to stare into her dark almond-shaped eyes. "You know, I miss home too. I only wish I had the nerve to tell you how I felt about you while we were still back there. Maybe we could have enjoyed each other's company a little more if I had.

Things might have been different if I would have told you how I felt about you before we got into this mess."

Megan pulled her face out of his hand and sat up straight. "That's just it, Ben. Even if you would have said something, it might not have made any difference. I only had mixed feelings for you then. I really didn't know I was in love with you yet. If things would have happened any differently, we might not be here together right now."

A sudden feeling of dread came over Ben when he realized what she was saying. "I guess God does work in mysterious ways," he said. "How do you feel about me now since we've been dragged to who knows where in the world, and you've had time to realize that I couldn't do a thing to stop it?"

Megan shook her head. "I don't know if I would have ever fallen in love with you if we wouldn't have been forced to live together the way we were."

Ben grimaced. "I just can't help feeling guilty about you having to spend the rest of your life here in this backward land. Do you really love me enough to overlook my being so inept? I mean... I've got a lot to learn about being a good husband. We really haven't been able to spend more than a couple of nights together since we got married. How long's it been, over two weeks ago now?"

Megan stood up and glared down at him with wide eyes. They stared at each other for several seconds before she finally stretched her hand out to him. "I think we were together long enough, Ben," she said. "Now, why don't you come back to the tent with me and let me show you just how much I do love you?" she added in a husky whisper.

Ben smiled as he reached up to take her hand in his and stood up beside her. Looking into her eyes, he felt reassured when she smiled back at him. Then he drew her into his arms and kissed her with all the pent-up passion built up him.

They remained in their tender embrace for several seconds before their lips finally parted, and they started back toward the camp. Their pace was a quick one. At least six days had passed since they had the opportunity to share the same bed together.

Chapter 28

Eleven men prepared to leave the rogue camp for Plantation Quander before dawn. The previous evening, they decided that the women would remain behind in the safety of the camp with two men left to guard them. If the rescue attempt was successful, the rest of the men would return to the camp for the women before moving on toward the Southern Mountains. If everything went well, they would be on their way south by noon. The two men left behind to guard the camp had orders to take the women and children south into the safety of the mountains by themselves if the rescue party failed to return before nightfall of the next day.

While the rest of the men were preparing to ride out of camp, Mota stood talking to Tolan with a glum expression on her face. "Bring our daughter back safely, my love."

The giant Pack leaned low over the side of his mount and kissed her tenderly. "I will not return without her," he said in a reassuring manner.

Bander rode his mount up beside Tolan's. "Nor will I." He held his spear up in his right hand. "I intend to fight until I have set the woman I love free."

Ben and Megan stood holding hands as they talked quietly to each other a short distance away.

"Please be careful, Ben," Megan whispered so only he could hear her. "I thought I would go mad back in Jando Village when I thought we would never see each other again. I really don't think I can go on without you now."

He hugged her and kissed her on the forehead. "Don't worry, darling. I'll be careful. There's too much at stake for me not to be."

Zalon stepped out of the tent where he and Xanet had been tending to Tanel and walked over to Ben and Megan. "The girl has regained consciousness," he said, glancing at Megan. "She is asking for you."

Megan seemed totally confused. "Why would she ask for me? I hardly know her. We only met each other in the slave house a couple of hours before the auction."

Zalon shrugged. "Maybe because you are the only person in our group she knows."

"Yes," Ben exclaimed abruptly. "You were with her when she was branded, so you are the only one, as far as she knows, who can even try to understand what she is going through right now."

Megan regarded Ben silently for a moment. "Maybe you're right. I'll go see her. Be careful, darling." She stretched up on her tiptoes and kissed him before stepping back to wave before he turned to mount his horse.

Ben quickly returned her wave. "I'll be back by this time tomorrow," he said before riding off to join the rest of the column. He reined his horse in beside Bander's and glanced back over his shoulder to watch Megan walk toward the tent where Tanel was waiting for her. He couldn't help wondering what Tanel wanted to see her about. He didn't have much time to ponder the matter because Zalon rode by a moment later and gave the order to move out.

Ben glanced up at the sun. Half the gleaming orb had risen above the horizon line by the time the band of rogues reached the boundary of Lord Quander's plantation. They had been traveling for over an hour and only managed to reach the hills bordering the plantation. It would be at least another two hour's ride before they reached the house, and Ben was beginning to feel uneasy. He had noticed earlier that several horses had passed the same way only a few hours before them.

Bander rode up and reined his horse in beside Ben's. "We still have a long way to go before we reach our goal," he said, glancing up at the sun.

"Yeah, I know," Ben replied. He pointed down at the ground in front of them. "I noticed these fresh tracks in the trail ahead of us. Looks as if there were at least five horses with riders. Since there aren't any towns or settlements anywhere between here and the plantation, I wonder if those riders might have warned Quander that we're coming."

Bander glanced at the tracks. "Father and Tolan noticed those tracks earlier when we came back out on the main trail this morning. They share your concern that Quander may be aware of our coming, so they have devised an alternate plan in case we find Quander's guards waiting for us when we arrive."

"One thing about it," Ben said. "We won't know for sure until we get there."

The rogues paused just beyond the crest of a hill overlooking Quander's house. At Zalon's suggestion, they had taken an alternate route that allowed them to approach the buildings of the plantation from behind instead of the frontal approach they had planned on taking in their previous plan.

Zalon dismounted and moved cautiously forward to peer over the top of the hill overlooking the house. Being careful to use some small trees that grew near the top of the rise as cover, he glanced down into the barnyard below and returned to the rest of the party a few minutes later with news that caused them a great deal of concern.

"There is no doubt about it now," he announced. "Quander has definitely been warned of our coming."

"Calor," Bander exclaimed.

"I am afraid so, son," Zalon replied. "I counted six horses tied outside in the barnyard. Since we all know Quander does not own horses, I would say someone has ridden all the way from Jando Village to tell him about what has happened there. Who else could it be but Calor? He must have heard about Smandit being killed and his slaves missing and guessed who was responsible. Then he came straight back here to tell Quander." He fell silent for a moment while he watched his son's reaction. "It is up to you now, Bander. Do you still want to continue with this mission, or would you rather return to camp? Tala's life will definitely be in danger for sure now."

Bander didn't hesitate before answering, "I want to go on. Tala's life is at stake." He turned to Tolan sitting astride his horse a short distance away. "Tala is your daughter, and I know you love her, but so do I. I will not ask you to risk her life if you do not want to take the chance of trying to free her. I will accept your decision regarding this matter."

Tolan dismounted and hefted his spear in the air. "I say we go in. I would rather see my daughter dead than leave her here to remain Quander's slave."

Bander hefted his own spear above his head and swung around to face the rest of the group. "If any of you want to go back, then go now."

"I will be at your side when you attack," an all-too familiar voice responded.

Bander and Tolan turned at the same time to discover Ben standing behind them.

"Tolan and I both want to thank you," Bander said. "You have proven yourself to be a true friend. Are you sure you want to risk your life for our family?"

Ben shrugged. "I'll always be ready to defend the lives of my friends. Besides, Megan and I didn't help Tala and Mota out there in those mountains just so they could be returned to Lord Quander and enslaved again. That's not the only reason I'm willing to help you. If it were not for you two and your friends, Megan would still be back in Jando Village with that wretched blacksmith. I can never repay all of you for risking your lives to help us."

Zalon moved closer to address the rest of the group. "Very well then. Are the rest of you with us in our endeavor to free Tala?"

The humans in the group stepped forward to stand beside their leaders in a line of alliance.

"We are with you," Bistan replied. "Without the four of you, our dream of finding a new country will be lost forever."

Tolan raised his spear over his head. "Listen to me, my fellow Packs! I cannot ask any of you to risk your lives or those of your loved ones. Quander still holds your families down there in his barn. Now that the scales may have been tipped in his favor, the danger has increased considerably for all of us and our families."

In a bold response to their leader's words, the Packs all dismounted their horses and hefted their spears in the air. They all pledged their devotion to the cause in unison. "We will fight for freedom," they replied.

Ben was lying under a clump of bushes near the top of the hill overlooking Quander's house a few minutes later. He didn't know enough about the layout of the plantation to help the others deliberate their plan of attack, so he volunteered to keep watch. From his hidden vantage point, he could see the whole barnyard. He remained hidden there for at least half an hour before he finally caught a glimpse of movement in the barnyard below.

A guard suddenly darted across the barnyard from the main house and went inside the barn. He stepped back outside a moment later with a Pack woman and guided her toward the house at spearpoint.

Straining his eyes, Ben finally recognized Tala and the man ushering her toward the house as Calor. He waited until Calor escorted Tala under the roof of the veranda before creeping from his hiding place and running to tell the others what he had seen.

The attack started as planned. The first to fall in battle was the guard stationed in front of the barn doors. One moment, he was standing at his station seemingly unconcerned, and the next, he was on the ground with a spear in his chest. He only managed to let out a short gasp before his eyes closed in eternal sleep.

The second man to meet death didn't do so as quickly, or as quietly. He was stationed at the gate of the fence surrounding the buildings of the plantation and was the only person to see his fellow guard fall in front of the barn. It was his cry of alarm that alerted the rest of the guards to the attack. He lay dead with an expertly thrown spear in his back the moment he left out his warning cry.

Quander had at least twenty guards at his disposal, and every one of them was in the thick of the battle. They would have made short work of the twelve rogues if it hadn't been for the quick action of Phlander.

It was Phlander's spear that killed the guard stationed at the barn doors. Before the battle could reach its zenith, Phlander removed the bar that held the doors of the barn shut and threw them wide open before rushing inside.

Ben watched the plantation guard run inside the barn to free the cowering Packs within. He tried to go inside with Phlander but was delayed when one of Quander's men confronted him. Ben didn't know much about spear fighting, but he was forced to learn in a hurry. It took him a while; but thanks to his youth, superior muscle mass, and speed, he was finally successful in dispatching his adversary. But the delay was long enough for Phlander's fate to be sealed. Ben turned in time to see Phlander heft his spear high over his head and cry out to the Packs just before a dark figure silently skulked into the barn behind the unsuspecting guard. Ben desperately tried to warn Phlander, but the noise of battle drowned out his warning cry. The next few seconds passed so quickly that he couldn't do anything but watch the terrible scene unfold.

Phlander stood with his spear held high over his head. "We have come to free you. Tolan is with us and is fighting against Quander's guards in the barnyard. Come join us in the fight for freedom! Mighty Tolan will lead you to victory."

Several of the Packs took a few hesitant steps forward and glanced out into the barnyard. When they heard the noise of battle, they grew even more hesitant until one of them spied a familiar figure wielding a heavy spear in the midst of the battle. The excited Pack spun around and cried out to his fellow equines. "Phlander tells the truth. I can see Tolan outside even now."

Phlander hefted his spear over his head again. "Fight with us now! Fight for your free—"

Those were Phlander's last words. Before he could finish, he had been run through from behind. His spear fell to the floor, and his mouth flew open as he began to cough. He looked down at the spearpoint protruding from the front of his chest as bubbling red froth flew from his parted lips. He stood there for a moment, staring at the bloody spearhead, as if wondering what it was doing there, before sinking slowly to his knees. He silently knelt there on the barn floor for a moment before the spear was finally withdrawn from his back, and his lifeless form was kicked facedown to the floor.

Calor left out a triumphant howl after killing Phlander and then peered at the cowering packs. "I will do the same to any of you who try to come through that door," he yelled. He laughed as he backed out of the barn. He must have thought his victory over the Packs was complete because he didn't even bother to close the doors once he was outside. His evil smile quickly faded when he turned and found himself standing face-to-face with Ben Thomas.

"Hello, Calor." Ben's face was stern, but his voice was unsteady. "I saw you kill Phlander. Now it is your turn to die."

Calor raised his spear and spoke in a low growl, "You will be the one to die, Pack thief."

Ben raised his own spear in an awkward defensive position. "We'll see about that." Fear was building up in him, but he stood his ground. He couldn't afford to back down now. He knew Calor would kill him the moment he turned his back on him.

Calor suddenly lunged at Ben's midsection, and Ben knocked the deadly tip wide of its intended mark with a quick swing of his own spear, more out of fear than skill. For the next several seconds, the fight was thrust and parry, parry and thrust, with neither man able to gain an advantage over the other. Ben's confidence began to build in his ability to defend himself with the unfamiliar weapon. However, Calor soon found a weakness in his style and quickly took advantage of it. Every time Calor thrust at him, Ben shifted his weight and parried to the left. The ugly plantation guard quickly made a last-second change in his method of attack and shifted his own weight. The next time Ben parried to his left, Calor spun around to his right in a full circle. Before Ben could regain his balance, Calor had spun around and slammed the shaft of his spear across the back of his knees. The force of the stinging blow knocked Ben facefirst to the ground. When he tried to break his fall with his hands, his spear was jarred loose and went flying out of his reach. Ben quickly rolled over on his back in a last-ditch effort to save himself, but when he turned, Calor was already standing over him with his spear ready to deliver the fatal lunge.

With his spear aimed directly at Ben's heart, a sneer crossed the plantation guard's face when he saw the fear in his adversary's eyes. "The time has come for you to die, Pack thief." Then the look on Calor's face suddenly changed as his sneer was replaced with a look of shocked confusion. A stream of crimson suddenly appeared at the sagging right corner of his mouth and started to flow down over his chin. Without making a sound, the dirty guard toppled over backward with his eyes staring wide in death.

Ben tore his eyes off the corpse of his fallen enemy and looked up into the familiar face of the man standing over it with a bloody spear in his hand. "Bodon," he cried. "Where did you come from?"

The short plantation guard grunted as he nodded his balding pate. "I took my wife from the plantation when Calor returned and told Lord Quander what had happened in Jando Village. We have been hiding in the forest a short distance from here. I decided to stay nearby for a while to see if Bander would return with Tolan. I thought I might be needed here when I heard the fighting. As it turned out, you were in much need of my help."

Ben scrambled to his feet and clapped Bodon on the shoulder. "Thank God you showed up when you did, my friend. I would be dead right now if you hadn't."

Bodon merely nodded and bent down to pick up Ben's spear. Then he held the weapon out to him and spoke in a level tone, "You will need this. The fighting is not over yet."

Ben smiled as he took the weapon from the muscular little man. "Thank you for my spear, and for my life."

Bodon grunted his acknowledgment before turning to run inside the Pack barn. "You Packs, come out and fight for your freedom!" he shouted. "Calor is dead."

An excited outcry came from inside the barn, and the Packs came rushing out into the midst of the battle. There were over sixty-five of them, and they rushed from the barn with a killing vengeance.

The tide of the battle changed within minutes. Quander's men were outnumbered over two to one. Although the plantation guards were armed with spears, they soon began to fall to the sheer numbers of the Pack and rogue forces. Every time a guard became engaged with one of the rogues, there was a Pack there to pounce on him as soon as his back was turned. Before long, all of Quander's men had either run off or were lying on the ground dead or dying. Only a handful had managed to escape the terrible onslaught of the determined rogues.

Quander stood alone on the veranda of his stone house with a double-bladed war ax in his hands when the fighting finally ended. The bodies of several dead Packs and his two bodyguards lay on the ground near the foot of his throne, the bodies of the Packs having been badly hacked by his war ax. Tala lay there too, struggling to free herself from her bonds.

The surrounding crowd started to press in closer. Realizing the battle was lost, the flabby brute bent down and grabbed the bound Pack girl lying at his feet. He lifted her into the air by her mane with one hand and held the bloody razor-sharp blade of his ax to her throat with the other.

Tala's ankles were tied together with a thick rope, so she couldn't use her feet to keep her balance. The only thing holding her upright was Quander's hand wrapped in her long apple-red mane. She tried to stand on her toes to help relieve the burden from her entwined tresses, but her feet couldn't touch the ground, and she swayed helplessly in her master's iron grip.

Quander cried out to the angry crowd around him, "Hear me now, all of you! If any of you takes another step, I will cut the little she Pack's head off."

"If you do, this crowd will rip you apart, Quander."

Confused, Quander strained his eyes to see the face of an old friend. "Zalon, is that you?"

Zalon moved to the front of the crowd. "Yes, it is me."

"I never thought you would turn against me, old friend," Quander said, shaking his head slowly.

Zalon smiled and spoke in a calm voice, "Let the girl go, Quander! She cannot harm you."

Quander shook his head more vigorously. "If I do, this mob of madmen will rip me apart. You said so yourself."

"No, I will not let that happen." Bander stepped forward to stand beside his father. "All of this fighting and bloodshed was unnecessary. We only came here for Tala, and to free the Packs you so blatantly mistreat."

"You know I cannot just let the girl go, or any of the rest of my Packs for that matter," Quander growled. "They are my slaves, and you all know how I hate Packs. I would rather kill every one of them rather than let one of them go free."

Tala's eyes widened when she heard Quander's harsh remarks. She must have known he meant what he said because she increased her struggles to break free of his grip until he shook his hand to stop her. She tried to scream, but the gag in her mouth prevented her from uttering anything but short grunts.

Bander took a couple of steps closer. "Will you fight man to man for her then?"

Quander was clearly surprised by the challenge, but he only paused for a second before answering. "Yes," he said, nodding. "I am willing to do that. However, I must warn you that you will lose. No man can stand against my ax, and that is my weapon of choice."

Zalon interrupted the two men before they could challenge each other further. "No man can stand against you with that ax in your hand, Quander. What about hand-to-hand combat with no weapons?"

Quander threw his head back in a roar of laughter. "Very well, Zalon. Hand-to-hand, it will be. I need no weapons. There is still no man among you who can match me."

Bander threw down his spear and stepped forward. "Maybe not, but I can try," he exclaimed angrily.

The towering lord threw back his head and laughed again. After regaining his composure, he glared down at Bander. "Tell me, boy, why are you so willing to die for this pitiful Pack?"

Bander glanced at Tala and noticed the imploring look in her eyes. She had managed to gain her balance when Quander relaxed his hold on her hair and let her feet touch the ground. "Because I love her," Bander replied, casting Tala a sympathetic smile. "Forgive me for not telling you sooner, my love."

Quander released his hold on Tala's hair and left her to fall to the ground. "I would never have thought you to be a Pack lover, Bander. That is too bad. You will never have her now because you will be dead soon. Now prepare to die!"

"Wait," a baritone voice called out.

Everyone turned to see Tolan walking toward the front of the crowd.

"This is my fight," Tolan cried. "Lord Quander and his men have manhandled my family and my people for years. It is time to end his reign of terror over all Packs."

Bander hesitated a moment. Realizing Tolan wasn't going to back down, he backed away to give him room.

Tolan glanced at his daughter lying at Quander's feet and then at his young friend. "If I lose this fight, Tala will still have you. Now that she knows you love her, she will not want to lose you. I know you will take good care of my family if anything happens to me. I only ask that you will not leave any of my people behind when you depart from this plantation if I die." Bander slapped Tolan on the shoulder as the big Pack moved past him. "You need not worry about losing. Those muscles of yours are more than a match for that mountain of fat."

Tolan didn't reply. He just patted Bander on the shoulder and walked to the center of the circle.

Bander turned to look at Quander. "What about it, Quander?" he asked. "Do you accept Tolan's challenge? Or would you rather face me?"

Quander started to laugh again. "I will kill Tolan first, and then I will kill you," he roared. He assumed a crouched stance and growled through his teeth. "So, Tolan, I finally get to kill the Pack who started all of this trouble in the first place."

Tolan shook his head and replied in a low tone, "You only think you are going to kill me, my lord. But before you try, I want you to know one thing: I am the one who killed your brother. His neck snapped like a brittle stick in my hands."

At that moment, Quander chose to attack. He roared angrily and leaped for his enemy's throat with outstretched hands, but the combination of his enormous weight and Tolan's blinding speed caused him to miss his mark by two feet. Instead of grabbing Tolan's throat, he grabbed nothing but thin air. Before Quander could regain his balance, Tolan had stepped in close behind him and delivered a powerful chop to the back of his fat neck with the side of his hand. A loud cheer arose from the encircling crowd when they saw their champion strike the first blow.

Quander fell prone on his stomach with his face in the dust. He remained still for a few seconds before rolling over on his back and glaring up at the Pack with hate in his eyes. Then he grabbed a handful of fine dust and threw it in Tolan's face.

Tolan stepped back, momentarily blinded. Before the Pack could clear the dirt from his eyes, his gigantic opponent had regained his feet. Tolan was still unable to see clearly when a meaty fist hit him a tremendous blow in the face. The shock of the blow threw the Pack's head back with a force powerful enough to break an ordinary man's neck near the base of his skull. However, Tolan was no ordinary man. Thanks to the heavy muscles in his bull neck, the blow only caused the Pack to bark out in pain and grab the back of his head. Fighting to clear his blurred vision, he merely shook his head before launching a ferocious counterattack of his own.

Quander's massive girth slowed him down. Before he could deliver a second blow, Tolan was ready for him. Quander swung a hard roundhouse left, which Tolan easily eluded by stepping back. Then he quickly moved in to hammer a gut-wrenching blow to the plantation lord's midsection, which lifted him off his feet. Quander's feet hadn't even touched the ground again before Tolan delivered a second blow in the same place. A third and fourth punch landed on either side of his jaw before he even knew what was happening, and the plantation lord fell to the ground, coughing up blood and gasping for breath. Tolan stopped his attack and watched his former master groveling in the dust for a moment. Showing little emotion when he realized Quander wasn't going to get up, Tolan quickly turned and walked over to where Tala lay bound and gagged on the ground.

Bending down beside his daughter, he untied her ankles and helped her to her feet. After he removed the gag from Tala's mouth and started to turn her around to untie her hands, his poor hearing managed to catch a warning cry from the crowd. Tala turned her head to look behind her father and screamed in terror. Both warnings sent Tolan instantly into action again.

Wheeling around with blazing speed, the giant Pack reached up and grabbed the handle of Quander's double-bladed ax just before its heavy blade could split his skull. Keeping an iron grip on the ax handle, he snapped around behind Quander and pulled it tight against the front of his thick throat and steadily increased pressure with all the strength in his mighty thews. Tolan was exhausted, but he knew he couldn't let go. Not only his life depended on his strength now, but the lives of his daughter and future son-in-law as well.

Quander's tongue protruded from between his thick lips, and his eyes bulged as if they would pop out of their sockets as the ax handle slowly choked the life out of him. There was a tense moment, when the onlookers thought neither man would give, before Quander's body suddenly went limp and his hands slipped off the ax handle. He stood unmoving with his enormous body leaning back against the huge expanse of Tolan's chest for a moment. Then the mighty Pack finally let go of the ax and let it drop to the ground along with its dead owner. Justice had been served.

Bander rushed forward and took Tolan's forearm in his hands. "I knew you would not lose," he exclaimed. "Now you and your people are free. Free to follow Ben and the rest of us to a new land without fear of Quander, or anyone like him, seeking revenge."

Tala rushed forward, and Tolan threw his arms around her. The filly stood quietly sobbing against her father's wide chest while Bander untied her hands. As soon as she was free of her bonds, she threw her arms about her father's neck and kissed him on the cheek. "Oh, Father," she exclaimed, "I thought Lord Quander was going to kill you when I saw him coming at you with that ax."

Tolan bent down and kissed her on the forehead. He turned and looked down at his former master's corpse as if filled with a deep remorse. "I knew, if it came down to a battle of strength that I was the only one here who had a chance of defeating him. I am sorry I had to kill him. I would have preferred to let him live if I could have, but hate had completely destroyed his reasoning."

Zalon moved to stand beside Bander. "I know that your friends must be tired after such a battle, but we must get back to camp as soon as possible. The sooner we get out of this part of the country, the safer it will be for all of us."

Tolan nodded. "You are right. We should be going, but there is one thing we must take care of first." The giant Pack took his daughter's right hand in his and reached out to take Bander's right hand with the other. He had a broad grin on his face as he pressed their hands together between his and called out in a loud voice, "Now hear this, all of you! From this day forward, my daughter, Tala, shall be known as the wife of Bander! By my faith in the Great Creators, I proclaim it to be so."

Zalon stepped forward and placed his hands over those of the young couple and raised his voice to the crowd as well. "From this day forward, my son, Bander, shall be known as the husband of Tala! By my faith in the Great Creators, I proclaim this to be so."

The ceremony was a brief one, but to the newlyweds, it was the most wonderful one they had ever attended. After it was over, they embraced in their first long-awaited kiss of true love. Ben was the first to greet them when they started through the crowd of well-wishers.

Bander embraced his friend and spoke to him in earnest, "Now it is up to you to lead us to our new country, Ben." He raised his hands and motioned for the crowd to be silent. "Your dream has become ours, Ben Thomas. Lead us to our new country and freedom!"

"Yes," Tala broke in, "lead us to our new country and freedom!" The whole crowd soon took up the cry along with them.

Chapter 29

Seventeen horses returned to the camp the next morning, six more than had left the previous day. Thirteen of them carried riders while the other four pulled two wagons filled with Pack women, children, and supplies. The second wagon held the supplies that Zalon had ordered the men to take from the plantation. This had forced the men to walk, but none of them had complained about not being able to ride in the wagons with their families. They all knew the supplies would be needed during their long journey south. Ben, Zalon, Bander, Tala, and Tolan rode the four horses at the head of the column while the rest carried riders bringing up the rear. Ben rode his horse slightly ahead of the others while Bander and Tala rode directly behind him. Zalon and Tolan rode along on either side and slightly behind Ben while Mota, who had run out to meet the returning party, walked beside Bander and Tala's horse, talking excitedly with the newlyweds.

Ben's eyes came to rest on Megan and Tanel sitting beneath a giant monarch of the forest as he rode into camp. He tried not to act too surprised, but he felt his face turn crimson when they both looked up and waved to him at the same time. He wasn't exactly sure what to do, so it was a great relief to him when they both smiled and cried out, "Welcome back," as he rode past them on his way to the tent. Megan helped Tanel to her feet, and they walked over to greet him when he dismounted.

Tanel's leg was apparently well enough for her to walk on it without causing her too much pain. Although it was heavily bandaged, she still required some help from Megan to support her weight until she sat down on a stone beside the tent. Ben thought about offering to help her sit down, but he thought that he had better stay as far away from her as possible for a while.

"I'm so happy you made it back safely," Megan exclaimed, throwing herself into his arms and smothering him with kisses.

"Yes," Tanel added hesitantly. "We were worried about all of you. We can thank the Great Creators now that you have returned safely."

Ben glanced at Tanel before turning his attention back to Megan. "I take it the two of you have been getting to know each other better while I was gone."

"They have been doing just that," Xanet said, walking up behind Ben. "And I must admit that *you* have been the main subject of their conversations during the past few hours."

Megan looked up into his eyes and caressed the side of his face with her hand. "Tanel and I want to talk with you later. Maybe after we stop to make camp tonight, if you have time then. We can't waste time telling you what we were discussing right now because we have to pack up and get moving right away."

Ben glanced at the two women and nodded before turning away to tend to the business at hand. "All right, we'll talk later." *I wonder what they want to talk about,* he thought.

It really didn't matter because the group's business demanded his and his friends' undivided attention for the next four days.

※

On the fourth day after the battle at Plantation Quander, the band of rogues now consisted of over seventy Packs and humans. Although the Packs outnumbered the humans by at least six to one, they left most of the decision-making to the humans. It would be a long learning period before most of the equines would gain enough self-confidence to make any important decisions concerning the group as a whole. The only exceptions were Tolan and his men and Mota and Tala. Those few alone had enough confidence in themselves to make up for what the others lacked.

Zalon had chosen to march the tribe hard during the past four days. He was worried that the few guards who had escaped from Quander's plantation might have gathered together to follow them or that they might have returned to Jando Village to muster support from the other local plantation lords and form a posse to come after them.

Ben's only regret was that Din was not one of those among the dead. A thorough check of the bodies of the dead plantation guards failed to produce his remains, and Ben had a funny feeling that he hadn't seen the last of the little weasel.

Sundown was fast approaching when Zalon finally called a halt to the day's march. The leadership of the humans and packs was his sole responsibility. Although he seemed to feel extremely uncomfortable in his new role as chief, he didn't turn it down when Ben and Bander asked him to assume the position, if only temporarily.

Ben knew it was his fantastic idea of a new land where all people could live together in peace and freedom that caused the rest of the group to embrace him as a leader of their newly formed tribe, but he refused the position of chief when it was offered to him. He felt he was too young and inexperienced to accept the leadership role. However, he did agree to be Zalon's personal consul when he was asked to fill that position. Only after he agreed to be Zalon's personal representative did the older, more experienced man reluctantly step forward and take command of the optimistic group.

After they stopped, Bander rode up to Zalon and Ben and reined in his horse between theirs. Tala was seated behind Bander on his horse's back: a position she had been reluctant to relinquish since the day she had ridden off Quander's plantation with her new husband. "We have traveled far these past four days, Father. Do you think we can rest for a couple days before we move on again? Those who have to walk are growing weary."

"Yes," Tala added. "The little ones are getting very tired as well and are becoming a burden for their mothers. We could all use a good rest."

"I cannot think of any reason why not," Ben broke in. "There haven't been any signs of anybody following us." He turned and looked at Zalon. "Besides, I would like to have a council meeting with the other tribal advisors tonight before dinner, after we set up camp. That is, if it is okay with you, Zalon."

The chief gave Ben a thoughtful nod and then turned to Bander. "Tell Tolan there will be a meeting after we set up camp!"

"I will tell him," Bander replied, turning his horse to ride back along the column to inform Tolan of the sudden and unplanned decision.

The tents were pitched, and the campfires were burning brightly two hours later. Most of the occupants of the camp were busy cooking their dinners. However, one particular fire wasn't being used for cooking. It was the council fire of the tribal leaders.

Ben stood beside the fire burning at the center of the small circle of men he was addressing. "Zalon, you said you have traveled this way before. Do you have any idea what we may run into on the trail south?"

Zalon thought a moment before answering, "Many years ago, during my early days as a plantation guard, I came this way with two of my fellow guardsmen. The three of us went as far as the top of the great mountain range in search of wild horses for our home plantation. From there, we saw the vast grasslands that lay far below, but we never got to explore them. We intended to explore the strange land the next day, but my companions discovered a herd of wild horses in the foothills before we could do so. So instead of exploring the grasslands as we originally intended, we went after the horses and managed to capture six of the beasts. Not wanting to take a chance of losing any of the valuable animals while exploring, we decided to return to the plantation with them the next morning." He fell silent for a moment and then added, "I always intended to return one day and explore those grasslands, but something happened that just seemed to prevent me from coming back."

Ben waited a few seconds, and when he realized Zalon wasn't going to tell him what happened, he asked, "Well, what kept you from returning to explore the grasslands?"

Zalon suddenly started to laugh. "I met Xanet," he replied. "She was the daughter of the plantation lord I worked for. We fell in love and were married six months later. Needless to say, we have been together ever since. After Xanet's father died, I inherited the lordship of his plantation. I spent the next eighteen years as a plantation lord before I was forced to relinquish my title and moved to Jando Village."

Ben couldn't help smiling. He wouldn't want to go anywhere without Megan either; they had shared too many experiences together already.

Tolan didn't laugh aloud, but he did crack a wry smile. "I never had a chance to explore much more than the hills around Quander's plantation after my escape," he said. "However, I do know how the love of a woman can slow you down," he added, winking at Ben.

Ben shook his head and smirked at his older companions. "I'm afraid that isn't always true," he replied. "Megan and I have traveled a long way together."

Zalon suddenly grew somber. "That is why the tribe relies so heavily on you, Ben. Despite your youth, you have more experience at surviving in this wilderness than any of us."

"That is true," Tolan added. "Mota and Tala have told me how you used a strange weapon to kill the mithor that attacked them. Perhaps you will show us how to make such weapons one day?"

Ben nodded toward his giant friend. "If my calculations are correct, we are only a short distance from the hills where Calor captured us. Bander knows the way better than I do. He can lead us there tomorrow while the rest of the tribe is resting. We can retrieve the weapons then if they are still there."

"So be it," Tolan exclaimed. "You three will ride to the cave tomorrow and retrieve the weapons while I remain here and watch over the camp."

The following morning Ben, Bander, and Zalon set out for the cave that Ben and Megan had set up housekeeping in almost five months earlier. He hoped their bows would still be in good condition when they reached the cave because they never had a chance to store them properly before they were captured. With any luck at all, the bows and arrows would have remained undisturbed since they had last been used. Mice or rats could easily have chewed on them during the time they were gone. Both bows had been left in a corner of the cave along with the two quivers of arrows. Din didn't realize the value of the strange weapons, or he would have brought them along when he caught Megan inside the cave. Ben couldn't help thinking how different things might have turned out if he would have remembered to take his bow with him that day. But that was in the past. He had to think about how the weapons could help his tribe now.

It took most of the day for them to reach the little canyon where the lair was located. Thanks to Bander's leadership and good sense of direction, they were able to find the cave quickly.

They approached the lair cautiously in case another mithor or some other wild animal might have taken up residence there after it stood empty for so long. It turned out that their caution was unwarranted. The cave was still unoccupied, except for a family of mice and a few other small animals that had moved in during the owners' absence.

Zalon remained outside on lookout while Bander followed Ben inside the cave. Ben lit the torch, which he found still standing outside the entrance, and used it to burn the cobwebs out of the doorway.

Once they were inside, Bander got his first look at the place where his wife and mother-in-law had remained in hiding for so long. He studied the stone walls around him carefully. "So this is the place Tala has told me so much about," he said.

"This is the first place Megan and I chose to call home after we were brought to Gildor," Ben replied.

Bander pointed at the fur blankets on the floor near the firepit. "Is that where Tala and Mota slept?" He seemed very interested in anything that had to do with his wife's brief hidden past.

Ben understood why because it was the only time Bander had ever lost total contact with Tala since he had known her. He kicked at the musty blankets with the toe of his boot. "Yes, she and Mota slept on these blankets Megan and I gave them."

Bander looked down at the blankets, now covered with a heavy layer of dust, then at the bed in the back of the cave. He had a solemn look on his face when he turned to look at Ben again. "Tala told me that she would have gladly shared your bed as a second wife if you would have allowed her to."

Ben flashed a nervous smile and nudged Bander in the side with his elbow. "I knew that a girl as beautiful as Tala had to have someone who loved her. I told her that, but she didn't seem to think I knew what I was talking about at the time. It's a good thing you showed up when you did, or things might have been a lot different. If Tala and Mota would have stayed with us much longer, they just might have persuaded me to take Tala as a second wife one day."

An amused smirk crossed Bander's face, and he chuckled softly. "I guess it was a good thing I showed up when I did then," he replied, slapping Ben on the back. "Otherwise, you would certainly have your hands full catering to three women now."

Ben shot a puzzled look at his friend and shook his head. "I really don't think Mota was interested in me, Bander. She loves Tolan too much to take up with another man. Besides, she seems capable of taking care of herself when she has to."

"I was not referring to Mota," Bander replied in a more serious tone.

Ben walked over to the corner and picked up his bow. "Who then?" he asked, inspecting the string on the bow for damage.

Bander seemed surprised. "You mean to tell me that you really do not know? Megan has not told you what she and Tanel were talking about the other day while we were off attacking the plantation?"

Ben shook his head nonchalantly as he continued to inspect the bow. "Not really. We haven't had much time to ourselves these past four days. I've been so busy tending to all the tribe's problems that I've barely had enough time to talk to Meg at all. I hate it when my responsibilities keep me from spending time with her." He had just started to inspect the arrows in his quiver when he suddenly felt Bander's hand on his arm and turned to look at him. "What is it, my friend?"

"You have not caught on yet, Ben. Mota was not one of the women I was talking about when I said you would have your hands full catering to three of them."

"Well, you didn't really answer my question," Ben retorted.

Bander threw his arms up in disgust. "That is what I have been trying to do, but you are not listening to me. You would rather inspect your weapons than listen to what I am trying to tell you."

Ben shrugged and put the quiver down. "You're right. I haven't been paying much attention. I'm sorry. Please go on. I'm listening now."

"I was talking about Tanel," Bander replied. "She is in love with you." "But... but that's impossible," Ben stammered. "We only met each other a few days ago. I haven't even been very nice to her since she tried to put the make on me back at the inn."

Bander shook his head slowly. "Nevertheless, what I am telling you is the truth. I do not understand the way women think any better than you do. Mota told me about this surprising development yesterday. She must have thought that Megan had mentioned it to you by now."

Ben shook his head as he picked up Megan's bow and started to inspect it. He tested the string with nervous fingers as he thought about what Bander had just told him. "I've got to talk to Megan when we get back to camp," he mumbled to himself. *Lord only knows what she's been thinking these last few days. I hope she doesn't think anything happened between Tanel and me that night at the inn. I'll kill Tanel if she tries to drive a wedge between us.*

The return trip to camp seemed to take forever to Ben. He rode slightly ahead of his companions and never looked back. While Bander and Zalon kept a steady conversation going between them, Ben was silent and remained deep in thought. He loved Megan with all his heart, but he was worried that Tanel's admission of her love for him might be a ploy to drive them apart.

It was early the next morning when the weary travelers rode into the sleeping camp. The only people awake were the men on guard duty. One of them waved to them as they passed by, but Ben barely noticed him. His thoughts were on other matters. He rode directly to his and Megan's tent and dismounted. Bander took the horse's reins from him and offered to take care of the animal. After he watched Bander lead the animal away, Ben turned and stepped into the tent. The dim light of a small oil lamp revealed that Megan was still fast asleep. He thought about waking her up and asking her what she and Tanel had wanted to talk to him about, but decided it could wait until after he had rested first. Anything she had to tell him could wait until morning. They would both be able to think better when they were wide awake. He quietly slipped out of his clothes and slid under the blankets beside his wife.

Chapter 30

Ben awoke to the tantalizing aroma of hot stew drifting into the tent. He propped himself up on one elbow and inhaled deeply. It was the first time he had smelled good hot stew since Bander had secretly fed him and Megan that night on Quander's plantation. Sitting up, he glanced over at the pile of blankets beside him and discovered that Megan's side of their crude bed was empty. *Maybe that's her cooking the stew*, he thought. His stomach started to rumble as he kicked off the rest of the blankets.

He quickly dressed and poked his head out through the tent flaps to let the morning sun shine full on his face. Turning his eyes toward the cooking fire, he saw Bander sitting on the opposite side of the fire, anxiously watching her as she stirred the contents of a pot sitting over the flames. Tala soon joined them at the fireside with a load of firewood in her arms. After carefully stacking the wood beside the fire, she sat down beside Bander and leaned over the pot to take a deep whiff of its delicious contents.

"The stew smells very good," Tala said, leaning back and looking across the fire at Megan.

Ben stepped out of the tent. "So… I sleep a little too long and look what happens! I find my friends waiting to steal my breakfast."

Bander looked up, shrugged his shoulders, and smiled as he held his hands out at his sides. "You will have to forgive us, Ben. We did not know when you intended to get up, so when Megan asked us if we would like to join her for breakfast, we happily accepted the offer."

Megan looked up at Ben as she stirred the hot brew with a wooden spoon. "Naturally, me being the kindhearted person I am, I offered to share your breakfast with Bander and Tala."

Ben smiled at her and nodded. "I hope you made enough for all of us. I could sure use a good bowl of stew right now. I think I ate at least ten pounds of dust riding to the lair yesterday. The dust must be in my stomach yet. I can still taste it."

Megan poured some of the pot's contents into a wooden bowl and held it out to him. "This ought to stick to your ribs. It has some of the smoked meat in it that the men took from Lord Quander's plantation."

Ben took the bowl and thanked her. He took a sip of the hot broth while he watched to see if she showed any signs of uneasiness. He figured she would let him know if she wanted to talk to him. *She seems happy enough*, he thought. *Maybe she isn't too upset about this matter concerning Tanel.*

Megan continued to stir the contents of the pot for another minute or so and didn't look up until after she had poured some of the steaming hot mixture into two more bowls. Bander and Tala sat sipping at the hot stew and commenting on how wonderful it tasted a moment later. Megan poured herself a bowl and set the half-empty pot down over the fire again. Then she turned to the newlyweds. "Why don't you two take the rest of the stew to your parents after you finish yours?" she suggested.

"Thank you. We will do that," Tala replied excitedly. "I am sure they will truly enjoy it."

"Are you sure the two of you have enough for yourselves?" Bander asked between sips.

Megan nodded and gave Ben a quick glance. "We have more than enough," she replied.

Ben noticed the look of quiet urgency in her eyes. He knew she was ready to talk to him alone. "Megan and I are going for a little stroll," he said. "We'll see you a bit later."

Bander gave Ben a knowing glance and nodded. He knew Ben and Megan were about to have a serious chat.

The young couple walked away slowly, neither of them speaking until they were well away from the campsite and out of earshot of the others. They stopped beside a flat boulder where Megan sat down to finish her stew while Ben leaned against the bole of a tree to finish his. After she had finished her stew, Megan set her bowl aside and threw her head back to let her face be bathed by the early-morning sunlight for a moment.

Ben couldn't help thinking how beautiful his young wife looked sitting there in the skimpy slave garb she still wore. He wanted to take her in his arms and kiss her just then, but he restrained himself. "I found your doeskin shorts and vest in the cave yesterday," he said, finally breaking his silence. "I brought them back with me last night. They're still wearable, but they'll need a little mending and have to be washed first. I'm afraid the rats and mice ruined your boots though. There wasn't much left of them."

Megan turned to look at him and tilted her head to one side, all the while grinning deviously. She spoke in a husky tone as she ran her hand slowly up along her left thigh and watching him with half-closed eyes. "What's the matter, Mr. Thomas? Is there something wrong with the outfit I'm wearing now?"

Ben shook his head and fought to swallow the lump in his throat. "Not exactly," he replied. "But it does remind me of something from a bad fashion show I saw on TV once."

Megan reached down and slowly ran the edge of the open revere at the front of the short skirt between her fingers. "Well, maybe I can use it for a nightie. What do you think of that?" she asked, striking a seductive pose.

"*Great,*" Ben blurted, his voice about an octave higher than normal. "But I don't think it's quite adequate for everyday use."

She let out a deep sigh and let the sheer material drop from her fingertips. "On a more serious note, Ben, we really do need to talk."

"I know you've been waiting to tell me something for the past couple of days, Meg," Ben replied. "I'm sorry if I've been ignoring you. I didn't mean to."

"It's okay, honey. I know how busy you've been since being appointed chief consul. You're doing a wonderful job, and I'm very proud of you."

Ben moved to sit down beside her on the boulder. "Bander said Mota told him that you and Tanel had a long talk. He also told me that I should ask you what that conversation was all about. So I'm asking you now. What did you and Tanel talk about, and what does it have to do with me?"

Megan brushed a stray lock of raven hair away from her face and turned to look up into Ben's questioning eyes. The slight hint of a smile played on her lips as she spoke, "We did talk for a long time the other day after you and the others left for Quander's plantation. While you were gone, I found out, quite by accident, that Tanel is in love with you."

Ben shook his head in dismay. "I don't understand how she can be in love with me. We only met for the first time the night before the auction, and then it was only for a few minutes. I didn't like the way she came on to me, so I wasn't very nice to her."

"Sometimes that's the way it happens," Megan replied. "Love at first sight isn't a myth, you know. It really does happen sometimes. That's exactly the way it happened with Tanel."

Ben sat silently staring at the empty bowl in his hands. A grim feeling suddenly entered his heart as he said, "Tanel is a very beautiful girl, and I'm sure that most men would love having her as a wife. But I can't return her love. You're the only woman for me, Meg."

Megan leaned close and kissed him on the cheek. "I know that," she whispered. "And Tanel knows it too."

Ben slipped his arms around Megan and drew her close to him. She relaxed and let her body rest against his as they embraced in a loving kiss. They remained embraced in each other's arms for several seconds before Megan finally pushed away and sat back to stare into Ben's eyes, as if waiting for him to say something.

"What do you think we should do?" he asked.

"Tanel is very confused right now. She told me all about what she did while you were in her husband's inn—about how she tried to seduce you, I mean. I know why she did it. The poor girl has gone through a living hell, Ben. Life hasn't treated her very kindly."

Ben gave Megan a perplexed look. "What kind of living hell? She never bothered to tell me why she acted the way she did."

Megan left out another sigh. "Both of Tanel's parents would have been sold as slaves for failing to pay their taxes if she hadn't agreed to marry Porat. She only married him to protect them because he offered to buy their way out of debt if she agreed to do so. It turned out that it didn't matter if she married him or not because both her parents died of the plague shortly after she married him."

"I see," Ben said angrily. "Porat saw an opportunity to hook himself a beautiful young wife and used his money and influence to get what he wanted. He never treated her very well, did he?"

Megan shook her head. "Not really. I might have acted the way she did if the shoe had been on the other foot. There's another reason she wanted to get away from Porat."

"Oh! What's that?" Ben asked.

Megan stared up into his eyes and answered in a low whisper, "Tanel is almost two months pregnant. She will begin to show in a few more weeks. She's already beginning to suffer from morning sickness."

Ben took a deep breath and let it back out slowly. "It isn't Porat's child, is it?" He thought he already knew the answer to that question.

Megan shook her head. "No. Tanel didn't want him to know about the baby. She was afraid he would sell it after it was born. She said Porat wasn't above doing anything for money, even if it meant selling her baby for personal gain."

"What about the father?" Ben asked.

"Just one of many men Porat made her sleep with. She doesn't know who the father is and really doesn't care. The only thing she knows right now is that she wants to keep her baby. It's part of her, and nobody can take it away."

"She really has been through it then, hasn't she?" Ben sighed. "Forced to live the life of a prostitute just to satisfy her greedy husband's want of money."

Megan nodded. "Tanel never told Porat about the baby because she was hoping to find a man, any man, who might be willing to take her from Jando Village and treat her and her baby kindly."

After they had finished discussing Tanel's hardships, they sat in deep, silent thought for a while before Ben finally spoke again.

"I love you, Megan. So I hope you'll understand why I'm going to say what I'm about to suggest. After what you just told me, I think Tanel needs and deserves our help."

Megan stood up and clapped her hands. "I just knew you would not let her down. I talked it over with her already, and we both agreed that you and I should be her baby's godparents. We'll help her raise her child, and if anything happens to her, we'll raise it as our own."

Ben stood up beside her and chuckled. "This really means a lot to you, doesn't it?"

"Yes, it does, darling. But it will mean so much more to Tanel, knowing that someone cares about her and her baby."

They talked quietly for several more minutes before starting back to the campsite. Megan ran off to find Tanel and tell her about the decision she and Ben had come to. She was gone for quite some time before she returned with the beautiful ex-wife of the innkeeper in tow.

Ben was standing in front of the tent replacing the frayed string on his bow when Megan and Tanel found him. He noticed Tanel had tears in her eyes when he stood to greet them.

She wiped the tears away as she spoke in her naturally husky voice, "I want to thank both of you," she said. "And I promise that I will not be much of a bother to either of you," she added, bowing her head and starting to weep quietly. "At least my baby will have a father now, even if you are only the godfather."

Ben put his arms around her and gently kissed her on the forehead. "I'm so sorry I misjudged you, Tanel. I will try to set a good example for your child to follow."

Megan stepped forward and put her arms around both of them. "From now on, you will be like a sister to us, and your baby will be a welcome member of our family."

Tanel turned her watery eyes toward the ground. "I want to thank both of you for your kindness. I do not know what I would have done if you would not have offered to help me through these hard times. I will never set my designs on another woman's husband again."

Ben gave her a satisfied nod. "Megan and I will be here to make sure that you never have to."

Zalon gave the order to break camp before sunup the next morning. He wanted to put as much more distance as possible between Quander's plantation and the tribe before they stopped to camp again.

It was over an hour since the men started loading the wagons, and Ben grew more impatient with every passing minute. Only a few members of the tribe noticed the young consul's concern as he kept a watchful eye on the forest while they loaded the wagons. He couldn't shake the ever-present feeling that someone was watching them. Even after the tribe left the campsite and headed south again, he still couldn't shake the feeling that someone was watching every move they made.

Chapter 31

The day passed quickly without any serious incidents, and almost every member of the tribe seemed to have a carefree attitude. After their two noble advisors assured them that they were not being followed by anyone, they became even more confident when the word spread throughout their ranks that their young chief consul was going to teach them how to make weapons that could kill from a greater distance than even the mighty Tolan could hurl a spear.

When the daylight started to give way to dusk, Zalon called a halt to their march and ordered camp to be set up. He chose a small glen in the foothills for their campsite. The same grasslands that Ben and Megan had crossed months earlier lay just below them.

Ben asked Bander to go with him and spend the following day cutting saplings that would be used to fashion the bows. He had already asked Megan and Tanel to hunt for straight sticks that could be used to make arrows. Mota, Tala, and Xanet promised to look for tough leaves and bird feathers that could be glued on the arrow shafts as fletching. Since no one else knew anything about fletching arrows, Ben decided to take on that chore by himself. It was up to Zalon and Tolan to show the rest of the men how to cut and shape arrowheads from the cache of spare spearheads Bander had taken from the bunkhouses back on the plantation. All these things had been discussed, and the assignments were handed out accordingly before the camp was plunged into darkness for the evening. The only fires left burning two hours later were those used for cooking, and they soon burned themselves out.

Eight guards had been posted at various points around the campsite. Zalon selected strategic locations so no one could leave or enter the camp without being seen by at least one of the guards. The sky was clear, and long after the fires had gone out, the moon still gave off enough light for them to see anyone who might try to sneak by them. The lead guard would give an almost-silent signal for the rest of them to rotate positions every half hour. This prevented them from falling asleep during their tiresome watch until their replacements arrived four hours later.

The breaking of dawn brought new life to the camp. The women awoke first and lit the cook fires in the center of the ring of tents. The men awoke soon afterward to eat the breakfast the women had prepared for them. After breakfast, most of them broke up into small hunting parties and marched off into the forest to hunt for their next meal.

It was an hour past dawn, and only a handful of men remained in the camp to guard the women and children. The guards who had been relieved of duty at sunrise had already retired to their tents for some much-needed rest. Soon the only activity in the camp was that of the women cleaning breakfast dishes in the brook running along the western border of the little glen and that of their children playing nearby.

Ben and Bander had discovered a stand of saplings about two hundred yards from the camp. The saplings were just what they were looking for, so they eagerly started cutting the young trees with their hunting knives and stacking them into a bundle. Ben instructed Bander to cut only those saplings under two inches in diameter because anything thicker would be too hard to draw back after it was fashioned into a bow. He let Bander pull the string back on his own bow to help him judge how limber the saplings had to be. After he gave the matter some more thought, Ben did cut one sapling about two and a half inches in diameter. "Tolan might be able to handle a bow with a heavier draw than the rest of us," Ben said, winking at Bander. "But even a strong man like him might shake and not be able to shoot an arrow straight if it's any thicker than this."

When they finished cutting the saplings, Bander approached Ben and asked if he could flex his bow one more time. "This weapon bends so easily that I am afraid it is not strong enough to kill anything," he said, slowly pulling the string back with his fingers.

Ben chuckled. "It may feel weak to you now, but it will grow harder to hold with the more time it takes you to aim at what you want to shoot. You will learn that it can shoot an arrow much farther than you can throw your spear accurately."

"You keep telling me that, but you must remember that I have never seen one of these weapons used before. Its true strength will not be revealed to me until I see it in use."

Ben shrugged and smiled. "I'll show you how it works right now. I'll make sure you get the first one we make because I'm that sure you'll want it when we're finished with it."

Bander put his hand on Ben's shoulder. "Thank you. If I receive the first one, I swear I will only use it to hunt for food and defend the tribe from our enemies."

"That's the only times it should be used for killing," Ben replied, drawing an arrow from his quiver and nocking it on the bowstring. He raised the bow and slowly drew the string back and carefully aimed at a nearby tree. Just as he was about to release the arrow, a scream echoed through the forest, and he quickly lowered the bow and glanced at Bander.

Bander pointed toward the forest behind them. "It came from that direction."

Leaving the stack of freshly cut saplings, both men ran in the direction the scream came from. Ben tightened his grip on his bow as he ran alongside his friend. He increased his speed when he heard another scream and realized it was Megan. A moment later, he caught a glimpse of her dark hair as she ran through the trees calling out to him.

"I'm over here, Megan," Ben yelled.

Megan stopped for a moment when she tried to determine the direction Ben's voice had come from, which turned out to be a serious mistake on her part. She was suddenly knocked to the ground by a sharp blow from behind. Her assailant had been gaining steadily on her and had caught up to her when she stopped to get her bearings.

By the time Ben saw Din, it was already too late. The grimy little plantation guard had thrown his spear at Megan and knocked her to the ground before Ben could call out a warning. He thought he had just seen his wife killed before his eyes. "No! My god, Megan," he yelled.

Din paid no attention to his enemy's sudden outcry. He kept his eyes glued on Megan. After he saw his prize fall, he immediately ran forward to retrieve his spear and point it at the back of her exposed neck. Megan lifted her face and looked in Ben's direction, her eyes full of fear, while Din stood over her with the sharp point of his spear pressed against the base of her skull. A wicked smile crossed Din's face when he finally looked up at Ben. "If you come one step closer, I will kill her," he yelled.

Ben stopped where he was. Relieved to see that Megan was still alive and apparently unhurt, he forced himself to keep his tone under control when he spoke, "If you hurt her, Din, I'll see that you die a very slow and painful death."

"Ben," Megan sobbed, "he killed Tanel. He ran her through with his spear." She didn't realize it, but in her stunned confusion, she had cried out in English.

"Quiet, woman," Din demanded. "You are talking gibberish."

An idea suddenly formed in Ben's mind. *If I can get Din's attention off Megan for a second, I might have time to shoot an arrow at him.* "Listen to me carefully, Meg," he said in English. "When you feel that spearhead move away from your neck, roll away quickly! Understand?"

Megan blinked her eyes and replied in a surprisingly controlled tone, "Yes, but please hurry. There's no telling what this crazy man might do next."

Din pressed the point of his spear tighter against Megan's neck. "I said be quiet!"

Ben called out in a harsh tone. "You killed our friend, Din. You will die for that." He raised his bow and drew the string slowly back and took aim.

Din glanced at the flimsy weapon in his enemy's hands. "Am I supposed to believe that you are going to try and kill me with a sapling with a piece of string tied to it and a flimsy stick?" he roared, half-snickering.

"That's right," Ben replied, aiming at Din's right shoulder.

"Well then, go ahead and try," Din yelled before breaking into another fit of laughter.

Ben noticed the little imp's spear had moved a few inches away from Megan's neck when he started to laugh. He called out in English as soon as he saw the opening, "Roll away now, Meg!"

Megan immediately rolled to one side after she heard Ben yell. As soon as she was clear of the menacing weapon, she got up on her hands and knees and scrambled away as fast as she could.

Din drew his spear back when he realized his prize was getting away and prepared to throw it at her again. This time, the spearhead was pointing forward. However, before he could launch the deadly missile, a terrible ripping pain tore through his chest, causing him to drop his spear to the ground before crying out in agony. He grabbed the thin shaft jutting from his right shoulder with a startled expression on his impish face and turned to look at Ben. He only had a few seconds to react to the first arrow before another wave of pain shot through his body when a second arrow tore into his left shoulder. Then he fell to his knees and let out another cry of anguish.

Ben's face was emotionless as he watched Din kneeling on the ground, weeping in pain. "That first arrow was for Tanel," he said, nocking another arrow onto his bowstring. "The second one was for Megan," he yelled, taking aim again. "And this one is for me," he added, letting the string slip from his fingers.

The twang of the bowstring was the last thing Din ever heard. The wooden shaft flew straight and true. In less than two seconds, there was a sickening thud when it struck solid flesh. This time, there was no cry of agony. Instead, a quiet grunt escaped from between Din's thick lips before he fell over backward with the third shaft impaled in his cold heart. The three onlookers watched as Din's body quivered only slightly before becoming completely still.

When she was sure Din was dead, Megan jumped to her feet and rushed forward to throw herself into Ben's outstretched arms before breaking into tears. "Oh, darling," she said. "That terrible little beast killed poor Tanel. She tried to help me when she saw Din attack me, so he ran her through with his spear. She's lying back there in the woods."

Ben hugged Megan tightly, and he started to weep along with her. A day that had started out with the tribe in such high spirits had turned into one of tragedy.

✷✷

The whole tribe mourned Tanel's death. Even though they barely had time to get to know her, they mourned her death because of the grief it caused their chief consul and his wife. That night, they held a memorial service for Tanel on the hillside overlooking the campsite.

Bander and Tolan dug the grave, and Zalon insisted on conducting the funeral service himself. All the members of the tribe retired to their tents for the rest of the evening after the service, except for the six men who remained outside to guard the camp. Zalon told Ben that the traditional time for mourning in Gildor was one day, and that was how long they stayed in their tents. At sundown the following day, the mourning period was officially declared over, and the camp came back to life.

The cooking fires were lit, and the women started making dinner for their families. Megan was no different from the rest; she lit a fire and started to roast the leg of an abok that Bodon and Bistan had given to her and Ben.

The two men had killed the abok while hunting together the day Tanel had died. The memory of how happy the two looked when they triumphantly marched into camp with the stag tied to their meat pole was still fresh in Ben's mind and how those looks turned to despair when he told them about Tanel's tragic demise. They silently hacked a hind quarter off their kill and gave it to him before offering their condolences and sorrowfully walking away.

After the venison was cooked, Megan returned to the tent to tell Ben that his dinner was ready. When she stepped inside, she found him sitting in the dark with his face buried in his hands. "Why are you punishing yourself so, Ben?" she asked. "I feel terrible about Tanel's death too, but I know it wasn't your fault. There wasn't anything that you or I could have done to prevent it, or anyone else for that matter."

Ben remained silent for a moment before turning his glazed eyes up to look at her. "I can't help thinking that there must have been something I could have done," he replied somberly. "Maybe she would still be alive if I would have thought to keep the two of you with Bander and me while you were looking for arrow shafts."

Megan shook her head. "Believe me, darling, there was nothing you could have done. You can't keep every member of the tribe in sight every minute of the day. There's always going to be danger of some sort lurking around. No one knew that Din was following us. Besides, he would have eventually tried to kill you and take me with him even if there would have been fifty people around. Remember how determined he was to make me his slave? Remember when he said he wanted to kill you and make me his woman one day? We couldn't spend the rest of our lives walking around in a crowd. He was bound to catch one of us alone sooner or later if he kept dogging us."

Ben nodded as the memory of Din's threat came rushing back to him. "I guess you're right. I had a feeling someone was following us, so maybe I should have been ready for him. I just wish he would have come after me first."

Megan put her hand on Ben's shoulder and gazed into his gray eyes. "But he didn't," she said. "That's something you'll just have to learn to accept. You can't always be ready for everything that's going to happen. Tanel's life may not be the only one we lose while we're searching for a new land to live in. As chief consul, you'll have to get used to that idea. We could very easily lose more lives before we find a new place to live."

Ben shook his head and stood up. "You're a good teacher, Meg. I'm still learning things about you that I never knew before, even now that we're married."

Megan reached up and touched his cheek with her fingertips. "You're a fast learner too," she replied. "I'm just glad I have something to teach you. You have already taught me so much already. You're the one who taught me what true love really is."

He slowly took her in his arms and kissed her. The feel of her moist lips against his still gave him a thrill when he realized just how much he really loved her.

Chapter 32

Four weeks had passed since Tanel's untimely death. The tribe finally made its way out of the mountains to the vast grasslands that Ben and Megan had traversed months earlier. It only took a few days for Ben and Megan to trek up through the mountains by themselves then, but traveling now with two wagonloads of supplies and over seventy people required that they take a more indirect winding route down to the plain. The wagons just simply couldn't travel over the same rough terrain that people and horses could. Precious time was lost, but it couldn't be helped; the supplies were critical to the tribe's survival. Luckily, no one was following them, either because they lost the trail or because they figured the tribe's numbers were too great to take a chance on trying to capture them. The evidence left behind at Quander's plantation proved that the tribe could be deadly if confronted.

During their third day on the plain, Tala came to Ben and Megan and pointed out the place where they had first laid eyes on each other. Ben remembered the spot very well, but Megan was a bit confused. She remembered that she was suffering from a severe case of sunburn when she saw the equine girl, but her memory was a bit fuzzy on where it was she had first seen the beautiful Pack.

Zalon ordered the tribe to set up camp a short distance beyond the old campsite. It was almost dark, so he decided to stop there and let the tribe rest instead of pushing on through the night.

After dinner that evening, Bander and Tala came to visit Ben and Megan. They found the young chief consul and his wife sitting outside in front of their tent. When Ben saw them approaching, he invited them to sit down and join him and Megan beside the fire. "Welcome, my friends. Have a seat and visit with us for a while." After they thanked him for his hospitality and sat down, Ben noticed Bander had a perplexed look on his face. "Is something bothering you, Bander?" he asked.

Bander nodded. "Today, when I saw the campsite where you and Megan stopped on your trek across the plain, I realized that you really must be from a different place other than Gildor. Very few healthy Gildorians could have crossed this plain without food or water. Yet you managed to do so with your wife, who, according to Tala, was ill at the time. That alone is a feat worthy of much admiration."

"I told you a long time ago that Megan and I weren't from Gildor," Ben replied. "Didn't you believe me then?"

"Oh yes," Bander exclaimed apologetically. "What I am trying to say is, I never realized just how special the two of you are until today. You brought so much knowledge here to Gildor with you that we cannot even hope to comprehend it all. Yet you chose me to be your closest friend over all the others with whom you have come in contact. I do not know why you chose me, but I am glad you did. I will always try to be worthy of that honor."

Ben was flabbergasted. A great pride swelled within him as he thought, *I should be the one to feel honored to have such a friend as you.* Leaning over the dying flames of the fire, he took Bander's hand and shook it. "This is how friends greet each other where Megan and I came from. I would like all our friends to greet us in this manner from now on."

Bander nodded. "Thus, it shall always be."

Megan moved closer to Tala and put her arms around her shoulders and gave her a hug. "This is another way of expressing close friendship where we came from," she said.

Tala smiled and returned the hug. "Thank you, Megan. Not so many months ago, I dreamed of having a kind and caring mistress like you. Now I am a free woman, married to a full-blooded human, and I know a beautiful human woman who chooses to be my friend rather than my owner. I never dreamed that such a thing would ever come to pass until I met you and Ben."

"That is right," Bander added. "It is your dream that we all follow now, Ben. May your children grow to be as wise as you."

Ben's face flushed. "I'm afraid it will be a while before Megan and I have any children to learn anything from me."

"Oh, I don't think it will be all that long a wait," Megan replied with a smirk.

Ben gave her a questioning look. Megan didn't bother to say anything more. She didn't have to; her eyes said it for her.

"You mean... are you trying to tell me..." Ben suddenly found it hard to talk because his tongue started to get in the way of his words.

Megan slowly nodded and broke into a broad smile. "Yes, darling, I'm going to have your baby. Xanet examined me a few days ago, and she seems to think that I'm about five or six weeks along now."

Ben flew to her and picked her up in his arms. Wheeling around in a circle with her locked in his arms, he threw back his head and yelled at the top of his voice. "Did you all hear that? We're going to have a baby."

It didn't take long for the word to spread throughout the camp or for other members of the tribe to start gathering around them. Everyone wanted to congratulate them. A celebration that lasted far into the night was held in honor of the great event.

Bander and Tala were the last ones to leave, but not before Bander made Ben promise to start teaching the men of the tribe how to make bows and arrows. Ben had put the project on hold after Tanel's death, and Bander reminded him that it was time to start working on it again.

After things had quieted down and Bander and Tala had left, Ben turned to Megan. "I'm not tired yet, are you?"

"No, not really," Megan replied.

"Let's take a little walk then," Ben said, taking her by the hand and leading her toward the edge of the camp.

Before they could reach the camp's perimeter, a guard called out for them to stop. The young couple swung around to see Bodon walking toward them.

Bodon lowered his spear as soon as he recognized them. "I am sorry for stopping you, my lord, but I wanted to make sure no strangers were in the camp."

"It's all right, Bodon," Ben said. "Megan and I are just going for a little walk before turning in for the night."

The chunky guard nodded his bald pate and smiled at the young couple. "Please do not wander far from camp," he said. "I need to know if any danger threatens you and Lady Megan while you are out there."

"Way to be alert there, Bodon," Ben said, saluting him with his right hand raised and the fingers spread wide apart. "Keep up the good work, my friend. I promise we won't go out of your sight." He slipped his arm around Megan's waist and turned to continue out of the camp.

"You're learning," Megan whispered, falling in step beside him.

Ben looked into her eyes. "What do you mean?"

"You're learning how to be a good leader," she replied. "You're learning to teach as well as commend those who do their jobs well. You'll be an excellent chief consul, Ben. Our children will be proud of you."

The young lovers strolled out to the top of a grassy knoll forty yards beyond Bodon's watchful eyes. Ben slipped his other arm around Megan's waist and drew her to him and sighed as he looked out over the moonlit plain. Megan leaned forward to let her head rest against his broad chest while he stood holding her for a few seconds. Then she suddenly leaned back and looked up at him.

"What are you thinking about?" she asked.

"Oh, a lot of things," he replied, drawing her back to him again. "Mostly about tomorrow. I promised to start teaching the men how to make their own bows and arrows. And about moving on again after that. In a couple more days, we will be in Bondo territory. I have to make sure the people of our tribe are ready to defend themselves against those monsters."

"Don't worry, you'll have them ready. You taught me how to shoot a bow well enough to kill a mithor, didn't you?"

He glanced down into her pretty dark, almond-shaped eyes. "I guess I did at that." He chuckled before turning to look out over the plain and sighing again.

Megan reached up and turned his face back toward her. "Now what's bothering you?"

He put his hand on her bare belly between the hem of her short vest and the waistband of her shorts. "That," he replied, smiling sheepishly. "I'm going to be a father, and I'm not sure if I know how to be a good one."

"You don't have to worry about that either, darling," Megan said, rising up on her tiptoes to kiss him. "You'll be an outstanding father."

Back at the edge of the encampment, Bodon smiled as he watched the silhouettes of the young lovers against the backdrop of the moon. "May you have a strong son to take your place when the time comes, my lord," he whispered. "Until then, may you live a long life and guide our tribe wisely."

About the Author

Arthur L. Woodring was born and raised in the small community of Scotch Hollow, just a stone's throw from the small town of Osceola Mills located in central Pennsylvania. Arthur and his wife still live in the little hamlet he grew up in. Always the daydreamer, he took up writing as a hobby thirty years ago. That is how his Gildor series got its start. He spent his days working in an injection molding facility where he molded electronic connectors for computers and cell phones and then would go home and spend his spare time writing at night. He has a few more ideas for books in his head and would like to share them with the rest of the world, along with his Gildor series. The books he has written are for his grandchildren and their children to enjoy, along with the rest of the world—his legacy to them.

www.ingramcontent.com/pod-product-compliance
Lightning Source LLC
LaVergne TN
LVHW091534060526
838200LV00036B/609